AMERICAN WEST

Twenty New Stories from the Western Writers of America

EDITED WITH AN INTRODUCTION BY

LOREN D. ESTLEMAN

FORGE®

A Tom Doherty Associates Book
New York

AMERICAN WEST: TWENTY NEW STORIES FROM THE WESTERN WRITERS OF AMERICA

This book is printed on acid-free paper.

Design by Jane Adele Regina

A Forge Book
Published by Tom Doherty Associates, LLC
175 Fifth Avenue
New York, NY 10010

www.tor.com

Forge® is a registered trademark of Tom Doherty Associates, LLC.

Library of Congress Cataloging-in-Publication Data

American West : twenty new stories from the Western Writers of America; edited with an introduction by Loren D. Estleman.—1st ed.
    p. cm.
  "A Tom Doherty Associates book."
  ISBN 0-312-87317-4 (alk. paper)
  1. Western stories. 2. Short stories, American—West (U.S.) 3. American fiction—20th century. 4. West (U.S.)—Social life and customs—Fiction. I. Estleman, Loren D. II. Western Writers of America.

PS648.W4 A57 2001
813'.087408054—dc21

00-048446

First Edition: January 2001

Printed in the United States of America

0 9 8 7 6 5 4 3 2 1

Copyright Acknowledgments

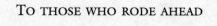

TO THOSE WHO RODE AHEAD

Contents

INTRODUCTION:
The New Westward Expansion

Loren D. Estleman

A veteran photographer lays out her equipment to make a portrait of a Sioux legend in the literal last days of the last year of the old frontier. . . .

Two close friends, survivors of Vietnam and the Rites of Passage, square off over the carcass of a deer, unaware of the true depth of their conflict. . . .

A pioneer in the early wilderness stalks a giant bear and comes face-to-face with the Great Mystery. . . .

One family's struggle to settle the arid Southwest is observed by the piano whose music accompanies all the joys and sadnesses of its years. . . .

A benevolent spirit haunts a stretch of wild river, determined to prevent an old tragedy from repeating itself. . . .

A legend of the modern West withstands the ravages of climate, economics, and a mountain lion's wrath, only to be struck down by harsh words and uninformed opinions. . . .

This is not the stuff of what is patronizingly referred to as the "traditional" western; a world where it is always a few years after the Civil War and many years before the turn of the twentieth century, where two tall men square off daily on a dusty street, daring each other to draw and fire his six-gun first, and where all the women are either cowering in the root cellar while their men defend the homestead against Indian raids or flouncing about some saloon in sequins and feathers, charming cowhands into buying them a drink or an hour in a room upstairs.

It was a fun world, and an exciting one, until it wore out its welcome sometime around the late sixties, when too many assassinations and a war that was more miserable than most convinced us that good does not always triumph over evil, people are more complicated than Swiss clockwork, and when it's a question of your life or someone else's, you're better off not giving the other guy a chance to draw at all.

These were not new discoveries, although the collective experience of a population in tune with the world led to a wider understanding of their importance. Authentic western gunfights were largely a matter of gaining the upper hand over one's opponent, women who proved they could compete with men were quickly accepted as equals—and in many cases superiors—and much of the drama of the frontier had to do with a race against time and the incursion of civilization from the East; sometimes from as far east as Russia and Japan. The West did not exist in a vacuum.

There are those who decry the demise of the traditional western, but they are mourning the passage of the kind of story that was responsible for the genre's subliterary status. The classic westerns— Jack Schaefer's *Shane*, Owen Wister's *The Virginian*, Dorothy M. Johnson's "A Man Called Horse," Walter Van Tilburg Clark's *The Ox-Bow Incident*, Thomas Berger's *Little Big Man*, to name a bare handful—were never bound by tradition, attempting to portray the West as it was and is and to expand the horizons of its literature. More recently, such monumental works as Larry McMurtry's *Lonesome Dove*, Cormac McCarthy's *All the Pretty Horses*, and Jane Smiley's *A Thousand Acres* have done just that, moving the fiction of America's wide-open spaces physically from the genre racks that have been dominated for decades by Louis L'Amour and Zane Grey to the modern literature sections alongside the titles of Ernest Hemingway, Joan Didion, and Kurt Vonnegut. These books have sold in the millions and compete for all the literary prizes worth pursuing. Yet the myth persists that the western is moribund.

To lump the work of the truly gifted writers in this form with that of the hacks is as great an act of ignorance as to state that all mysteries involve creepy mansions, grim butlers, and exotic poisons, as if the detective genre died when Monogram stopped filming

Charlie Chan. Dashiell Hammett, Raymond Chandler, and P. D. James took violent death from the musty libraries of the English aristocracy to the gritty alleys of urban America and the even darker and more frightening venue of the subconscious mind. Similarly, Willa Cather, Oakley Hall, and Glendon Swarthout snatched the struggle for order in the old frontier out of ornate saloons where a piano player in a derby hat pounded out endless choruses of "Buffalo Gals" and placed it in the ice-locked mountain passes and claustrophobic hotel rooms where much of it actually took place.

Gunplay on Main Street, Indian uprisings, range wars, and gold and silver strikes are as much a part of the expanding vista as they were of the shoot-'em-ups of old; today's writers, and the greats of the past who inspired them, seek to place those events in a realistic context rather than exploit them merely for the sake of noise and color. Bullets do savage things to mortal flesh, and their victims are always mourned by someone. Sudden wealth can be as disastrous as disappointment and despair; the effects are as dramatic as the strike itself.

Some have found a truer picture by flipping the negative. Douglas C. Jones, whose *Arrest Sitting Bull* and *Winding Stair* captured the pathos of Indians caught between the old ways of their people and the White Man's Road, borrowed a leaf from science fiction to present the Battle of the Little Big Horn from a new perspective, asking: What if Custer had survived? *The Court-Martial of George Armstrong Custer* stands head and scalp above all the conventional accounts of that epic affair.

After the consciousness-raising sixties, the American western came under fire for its portrayal of minorities, particularly the Indian, whose grand tragedy was as well-known—and as widely condemned—in the Gilded Age as in the Age of Aquarius. The charge of racism is false. Except in the trashiest paperbound fiction and creaky low-budget films so obscure that few if any are available on videotape, the members of the native tribes have never been dismissed by writers or directors as thoroughgoing villains. This is true as far back as 1912's *The Squaw Man* (Cecil B. DeMille's film based on Julie Opp Faversham's 1906 novel), about the trials of a white-Indian marriage.

Even the Hollywood of demeaning black stereotypes and demonized Asians took time, in every major feature pitting whites against Indians, to explain and sympathize with the natives' claim to their ancestral lands. Although often inaccurate, sometimes embarrassingly burlesque, at worst (as in John Ford's *Stagecoach*) reducing the mounted warrior to a faceless cypher to be shot spectacularly off his horse, the "oater" of the old-time silver screen was rarely so insensitive as to miss the dramatic implications of a lost cause. Those moguls knew a good story when they saw one. Yet the calumny lives, not entirely through ignorance. A few seasons ago, seeking to expose the racism of the old (pre-Clinton) Hollywood, a TV documentary on the western cinema aired a montage of sequences featuring oafish characters whose silly oxymorons about Indians were clearly intended to be jeered at in their own time. After screening many thousands of feet of ancient stock, this was the only "evidence" the crew could uncover. Rather than admit to their own politically correct prejudices, the producers presented the out-of-context footage as if the laughable lines represented the opinions of the writers and directors. The performance was unscrupulous and clumsy.

The efforts of the pioneers of realism have had a profound effect upon the western's potential as a medium of artistic expression. No longer confined to that narrow historical alley between Lee's surrender at Appomattox and the official closing of the frontier in 1890, today's western writer may set his or her story in prehistoric times, the modern age, or even the future and still be assured that it will find an audience. Freed from the stereotype of the rugged white male hero of Anglo-Saxon ancestry, he or she may select a Negro cowboy, a Mexican priest, or a woman rancher as the focus of the tale, widening its scope and plumbing the depths of human experience without compromising the integrity of history; for these types not only existed, but were commonly encountered in the mountains and deserts and plains of our unexplored continent. The lure of the frontier was the promise of a second chance, a place where one could leave behind the failures, prejudices—even the crimes—of his or her homeland and start over fresh. The lure is even stronger today, when all the paths have been found and the deepest seas plundered of their treasures. Great stories have been based upon this theme, from *The Odyssey* to *Centennial*. Greater ones are still to be told. Frontier writing may itself be the last frontier.

The evolving western is told from the point of view of blacks and Indians, Hispanics and Asians, Jews and Gentiles, Mormons and Catholics, women and men; often *by* blacks and Indians, Hispanics and Asians, Jews and Gentiles, Mormons and Catholics, women and men. It is about the cooling of a continent at the beginning of humanity and the swarming plains at the end of the millennium. It is about a naked warrior scaling a mountain in search of his vision and a Vietnam veteran crawling into a lodge to forget his past; a pair of friends planning a prank to lighten the Great Depression and a female pioneer dealing with a depression of a more personal kind; a miner retreating into the hills to defend his claim and a woman walking torturous miles to save her child; it may even be about two tall men squaring off on a dusty street. It is about America, it is about life. Whether the story's central figure is a hangman or a midwife or a cowboy who hates tomatoes or a Mexican stonesmith or a family of frightened homesteaders—or, yes, even a piano—you may be certain that it is a narrative of the American West.

The Snows of August

JORY SHERMAN

Jory Sherman was a member of the San Francisco community of beat poets that included Jack Kerouac. He is also one of the best western novelists of all time. "The Snows of August" contains elements of Ernest Hemingway and Ambrose Bierce, but don't be fooled; when you read a story about bear hunting and you come away smelling of bear, that story is all Sherman.

THE SUN GLAZED THE SNOW UN-
til it shone like a carpet of smashed diamonds, blinding to the sight. Cal Reese squinted his eyes to block out the glare as he followed the tracks that had broken the crust, leaving shards of cracked plates that looked like blanched slate tablets strewn helter-skelter along the ridge by some monstrous schoolboy scurrying home after the last bell had rung.

Half blinded by the sheer cruelty of the light, Cal looked up at the pine-studded rimrock that towered above him like some ancient city cobwebbed in white dust, and the sight gave him some relief from the blinding dazzle that made his eyes feel as if they had been rubbed with sandpaper.

He could smell the bear, smell its rank, carrion-wallowed hide, thick as its winter coat in his nostrils, and the scent stirred the juices in his belly, made his stomach roil and undulate with hunger, a hunger that had been gnawing at him for days, a hunger that no stink could assuage.

Cal stood there a moment to calm himself, to align his scattered senses and to think about the people waiting far below the slope, huddled together next to their wagons, the eternal fires burning through the day like forlorn beacons in the hope that some rescuer would come, some savior would pass by with a wagonload of food and a friendly face, a warm smile.

Tears stung Cal's eyes as he thought of his wife, Suzie, and his son, Billy, and Billy's little brother Eddie. Their bright eyes seemed to burn into his senses and he could feel the pleading in them, could feel the silent accusations in their hungry gazes.

In his mind he saw the wagons, nearly covered with drifted

snow, could hear the old people rummaging through them looking for a scrap of food, a piece of cured bacon they had somehow over-looked, a pinch of flour, a few desiccated beans, anything to chew on, to fill their empty bellies.

The men had not hunted for days, but he had seen them venture out from the protection of the wagons and flounder in the deeps of a snowy sea and come back frozen mindless without seeing so much as a bird track.

Where were the snowshoe rabbits they had heard about on the other side of the pass? Where were the deer and the elk, the beaver, the ermine, the mink? They had not even seen a wolf, although folks had said the mountains were full of them, and they had searched the night for their long lean shadows and watched beyond the fire for their dancing eyes and listened for their mournful keening in the deep silence of stars, cold stars, scintillating like brilliant fireflies so far away from the bleak snow-glazed moon.

And, sometimes, the stars looked to them like distant campfires burning on an open prairie and Cal would hear the children sobbing, the women weeping, the men clearing their throats for words that would not come, could not be uttered in the midst of such hope-lessness, and there was no sun-drenched prairie, no friendly camp-fires burning in profusion on a desolate plain, but only the ageless stars impervious to time's inexorable seep of fine sand through the hourglass, and the loneliness rose up in him like some powerful smothering thing that blotted out all hope, leaving only the desolate feeling of despair in an empty heart.

Cal shook his head as if to rid himself of the thoughts that threat-ened to plunge him back into those dark gelid nights when he had gazed upward at stars and suddenly realized that there was no God, not on earth, at least, no God, no salvation, no rescue. No hope.

Cal stepped out from where he had stood for what seemed like hours, but had only been a few seconds, and realized his shoes had already begun to stick to the snow. He climbed ever higher, follow-ing the bear tracks, willing himself to stay warm, moving his fingers inside his stiffened gloves to restore circulation, wriggling his toes inside his boots so that they would not turn black and die.

Cal reached the ridge, and tugged himself over it until he stood, shaking, on its very spine, and from that promontory he could see for miles in nearly every direction. Snow-clad peaks jutted from the land, scraped the blue sky like divine towers built by long-ago gods and the air was silken and thin as a spider's spinnings, sharp in his lungs, filled with invisible razors.

He could not look at the spectacular vista for more than a moment. The vastness of the land overwhelmed him and he felt small and weak, an inconsequential being in a kingdom of unspeakable majesty. He could not lose hope again, not now, not when he was so close to his goal. The bear spoor was strong there, the musk so powerful he felt drenched in its smoldering musk.

There, on the heights, he felt suddenly uplifted and he closed his eyes again against the blinding glare of light and became part of the sky, floating atop the world as if he were wraith and bondless in that split second of eternity. Light-headed and giddy from the climb, Cal filled his lungs and let his heart slow to match the inner peace that pervaded his being.

The bear was close now, and he knew he had to press on, to follow the tracks and make the kill. Cal opened his eyes, squinted to shut out the blare of sun glancing on sheets of ermine snow, and found the track a few yards away. He followed the ridge, the trail winding through the pine and blue spruce, the mantled boughs dipping low, casting soft shadows like pale blue scarves.

He ducked under the low-hanging branch of a stately spruce and eased through its comely shade, able to open the aperture of his eyes wide once more. The bear had dislodged clumps of snow that had fallen on the trail, marring the pristine flatness, rumpling the smooth surface of the path that was obviously an old game trail. He shivered in the sudden chill and his teeth clattered like tumbling dice carved out of bones.

The snowstorm had caught them so sudden, turned into an August blizzard that left the wagon train stranded in a long deep valley. None of them had expected it, and none were prepared for its high winds, its whirling fury. The snows had lasted for a week and only today had the sun come out, so feeble and weak it had not energy to melt a single flake, it seemed.

A month ago, only. It seemed to Cal like a year, for on that first night he had made a stupid mistake, and the Rockies were not kind to those who made mistakes. He had seen the wilderness take others with its mindless blunt force on the long journey out from Kentucky, across the Mississippi, and along the Missouri. Young Jeb Morris had drowned, old Nate McBride had pulled his flintlock from his wagon muzzle-first and it had fired, blowing a hole through him big enough to fit a fist through, and Molly O'Keefe had broken her ankle so bad, they had to cut her foot off and then the leg had become infected and they had to saw that off, too, and the shock killed her two days out of Council Bluffs.

He had let himself get in between the oxen and the wagon and when he tried to free a clump of snarled harness, one cow had kicked him in the leg, right up near his groin, and the hoof had broken the skin going in and torn a chunk of meat out of him coming out.

Bob Purdy and his woman, Mary Beth, had packed the wound with snow and mud and moss, but that all dried up and after it snowed, they could only pack it with cold snow that burned worse than the raw wound.

But the leg did not hurt now and he paid it no mind as he followed the narrow indentation along the ridge that marked the old trail, where deer and moccasin tracks had worn it down to rock, probably, and he felt light in the high air, whole and virile, despite the teeth of the chill that hung in the shadows like ice in a cave.

The bear scent was overpowering now, fat, cloying, pervasive along the trail. The bear was moving more slowly, padding on all fours, and he saw tufts of its thin summer hair clinging to the bark of trees it had rubbed against in its passing.

A gust of wind caught him as he walked into a cleared stretch above the rimrock and he thought he smelled Suzie's lavender water on the fresh breeze and a longing rose up in him that almost blotted out the bear scent. He saw her tending the fire when it was her turn, leaning down to push more green wood into the furnace of its heart, and he, gritting his teeth at the pain in his leg, helpless to give her a hand, and little Eddie trying to help, while wise old Billy looked on, teasing him as only an older brother can do, and their antics were like warm brandy in his belly and he had not felt the cold nor the shooting pains that streaked through his leg and groin.

God, why had he pulled up stakes in Kentucky and headed west with this accursed train, like so many others who had gone before? He recalled the tales of those who had returned, stories of rich green land by the sea in Oregon and California and his wanderlust had gotten so strong, he could no longer plow a straight furrow or root himself to a farm that had disgorged him during many a sleepless night and daydreaming morning when the mist rose from the river and the wild geese called from the heights of the heavens as they flew north in the spring, filling the sky with their ragged vees and their bugling cries.

The second storm had been worse than the first, barreling down on them just as they thought they had a chance to get out of the valley and cross the mountains before winter imprisoned them. The wind drifted the new snow atop the old, and they watched their food supplies dwindle and disappear, and during the night, they had heard the elk herds crashing down the mountain, passing them out of rifle range, and mule deer had gamboled through heavy drifts and disappeared before any man could prime his pan.

Then, the oxen got loose during the blizzard when a cougar appeared out of the woods and attacked one of them, tearing out its throat and dragging it back into the timber. The snow covered its tracks and none of them were able to find the slaughtered ox when the food ran out, though they searched for days in the still, empty woods.

Mistakes, Cal thought. They had made a passel of them after the first blizzard made their Indian-summer world vanish and brought the early winter down on them as if they were accursed. He could still hear the children crying in the night, their bellies swollen, distended into hollow gourds, their eyes shining with pain and fear each morning as they stood shivering by the fire, the fire that was never warm enough and lashed at them when the winds whipped through the valley, and whose tent had caught on fire? Purdy's? Hawkins'? Purdy's, he thought, and they all tried to beat out the flames, but Purdy's kerosene bottle exploded and spread the fire to all corners of the tarp and Bert Purdy and his wife broke down and cried their hearts out because they had lost their Bible and some letters from family in England. But, the Hawkins family took them in for two nights before they all started quarreling and Bert and Hattie said they would walk down the mountain and left before anyone realized they were serious, and had never returned. Now, everyone blamed Sid and Mandy Hawkins for booting the Purdys out and causing their deaths, most likely, from critters or frost, it made no difference.

Mindless, senseless things they all had done on this journey. In the pure air of the mountain ridge, he saw everything so clearly, and all at once, as if the knowledge had come from some divine revelation.

Suzie, I'm so sorry, he thought, and a deep sadness gripped him once again and he wondered if he was not making another mistake in following the bear. Had he blazed the trees on the way up? No, he had not thought of it until now, but as he looked around him, he saw that this was a place that he had seen before, before the snows. It was much different now, but he recognized the view, the landmarks.

Ahead was a huge boulder and a wide-open place, in which there was a massive juniper tree with a thick trunk. When he walked to it, he knew what he would see and, sure enough, there was a flash of light wood where the rope had rubbed away the bark.

Cal stood at that place and looked down the slope. He could not see the smoke from the fire, but he saw the place where the wagons had gained the floor of the valley. At intervals, he knew, buried under drifts, were the stakes they had driven, the trees they had used when they winched the wagons down. It had been a slow, agonizing process, fraught with peril, but one by one they had lowered the wagons, the men gradually letting out rope to ease each one down gently. His back hurt with the thought of it, the strain he had felt holding the ropes that held the heavy wagons.

They had performed that same ritual many times before in these mountains. He remembered the men squatting in a circle as they discussed the strategy each time they came to a place too steep for the oxen to pull the wagons down safely. And this was the last place they had done that, right here, so very long ago, it seemed.

Cal heard a noise that seemed out of place, disconnected from anything certain or natural. It took him a long moment to discern its source and meaning. He turned around, looked beyond the juniper to the east, and his gaze lingered on a jutting granite peak that he remembered. They had used that for a sighting when they brought the wagons here, a beacon so that they would not lose their bearings. Hawkins had sighted it, and guided them toward it, for it was visible for many miles, even from some of the deep canyons they had traversed, places where they had to drive stakes to haul the wagons uphill, hard, treacherous work, with the men cursing and the women and children pushing from behind like pyramid builders moving stones of immense size under the snap and sting of the overseer's whip.

Then, it came to Cal where the bear was headed. Around the face of the rock outcropping was a ledge, a rimrock path, and in the center a cave they had all talked about, dark and brooding, mysterious.

The bear, Cal knew, had been caught by the blizzard, the same as they, and was heading for its den high up on the rimrock. The sound he had heard was the slide of shale, after a dislodged rock had tumbled down the cliff face and into the trees.

He must hurry, he knew, cut off the bear before it reached the cave. Quickly, Cal rounded the juniper and headed for a spot where he knew the bear must be, a long sloping pile of detritus that would give the animal a ramp to climb. That rock he heard must have been among those at the very bottom, above timberline.

Cal started to run and was surprised that there was no pain in his groin. The gunpowder Purdy had poured into it and lighted with sparks from his flintlock must have seared the wound shut and it must have begun to heal. But, wasn't it only last night that he had screamed with the pain of it, screamed until Suzie had to stuff a sock in his mouth?

No, that must have been the day before, or a week ago, he reasoned, and he ran, the air no longer burning his lungs, the excitement of the hunt electric in his veins, strong in his quick beating heart.

He ran through a copse of trees and broke into the open and there, at the base of the rock pile, the bear had found carrion and was wallowing in it, an elk carcass that smelled to high heaven, grisly, horrid in the stark light of morning. The elk must have fallen from the cliff in the dark, and smashed its heavy body on the rocks below.

As Cal drew closer, he heard the bear grunting, and the sound was like people whispering in a rooming house like the one he and Suzie had stayed in for a time back in Virginia after they were married and before the westward urge had come upon them. Suzie no more than a girl, and he just off the family farm, happy to be the one she loved, but not knowing what he was going to do, or where he was going to go after the honeymoon.

They had followed Joe Walker's clan to Kentucky and had fallen in love with the woods and the green hills, and land was free, with no taxes to bear, and then Suzie had become pregnant and Billy had been born, and they meant to stay there forever after little Eddie came along, and then Joe Walker had come back talking about grand mountains and a land by the Pacific Ocean that was even better than Kentucky or Tennessee, and Cal could think of no other place to raise his family. Others shared his vision and before long, they had all sold their properties and bought wagons and oxen and said good-

bye to all their friends who could not see beyond the valley of the
Ohio, and set out for Oregon, where it was forever green and crops
could be raised with only a thought and a prayer.

Cal jolted to a stop as the bear rose up on its hind legs and
looked at him with small fierce porcine eyes. Cal fumbled for his
priming horn and lifted the rifle, opened the frizzen. With shaking
hands, he poured a tiny amount of fine powder into the pan, blew
the excess away, and closed the frizzen.

The bear let out a mighty roar and the sound echoed from the
rimrock and the towering rock above it and it seemed to Cal that
he could feel the hot blast from its breath as he put the butt stock
to his shoulder and took aim.

The bear did not charge just then, but stood there, snarling and
bellowing, and Cal lined up the rear buckhorn sight on the Kentucky
rifle with the front blade and leveled it at the bear's heart. The barrel
wavered for a moment until Cal took a deep breath and held it, then
steadied on the target and it seemed so easy to gently squeeze the
trigger and listen to the flint strike the frizzen and shower tiny sparks
into the pan, then the little huff as the powder caught fire and exploded through the blowhole and into the chamber, setting off the
main charge that would propel the .64-caliber lead ball and ticking
patch out the muzzle at high velocity.

Then, the bear fell to all fours and charged Cal, moving at great
speed, its hackles bristling, its fur rippling as its muscles flexed beneath its dark coat.

Cal stood his ground and as the bear approached within a few
yards, it stood on its hind feet and roared.

And in that moment of utter clarity, Cal saw the bear as something other than animal, as something godlike and powerful, huge,
towering, facing death with no fear in its heart, and he wished he
had not pulled the trigger and could stop the lead ball from speeding
toward the grizzly's heart.

In those last seconds, there was an awesome roar in Cal's ears
and a cloud of smoke billowed out from the barrel that spewed a
bright orange flame and the smoke blotted out the bear, the high

granite peak, and all that lay before him as if none of it had ever been there but was only a vision of something torn out of a half-remembered dream, a fragment of fantasy from a distant childhood when he made mud pies at the watering trough while his father plied the pump with strong brown arms and whistled some aimless tune that reminded him now of the bullet's faint whine as it sped through the thin crisp air straight at the mighty heart of the bear.

The bear opened its arms and covered the last few feet to lock Cal in its crushing arms.

The bear clasped Cal in its powerful embrace, locking him in a final dying caress, and Cal saw the black hole of death as it blocked out all light in that final, fatal moment.

Then, there was a flash of blinding brightness nobody saw, that was whiter than the snow, as dazzling as an explosion of a photographer's phosphorous in a pan, more brilliant than the brightest star, that seemed to wash over the land in one infinitesimal moment and consume Cal and the grizzly and sweep their spirits away in a single breathy exhalation.

Once, a few days after they had been in the mountains, he had stood at the edge of a small lake at twilight. The water was perfectly flat and motionless, the color of a pewter plate. He could feel the darkness coming on in the stillness. Suddenly there was a brief flash of light and the lake shimmered for a split second like a signaling mirror, bright as nickel or mercury. And, then the light disappeared. He had wondered all these days where the sudden light had come from and where it had gone.

"When did he go, Suzie?" Hawkins asked, staring down at Cal, who had been sitting on a chair wrapped in blankets. Cal seemed to be staring beyond the fire, into the cloud-flocked sky.

"A few minutes ago, I think," Suzie said.

Luke Morris, standing with the others on the opposite side of the fire, leaned over to whisper to his wife, Lorene. "At least we won't have the stink of gangrene no more."

"Shush," Lorene said.

"Mighty sorry."

"Thanks," she said. "I think he wanted to go, at the end."

"Ah."

"No, I mean it. He was very sick, and he was tired, and I think he was worried about us, about me and Billy and Eddie."

"I'm sure."

"I'll miss him," Suzie said.

"We all will. Cal was a fine man, truly a fine man."

Billy and Eddie were fastened to their mother on either side of her, clinging to her as the young of the opossum, and neither did they speak nor cry as they looked at their father sitting there, as if alive, in that old chair their mother had brought out from Kentucky because her father had made it from an ash tree and she said they'd need it in Oregon when they got there.

"Good-bye, Cal," Suzie said, and then bowed her head and began to weep softly. Hawkins drifted away in an awkward shuffle, and the two boys hugged their mother and burrowed in closer to her warmth and tried to hold back their tears.

Then, there was only the sound of Suzie sobbing and the murmurs of the others who had endured one more tragedy among them and were marveling at the sudden wind that had sprung up, and suddenly the sun seemed to warm them even as high up above them they heard the soft sough of a building south wind that they knew would bring the thaw to their frozen valley, where they had managed to survive all that God and nature had borne against them to test their faith. And the wind, like a river of air, picked up speed and blew warm breath all along the snowy valley and beyond until the trees soaked up the sobbing sound and swallowed its brief gusting moan and, for a long moment, as if God were holding His breath, granted a deep, peaceful silence that was beyond all understanding.

The Guardians

DON COLDSMITH

Fans of the Spanish Bit Saga, Don Coldsmith's sweeping chronicle of the explo-
ration of and struggle for independence in the
early frontier, know it's a mistake to make plans
for the weekend once they have begun a Coldsmith book. His understanding of the great
events that shape nations is founded upon a
deep empathy with the emotions of ordinary
people fighting to survive.

JAMES IMPATIENTLY FLAPPED THE reins on the rumps of the horses, and they broke into a lazy trot. *Too slow,* he fumed to himself. He wanted to rush ahead, to be home with Rebecca. He had been gone nearly a week, much longer than they'd planned, and he was concerned about her. He'd hated to leave her, anyway. They'd been married less than a year, and she was still frightened over the unfamiliar landscape on the Kansas frontier. Wide skies, fewer trees than back home in Ohio . . . And Indians — She was still terrified of Indians. It was only a few miles farther west that the reservation was located. Too close for comfort. For her comfort, anyway. He was sure that she worried constantly about it. Well, she said so, often enough. It was true that they sometimes saw Indians, usually one or two braves, riding horses, carrying weapons. They would leave the reserve to hunt buffalo, which was permitted. But since he'd homesteaded here, James had seen more Indians than buffalo. Mostly the herds were farther west now, it was said. Maybe even a couple of days' travel.

Still, a lot of people were uncomfortable about the Indians. What if they left the reservation and took up raiding? And that was just the "tame" ones. The Cheyennes were known to come this far east sometimes, and some of them were still pretty wild. Not to mention Kiowas. . . .

But he had convinced Becky (and himself) that this trip was really necessary. Six neighbors, traveling together for safety to take their first crop of wheat to the mill. Three days — one day's travel to Topeka, one to get the milling done, and one to travel home. They weren't as concerned about Indians as they were about bushwhackers. There was a lot of talk about war. It was known that terrorists were raiding isolated farms and homesteads along the Missouri border. A lot of people had been killed. Some families had been raided by *both* sides.

It was not so much a matter of a man's political views as it was a view to survival, James figured. He hoped that they were far enough west to be out of the main part of the border killing. But it was hard to be sure.

"You'll be fine, Becky," he had assured her as he left. "Looka there, you can see the Phillipses' house yonder. Not a half mile away. You get skeered at all, you run over there. Stay with Hannah. We'll be back on Wednesday. Three days. Only two nights. But go on over there now if you want."

"No, the cow needs milkin'," she'd said. But he knew she was afraid.

Now they were on the last stretch. His team, a mismatched pair of old mares, was working up a lather in the warm sun. He really ought to give them a breather, but they were back so close to home now. Just a couple more miles.

"Don't push too hard, James," called Ben Phillips from the wagon behind him. The others were strung out behind Ben.

Three days. . . . They'd been gone five. They'd gotten to Topeka the first evening, and found that the mill was broken down.

"Waitin' for parts from Kansas City," said the miller. "I'm sorry, boys."

"How long will it be?" asked Mercer, one of the other neighbors.

"Don't know. May have to order out of St. Louis. Tell you what, though . . . there's a mill at Lawrence. They'd take your wheat."

"That's a Union town, ain't it?" asked Phillips. It wasn't a question, but a statement.

"Well, so's this," said the miller. "You wantin' politics, or your wheat ground? There's Lecompton, the capital, partway to Lawrence, and it's secesh. Don't know if they've got a mill yet, though."

"No, no. We'll think about it. Maybe we go on to Lawrence."

They discussed the matter at length, and it was decided to take the six wagonloads of wheat on to Lawrence. Three *more* days, thought James. But in the long run, it would be more practical. David, the Phillipses' son, would ride back home on a borrowed horse to tell the womenfolk what was the trouble, and then stay there till the men got home with the flour. But that had been four days ago. Nearly five. James was worried about Rebecca.

REBECCA HAD BEEN IN A STATE OF NEAR-PANIC SINCE SHORTLY after the men left. The day was hardly started when she spotted the two Indians. They sat on horseback on the low ridge overlooking the house and outbuildings. They were apparently engaged in conversation, and their attention was riveted on the homestead. One, in fact, actually pointed to the house. That in itself was odd. Indians rarely pointed. Then the other nodded toward the distant Phillips house and rode away in that direction.

Terror gripped her as she watched the remaining brave start to walk his horse slowly around the house and farmstead, a hundred yards or so from where she cowered. As he progressed, Rebecca scurried from one window to another, peering out to see if the threat was increasing. What could she do? *Have to think, now. . . . Don't panic.* What had James taught her about the rifle?

She hurried over and took the long weapon from its pegs over the door. She hated its looks, the feel of its cold metal. James had insisted that she learn at least the rudiments of its use for self-defense. She had paid little attention. It seemed unlikely that she would ever have to bag game to eat. The other use, to shoot or threaten another human being, was even more unlikely. Her people were Quakers, "Friends," and as such didn't hold with killing folks. Not that Indians were "folks," exactly.

But this one was far too interested in the homestead. He made several circuits around the place during the rest of the day. From fright, Rebecca progressed to indignation over the sheer boldness of the savage. Then anger. . . . He had no right to intrude in her life, the life that she and James were carving for themselves out of the frontier. To top it all, she strongly suspected that she was with child. She hadn't told James yet. *I will not let this heathen take that from us,* she vowed. She must fight, kill if need be.

Rebecca looked at the rifle again. It was always kept loaded, but uncapped. Maybe she *could* use it if needed. And the way it seemed, it might be needed. Experimentally, she lifted the gun and squinted down the barrel. *Put the front sight in the little notch in the back sight,* James had instructed. *Then line that picture up on whatever you need to hit.* He'd made her fire a shot or two, but she didn't like the smoke or the noise.

Now it might be different. Maybe a shot in the direction of the savage on the hill would make him back off. She might try it. She opened the cap box and carefully fitted the little cup over the cone, pulling the hammer back to do so. She lifted the gun to her shoulder again and sighted through the open window at the horseman. Waveringly, she lined her sights and slowly swung the barrel toward the Indian on the horse. He sat lounging on the animal's back, hands folded across the withers. The absolute gall of the man! Her finger started to tighten on the trigger. . . .

No! I can't, she realized. *I couldn't do it.*

She removed the cap from the nipple and lowered the hammer carefully. So now what to do? The cow should be milked and the chickens fed. The chickens would be all right, she guessed, foraging for grasshoppers all day. They ought to be shut up for the night, of course. But poor Buttercup wouldn't tolerate her swollen udder very well. Rebecca felt like crying.

The sun was setting now, the shadows lengthening. . . . Wait! What had James suggested if she needed help? Go to the Phillipses' house. Of course!

She unbarred the door and stepped outside into the cool of the evening. She didn't want to look, but she must. . . . Yes, he was still there. Maybe she could sneak around the other side of the house. Unseen, and make a run for it. Only half a mile. . . .

She took the rifle, mostly so as not to appear helpless. Might as well have left it behind, as it turned out. She was seen before she'd traveled a hundred yards. The Indian turned his horse and, at a walk, began to travel parallel to her line of retreat, following the ridge.

What to do? Stop and try to shoot? Run on toward the Phillipses' place? Her courage failed her and she sprinted back toward the house, gripping the rifle tightly. The Indian turned his horse and rode back.

Gasping for breath, she hurried inside, slammed and barred the door, and sank to the floor, sobbing. They'd attack in the darkness, she was sure. Probably burn the house, and grab her when she tried to flee. Then . . . She didn't even want to think about it.

She spent the sleepless night crying and hugging the rifle and listening to Buttercup's indignant bellowing over her discomfort.

REBECCA WOKE IN A PANIC. IT WAS DAYLIGHT. SHE'D DRIFTED off in spite of herself. Frantically, she dashed to the window. Yes, he was still there. Or was this *another* Indian? She couldn't tell. *They all look alike,* she told herself.

The morning dragged on, and the savage didn't seem to want to come any closer. He just sat, watching, occasionally riding the circuit around the farmstead. Buttercup's pleading cries were getting on her nerves now. Maybe she could go and milk her out, at least partly. The threat hadn't seemed to increase any, except when Rebecca had tried to leave. She'd take the gun and go to the barn with her milk pail. She thought she could position the cow and herself so that she could watch the intruder while she milked. Even a little milking from each teat should provide some relief for poor Buttercup.

The hens, not having been shut in for the night, were already out foraging. They'd be all right, and maybe she could toss them a little grain.

From the different angle at the barn, she could now see that there was another Indian up at the Phillips place. She couldn't see the Mercers' house from here, but wondered if all the neighbors were under siege. She'd heard no shooting, though. Strange doings. . . . Maybe they planned to attack everywhere at once. The men would be back tomorrow night. Would that be too late?

She quit the halfhearted job of milking, knowing that it was inadequate but hoping it would help some. She hurried back to the house, milk pail sloshing in one hand and the rifle in the other. She slammed and barred the door and sat down, sweating and trembling.

LATER THAT DAY, AS SHE WATCHED THE INDIAN, SHE HEARD hoofbeats in the other direction. *Oh, Lord, they're coming,* she thought, rushing from the back window to the front, rifle in hand.

"Halloo, Miz Brighton," a voice called. "It's me, David. David Phillips."

Rebecca flung the door open and ran outside. Never had she been so glad to see anyone.

"David!" she exclaimed. "Indians! See?" She pointed to the ridge. Then, "You're back early. Where are the others? Are they . . ." Terror gripped her again.

"They're fine," explained the lanky teenager. "The mill's broke down in Topeka. They had to go on to Lawrence. They'll be back Friday night. Sent me to tell. But what's this about Indians?"

She motioned him to the corner of the house and pointed to the ridge.

"There's been at least one, all the time," she blurted. "They ride around and around. There's one up at your house, too. Friday, you say? This is only Tuesday!"

"Hmm," said the boy thoughtfully, probably wondering what his father would do. "Tell you what . . . you come up to our place with me. We'll see what my ma thinks about this. I'll walk with you and lead the horse. Bring your gun."

"Maybe they'll burn the place," she said fearfully.

"Mebbe. If they do, better you ain't in it, though."

There was no trouble on the half-mile trek to the Phillips place. Hannah hurried them inside. She, too, was puzzled over the behavior of the Indians.

JAMES KNEW NOTHING OF ALL THIS AS HE DROVE HIS SWEATING team into the barnyard. It was Friday, and the sun was low in the west. A long worrisome week was over. In the wagon bed under a tarp was a pile of cotton sacks bulging with newly milled flour. Even with all the trouble, it had been a satisfactory trip. He'd sold some wheat to the miller, and traded some more to the miller in exchange for grinding the rest. Now he was home.

He pulled the mares to a stop, leapt down, and ran to the door, jerking it open to rush inside.

"Becky?" he called.

There was no answer. The house was empty. He stepped back outside, glancing up the road to where Ben Phillips was just topping the hill.

There was a flash of movement to his left, and he looked in that direction. A tall warrior on a spotted horse was trotting slowly down from the ridge, straight toward him. The Indian's right hand was raised in peaceful greeting, the open palm displaying no weapon. Now another Indian hurried down from the direction of the Phillips place and reined in near the other.

"Hallo," began the first Indian, hand still raised.

"What do you want?" demanded James. "What are you doing here?"

"Your woman is there." The warrior pointed to the Phillips house. "She is safe."

"You talk good," said James cautiously, "but I asked what you want."

"I have been to white man's school," explained the Indian. "I came to tell you . . . we saw that your men were all gone, with the wagons of grain. We know that the white man is busy killing each other. There is danger . . . bad men around . . . we looked after your women until you return. Everybody's house . . . we protect from raiders."

But there were no raiders, James started to protest, but then he paused. *There could have been*. It had been risky to leave the women alone, and it had been longer than expected. He felt embarrassed.

"What is it?" called Ben Phillips as he drove into the yard, picking up his gun from under the seat.

"Put it away, Ben," said James. "These fellers, here, saw we were gone and decided to look after things in case any raiders came along."

"What do they want?" asked Ben, still suspicious.

"Didn't say, yet." James smiled. "I expect, though, that they'd relish a sack of flour. Or maybe bread, when the women bake."

"Yes, that would be good," said the educated Indian. "We will come back, no?"

"Yes . . . tomorrow?" suggested James.

"It is good," said the Indian, reining his horse around and urging it into a trot. "We will come!" he called over his shoulder.

NOTE: This story is based on an actual incident which occurred in Wabaunsee County, Kansas, about 1860. It was related to me by the descendants of the families involved, who still live in the area. Only the names are changed. The danger was real, as the principal guerrilla terrorists, John Brown for the North and William Quantrill for the South, were raiding within a day's ride of those homesteads.

Don Coldsmith

A Piano at Dead Man's Crossing

JOHNNY D. BOGGS

Johnny D. Boggs is a novelist and photo-journalist whose credits include *Boys' Life*, *Louis L'Amour Western Magazine*, *Cowboys & Indians*, and *The Santa Fean*, as well as his *Hannah and the Horseman* series of novels. His moving narrative of the life of a piano makes those of us who have written only from the perspectives of people and animals wonder what we were thinking.

SHE STANDS IN FRONT OF THE
plate-glass window where she has been on display for eighteen
months, baking in the sun as passersby hurry down the boardwalk
to buy whatever Prescott has to offer. The PRICE REDUCED sign put
up a week ago by the man with the reddish gray dundrearies does
no good. Few stop to even window-shop.

A year has passed since someone touched her ivories. A plump
woman named Gossamer Jane had rubbed her pasty fingers over the
double-mahogany-veneered case and played a few bars of some min-
strel song called "Oh, Dem Golden Slippers."

"The girls'll like it," Dundrearies had said. "Gossamer Jane's will
be the class of Prescott."

The woman laughed and stepped away. "Two hundred is too
steep. When you come down to seventy-five, lemme know."

"You'll never get it for seventy-five, Jane. I promise you that."

"We'll see," the woman said.

She hadn't returned.

Prescott booms. People come here to wash down the Arizona
dust or to visit places like Gossamer Jane's. They need grub, the
"law," or Doc DeWitt, maybe "a bath and a shave." No one needs
an upright grand piano.

Seven and one-third octaves. Double-roll fall board and full
swing music desk. Hand-carved panels and Queen Anne trusses.
Double repeating action. Nickel-plated hinge on the fall board. Ivory
keys and ebony sharps. Three pedals. Eight hundred pounds. Nothing can match her in Prescott.

Some locals call her Harrigan's Folly.

A man stops in front of the window and runs long fingers

49

through a rough matted beard. He wears a muslin shirt, stained canvas suspenders and brown trousers caked with dried mud and drier dust. A flat-brimmed, low-crown Boss of the Plains that John B. Stetson wouldn't claim tops his narrow head, and something bulges in his left cheek as he stares through the glass. Finally, he spits a brown waterfall onto the boardwalk and walks away.

Good. He's no musician, and it's better to cook in Harrigan's Dry Goods than to be chopped up for winter kindling.

The bell over the door chimes. Dundrearies rises from his perch behind the counter and puts on his fake smile.

"Good afternoon, sir. What can I do for you today?"

"Like to see that pianer."

After recovering from shock, Dundrearies uncovers her ivories and steps back. The bearded man hesitates, then pounds a few keys and sharps that result in a groan. He jerks back.

"I'll take 'er," he says.

"Sir?"

"Said I'll take 'er. How much?"

"Er. Two hundred and eighty dollars in U.S. script. Or two-twenty-five in gold. That's a bargain, like the sign says."

Haggling should come next, but the man nods and hefts a pouch from his trouser pocket. Doesn't he know he's being cheated?

They weigh gold dust on the counter scales, and the clerk writes out a receipt. He can't contain his grin until the bearded man says, "Sign says you'll deliver anywhere in the territory."

"Yes sir. For the piano, that would be, oh, ten dollars extra."

"Done," says the new owner, walking to the map that hangs on the far wall. He stretches a long arm up to the far right-hand corner of the map, then drops down, tracing a bony finger past Fort Defiance, Saint John, on down until he reads "White Mountains." He jabs at a place and says, "Here. You can get directions from Jake's at Springerville. How long?"

Dundrearies slowly shakes his head. "A month, maybe?"

The man hands him a couple of gold coins. "Pleasure doin' business with you."

The bell over the door chimes, and the owner walks down the boardwalk whistling "The Blue Tail Fly."

Dundrearies stares at the map.

"Shit," he says.

WRAPPED IN A TARP, SHE SITS IN THE BACK OF THE LONG WAGON. Branches slap the dust-covered canvas, showering the wagon bed with the scent of pine. Above the sound of the wind, the creaking of metal-rimmed wheels over malpais rock, she hears Logan, Mc-Intosh and Prosser—the men Dundrearies hired in Prescott—sing some song she has never heard:

> "Jesus Christ! Keep movin',
> you son-of-a-bitchin' mules
> That bastard, Harrigan
> I'll kill the damnyankee
> Move, you dumb mules
> Damn your hides, I said move."

The hemp rope that bites through the canvas and into the mahogany snaps from the strain as the left rear wheel slams into a hole. The tailgate opens, and she slides out, flips once, and crashes against the rocks to an out-of-tune dirge.

Prosser sings another verse of his song. Logan and McIntosh join in.

> "Don't just stand there, you scalawags
> Help me get that piano back on the wagon
> Set the brake, you worthless oaf
> Harrigan. I'll rip his guts out
> What the hell is this?

Leg's busted off. Throw it in the back
Lift on three. One . . . two . . . three."

The busted leg, with its engravings now scarred and dirty, doesn't hurt. The men slide her onto her back, ignoring the rips in the canvas tarp and scratching the mahogany even more. The keys sound awful, but Prosser, Logan and McIntosh go on with their songs. The wagon gets stuck in the first crossing of what Logan calls the West Fork of the Black, and the mules sing at the crack of the long snake Prosser swings. Thrice more they cross the flowing water, then begin a harrowing climb over loose rock and dead branches until they reach the meadow and see smoke from a cabin's chimney.

"What the hell happened?" the owner asks after Logan and Mc-Intosh have cut away the canvas.

"Mister, you try haulin' a piano up the Grapevine and 'cross Dead Man's Crossing," Prosser says. "It's a wonder that piano's in one piece."

The owner holds up the broken leg. "I wouldn't call it one piece."

A musical voice from inside the cabin breaks a lengthy silence. "Seth, I can't wait any longer. I'm coming out."

"Come ahead, Nora."

Nora's eyes match her calico dress, sparkling. This woman doesn't belong here. Her mouth falls open. "It's beautiful."

Seth examines the piece of leg in his right hand. "Reckon we can wrap some wet rawhide around it and she'll be as good as new. Well, play 'er, Nora. That's what I got 'er fer."

Nora brushes dust and needles off the cover, lifts it and hits an F. "She's out of tune, but I guess that's to be expected."

Logan has found a crate and brought it over. Nora thanks him, sits down and plays "Lorena." Afterward, they move her inside, where Nora performs "Amazing Grace." When Seth offers to tip the Prescott freighters, Logan tells him the music has been payment enough and they'd best be on their way. Prosser calls Logan a stupid son of a bitch as they walk out the door, but Seth and Nora don't hear.

WHILE THE BEARDED OWNER NAMED SETH LACKS MUSICAL AM-
bition, the woman, Nora, has an angel's touch. Her long fingers not
only grace the ivories and ebonies, but they are strong enough to
pull on the wires until a C almost sounds like a C. Maybe she'll
never be tuned properly—as she had been back on the corner of
Clark and Kinzie in Chicago before being shipped off to Prescott—
but the music Nora makes here on this mountain up from Dead
Man's Crossing sounds wonderful.

Nora knows everything, from "Barbara Allen" to "I'll Take You
Home Again, Kathleen," from Johann Sebastian Bach to Stephen
Foster. Nora waits until the morning light is perfect, then sits on
the pine stool Seth has made. She plays, sometimes humming along,
sometimes even singing. Delicately, she closes the cover over the
keys and goes about her chores. At evening, she plays again, occasionally scolding Seth for leaving his coffee cup on the piano top.
No one else hears her until this Sunday.

Children dance a jig outside, while the silent, smoking flutes of
Seth and the other men overpower the smell of peach cobbler and
elk roast. She has been hauled outside, where everyone can hear, and
Nora has been coaxed to play "Oh! Susanna." Men, women, and
children are still applauding as the man in buckskins reins his lath-
ered horse to a hard stop in front of the cabin.

"Apaches wiped out Carr's command! Fort Apache's been
burned to the ground."

Seth calmly removes his half-smoked flute. "Now, I doubt that."

"Suit yourself," Buckskins says. "I'm just spreadin' the alarm.
These mountains is about to go up in flames!"

Seth tugs on his beard after Buckskins gallops off. The men bring
her inside and pass around a clay jug. She has heard of men playing
these jugs, but the only music these men make is an occasional belch.

Shortly after supper, new riders arrive, their black hair dancing
in the wind as they sing and dance to another new melody in a
strange language. It offends one of the ladies, who faints, while men

grab long sticks like those Dundrearies sold. These instruments clang harsher than cymbals. They boom without rhythm and produce a bitter smell and thick smoke. Something thumps against the logs and splinters the shutters. One man yelps and slides down the wall, while a woman—it's Nora—runs to his side and sticks a bandanna against his shoulder.

The children cry.

"It's all right!" Nora tells them. "It'll be all right!"

The other women seem transfixed by the music and excitement. The clay jug Seth has left on top of her explodes and sprays the pine walls with a foul-smelling liquid.

The children cry.

Seth works the lever of his long stick and braces himself against the thumping wall. "Play somethin'!" he shouts.

Nora looks up at him, bewildered. "To quiet them kids," Seth says. "To let them 'Paches hear our medicine. Play somethin'!" He slams the big part of his stick against his right shoulder, spins around and strikes another harsh, loud note.

Nora crawls to her, whispering to the children, and lifts the cover. She pulls herself up, crying, and begins to play, missing a few notes, sounding terrified:

"We will welcome to our numbers
The loyal, true and brave
Shouting the battle cry of freedom
And although he may be poor
Not a man shall be a slave
Shouting the battle cry of freedom."

"Sing with me!" she repeats. And after another verse, the children obey, hesitantly at first, then louder, trying to carry their voices above songs of the long sticks. Two women join in. Even the man leaning against the wall with a sticky, crimsoned bandanna pressed against his shoulder mouths the words.

"The Union forever
Hurrah, boys, hurrah
Down with the traitor
Up with the star
While we rally 'round the flag, boys
Rally once again
Shouting the battle cry of freedom."

They play and sing like that for an hour. Slowly, the men, sweaty, faces blackened, step away from the windows and door and lean the long sticks against the wall.

"I think they've had enough," says Llewelyn, someone called a Welshman. "So have I," adds another man.

Seth smiles. "I think Nora's pianer music scared 'em off. Play us another song, gal. Somethin' we can all sing along to."

"Something less Yankee, though," Llewelyn says weakly.

Nora smiles despite her tears and begins "Green Grow the Lilacs." The men don't play their noisy long sticks this time, and those long-haired musicians outside, the 'Paches, will never return for another concert. Nor will several of the men, women, and children inside the smoke-filled cabin today.

SHE HASN'T BEEN PLAYED IN TWO DAYS. NORA IS IN THE ROOM where she and Seth sleep. A tired old man with a black bag has arrived. He is inside with Nora. Seth sits on the piano stool, wringing his hands.

Outside, a wolf yodels to the sky.

Seth bites his lips.

Nora's screams are painful to hear. Seth drops his head. The stranger scolds Nora. She moans. Seth looks up. Nora and the man have grown silent. Then a new tenor breaks into a strange chorus. Slowly, Seth rises off the piano stool as the stranger pushes past the bearskin that divides the cabin. This man wipes his wet face with a white rag. He looks at Seth. The music continues behind the bear-skin.

"Well," the man says, "you're supposed to give me a cigar, Papa." He smiles. "You got a girl."

Seth jumps so high he almost punches a hole through the roof. He dances around the stool, hugs the newcomer, and says, "I ain't got a cigar, Doc. How 'bout somethin' stronger?"

SOMETIMES SHE MISSES THE 'PACHES AND THE DRUM OF THE long sticks. Visitors are few, and the wind moans frightfully. Outside stands a sheet of white, and Nora's fingers are cold on the keys as she softly follows "Oh, My Darling Clementine" with "Shall We Gather at the River." The girl, Lorena, sits at Nora's side, softly kicking the base and occasionally the rawhide-covered busted leg.

Nora finishes the chorus and pushes away.

"Your turn, Lorena," she tells the girl.

"I don't wanna, Mama."

Nora smiles. "It's your turn."

Lorena hits the ivories hard, like Seth had done back in Prescott so long ago. Nora's face hardens and she slaps the girl's left hand. "Do it right," she says.

Lorena plays a gospel song, not as well as Nora. It must not please Nora because she moves away and leans against the wall, holding her stomach. She is bigger now, as she was before Lorena joined them. But she is also paler. Trembling, she collapses into a chair by the table. Lorena stops playing, turns.

"Mama?" she asks timidly.

"Go find Papa. Hurry."

SETH AND LORENA WAIT. THE MAN WITH THE BLACK BAG HAS returned. The room behind the bearskin has become silent. No new songs from Nora. No tenor joining in for the chorus. After a long time, Black Bag steps from behind the bearskin. He says nothing.

"Lorena," Seth says. "Why don't you practice your pianer music?"

"I don't wanna, Papa."

"Please. Play somethin' for Mama."

Lorena starts with "Johnny Get Your Gun," thinks better of it, and turns to "Jeannie With the Light Brown Hair." She doesn't concentrate, misses several notes.

Seth and the doctor shake hands, and as Black Bag disappears behind the bearskin, Seth walks into the whiteness outside and returns with a small wooden box, too small to carry an accordion. He, too, walks behind the bearskin, while Lorena finishes the Stephen Foster song and begins "Lorena," for which she is named. As Seth and Black Bag carry the small box outside, Nora hums a new tune, a mournful wail that grows louder, like the wolf's song.

Lorena bites her lips, sniffling, but continues to strike the keys.

A NEW SMELL HOVERS IN THE AIR, THICK AND CHOKING. LIKE A hundred fireplaces going strong in the worst winter. The sky out the window, normally a crisp, clear blue, has turned dark gray.

This is hot, much worse than baking in the window at the place in Prescott. What was that name? Pine smoke serpentines its way through the open window. Usually smoke confines itself to the fireplace and chimney.

The door bursts open. Lorena and Nora, their dresses torn and dirty, their hands and faces blackened, stumble inside, supporting the young son of the Welshman Llewelyn between them. They ease him into one of the chairs by the table.

Nora turns her head and coughs harshly.

"I'm sorry, Missus McCullough," the boy, a young man actually, says.

"Hush. Lorena, get some water. Let me see that hand, Gwyn."

They wash Gwyn's mangled hand, pink and black and red and purple, and wrap it with sheets ripped off Lorena's bed. Outside, the strange clouds have blackened. Nora suppresses another cough and rises. "You two stay here," she says, walking toward the door.

Gwyn weakly rises from his chair. "I'm helping, Missus Mc-Cullough," he says.

Lorena accompanies him. "It's my home, too, Mama," she says.

Nora smiles. "Let's go," she says.

They are gone for ages. The sky darkens more, the heat intensifies, but the wind has changed directions now, and the gray-black clouds drift away. Somewhere, a drumroll sounds. The winds pick up. And now there is a pattering on the roof, a strangely familiar sound. Rain. Yells are heard outside. Someone breaks into a song. Some time later, the door bangs open again. Their voices are recognizable, but the soaking clothes and streaked, grimy faces and hair aren't.

Yet this is Nora, with scarred, soot-colored hands and matted hair, who sits on the stool at the urging of the others. She wipes her filthy hands on her ragged dress and stains the ivory keys as she tries a few cords.

"Play!" the man with Seth's voice says. "We gotta celebrate."

Nora looks at the ceiling. "Well," she says, "this certainly seems appropriate."

"A Hot Time in the Old Town" bangs out.

Seth, Lorena, Llewelyn and Gwyn howl with laughter.

Lorena looks like Nora had when she first saw her: sparkling eyes. Only the dress is white, not calico. And Nora sobs.

Seth puts a lanky arm over Nora's shoulder.

"Ain't no need in cryin', woman," he tells her.

"I'll cry if I want to," she tells him.

They have moved her outside into the pasture, where Nora plays the "Bridal March" and Seth escorts Lorena to the copse of aspens where a red-haired man waits with Gwyn. Lorena and Gwyn repeat some words, kiss, and everyone—it looks like more people than had ever been in Prescott—claps.

Later, as smoking flutes and clay jugs pass among the men, Nora launches into "On the Banks of the Wabash, Far Away," some Beethoven, and, finally, "Buffalo Gals." Lorena plays, too, "The Sidewalks of New York" and "Listen to the Mockingbird." The party seems to last forever, but finally Lorena kisses Nora and Seth and climbs into a buggy with Gwyn.

They have been on these so-called Sunday drives before, but this time they don't return. The guests leave, too, after Llewelyn, Buckskins, Black Bag and Seth move her back inside the cabin. When Seth and Nora are alone, Nora sits on the pine stool and plays "Lorena."

After the last verse, Nora falls into Seth's arms and cries.

"A MAN CAN'T MAKE A LIVING ON ONE HUNDRED AND SIXTY ACRES in this country," the man with the gray derby says. "Not in this day and age."

Seth studies his coffee cup. "We've made do, Nora and me."

"Scraping by. Listen, you've got some good summer pastureland up here. Selling to my client is the way to go. You can get out of this shack, get closer to your daughter, your grandbabies. This is a new century."

"Your client needs more than my quarter section for his herd."

Gray Derby sighs. He looks across Seth's shoulders and sees her. "My God," he says, "how did you get that thing up here?"

Nora smiles. She has come out of one of the new rooms, the one Seth, Llewelyn, and some other men added a long time ago to give Lorena a place of her own. "It was a wedding present," Nora says.

"You play?" Gray Derby asks.

Nora shrugs.

"Please, may I impose?"

Nora lifts the cover and pulls out the song book Lorena has sent. Nora plays, sings.

> "No one to see while we're kissing
> No one to see while we spoon
> Come take a trip in my airship
> We'll visit the man in the moon."

Gray Derby thanks her. He shakes Seth's hand.

"Mister McCullough," he says, "I'll deny saying this, but if I were you I'd never sell this land."

SHE HASN'T BEEN PLAYED SINCE NORA TRIED "MY MOTHER WAS a Lady" months ago. That rendition had been cut short by Nora's hacking cough.

Nora is in the room, the one with the door instead of the bear-skin that had hung for so long. Seth is with her, but Black Bag, the man who usually came during times like this, is not here. White flakes fall outside.

She realizes now that Nora has changed. The eyes no longer sparkle. The dark hair has turned gray, and the face is leathery and wrinkled. Nora's fingers had ached when she tried to play her.

They are both old.

Seth opens the door, softly closes it behind him and staggers to the table. He leans on this for support. His lips tremble. His entire body shakes. He weaves around the chairs and sits on the stool he made out of the trunk of a pine. The hinges squeak as he opens the lid and stares at the ivory and ebony keys. He tries to strike a G, misses, and pounds the keys with his elbows, burying his face in his hands.

He cries.

Hours later, Llewelyn arrives. He, too, has grown old, but the two men bring a large wooden box into the room. Both men fight back tears as they carry the box outside. They are gone for a long time. Nora, she seems to understand, will not return.

Later, many people come through the door. Some of these look like those who came when the 'Paches had their concert. Gwyn is here, holding Lorena close as she sobs on his shoulder. The strangers talk among themselves. They fill the table with pies and chicken, with ham and potato salad. They talk about Nora, but no one suggests a song.

Why?

When they are gone, when Lorena has kissed Seth's cheek and Gwyn has shaken his hand, the old man again sits on the pine stool. He swallows and heads into Nora's room, returning with a linen sheet. This is draped over her.

She will sit like that for years.

HEAT FOLLOWS COLD. COLD FOLLOWS HEAT. VERSES AND REfrains are repeated, but no one plays her. She has forgotten so many songs from sitting uselessly underneath her shroud. Rats have chewed on the rawhide patch so that her busted leg has almost fallen off.

"Seth!" a man sings. "Seth McCullough. It's Pryderi Llewelyn. You there?"

There is no answer. The door opens. Relying on a cane, Llewelyn hobbles inside. He glances across the room and moves to Nora's place, where Seth went in some time ago. Llewelyn slowly opens the door, closes his eyes for a minute, and stumbles inside. A few minutes later, he is back out, shutting the door. He inhales deeply.

Another man, a stranger, comes inside. Llewelyn looks at him.

"He's gone," Llewelyn says.

The man nods. "Damned shame. Reckon he was up in years, though. Hell of a long life, especially up here."

A NEW SOUND PUTTERS OUTSIDE. THE DOOR OPENS. GWYN LLEWelyn opens the door, mopping his older face with a calico rag. Two bronze-skinned strangers, equally sweaty, follow him inside. Outside stands a weird wagon, rubber tires instead of spoked wooden wheels, and no horse to pull it.

Lorena walks inside. Two dark-headed boys follow her.

"That was an adventure," one says.

The other chimes in, "Reckon we'll get that many flats on the way down, Daddy?"

Gwyn is too out of breath to reply.

Lorena pulls the dirty sheet away and drops it on the floor. "A piano!" the second boy exclaims. "It's a piano!"

"How did it get up here?" the first child asks.

"Your grandpa had it brought up for your grandma when they were first married," Lorena says. She lifts the covering, rubs her fingers across the keys. "Out of tune," she says, "but I guess that's to be expected."

"What happened to that leg?" the first boy asks. "It's all busted up."

"It's perfect," Lorena says.

"Go outside and play," Gwyn tells the youngsters. He turns to the bronzed men. "Y'all get the truck ready."

When they are gone, Gwyn puts his right hand on Lorena's shoulder.

"Honey," he tells her, "this is no good. We had a hell of a time getting up here in that truck. We'll never make it down with that old relic."

Lorena pulls away from him. "You promised," she tells him.

"But—"

"But nothing. My father had this brought up more than fifty years ago. Mama taught me to play on this. She played it on our wedding day, in case you've forgotten. We've sold the land. I'm not selling this."

Gwyn shakes his head. "We'll never make it, Lorena," he said.

Lorena smiles. "We'll make it." She plays "The Flying Trapeze." Gwyn walks outside and serenades the bronzed men.

"We'll throw a tarp on the bed
And wrap another over her
This is a family memento
And I'm not paying you to be careless
It's a hell of a way across Dead Man's Crossing
And on to Springerville in this piece of junk."

Wrapped in a canvas tarp, she stands on the back of the strange wagon, baking in the sun. Lorena and Gwyn sit up front in the metal cab of the puttering wagon. The bronze men and the two boys rest in the back, staring at her.

Humming a polka, the horseless wagon lurches forward, turns around and heads toward the first crossing on the West Fork of the Black. She doesn't know where she's going—Phoenix, she has heard one of the bronze men say—and she will miss Nora, Seth, and the log cabin where she has been played for so long.

Lorena will be good to her, though. Nora saw to that. The wagon groans as it awkwardly fords Dead Man's Crossing. Gwyn is lucky. He should have been here when her banks were full back before the 'Paches sang harmony and the men played their long sticks.

One of the boys begins whistling a song. The other joins in. The bronze men smile.

She doesn't know this song.

But she will learn it.

Traveling Princess

LENORE CARROLL

D eath and danger in the old West had no need of bandits or hostile Indians. This tale of one woman's courageous coming-of-age is emblematic of the work of Lenore Carroll, who established herself as one of our finest writers of American historical fiction with the publication of *Annie Chambers* in 1989.

June 1846

My journal tells a story tonight different from what it has ever done before. The curtain rises now with a new scene. This is the third day since we left Brother James's. Tuesday evening we went into Independence; there we stayed one night only at Mr. Noland's Hotel. On Wednesday I did some shopping.

Once we began, I had thought we were well under way, but all sorts of things shifted and tilted, and the wagons had to be repacked at Westport after two days. I cannot find one small trunk. I can only hope it comes to light before all my available clothes are soiled.

Last night Samuel confided that his brother James is already en route to Santa Fe. President Polk sent him to parley with Governor Armijo. General S. W. Kearny is moving toward Santa Fe from the West. James's task is to persuade Governor Armijo to surrender to Kearny. If he fails we may find a war instead of trade when we arrive. Samuel is confident that James will succeed. He listens to my timid fears, scoops them up and devours them with his confidence.

Thursday 11th

Now the Prairie life begins! We left "the settlements" this morning. Our mules travel well and we jogged on at a rapid pace. The hot sun, or rather the wind which blew pretty roughly, compelled me to seek shelter with my friends—the carriage & a thick veil.

The teamsters were just catching up and the cracking of whips, lowing of cattle, braying of mules, whooping and hallowing of the men was a loud and novel scene rather. It is disagreeable to hear so much swearing; the animals are unruly 'tis true and worry the patience of their drivers, but I scarcely think the men need be so profane.

For our first supper, I ate fried ham and eggs, biscuit, and a cup of shrub and enjoyed a good night's rest. It was sweet indeed.

After we left Independence it took a few days to clear wooded areas and meet the Prairie with its open vistas. My maid and I ride in the Dearborn and oh! the dust is terrible. Samuel put us nearer the front of the train when he saw our plight. At the end of the day we looked like millers with masks of dust on our faces.

Samuel has bought trade goods—iron implements and forged steel, also, household items such as Dutch ovens and warming pans. We have enough household goods of our own in several wagons, plus our clothing and personal items. We left nothing behind that we thought would contribute to our comfort. When we stop moving at the end of the day, I am pathetically grateful for simple comforts—a large washbasin, a chair with a back, our own bed. Supplies to feed all the men and animals fill several more wagons.

A few months ago I was a girl in my father's house in Kentucky and now I am a traveling princess on a trading expedition. If Magoffin has any doubts about the wisdom of what he is doing, he hides them. I have been too caught up in the excitement to be frightened, but I shall have time now to worry as we roll westward day after day. Will I be the woman Samuel expects? I do want to be brave and strong and not weep or complain. He is good to me and I find myself changing in spirit as well as body. I pray for strength.

Saturday 13th

We are going to "noon it" now. We are up on the Prairie with not a tree near us. The sun is very warm.

Josiah Gregg's book prepares me for some of the events of the trail, but he left out important things. To me a stand of wildflowers is as important as a mountain or rock formation. None of the flowers, of which there are innumerable quantities and varieties, have gone to seed as yet, so I must press them in a book to take home. We found some beautiful roses and one flower which, for want of a better one, I have given the name of the "hour glass" from its peculiar shape. It is brown and yellow, with a fuzzy pale green leaf. The little flowers, the leaves of which turn in both ways, up and down. The flowers are very small and hang in a thick cluster at the top of the stem.

At 110 Mile Creek

I can say what few women in civilized life ever could, that the first house to which my husband took me after our marriage was a tent; and my first table was a cedar one, made with only one leg and that was the tent pole.

Each day I grow more fond of Magoffin. He explained how he computes the costs against the profits on the hard goods we carry. My attention flagged and I nearly dozed when he asked my opinion about managing the teamsters. Then I came awake, as though struck by lightning. I realized he was talking to me the way Papa talks to his foreman—as though I were his business partner. We discussed the teamsters, who tend to be short-tempered amongst themselves and prone to fistfighting. I suggested contests like foot races to work off their bad spirits. Samuel was not overly enthusiastic, but he did allow it would give them an outlet.

Samuel is kindness itself to everyone, but he paid me the supreme compliment of taking me seriously. I am 18 yrs old and have never managed anything more complicated than a Fourth of July picnic, yet he treats me as an equal although he is 20 yrs older. I'll not pine for poetry or romance when he had given me this tribute.

Last night, in his passion, I misheard what he said. "Who is she?" I demanded righteously, ready to take offense. He looked utterly nonplussed and lost his erection. (That mysterious event I have so recently learned.)

"What name?" he asked.

"You called out 'Alma, Alma.' Who is she? Some mistress you prefer to me?"

He burst into laughter. I was angry.

"*Mi alma* is Spanish," he explained. "It means 'my soul.' "

I apologized, embarrassed at my ignorance and lack of faith. He showered me with all the Spanish endearments he knew—*mi corazón, mi amor, querida*. I hope other couples arrive at pet names so affectionately. I call him *mi alma* now and no one knows our secret.

I SEE THAT I WRITE SHORTER DIARY ENTRIES FOR MY FAMILY THAN I do for myself. I must do better so that when I return they will have a record of what I observed.

Camp No. 7

Last night we heard a wolfish kind of serenade! Just as I had composed myself for sleep after fanning off to some other quarters the mosquitoes, the delightful music began. Ring, my dear, good dog, was lying under my side of the bed and he flew out with a fierce bark and drove them away. Then the flying tormentors returned and it was slap! slap! while *mi alma* breathed sweet sleep at my side.

Diamond Spring

Last night the mosquitoes were so thick I was afraid to leave the carriage and go into our tent to be closed up with them. Samuel told me to run straight into the tent and into bed without taking off hat or shoes. I dashed from the carriage through the flap and he pushed me under the mosquito bar. I checked to see if I was alone, then I stripped down to my shift in an effort to cool off. The next day I discovered that the impudent pests had left lumps the size of peas all over my face.

• • •

I SENT SAMUEL TO DO THE SAME SERVICE FOR JANE. THANK HEAVens, she is always ready for something new. For once Sandeval and Tabino got her tent up pronto and Samuel pushed her inside her net.

I am less nimble than Jane as I slowly change shape. Samuel says he can see no change, but my bodice is too snug and I must lace my stays more loosely. They are loose already because of the heat, which is oppressive. No one mentions it, so I think it must be my condition.

When Samuel returned I lay almost in a perfect stupor, the heat and stings made me perfectly sick. Samuel took off my shift and bathed me, very matter of factly. I found it unspeakably tender. Later, about 11 o'clock, *mi alma* came and raised me up onto my feet without waking me. He led me outside where the whole scene had entirely changed. The sky was dark, wind blew high, the atmosphere was cool and pleasant and no mosquitoes!

I thought I loved him when we married, but I did not know him well. I loved only those aspects that were public. Now I know him to be a good manager of his employees, a calm and reassuring traveling companion and an ardent lover.

Thursday 25th

Here I am in the middle of my bed, with my feet drawn up under me like a tailor. I have taken refuge from the rain, which from the time we went to bed last night till this time, 3 P.M., has continued to fall, driving against the tent as though it would wash us away every moment. But we continue dry over head and that is something. We rose late this morning and had nothing to do. We ate and came back to bed and sat in the middle of it to keep our feet dry. The water ran in one side of the tent and out the other like a little spring.

Mi alma soon tired of sitting with his feet as high as his head and so put his head in my lap and dozed a little and talked a little.

Soon we both lay down, but not for a nap, but then Colonel Owens came to see how we fared in the rain.

Whatever happens, I enjoy it still. It is all part of the "variety of life," which adds "spice." Of course it must be enjoyed.

Each night Samuel and the wheelwright inspect all the wagons. The wooden wheels shrink inside the iron rims. The blacksmith must set up his forge and anvil and repair broken axles and shape shoes for the mules.

My duties include feeding the horses, also the chickens and ducks in their coops, and Ring, our noble brown and white hound.

We number: fourteen big wagons with six yoke of oxen each; one baggage wagon with two yoke; one Dearborn carriage with two mules (which concern carries Jane and sometimes me); our carriage with two more mules; two men on mules driving loose stock consisting of nine and one half yoke of oxen, two riding horses, and three mules. Mr. Hall supervises twenty men, three of which were tent servants. Additionally, for our use: two horses, nine mules, some two hundred oxen, and the dog.

Ring is my companion during the day and sleeps beside us at night. He is hopeless for retrieving the partridges Samuel shoots. Ring knows the birds are good for something, but he has not been trained for hunting.

Besides the insect I think of as an alligator in miniature, Jane and I are careful when we walk. Yesterday I carelessly stepped almost onto a large snake. It moved, and I screamed and ran off like a ninny.

At Council Grove we found ripe gooseberries and raspberries and nearby, wild plums, but they were not ripe.

Sunday June 28th

On this my third Sunday on the Plains, my conscience is troubled. May my heavenly father grant me pardon for my wickedness! On this Holy Sabbath, so much like a regular day of the week, I took out my week's work, knitting. How could I ever have been so un-mindful of my duty and my eternal salvation!

June 29th
Cross Creek

Jane and I found enough gooseberries for a fine pie and tonight we enjoyed a dinner of boiled chicken, rice, and dessert of wine and gooseberry tart.

I have seen a perfect city of prairie dog dwellings, stretching for acres. Wolves are heard at night. We expect to see buffalo soon. A Mexican man in Colonel Owens' company died. He had consumption. Poor man! Only yesterday I sent him soup from our camp. Interring on the plains is necessarily very simple. The grave is dug deep to prevent wolves from getting to the body, then stones are put over the corpse, earth thrown in and sod replaced. The Mexicans always place a cross at the grave.

July 4th
Pawnee Rock

Yesterday was a disastrous celebration. We stopped at Pawnee Rock, which has an awe-ing name since this tribe are the most treacherous and troublesome to the traders. Samuel stood by to watch if any Indian should come up on the far side of the rock while I cut my name, among the many hundreds inscribed on the rock and many of which I knew. It was not done well, for fear of Indians made me tremble and I hurried it over.

We rode briskly to overtake the wagons and had gone some six miles to Ash Creek. No water ran in the creek and the crossing looked pretty good with a tolerably steep bank. Magoffin hollered "Whoa" to stop the carriage so we could get out and walk down to save the mules. But the mules kept going—over the verge. Samuel hauled on the reins. I shrieked and the carriage whirled over the edge, flew off, and crashed. The top and sides broke into pieces with a shattering noise. Samuel caught me in his arms as we fell. I was stunned at first and could not stand. Samuel carried me in his arms to a shade tree, falling once as he struggled up the bank, and rubbed my face and hands with whiskey until I came to myself. We were both bruised. He could have saved himself if he hadn't clasped me as we crashed. I should perhaps have been killed without his shoulders keeping the top off me. I sought Jane's carriage.

I am rather the better of my bruises today. I fear I am yet to suffer for it.

We stay at Pawnee Rock. A respectable crowd now, we number seventy-five or eighty wagons of merchandise, besides those of the First Dragoons, which have joined us. I hope the soldiers' uniforms frighten any Indians that might have had plans to attack us.

We see bison now. I am uneasy when Samuel goes hunting. There is danger that the excited hunter seldom thinks of. His horse may fall and kill him; the buffalo is apt to whirl—and fatal accidents occur. To placate me, Samuel presented me with marrow and I found it a subtle and delicate dish. I have trouble keeping down the salt meat we brought. Even my father's country ham no longer tastes good. I drink shrub, mixing crushed fruit with sugar and water. It suits me better. Samuel thrives on cold food, rain, wind, accidents, and no water. I could complain, but I choose to think of this as part of our adventure together.

I can bear anything with Samuel beside me. He is strong and confident. He explained why New Mexico must become part of the United States. Manifest Destiny is a huge undertaking and we are but a small part of it. Our little train, dwarfed by the expanse of the prairie, is moving with the times.

In the early morning, I walked out a bit for exercise. I picked wildflowers until I could hold no more. Their scent faded as I plucked them and they wilted soon after, but the little spots of color in the dun and ocher grass are alluring.

All of my life I have been taught to resist temptation, to be silent, to be well-mannered, to be seen and not heard. Now I am learning I can enjoy myself and it is acceptable to Samuel. I now talk to the head teamster and give orders to the house (actually tent) servants directly. Jane washed our small clothes in the creek and they dried in an hour, where she hung them on bushes. It is getting harder to bend over. Samuel accommodates my belly now with inventive games. No matter how I feel, when I see the love in his eyes, I know I would do it all again.

Saturday 11th
Camp 31st

How gloomy the Plains have been to me today! I am sick, with sad feelings, and everything around corresponds with them.

We see thousands of bison. The plain is dead level here and this morning we saw several elk, tossing their noble heads and moving with majestic pride.

Tuesday 21st
A Shipwreck on Land

We stopped early last afternoon with a storm blowing overhead. Spattering rain hit the carriage roof, died and blew again. We ate supper, then the men got tents up in the loose, dry sand before the storm proper arrived. It was only eight o'clock when we went to bed, but it seemed later because of the somber sky.

The storm crashed overhead with torrents of rain, lightning shattered and peal after peal of thunder rang. As the storm came closer, the lightning's glare and the thunder's boom were simultaneous. The ground shuddered and the tent canvas strained. My bed was a boat in a stormy sea. The rain poured down and the wind gusted. I could almost feel the tent pegs loosening.

I called to Samuel, but he couldn't hear, but he must have sensed the danger because he sent José, Sandeval, and Tabino to remove Mrs. Magoffin. However, before they could extricate me, the tent collapsed.

I screamed in horror. I struggled to brace the heavy fabric, but it weighed too much. The wet canvas leaked where it touched me. I sobbed for Magoffin and struggled to breathe. My big belly made me awkward and the canvas trapped me. I felt I should drown.

Then I felt the canvas lift and Tabino hoisted it up while the other two hauled the main pole up. José held it and Sandeval pulled me out and carried me to Samuel, who wrapped me in blankets.

"Stay here," he said, and sat me inside their carriage. "I've lashed this to the wheels of the baggage wagon to keep it from turning over in the storm." Later, when I calmed enough to stop shaking, I found Jane's carriage. I couldn't sleep, but it was warmer.

The next morning Magoffin mounted a horse bareback with only a halter and rode through the flooding water. He looked as charming as a mill boy with his feet drawn almost up to the horse's back. He drove the reluctant oxen across the racing creek.

TUESDAY I WAS TAKEN SICK. WE STOPPED AT THE RIVER AT NOON. We found it better to go on to the fort as two or three companies had gone ahead and the doctor with them.

Friday morning I was no better and *mi alma* sent a man ahead to stop the doctor. Now that I am with the doctor I am satisfied. He is a polite delicate Frenchman from St. Louis. He is an excellent physician especially in Female cases and I have great confidence in his knowledge and capacity of relieving me although mine is a complication of diseases.

I AM TERRIFIED OF BEING SICK OUT HERE ON THE PLAINS, EVEN with a good nurse in Jane and the kindest husband in the world who would gladly suffer in my stead. I am to stay quiet in the carriage, but how can I be quiet when every rock and rut tosses me about? I long heartily for my mother and sisters. I am bleeding but as long as I can feel the little one shift and move I am reassured.

How do less fortunate women face adversity? I pray and each Sabbath read Dr. Beecher's sermons, but if I were at home, I should give in to these discomforts and stay in bed. Last night I gave in a little. "*Mi alma,*" I said, "I feel poorly."

He took me in his arms and a groan escaped me. I am still bruised from my crash and feel so weak. I am afraid the child will come too soon.

"Are you ailing?" he asked tenderly.

"Yes," I said. I could not tell him all, but I think he knew.

"I will see what I can do," he promised. He told me I was strong and brave and that I must stay in bed and do what the French doctor prescribed. I may recover yet.

July 27th
Bent's Fort

On our way here I saw soldiers encamped, a novel sight to me. The fort fills my idea of an ancient castle. It is built of adobe, with walls very high and thick with rounding corners. There is but one entrance. It is ninety or an hundred feet square. Inside the fort are twenty-five rooms which open on a huge patio and commons room. Servants sprinkled the dirt floors with water several times a day to prevent dust in the many rooms—bed chambers, dining rooms, a blacksmith's shop, and an ice house. Animals are kept inside the walls. They have a well and a billiard room.

Samuel has persuaded William Bent to give us rooms and I rested in a parlor and listened to *las señoritas* of the fort while the men took our furniture up. Our room has two windows, one which looks out on the Plain and the other which looks in to the patio. We take our meals in this room. Dr. Messure brought me more medicine and advises *mi alma* to take me to Europe. The advice is better than the medicine—anything to restore my health. I never should have consented to take the trip on the Plains had it not been with the hope that it would prove beneficial, but so far my hopes have been blasted for I am rather going down hill than up and it is so bad to be sick and under a physician all the time. How prone human nature is to grumble and think one's lot harder than any one of his fellow creatures. I must quieten my rebellious heart! I am thinner by a good many pounds than when I came out.

My body has absorbed so much abuse that I feel the child is trying to escape. I feel so ill. Even with Samuel, I am dreadfully frightened.

July 30th
My Birthday

I felt rather strange, not surprised. I was sick with strange sensation in my head, my back, and hips. I was obliged to lie down most of the time, and when I got up to hold my hand over my eyes.

There was the greatest possible noise in the patio.

The pains began. The doctor came, but once the waters broke, he could do nothing except attend me.

Children cried in the patio. Horses neighed, mules brayed, men scolded and fought. Servants quarreled. Nothing stopped while I labored. The pain grew and came oftener, until I could scarcely get my breath between spasms. I had never experienced such pain—it grasped my body, wrung it and cast me out. And each time I disappeared in it, another shipwreck. I screamed. Samuel disappeared, then returned, looking worried. "This is women's work," he muttered, and left again.

"Is there nothing you can do?" I begged the doctor. Pain stiffened me. I clawed at the bedclothes. The pain lifted me from the bed. I thought I would split apart. My hair lay plastered to my face and neck. If Mama were here, she would know what to do. Mama had lots of children. My sister would bring me a napkin wrung out in cold water from the ice house.

I lost myself from the pain.

"Push," said the doctor. "It is time."

I had no strength left to push. I was too tired. I went away again.

"No, madame!" The doctor raised my shoulders. "It is almost finished. Push!"

And I reached down beyond fatigue and found strength and pushed, felt a new, ripping pain, pushed, and the doctor reached for the baby.

I faded and came back again. Where was the child? I could feel all the warm wet fluids in the bed. Where was the child?

"My baby!"

The doctor worked at a basin of water placed on a chest, his back to me. He shook his head.

"It was kicking this morning," I said.

He shook his head again.

"No!" I wept. I struggled to sit up. "No! Let me see it."

I forced myself to become calm. The doctor wouldn't do as I asked if I was hysterical. I bit my lips and tried to breathe.

"Please," I begged softly.

"It came too soon. It is too small," said the doctor. He lifted the tiny body from the water and wrapped it in a towel. He brought it to me, and helped me prop myself up to take it.

"No," I whispered. "Sometimes they are big enough."

Then I saw the tiny face, white, eyes closed, flecks of blood streaking the cheeks. The doctor hesitated, then he handed me the bundle and pushed pillows behind my head.

I unwrapped the tiny, perfect infant. I counted the fingers, all the toes. A fine swirl of black hair, long earlobes, the cord. A beautiful, perfect boy. Tears ran unabated. A fly buzzing in the room landed on the small white face. Then I knew he was dead. "No," I murmured. "Not now. I wanted you so much. You are our first child." The doctor took the bundle and covered the face.

Later, after I was again in order, Samuel went to William Bent and asked if he might bury the infant.

Outside the fort, an Indian woman, perhaps an Arapaho, gave birth to a fine, healthy baby almost at the same time and half an hour later walked to the river and bathed.

Friday 31st July

I am forbidden to rise from my bed, but I am free to meditate. I slept, woke to weep and slept again. Most of all I wished for my family—all the cousins and aunts and my mother who could have told me what to expect. I could have asked how to bear the pain. They would have comforted me.

The fort is agreeable enough in itself, but with it are connected some rather unpleasant reflections—something rather sad, though I will not murmur at the chastening hand of Providence.

It is just 12 days since we came and 8 days since I left my room. Within that short space of time many things have occurred, both to myself and others. . . . In a few short months I should have been a happy mother and made the heart of a father glad, but we were deprived of that hope.

August 4th
En route west of Raton

Once we left the fort, we proceeded to Santa Fe with me lying in the carriage. My spirits lifted when I gazed on the mountains. What bride lives who had such a beginning, such despair and exaltation? I saw rain falling miles away in a purple veil. In the afternoon, the sun's dying rays threw claret shadows deep into the rocks. The air was cool in the shade and invigorating as wine. I thank God that I am mending and anticipate further novel events. I trust Samuel, *mi alma,* and pray.

Requiem for Rosebud

KEN HODGSON

Ken Hodgson's first published western novel, *The Hell Benders,* carries the endorsement of Elmer Kelton. His lifelong experience of the mining business and sure hand with narrative combine to create a compelling story of a pragmatic hero and his loyal partner.

of folks, some God-fearing and some that gives a preacher his purpose in life. Then there was Rosebud. It's an awful pretty name to waste on a town run by greed and evil. But that's what they called the place.

Gold is what caused Rosebud to be born there in the middle of nowhere. I should know, I was the first to find it. The problem was getting the gold out and living to enjoy the rewards.

It seems like it was just the other day instead of over five years ago that Rosebud and I first found gold thereabouts. Now Rosebud is my burro. Generally she's of tolerable good humor, but there's days when her female side comes to the forefront. If'n she hadn't gotten a burr under her blanket though, we'd likely never struck it.

I'd been following color up this one gulch for weeks. The last time I'd found pay rock was back in '74, so even a little color showing in the pan looked plenty good.

Folks who don't know beans about mining don't understand just how hard it can be to find a vein even when you've got it pinned down to a few hundred feet. I was so close I could smell it, but after several days I was getting powerful discouraged. Then one cloudy afternoon, Rosebud came wanderin' down to the spring for a drink and stepped square on top of a big rattler.

That burro flew straight up in the air and came down kickin'. Ole Rosebud never could abide snakes. Well, she drew back her hind legs and I reckon that rattler plumb starved to death before it came back to earth. That's when I seen it. Shiny wires of glistening gold right there where Rosebud had kicked that snake. By the time it got too dark to work I had opened up a narrow vein of white quartz shot plumb through with yellow metal.

The next morning I staked out a claim, naming it *Rosebud* after my burro. It was more'n fair, after all, she's the one that found it. Now, gold ain't worth nothing until you sell it and a claim ain't neither until you record it in the courthouse. That's when the trouble generally starts and I've been around long enough to learn to plan for it.

I headed for Pioche and sold what gold I'd brought out with me to a crooked assayer. There was over a hundred ounces in those ore sacks for sure—some of that rock was half gold—but I only got ten dollars an ounce. The scalawag kept moaning about it not being pure and all. Finally I took his offer. A thousand dollars is a lot of money and I needed to be moving, so I didn't have time to argue. Just *talk* of someone finding rich ore like what I'd sold had started gold rushes before.

After I left the assayer's, I filed the claim. Then I bought a passel of supplies at McVey's General Store, including several cases of Giant powder and plenty of ammo. I stowed what I could carry in Rosebud's saddlebags, then headed down to the livery to see Slim Matteson.

Slim looked up from a harness he was mendin', gave me a surprised smile, and said, "Well, Matt Wheeler, you're a sight for sore eyes. I figured you was buzzard bait."

"And you're still just a sight," I replied. "But it's good to see you anyway," then added seriously, "I finally made a strike."

Slim dropped the harness, jumped up like he'd been settin' on an ant bed, and said excitedly, "Where'd you find it and how rich is it?"

I tossed him a chunk of ore that probably had a half pound of gold in it and watched him examine it closely as a doctor does a newborn baby.

"East of Pioche in a rugged canyon of the Mahogany Mountains," I replied. "But it's not opened up enough to tell how big it will be. Right now the vein's only two to three inches wide."

I'd been in on too many mining deals for me to get my hopes up until we'd done a lot more work. Greenhorns think every vein is as wide as Fanny's bottom and longer than a wagon track.

"Just a few tons of high-grade like this will set a man up for life," Slim muttered dreamily without taking his eyes from that rock.

"Mining it ain't the problem, Slim. It's gonna be getting the ore out and sold without developing some unwanted holes in our hides," I said, bringing him out of his daydreaming.

Slim's handlebar mustache drooped so that it made him look sorrier than a starving hound. "Well, I reckon since I grubstaked you, we've got some work cut out for us. I'll get the mules together so we can pack the supplies we'll need. You'll take care of the rest?"

"Yeah," I told him. "I'll head over to the telegraph office then we'll go fetch the rest of the supplies so we can head out at daybreak. I've a real hankerin' for a good meal and a roof over my head for a change."

"A bath wouldn't cause you a lot of damage," Slim said absently, still staring at that piece of gold. "I'll even fill up the tub for you. I 'spect you won't be going to the hotel."

A chill trickled down my backbone. Charlie Voss owned not only the hotel but the saloons as well. He also was behind nearly every killing and claim-jumping that happened in these parts.

Sheriff Cox knew all about what was going on but for some reason when he played poker at one of Charlie's joints he always won big. Asking the sheriff for help was kind of like bringin' in a pack of coyotes to guard your sheep.

"Yeah, Slim," I said. "I reckon I'll sack out here and hope to live through whatever you cook up for supper. It'll be safer eatin' your vittles than going to Voss's place, especially once word of me selling that gold hits. I ain't sure about that bath, though. Flapjack Henry didn't live a day after they gave him one at Doc's."

"Flap was snakebit," Slim groaned. "That bath they gave him had nothing to do with his shakin' hands with Saint Peter."

"Well, I don't know if'n I want to take the chance or not," I replied testily, as I departed for the telegraph office.

· · ·

WHEN WE LEFT THE NEXT MORNING TO HEAD UP TO THE CLAIM, I was spankin' clean. Slim's got a real thing about bathin' regular. I suppose he'd take one ever' week if the town had enough water.

I reckon there must have been a couple of hundred wide-eyed pilgrims following us. It was a lot like leading a Fourth of July Parade. That wasn't any surprise to me. Gold does that to folks. Slim was mighty concerned, though. He'd never been in on a gold rush before. But I'd put his name on the claim papers for a full third interest, so he didn't have any choice. Slim had furnished me with beans and powder for the past year. Now that I'd made a strike, it was time he joined in on a little of the fun.

"Couldn't you have made a couple more trips and then we'd have enough boodle to hire us some help?" Slim complained, as he struggled with the head-and-tail string that was leading five loaded pack mules behind him.

"I could have," I said, "but it would have been mighty risky. All a body would have to do was plug me and take the mine for themselves. Now it's a matter of record who owns it. Even Charlie Voss can't get around that fact easy."

"Reckon you're right," Slim said, after cussin' out the lead mule proper-like. "Voss is as mean as a peeled rattler. I 'spect he'll be planning on stealing our diggin's anyway."

"Slim, ole friend, I'm counting on it."

A FEW DAYS AFTER WE ARRIVED AT THE MINE, THE WHOLE DAD-blasted countryside was covered with claims. Folks who didn't know pay rock from cow chips were slingin' dirt out of holes like a badger burrowin' in for the winter.

Slim and me spent the first couple of days building a lean-to for shelter. A few feet from the mine there was a overhang of rock. We faced it off with some poles and while it wasn't much for looks, it would keep the sun off. The place also gave us a good view up and down the gulch.

Then we started tunneling, saving the high-grade and stashing it in canvas bags and burying them under fresh rock from our diggings.

After we'd had our beans for dinner one day, a man leading a burro came up the gulch heading straight for our mine. As soon as I made out who it was, I lowered the hammer on my Winchester.

"Well, come on in and have a plate, Mose," I hollered.

I'd known old Mose Taylor for years. He was chasing gold rushes when I was still a pup.

Mose finished off the rest of our beans, then bummed a long-nine cigar from me. He pulled a fagot out of the campfire, lit his cigar, then set back and began filling us in on what was going on.

"There's a town growin' up on that flat where the gulch makes that sharp bend," he said. "And it never fails to surprise me how fast a saloon can sprout up when the spirit calls."

I raised an eyebrow and said, "Reckon I wouldn't be struck dumb if you told me it was Charlie Voss that was the one peddlin' the tarantula juice."

"Nope," Mose said. He took a drag on his cigar and went on. "It's him, all right. He's got a couple of toughs workin' for him by the names of Sam Kincaid and Vance Perkins. Aside from his saloon—he calls both it and the town 'Rosebud,' by the way—there's a dozen other buildin's thrown up."

"I reckon he's trying to soften me up by naming the town after my burro," I said.

Mose chuckled then coughed deep for a moment. I never could see how a man could breathe cigar smoke through his lungs and live. I mainly just chew the ends off of 'em.

"No, Matt, it ain't that, it's just that no one else seems to be findin' gold. Yours is the only strike so far. That's why he named the town after your mine. It ain't because he's feelin' kindly toward you, it's because the Rosebud is the only rich mine hereabouts."

That news was worrisome; if other veins had been found, it would help keep attention from us for a while.

"No one's found anything?" I asked.

"Oh, a Swede by the name of Johnston found a little ore below town a couple of days ago. He apparently didn't know much about dynamite. He blew himself to smithereens. Since he hadn't filed a claim, Kincaid jumped it. And would you believe he deeded it over to Charlie Voss before the Swede was even planted? He's got a couple of hired men diggin' the shaft deeper, but they ain't found nothin'."

"How does a man blow himself up?" Slim asked with concern.

Slim was plenty scared of dynamite, so I done all the blasting. I looked at him seriously. "The same way we'll have an *accident* as soon as Voss thinks he can take us out and wind up with the mine. That's the reason I filed the claim. He can't jump ours as easy as he did the Swede's."

Slim shuddered, dropped the subject of dynamite and took to looking around all worried-like with his hand resting on his gun.

"Tell me a little about the Rosebud Saloon," I said.

Mose cocked an eye and said, "Well, the place ain't nothin' but a clapboard shack. Charlie's got some planks set on whiskey barrels for a bar. There's five or six little rooms in back for some soiled doves. I understand he's got a bevy of 'em. Why, he's even got a honky-tonk pi-aner. Can you believe it? They've got a road fixed up out here now you can bring a pi-aner over."

"What about the girls, Mose?"

He shot me a grin and said, "You ain't fixin' to go pursuin' any basic urges, I hope. I reckon that wouldn't be healthy."

"No, Mose, I just want to know about them, that's all."

"Well sir, I've been away from the almighty dollar for so long I can't recall whose picture's on one. I only stopped by the general store an' bought a dime's worth of coffee. Charlie's boys wouldn't let me inside the Rosebud. Payin' customers are all that's allowed."

I reached into my pocket, brought out a couple of five-dollar gold pieces, and tossed them into Mose's lap. He blinked a couple of times to make sure his eyes weren't deceiving him, then glanced at me like I'd just grown horns and asked, "What in tarnation is this for? You ain't a tryin' to give me a job, are you?"

Mose had a reputation for being as nervous around work as a chicken eyeing a hawk. "Now Mose, I wouldn't insult you none by asking you to risk gettin' a blister. What I'd like you to do is go spend that money in the Rosebud Saloon."

The old man was running out of strange ways to look at me. He shook his head and grabbed up the coins. "My pappy always told me to never take advantage of a crazy man, but in your case I'm goin' to make an exception."

"There *is* one thing I'd like you to do." That wiped the smile right off Mose's face.

"An' jus' what might that be?"

"I want you to come back and tell us what Voss is up to, and I especially want to know about his girls."

Mose went back to shaking his head and grinning. "I rather planned on checkin' 'em out, Matt. It's just reportin' on the details that I ain't used to."

"That's not what I meant," I said, to his obvious relief. "All I want you to do is let us know what Charlie's up to and the names of his ladies. If you'll do that, there's a fair to middlin' chance I might find a few more gold pieces for you."

The old man left smiling like he'd found the mother lode. Slim eyed me mighty cautious when I grabbed several sticks of dynamite and started tying them into bundles with some twine. He come as close as he felt comfortable and said, "That old man might have been on to something when he called you crazy—just what, may I ask, are you up to?"

"Equalizing the odds a mite," I replied. "Come hell or high water, Voss will try to jump our mine. You can bet your hole card it won't be him personal—that ain't his style—he'll send his hired help. I plan on giving 'em more than they're expecting to find."

Slim didn't seem any too certain about me not being cracked after I explained what I was doing, but he went a safe distance away and started cutting the ends out of a coffee can with his knife.

Across the gulch near the top of the hill was a jumble of boulders. It was an easy rifle shot from there to our mine. I figured it to be the perfect place for an ambush to come from.

I took one bundle of dynamite and stuck a few blasting caps in the gaps where the string tied the sticks together. Then I grabbed a coffee can lid and climbed up to that rock pile. After I found the right crevice to stick it into, I covered the dynamite with some twigs from a pack rat's nest. I wedged the shiny lid in just so and went back to our lean-to. I was proud as punch when I stood in the mine entrance and saw the sun sparkling off that lid. It made a perfect target.

I set another bundle on the bank above the trail heading down the gulch. Slim even pitched in and helped me cover all but one side of it with a big mound of rocks, making it appear like a claim marker. One more lid and a piece of cactus later, we had a couple of surprises ready for any unwelcome visitors.

From then on, only one of us worked in the mine while the other stayed under cover with a Winchester kept at the ready. It was hard to guess just what Charlie Voss would try. There was always a chance he'd hire a shyster lawyer and try to jump our claim. The more I thought on the matter, the more I discounted it. Lawyers cost money and Voss was as cheap as a free drink. No matter how I sliced it, we were going to have a showdown with him. The only problem was, he called the shots as to when and how it would come down.

We had a fair amount of vittles laid back, and the little spring that ran by the lean-to had good water in it, so we could wait a spell. Like the doc told the lady whose baby swallered her wedding ring, "All things will eventually come to pass."

. . .

A COUPLE OF DAYS LATER ANOTHER PROBLEM AROSE: THE VEIN played out. It never was anything big, just richer than sin. First it narrowed to about an inch, then to a knife-blade width. The last blast I fired off showed nothing but gray granite that had as much gold in it as a tombstone.

There wasn't any gold in the floor of our little tunnel, but since we were doing a heap of waiting, I went ahead and put in a couple of shots. Not only was there no gold, that pretty white quartz vein disappeared. I called Slim in from his guardin' spot behind a big boulder near the mine entrance and gave him the sad facts.

"She was just a pocket, Slim. My guess is this one was just a little bigger than the one Mose said that Swede dug into."

"Won't the gold come back if we drive deeper into the mountain?" Slim questioned hopefully.

"Maybe," I answered. "Then again, maybe not. Lots of folks put all they've made and more into a hole in the ground trying to find a mother lode that simply ain't there. Besides that, partner, there's not even a vein. You can see for yourself there's nothing to follow. No, I think all the pay dirt the Rosebud's ever going to give up is in those canvas bags we've got buried outside."

Slim put that sorry hound dog expression on his face and whined, "You really think the mine's no good?"

"Dadgummit, Slim, what I'm trying to get through that block of wood you're packing around on your shoulders is, there is no mine. It was just a small pocket, that's all. Now don't go getting all bleary-eyed on me. We've probably got nigh on to a thousand ounces in those bags. If we get to an ore buyer that don't try to skin us, we should get maybe seventeen dollars an ounce. That ain't chicken feed in my book!"

I reckon it took Slim ten minutes to give up on trying to figger out what a third of seventeen thousand was so he just said, "I guess we've done pretty well for ourselves."

"We will for sure, if we can get out with it. Charlie Voss can have the mine. That'd be about the meanest trick I can think of to play on that skunk. He'll spend a passel of money digging more holes for sure. Our problem is, if we load up the gold on those mules and head out, we'll turn up dead in less than a mile."

"Well, Matt, what *are* we gonna do?"

"Fix lunch," I said, as I went to boil up a pot of beans.

MOSE TAYLOR MUST BE ABLE TO SMELL FOOD COOKING FROM A mile upwind. I'd just finished frying up some salt pork to add to the kettle when he came saunterin' up the canyon. He stared at that pile of rocks we'd buried the dynamite under for a minute, shook his head, then hollered at us that he was comin' in and for nobody to shoot.

He helped himself to a heaping plate of beans and grabbed a cup of coffee. After he'd eaten half of our grub, he bummed a cigar, then leaned back and commenced to yak while Slim and me rationed out the remaining pintos for ourselves.

"Charlie's got a real rip-snortin' joint," Mose said between puffs of cigar smoke. "Matter of fact, his place *is* Rosebud. He has the only business in town now that McVey closed his store and high-tailed it back to Pioche."

"No one's found any more ore?" I asked.

"Not enough to fill a bad tooth. The only reason folks are hangin' around is because of your mine bein' so rich. Oh, there's maybe a dozen hopefuls still diggin', but the smart ones has left."

"Tell me a little about Charlie's place," I said.

"Well, he waters that rotgut whiskey he sells for two bits a shot. But he only charges a dollar fer a visit to the back room," Mose said with a satisfied expression.

Then I noticed him eyeing a couple of beans stuck to the side of the pot. I scraped 'em up mighty quick and said, "I don't want to place a major strain on your intellect, Mose, but I reckon I'd appreciate a little more information; ten dollars' worth sounds about right."

The old prospector looked taken aback. "I was gonna get to it. That's the trouble with you young'uns these days, you've got no patience. Well sir, he's got his hired guns checkin' out every diggin' an' hopin' to dry-gulch someone with money. So far folks have been pretty lucky. There ain't no one outside that Swede that's found gold an' no one left in Rosebud's got enough money so's a body could make a profit by shootin' 'em."

"What's his business like?" I asked.

"Droppin' like an anvil," Mose replied. "When Charlie first opened, the place was a real fanny bumper. Last night they was only a few hopefuls. Things are so slow he's sent all but a couple of the girls back to town. He's only kept Liver Lip Lou and the Pioche Pig out here. I say, Matt, when a body sets eyes on either of those two, a silver dollar looks a sight better. There's a new gal who came out with him. Now there's a looker. But Charlie made it real clear— he has a way about him of doin' that—she was *his* girl an' it'd be too bad if anyone treated her like she weren't a lady."

I wolfed down the last of my beans, grabbed a cup of coffin varnish, and said, "Tell me a little about this gal of Charlie's. What's she look like and what's her name?"

Mose seemed happy talking about her. "She's a blonde. A little on the skinny side for my tastes, but she has looks that could clean out a bank. Her name's Mattie Kane. Charlie calls her his Candy Kane. He's real taken with her. I reckon he'd shoot a man who just looked at her too long. Charlie was in the outhouse when I had a chance to talk to her."

"You *talked* to her?" I asked.

"Yep, I sure did. That's why I come hoofin' out here. Candy— uh, Mattie—whispered in my ear and said to tell you that Charlie's had a will drawn up from you an' Slim here. You folks bein' his best friends an' all, you're leaving him the Rosebud claim along with all the gold you've mined."

"Plumb decent of us, but we ain't turned up our toes yet," Slim chimed in.

"I reckon Charlie figures to help us into the everlasting, just like he helped that Swede 'accidentally' blow himself to Kingdom Come."

"How's the mine lookin'?" Mose asked casually.

"Like a hole in the ground," I replied quickly before Slim could say anything. I wasn't ready for word to get around about the vein having petered out.

Mose drawled, "Boys, I'd like to stick around and see what you're fixin' for supper tonight, but I figure it might be time to move on. Healthier anyway."

I pulled a twenty-dollar gold piece from my pocket and handed it to the old man. He looked at me like a cat that just ate a canary and asked, "You want me to go back to Rosebud an see what's going on some more?"

"You've done fine," I told him. "Your luck might be better in another camp."

"Lately I've been thinking the same thing," Mose said. "Reckon I'll wander up toward Montana."

The old prospector finished his coffee, then bummed my last cigar. As he was leaving he glanced at me over his shoulder. "That new girl of Charlie's, the looker—do you know her, Matt?"

"Have a safe trip," I replied.

After Mose left, Slim commenced to worrying himself into a dither about getting dead. I had a flask of snakebite remedy in my grip. After a couple of pulls he seemed to settle down some.

There was no good reason to keep on digging in the mine, so I grabbed up my Winchester and told him I'd do guard duty with him. So that's all we done the rest of the day, just set there and talked, while waiting for the storm to blow in.

Trying to predict when Voss would make his move was kinda like figuring out what a woman might do and when she'd do it, only it didn't take nearly as long. From the way the sun was laying over the top of the hills, I reckon it was just midafternoon when Slim whispered from the shady side of a big rock, "Say, Matt, I caught a flash of something moving up by those boulders right where you said they'd come from."

I took a careful peek around the edge of the mine opening. My eyesight's tolerable better than Slim's. This time he was right on 'cause one of them rocks was wearing a hat.

"You stay under cover, pard. We've got visitors for sure."

He didn't have to be told twice. Slim flattened out like a horned toad, cocked his rifle, and aimed at that boulder nest.

"Don't go waking snakes yet," I told him quietly. "For all we know, they're just looking us over. Also, there's a fair to middlin' chance they might be moving in on us from the other direction."

I hadn't planned on ole Slim being so durn jittery. He up and made a run towards me and the mine. A bullet slapped into rocks behind him, just as he made cover.

"My guess is they ain't here simply to look us over," Slim gasped, catching his breath.

"Nope, they're here on business. But that little turkey shoot you provided gave 'em away. There's two men up there. One's right below the other."

"I'll take your word for it," Slim said.

"Put your hat over your rifle barrel and stick it outside a mite. I want to make sure we've got everybody out there pinned down."

"*We've* got *them* pinned down?" Slim croaked.

He was too shook to argue. The minute that hat of his saw daylight, two rifle shots cracked from the boulder nest. One bullet tore a ragged hole through his hat. That told me what I needed to know.

"It's got to be Charlie's two thugs," I said. "If he ain't hired any new help lately, we'll be okay."

Slim was looking a little on the peaked side, so I thought I'd put him at ease. I rested my rifle on a scrub oak branch that was at the mine portal and took careful aim at that coffee can lid. The sun was just right and it was shining away. I fired and a puff of dirt flared in front of it. Two more rifle bullets slammed into the ground in front of us as I jumped back for cover.

"You've really got 'em worried, Matt." Slim said.

"Somebody's been messing with my rifle," I growled. "They knocked the windage off."

This time I drew a bead and aimed a bit higher when I fired. Matt Wheeler don't miss twice. That boulder nest blew apart with the biggest bang you ever heard. When rocks quit falling from the sky, I walked out to check things over with Slim hot on my heels.

"By crackie, it worked," Slim said happily, eyeing the mountainside.

I agreed with him. That pile of rocks those outlaws had been hiding behind was simply not there anymore. "Whoever said you can't kill two birds with one stone didn't have any dynamite," I said.

"We still have to go through Rosebud to get out of this canyon," Slim said solemnly.

"I don't expect that'll be a problem shortly."

"*Now* what've you got up your sleeve that's likely to get us killed?"

"You worry too much, pard. We've pulled the claws out of the bear, I reckon it's time to go look him in his ugly face."

"We're going to Rosebud?" Slim choked.

"Not we, just me." Slim relaxed a little as I continued. "We can't leave all that gold here unattended. You plant yourself wherever you've got a good shot down the canyon and grab enough ammo so's that you might hit that other bomb before you run out, and wait for me. With any luck we'll make it out of here yet."

Slim shook his head and commenced to telling me how crazy people always come to a bad end. I listened to him ramble while I checked out my Colts. When I turned to make the walk down the steep gulch towards Rosebud, Slim told me, "You might have pulled the bear's claws, but have you thought about his teeth?"

"Yeah, I have," I replied more confident than I felt, as I started threading my way down the rugged canyon to Charlie Voss's saloon.

SAM GEORGE WAS PLAYING THE PIANO TO A HALF DOZEN drunken prospectors when I walked through the batwing doors into the Rosebud Saloon. It shook him so bad to see me, I think he actually banged a couple of notes in tune before he quit.

The Pioche Pig was nuzzled up to a fat drunk at the bar. Her eyes couldn't have opened any wider if someone had laid a hundred on her. She also knew who I was. Peg—that's her real name—peeled the miner's arm from around her and ran up to me.

"Matt, you get out of here," she whispered in my ear, pretending to hug me. "Charlie's fixing to kill you!"

"I know. Why don't you go tell him I'm here so's we can get on with it."

She jumped back, looked me in the eye, and said, "Matt, Charlie's as fast on the draw as they come. You're no gunfighter, are you crazy?"

"So many folks been asking me that question lately, I'm beginning to wonder myself. How about fetching Charlie?"

"Well, look who's come to town," a deep voice boomed from the dark hallway. "It's my good friend Matt Wheeler." The big man came into the light of the bar with a beautiful girl close beside him.

"It's me, all right," I answered, as Peg beat a fast retreat. "Your hired men won't be coming back. You might say they blew that little job you sent them on."

"Good help is hard to find these days." Charlie shrugged as the lithe blonde next to him gave him a squeeze around his waist. "Some things you have to take care of yourself."

"I'm calling you, Charlie, right here and now," I said with a lot more grit than I felt. The bar cleared out pronto. I stood before him, no more than twenty feet away, with sweaty hands over the handles of my revolvers.

"I hate to end a beautiful friendship like this," Charlie said, as he opened his black long coat to show off his nickel-plated .45.

The blonde stepped back from Charlie and melted into the darkness of the hallway.

"A sidewinder wouldn't call you a friend," I growled.

Voss's eyes narrowed to slits. "Then you can say hello to the devil," he said, and reached for his gun.

A shot fired inside a building makes one heck of a roar and echos something fierce. Charlie Voss hadn't cleared leather before he crumpled into a heap. I put my Colt back in its holster and yelled for everybody to stay out of the bar. Nobody gave me any argument on the matter.

The blonde came over and gave me a little peck on the cheek like she used to do when we were kids back in Missouri.

"Thanks a bunch, Mattie," I sighed. "I thought for a minute I was a goner."

"Not when your little sister's around. I've been pulling you out of scrapes all your life. When I received your telegraph, I came as fast as I could."

"Every time a prospector makes a strike, there's always a man like Voss trying to steal it from him."

"How's the mine doing?" Mattie asked.

I quickly filled her in on the sad news that it had played out. But when I told her she'd have over five thousand dollars coming for her third interest, she brightened.

I went back to the mine and helped Slim load the gold, while a few of the good citizens of Rosebud planted Charlie. If any of them ever saw the little hole in the back of his head made by Mattie's derringer, they never said anything. Most folks were simply glad to have him gone.

I USED MOST OF MY SHARE OF THE GOLD TO BUY A LITTLE SPREAD just south of Pioche. The water's good and raising cattle ain't such a bad life—fewer people shooting at you, anyway. Slim paid off the loan on his livery stable and avoids mining these days like a stump preacher does sin. Mattie took her cut and went back to St. Louis. The last letter I received from her said she was fixing to marry some politician. I'd say whoever winds up with her as a wife had better walk the straight and narrow.

A bunch of hopefuls took over our old mine and spent a fortune driving tunnels every which way. They never found a speck of gold.

Nowadays the town of Rosebud is nothing but a few falling-down buildings rattling in the desert wind. The place is dead as Charlie Voss. And no preacher will ever say any words over either of them.

Dead Game Man

SALLY ZANJANI

What is a "dead game man"? Perhaps only Sally Zanjani knows, or has to. This is a confident and controlled story of flight and pursuit, suggested by an incident in the life of frontiersman Jack Longstreet, the subject of a Zanjani biography.

EASY TO SEE IT NOW. EATING
breakfast outside the Chispa right after sunrise was a fool thing to
do. For the first few days after they jumped the mine, they'd been
more careful. Jack Longstreet watched sideways to the window by
the hour with his gun resting lightly on his arm. Billy Moyer and
George Morris acted so jumpy it made you itch just to watch them
cock their guns whenever a dog barked in the distance. Even Phil
Foote hadn't raised any particular objection to taking his turn as a
guard at night. Then the boss, Angus McArthur, who'd hired them
to take the Chispa from the Montgomerys, came driving up with a
wagon and team.

"Well, boys, I thought I better bring you a little whiskey and
beans," he said with a grin that stretched his wizened brown face so
wide it seemed to crack. "It looks like you're in for a long winter.
That's what the newspapers say."

Winter indeed. Moyer and Morris guffawed as they unloaded
the supplies and carried them into the rough board shack by the
main shaft of the Chispa. It was the tail end of the summer of 1895
then, with the sun burning down hot enough to roast an egg in the
sand. In fact, you could call it hell hot, even for the Ash Meadows
country down on the southern tip of Nevada, which wasn't exactly
known for its cooling breezes.

"Been pretty quiet, has it, boys?" asked McArthur.

They told him it had. So quiet Phil Foote found the silence
almost spooky. Not a shot fired, not a voice heard, not a man so
much as showed himself since the morning they moved in on the
Chispa, and Longstreet, in his soft Southern drawl with the dangerous edge on it, told the Montgomerys and their men they'd better

get on out and keep going, seeing as the Chispa was Mr. McArthur's property now and no one was coming in without his say-so. They took one look at Longstreet's Colt .44 and showed no disposition to argue, but the fury in Bob Montgomery's hard eyes made Foote glad that Longstreet was the one doing the talking.

McArthur nodded, looking well pleased. "Doesn't look like you boys are going to see much action," he said. "The Montgomerys say they want to settle the whole thing in court. Suits me. They let their assessment work on the Chispa slide and everybody thought she was a worthless mine, all played out before she hardly got started. That's when I staked out my claim to her, all fair and legal. I'm satisfied the judge is going to see it my way. But while the lawyers are jawing away up there in Belmont, you boys better keep holding the ground, just in case. No bloodshed, mind you. I don't want to go to jail as an accessory to murder. Just sit tight and face them down.

"By the way," he added, counting out each man's pay in gold coins, "you're famous now. The newspapers are calling you 'the professional fighters and desperate characters.'" He handed Foote a sheaf of newspaper clippings, with a wry look, as he shook the reins and turned the team south toward his ranch in the Pahrump Valley. "Well, likely they're not so far off the mark. When a man aims to take a mine, he doesn't hire himself four schoolteachers." Chuckling to himself, he drove away.

Once they heard the Montgomerys figured on fighting McArthur's claim with lawyers instead of guns, they'd eased up considerable, even Longstreet, who was maybe the wariest man living. Foote knew his ways. He hardly seemed to sleep, and never without the Colt .44 close to hand. Meet a stranger out riding and he'd slide down the far side of his horse, ready to cut loose. Let a stranger approach his campfire, and the stranger better walk slow and explain himself pretty good as he came, because Longstreet would be squatting back in the shadows in that Indian way of his with his gun. Foote sometimes wondered what had happened way back in the long ago to make the man so all-fired suspicious of everything that moved, but he knew better than to ask.

Anyway, even Longstreet had dropped his guard after McArthur
told them his difference with the Montgomerys was mainly over, so
far as shooting was concerned. Maybe being penned inside the shack
had a lot to do with it. Personally Foote didn't mind holing up if
the company showed themselves ready for a little betting action and
the surroundings were congenial. In a warm saloon, with a piano
tinkling in the background, a bottle of good bourbon at his elbow,
the cards rippling through his hands, and a soft blonde woman to
visit upstairs between games, Foote could go for days, even weeks
at a time without ever showing his face outside to see the light of
day. But being holed up in the shack by the Chispa, with Moyer
whistling strange little tunes between his teeth and Longstreet moving around the room from window to window to peer outside, his
big blonde restlessness putting Foote in mind of a caged mountain
lion—well, that was different altogether from the saloon kind of
holing up.

Foote could see the confinement grated on Longstreet worse
than anyone. Longstreet was a sagebrusher, always homesteading
out past the rim of nowhere with his Indian wives and his herds of
horses, always moving on someplace new when too many settlers
started coming in behind him. Maybe the outlaw brand had something to do with it too. Some said his long blonde hair hid the
shame of an ear slashed away from his head. Or maybe he just wasn't
the overly sociable kind. With Longstreet you could never tell.

So, edgy as he was, Longstreet hadn't squashed the idea when
Foote suggested it wouldn't do no harm if they took their breakfast
on the slope of the hill just outside the shack when nothing was
doing real early in the morning. After Longstreet gave a nod of his
big head, with the short blonde beard, Moyer and Morris naturally
went along with him.

It helped some to be going outside for just that little bit of time
when the sun bumped over the green timbered heights of the Spring
Mountains east of the Chispa before the heat of the day. The morning had a kind of freshness on it then, like the perfume on a new
woman before you'd taken her upstairs and found out she was no

different from all the rest. They'd all felt better for getting out in the open where a man had room to stretch and you could look out across the desert, instead of staring at each other's ugly mugs by the hour.

That is to say, it helped until the morning when all hell broke loose. Everything happened so fast that, thinking back on it, Foote still couldn't straighten it out in his mind. First, while Foote was sopping up the gravy with his bread, they heard the hoofbeats. He looked up toward the Indian camp to the north and saw the Indian woman riding in, long black braids flying, red calico dress whipped back by the speed of her galloping pinto pony. Then the firing broke out, a massive fusillade of guns from the buildings and the gully southeast of the Chispa. The woman's pony was shot from under her, but, being Indian, she knew how to ride and then some. Just as the pinto dropped to the ground, she jumped clear and started running toward them, zigzagging back and forth like a scared jack-rabbit. It was while Moyer and Morris were scrambling back into the shack after their guns that the bullet tore into Foote's belly. Dimly, through the fiery wave of pain that flooded over him as he stumbled back against the board wall of the shack, he saw the woman go down, too. She'd hardly fallen when Longstreet dashed out to her, scooping her up in his arms and running into the shack with the bullets whining around him.

How had Longstreet made it, being as big a target as he was, a good six feet tall and broad in the shoulders, coming through the rain of bullets with the woman in his arms, while Foote was a smallish kind of man—some called him weaselly—just crouching over his bread and salt meat? Foote couldn't see much justice in it nohow. He supposed, when Longstreet had pulled him inside the shack and the pain that seared his belly eased up enough to let him do any supposing, that his luck must have run out. If he'd been playing poker that morning, he'd likely have lost his pile, even with all the aces up his sleeve. When you fell into a losing streak, you couldn't change it, no matter what you did. And Longstreet? That day the big Texan would have won with nothing but deuces. If Phil Foote had learned one thing in the scattered saloons from Salt Lake City to the Arizona border, it was how to float along with your luck.

The gunfire ceased as rapidly as it began. How long had the whole bombardment lasted? Not over two minutes. Maybe no more than one. Nothing strange in that, thought Foote, trying to set his mind on something, anything, except the red-hot pain inside him. Once he'd played poker with a man up from Tombstone who told him the whole gunfight at the OK Corral took no more than half a minute. So maybe a minute was the regular time, long enough, anyway, to leave a man with the life seeping out of his belly along with his blood.

It didn't seem fair somehow that this should have happened to him. If he hadn't been obliged to skip over the Nevada border from Utah and make himself scarce for a while until that mess about the rich rancher and the marked cards died down, if it weren't for that whole cussed business, he wouldn't even have taken the trail into the Ash Meadows country. And he'd never have figured on making a little easy money with the bunch at the Chispa. He wished he could tell the Almighty it was all a big mistake. Longstreet or Moyer or Morris, they were the ones meant to take the bullet because they hired out their guns whenever they could. But not Phil Foote. He didn't really belong here at all.

The others stood ready with their guns. Apparently the woman was unhurt, though she walked a little gimpy from the fall she had taken. After Longstreet put her down, gripping her by the shoulders and running his big hands over her searching for wounds, she hovered behind him as he waited at the window. She was talking a mile a minute in the Indian lingo, which Foote knew Longstreet understood. After all, the man had lived so long out there in the far country with the Indians that he'd just about turned into one. When she fell silent, Longstreet turned to look at the rest of them, his blue eyes hardening with anger.

"Seems the Montgomerys never meant to settle things in court," he said. "That was just to throw us off our guard. They did it, too. Caught us like a bunch of silly schoolkids out on a picnic. While

McArthur was talking to his lawyer, they were sending down to San Bernardino for rifles. They hired them a couple of good guns to make sure: Harry Ramsey, up from Texas, and Pete Reed. They've got twenty-five men with rifles down there. She came to warn us and got caught."

"Jesus, twenty-five of them and only three of us left," said Moyer, his face looking pale and sweaty beneath the dark stubble of his beard. "We ain't got a chance, Jack."

"They won't stay twenty-five long if they decide to rush us," said Longstreet grimly, and added something in guttural Southern Paiute to the woman.

She started tearing cloth to bandage Foote's wound. In the dead silence, the harsh ripping sounds seemed to echo through the shack louder than gunfire. Then she bent over Foote to wipe away the blood with the whiskey Longstreet gave her and wind the bandage around the wound. Foote moaned, jolted by fresh pain when she shifted his body with strength surprising in a woman. With his head tilted up against Moyer's bedroll, he tried to concentrate on her hands as they flew around him. Strong hands, none too gentle but capable, hands that could shoe a horse, butcher a deer, crank a wind-lass like a man. He watched her coppery face, quick black eyes, high jutting cheekbones, full smooth lips pursed with concentration as she bent over her work. Generally speaking, Foote preferred another kind of woman, one with soft white pleasure-giving hands and a painted doll-like face, but every so often he fancied a change. If the pain hadn't been eating away at his innards, Foote could see how a man might get to wondering what kind of body the red calico dress concealed, how she might look unbraiding her coarse shiny black hair, and how she might taste when he parted those round com-pressed lips. Then, suddenly, the pain was all he knew. He heard himself groaning like an animal as she fastened the bandage firmly in place.

"Longstreet," a voice called from the direction of the gully. Though it might have been any man's voice, something in the note of hard triumph put Foote in mind of Bob Montgomery. "Longstreet, you better come out with your hands up, and the rest of 'em with you. We've got you surrounded with twenty-five guns. You haven't got a chance."

They all looked at Longstreet, waiting for him to say they'd be coming out. The silence lengthened until they realized he didn't intend to answer.

"He's right, Jack," said Moyer, nervously fingering his gun. "We ain't got a chance, not with twenty-five guns out there. And Phil's hurt bad. He needs a doctor."

"You want to go to the hoosegow?" Morris asked, licking his dry lips. His squinty green eyes slid nervously around the walls, and he twisted the red bandanna at his throat with absent fingers. "You want to?" he asked again. " 'Cause that's where we're going if we give up."

Foote watched Longstreet, standing impassive as a rock and saying nothing. No, Jack, you wouldn't much care for jail, would you? he thought. A little brick cell up north in the Belmont courthouse would get to grating on you even worse than holing up here in the shack. And you might have reasons beyond your general itchiness. Nobody knows who you really are or where you came from. No telling what might come out about you if you stood trial and went to jail.

"Can't be for long," scoffed Moyer. "We ain't hurt nobody. Not a one of us so much as fired a single shot."

Still Longstreet said nothing, but through the tides of pain that washed over his body in waves, Foote could feel his anger. Now that's a question I'd like to hear the answer to, thought Foote, if you were the talking kind of man. Why didn't you fire? Me and Moyer and Morris, we couldn't shoot. Fools that we were, we'd set down to breakfast without our guns. But how about you? You were wearing that famous notched Colt .44 of yours, just like always. So why is it, Jack Longstreet, that when all those guns busted loose from the gully, the most famous gunfighter west of the Utah border never fired a shot? I'm chewing it over, but I can't quite figure it out.

Moyer and Morris kept on arguing. "Even if we ain't hurt a fly, they'll git us anyways," said Morris. "When them lawyers and deputy sheriffs turn agin you, they find some dusty old law you never heard of. Might be stealing private property. Might call it trespassing. Might bring us in for carrying guns without permission or some such. You mark my words. They'll find laws you never heard of, and then they'll lock us up and throw away the key."

"It beats being dead."

It doesn't matter what they say, thought Foote, watching Longstreet. They could squabble from now till sundown, and nothing they say would make any difference. All that matters is what you say, and you're not of a mind to give up, are you? "Hey, Jack, come over here," he said, surprised by the faintness of his own voice. "I got something to tell you."

Suddenly aware that Longstreet's eyes were boring into them like a single jack drill, Moyer and Morris fell silent and turned hastily to their posts, Moyer at a window and Morris peering through the space where gunfire had blown away a piece of the wall. Longstreet came over to squat easily on his haunches beside Foote. The way he moved was one of the spooky things about Longstreet. The man was white. Burnt as brown as a cedar trunk, maybe, but the blue eyes and the long graying blond hair showed you plain enough that he was white. Why, then, did he always move like an Indian?

Longstreet's eyes rested on the place where fresh blood already darkened Foote's bandage. "How are you holding up, Phil?" he asked.

"I need a doctor, Jack. Need one bad. The pain—well, I believe a man doesn't hardly know what pain's about till he takes a bullet in the gut. I got to have some morphine."

The woman, kneeling now by Foote's feet, spoke low-voiced in slow careful English. "Your spirit, he wants go. Do not try you make him stay here."

Foote made a gasping noise that was cousin, several times removed, to a laugh. Pain from the movement left him so weak that he felt as though he were falling dizzily down the shaft of a mine.

For a moment the room darkened around the edges. "Lady, you haven't heard my spirit aright," he whispered hoarsely. "He's not leaving. He wants to stick around awhile. And he wants morphine."

Longstreet stepped over to the corner where they kept their supplies to bring the whiskey bottle. He poured the brown strong-smelling liquid into a tin coffee cup and held it to Foote's lips while raising the wounded man's head with one of his big hands. "Take as much as you can, Phil," he said. "Morphine won't do much for you that tangleleg can't do."

Foote drank slowly, but the whiskey welled back into his throat, mixed with the metallic taste of blood. He coughed, and the pain from the wrenching movement seemed to crush him, as though his body were being ground between the stones of an arrastra. "I'm telling you, Jack, I got to have morphine," he whispered. "Got cut up bad in Price once, and the morphine done me pretty good." He kept at the whiskey all the same, hoping it would dull the agony inside.

"Don't try to talk, Phil," said Longstreet gently. "Just take it easy. You know yourself there's not much can be done for a gut-shot man."

He was right about the talking, thought Foote. Talking hurt, swallowing hurt worse, just drawing breath was a torture almost past endurance. But he'd have to talk. Because if he couldn't convince Longstreet to run up the white flag, he knew he'd be lying out on the hill under a pile of stones before long.

"Some of these sawbones can fix up a man you'd think was done for." A moment passed before he could continue. "We go back a long ways, you and me. It's maybe ten years since you were trailing that horse thief into Utah and you cleaned me out playing draw poker in that saloon down Milford way. Me! When I'd just lifted the gold dust of every gambling man from Wyoming to the Colorado." Foote twisted his mouth in a grin of sorts and took a few more sips of whiskey, trying to gather up the strength from somewhere to push out a few more words. He watched Longstreet's blue eyes and sensed a flicker of the will behind them. Years of rippling the cards between his fingers had taught him how to read the changes in the men across the table from him the same way his old man, on the home ranch, could foretell the weather from a tiny shift in the wind. "You got to help me, Jack," he whispered, clutching at Longstreet's arm. "If you don't get me to a doctor, it's the same as killing me."

"Somebody's moving out there between the gully and the mill," said Moyer. "Can't see 'em plain enough to git a shot."

Again the voice called from outside, "Longstreet, we're about tired of waiting."

Foote watched the fury overtake the softening behind Longstreet's eyes as he rose and stepped over to the window. No doctor, no morphine. Jack Longstreet, it's that damned Southern pride of yours, he thought. Just because they caught you unawares out there at breakfast you've got to draw blood until you figure they've paid. Even if it kills us all.

"Ain't you going to answer 'em, Jack, one way or the other?" asked Morris.

"They start coming up that hill and they'll get all the answer they need," said Longstreet.

Morris started to say something and thought better of it. Again the silence seemed to pound like the beat of a drum. Hazily, Foote wondered if the vibrating sound that hummed in his ears was the pulse of his own blood running away from him. The whiskey that the woman held to his lips began to make the room waver and float. He tried to forget the pain and concentrate. That was something else he had learned in the saloons a long time ago. You couldn't daydream over your cards. You had to think hard, count carefully, remember every card, watch the expressions on the faces around you without seeming to do any of it. You had to know what they knew before they knew it. Then, sometimes, when you had hooked yourself into their heads just right, you could win on a lousy hand.

Slowly, as he had done so many times with the cards, he ran over every play in his mind from the beginning to the end. First the hoofbeats of the Indian woman's pony galloping in from the north, next the roar of guns, the downed horse, Morris and Moyer scrambling for the shack, the pain tearing through his gut, the woman running zigzag until she fell, Longstreet going through the bullets after her. It was like those drawings the old-time Indians made on the cliffs, stick animals and people and all kinds of funny designs that made no sense. But he'd always figured there was a meaning somewhere inside, if you just knew how to read it.

He looked at the woman kneeling beside him. No sweat shimmered on the smooth coppery skin of her face. The cup she held to his lips never trembled. Her movements were as slow and deliberate as though she had all the time in the world. She might have been grinding pine nuts in the sun-striped shade of a reed hut with a long afternoon before her, instead of getting ready to die in a blaze of gunfire as soon as the Montgomery crowd started moving in. Her serene face showed no sign of fear. Just watching her as she knelt in her pool of silence, asking no questions and making no arguments, calmed a man in a funny sort of way. For an instant her lively black eyes glanced over at Longstreet, and suddenly Foote saw what he hadn't seen before.

So that was it, he thought. If he hadn't been overly distracted with the pain, he might have wondered why Longstreet's Indian friends would send a squaw riding in with the warning. And maybe asked himself if she hadn't come on her own. Which would lead him to pretty soon figure out a woman's reasons for wanting to do a thing like that. Now he knew why she wasn't afraid to die.

He saw everything. He felt as though his thinking parts had somehow come detached from the pain in his body and gone floating up on the ceiling. He could look down on everyone in the shack and see inside them. Everything that had happened made sense now. Why, naturally, when the guns broke loose, Longstreet hadn't been able to shoot for fear of hitting her. Foote saw now why the big Texan had walked through gunfire to get her, even if the man didn't know it himself. He saw so much that he felt a little like God, if the

Almighty ever had the taste of whiskey in His mouth. And God just might at that, except He'd be drinking the best, the prime Kentucky bourbon.

Now that he saw everything so clearly, Foote decided he'd better do a little fixing too, just like the Almighty would have done if He'd taken the notion. Not for the sake of morphine. That didn't seem so important anymore. He figured on fixing lives, and as long as the Montgomerys held off making their move, he had time. The low angle of the sun told him that it was still early morning, just a little while since they sat down to bullets for breakfast. The trouble was that his mind was turning kind of blurry. Besides, he kept falling into a kind of blackness that was different from sleep. He'd open his eyes of a sudden and see everyone in the shack standing about where they'd been before, with nothing much changed. Except he knew that he'd been gone away somewhere.

"Jack, I got to tell you something," he said. Well, maybe he hadn't said it, because Longstreet didn't move. Maybe he'd only thought about saying it. Since the board walls of the shack got to wavering around like curtains, the things he really did got all mixed in with what he'd just thought about doing.

The second time he tried, some sounds must have come out, because the woman said, "Jack, he do like he want talk."

"You look sharp. They're going to start moving in anytime now," Longstreet told Moyer and Morris, and came over to squat once more beside Foote. His hand rested for a minute on Foote's forehead. His blue eyes met the woman's, and Foote could read the unspoken message between them: *He won't last much longer.*

Not yet, thought Foote, not yet awhile. I got some unfinished business here. He aimed his entire effort at making the words come out where Longstreet could hear them.

"Maybe you're right," he whispered. "A gut-shot man—he's played his last hand. But the Chispa's just a hole in the ground. She ain't worth dying for, not for the rest of you."

"Reckon we knew we might end up making smoke when we took the job."

"McArthur—you heard what he said, no bloodshed. He don't want us shooting it out and getting him hauled into court." Foote paused and closed his eyes for a moment. He realized a wounded man had some advantages. Not only could he look down on the whole world like God almighty, but also he could say things he'd never have dared give voice to when his hide was all of a piece. "It ain't the job, Jack. It's that goddamned Texas-size pride of yours that can't stand losing."

"I hired on to do a job, and I aim to finish it." No give. His eyes were the same blue as the mountains on the distant rim of the horizon and just as far from human touch.

Foote stayed silent awhile, working on the words. "All right, we hired on, you and me and Moyer and Morris. But what about her? She ain't hired on. She just risked her life to save you." Foote realized the spaces between his words were getting longer, but Longstreet was patient. He had that same Indian way of waiting that the woman did, as though time had stopped dead still. "Sure, you can shoot your share when the Montgomerys start moving in. But they're going to take us in the end. And she's going to die right here along with the rest of us."

Now he'd played his ace, and he thought he detected the subtle shift in Longstreet's expression that he'd been watching for. But he couldn't be sure. Maybe he didn't quite know everything as yet. Or otherwise said, he knew what folks ought to do if their own fool pigheadedness didn't keep turning them around wrong ways. He just wasn't quite clear on how to make them do it, especially a man like Longstreet who wouldn't hardly tolerate any telling. The struggle to force out the words kept getting harder all the time. He felt immensely tired, as though he'd been forking a stack of those bales of hay that had always seemed half again too big for him back at the ranch. Shoveling, maybe. Strange how just talking had gotten to be so much like shoveling a ditch all day in the hot sun with the old man's eyes lashing his back. So many years ago. He wondered dimly if your life turned back on itself in the end, like a dog chewing on its own tail. The thunking sound of the shovel kept pounding in his ears, but he tried to focus his eyes on Longstreet's face.

"Life never looked so good, Jack. Take it from me," he said. "If I was my rightful self, you wouldn't find me cashing in my chips just so folks could walk past my grave and say I got even. Did the famous Longstreet get caught napping? Don't matter much next to letting a woman like her die just to save your mule-stubborn pride, does it? Maybe you don't fancy getting locked up for a few weeks? Well, that don't matter much either, not when she's waiting back at the cabin and you got years ahead of you out there past Shadow Mountain where no one but a crazy man and a squaw wants to live.

"Save her, Jack. Let your fool pride get buried out there on the hill instead of you and her."

Longstreet looked at the woman, kneeling in her stillness. Rays from the morning sun shone through the window and made a fuzzy aura of white light around her shining dark head. Her black liquid eyes met Longstreet's. Speaking eyes, thought Foote. She said more with those eyes than most women did in a whole afternoon of chattering. But she asked for nothing. He saw Longstreet's eyes knot with hers, watched them soften and darken from their pale impenetrable blue, and knew he'd won after all. Or she had. He could have sworn that Longstreet almost smiled.

Longstreet stood up. "Boys, we'll be running up the white flag," he told Moyer and Morris.

Moyer slowly lowered his gun and leaned back against the wall, wiping the sweat from his face with his red bandanna. Even Morris looked relieved.

"Reckon we ain't got nuthin white," he said, blinking and looking foolishly around the shack, as though seeing it for the first time. "We tore up the sheet to bandage Phil."

"I have white," said the woman simply. She pulled down the petticoat from under her red calico dress and held it out to Longstreet with a shy proud smile.

Morris guffawed as though that were the funniest thing he'd ever seen, while Moyer started rummaging around for something to use for a pole.

"One more thing, Jack," whispered Foote, or at least tried to, but the first few times nothing came out. The woman saw that he wanted to talk, though, and drew Longstreet over to his side. "If'n I ain't going dancing next Saturday night, just supposing, there's something I want you to tell the newspaper fellas." Longstreet bent his bearded face close to Foote's to catch the words. "Phil Foote lived for the reputation of a dead game man and he played the string out."

Longstreet nearly smiled again. That made twice, the most Foote had ever seen in all the years he'd known Longstreet, but his face was dwindling, as though borne away on a rushing wind.

Foote heard him say from a faraway place, "Dead game man. I'll see they know."

The Heart of the Matter

MAX EVANS

He could smell buck deer in the nostrils of his mind." Max Evans is an American institution. Those who have read *The Rounders* and *The Hi Lo Country,* or seen the major motion pictures based on the novels, know that the post–World War II West bears his brand. He is a dedicated artist with range experience, an inexhaustible store of Hollywood anecdotes, and an abiding love for the men and women and horses of the land.

THE TWO MEN WERE SUCH GREAT friends they would have died for one another. No cliché, it was a fact. They had served in Vietnam together in the infantry. Each had on occasion drawn enemy fire to relieve the other.

They craved safety now. Security. They got it—as much as there is, anyway. For certain, they both had the sweating dreams of violent death and smelling again that exploding, unforgettable stench of war. They had their turns cringing at sudden, sharp noises and trying to make foxholes out of their mattresses. Even so, after all their miserable close calls in that tormented land, it would still be the guns of the Hi Lo country that would create their greatest grief.

Upon their return from the unpopular war, they gravitated to work on the steel tracks. Both their fathers had railroad backgrounds, and like their fathers, who had both fought in WWII, they were dominated by the duty of making the trains run on time. Simple.

Knowell Denny became section foreman at Hi Lo, New Mexico, in the northeast corner of the state. Luz Martinez started as a gandy dancer (spike driver) at Pueblo, Colorado, but soon advanced to also become a section foreman under the experienced tutelage of his father.

The friends met each fall—three years straight—in Walsenburg, Colorado, to hunt deer together. The fourth year, after celebrating a successful deer hunt in the Roundup Bar, Luz became sad. Knowell noticed, because his closest friend was a happy imbiber.

Luz finally confided that his wife had run off with his rich uncle. She had taken their only child, a girl, Lucia, and Luz was too broken-hearted to put up a fight for custody. He had left too much of his soul in the bloody, loamy, root-entangled earth of Vietnam.

Knowell took it on himself to have his friend transferred to Hi Lo. It was easy. There was a recently vacated section house six miles southeast of Hi Lo, so Luz moved in.

Knowell lived alone, as well, across the tracks at Hi Lo. His former wife had tired early of the isolation of the little town. She had stayed until their two girls and one boy were all of school age, then one day she took the railroad pass, all their savings, the children and moved to Oklahoma near her parents' farm. Knowell's kids came to see him for one week each summer. He took it well. He still cared about, and stayed in contact with, his wife. She remarried. He was glad. The only sign that anything bothered Denny was the slow, permanent bending of his skinny, six-foot body until he was five-feet-ten.

Luz was five feet seven inches of flexible muscle. At times he seemed twice that size. On other occasions he could shrink into himself and become almost invisible, like a shadow in an unlighted cave. He had a Hispanic/Apache face of bones that Rodin would have killed to sculpt, and his dark eyes gleamed from it like rare black pearls, sometimes as sad as slavery, sometimes as threatening as ingrained vengeance, and often as tender as the sigh of completed love.

He loved living just at the foothills of Sierra Grande. Some say it is the largest lone mountain in the world, because it is just under nine thousand feet high and takes a whole day to drive around it in a pickup. Knowell Denny was Luz's best friend, but the mountain was his twin soul.

Luz exulted in the moods of the mountain. The wind-scoured mass of rock dominated millions of surrounding acres with widely scattered malpais mesas like long, flat-backed snakes spewed from the fiery center of the earth, and mighty expanses of rolling gramma- and buffalo-grass covered rolling hills in between. Space in place. Chaotic order. The mountain would often gather all the clouds in the sky and draw the same fire and thunderous noise that had formed its own bulk from underneath.

Timberline is above twelve thousand feet on most of the mountains of the world. Here it was eight thousand. The reason? The wind. Ceaseless. Hot. Freezing. At different seasons, the mountain was green, then golden, then white, but the canyons were always deeply shadowed in blue and purple mists of grayish ghosts. The deer in its high parts, and the antelope in the foothills, were tough and cagey. They had to be to survive the mountain's turbulence, its coyotes, its cougars, and the hunting season. The season of killing.

Knowell Denny and all the other three hundred inhabitants of Hi Lo were actually on the northern foothills of Sierra Grande. The widely scattered cattle and sheep ranchers looked at it every day of their working lives for location, for hints of coming weather, for a companionship of terrible loneliness. No matter. Most were not conscious of these facts.

The volcanic mountain's base made such a wide, erratic circle its gradual-appearing slopes deceived the viewer. The cattle workers and the true hunters knew well it had thousands of hidden crevices and canyons. Endless secrets. It was a huge place of adventure and relaxation, a place that provided the winter meat Luz and Knowell loved so much. It was a place of destiny.

Just three years back Knowell had wounded a buck. He trailed it into rock-surrounded brush by following its stumbling tracks and scattered drops of blood. He had felt confident as he parted the bushes.

With lowered antlers, the buck made its last run. He struck Knowell in both thighs, hurling him back and down. One antlered point had ripped a gash in his right thigh. He was shocked, shaken, and astonished, but he would heal to hunt another season because the deer died with its head in his prone lap. Since that was the two friends' only kill that fall, they shared the venison with thankfulness and respect.

Just the season past they had hunted a uniquely formed rimrock canyon with Knowell working the top and Luz hunting the bottom, carefully staying several yards behind his friend's progress. If a deer was there, one or the other would get a shot. Care and skill. Slow and quiet movements. Hunters' blood working. The ancient way.

Luz felt a shot would open up—no, he knew it would. The canyon ended and he was alone. He was driven on up, on up the mountainside, by an old, old instinct. He could not see the tracks, but he could smell buck deer in the nostrils of his mind.

Luz entered the last rocky glade before timberline, and there he stood, broadside, majestic, in the autumn light. The mighty antlers caught the sun and made golden slivers against the blue background shadows. The regal head turned toward Luz. Their dark eyes met across the short distance. Luz raised the 300 Savage and placed the sights right behind the shoulder at the unmarked bull's-eye—the spot where the bullet would find the heart. His finger smoothly pulled the trigger. There was no jerk. The bullet exploded, the lead spiraling at immense speed through the barrel and out to the eternal kill.

Luz was so experienced, so skilled, he knew the bullet had been aimed and fired true. He lowered his rifle and started to move to the fallen animal. The mighty buck still stood. Unmarked. Motionless. Instinctively, Luz levered another shell into place, centered, and fired again. Smoothly. Accurately. The deer's stance and stare remained unchanged. A statue.

As Luz shoved the next shell into the kill position, he looked at the breech of the gun as if seeking an answer. When he raised the weapon to his shoulder, the animal was gone. Vanished.

Luz numbly moved to search for its sign, determined to track it until the soles were gone from his hunting boots if necessary. He could find no sign. Totally trackless. He circled wider and wider. No marks. Not a single vestige of disturbed earth or vegetation was visible. Then the one-fourth of his blood that was Apache told him what he had encountered. He had been greatly honored. Luz Martinez had been exposed to a *spirit deer*. He knew this extreme rarity carried a message of import. No matter how he concentrated and strained his mind, the omen escaped him. No matter how he struggled to relax and become open-minded to the portent, he could not recognize or receive it.

He told no one—not even his best friend. If so, he would be deemed crazy or worse. A quandary. Then, in the cycles of life, before the next hunt a year away, the mystification slowly eroded.

Unlike many, who were still tormented—even destroyed—by the graceless war and the loss of their immediate families, the two friends enjoyed more each year the wonder, the miracle of having been born.

Some of the ranching families successfully intermarried their young to breed and carry on their hard-lived traditions—a built-in security to ward off loneliness. However, a couple of railroaders had little chance of finding a wife or girlfriend in the tiny southwestern hamlet of Hi Lo. It was mostly populated by the very young and the very old. They solved this problem by splitting their vacations into four separate weeks instead of the usual month.

Luz and Knowell used their railroad passes to go to El Paso, Texas, then a cab would get them across the border to Juarez, Mexico. A week of debauchery three or four times a year sufficed.

They also enjoyed trout fishing a few miles east at Weatherly Lake. And on holidays they often made the three-hour drive southwest to Cimarron, at the foot of the Rockies, and fished the cold, fresh mountain streams nearby.

Knowell had a big television set which allowed him to have picture contact with the world. Luz felt such an instrument of imaginary travel, and ceaseless information would break the silent understanding of shared souls he had with the mountain. He much preferred reading—Jack London and Camus were his favorites—but he kept this as closely guarded as the spirit deer. However, on those weekends when the Denver Broncos played, Luz would go into Hi Lo and share the game with Knowell, who loved football only when the Broncos were winning.

Next to their annual hunt on Sierra Grande, the Saturday night poker game in the back of the Wildcat Saloon was their greatest recreation. The game had been going on as long as anyone could remember. As long as Hi Lo's existence. Sometimes it would last all night and on through the small Sunday church services. The game often included a couple of merchants, cowboys, ranchers, railroaders, pensioners, and then, of course, there was Emilio Cruz.

Emilio was the best poker player in this Hi Lo land. In fact, he had won his well-watered sheep ranch west of town in a single hand of the region's favorite poker game—High Low Split. So everyone played against Emilio. There was unspoken relief when he was busy and absent. Nevertheless, at the end of the year Luz would be about even, and Knowell would be a little ahead.

But as Luz said, "What the hell? We've had a million dollars' worth of fun."

Knowell had replied, "What else is there to do anyway? Besides, it gets everybody in out of the cockeyed wind."

The last poker night before deer season came about, and it was different. It was Luz's evening. He even took out Emilio Cruz early on with a 2, 3, 4, 5, 6 straight spade flush and bet it both high and low, winning against Emilio's three aces. Luz could not lose that night. He bluffed. He played cautiously. He played randomly. He was a winner. Luz had even run Knowell dry of cash, so Knowell was forced to sit out the game or write a check—which he never did.

The usual repartee of long-standing poker games varied off occasionally to the upcoming deer season.

Knowell was only slightly irked when he said, "Hey, Luz, if we both get bucks this year, I'll bet you a hundred-dollar bill mine's bigger than yours."

Luz, being silly from constantly winning as anyone would be, said, "You got it, partner. For a hundred extra I'll break a Boone and Crockett record."

It wasn't just the money. It was the ancient hunting pride. Everybody heard and knew. Luz was mostly a quiet, contemplative man, and this did seem a little braggadocio in a country where deer hunting was often from need, and had always been a religion.

Luz broke every cardplayer before sunup. A few even had time to get ready and attend church with their families. Luz did not even count the money. He was already looking forward to being on Sierra Grande with his best friend in just five days. A long, long five days.

Knowell always went to Luz's section camp house to spend the night before the hunt with his friend. They slept little. At daybreak they headed across the foothills. The antelope grazing, running here and about, made their nerves swell in anticipation.

An hour after sunrise, they stopped to rest their lungs a moment. They stood. Sitting would stiffen them in the cold air. But what a day. The wind was blowing at only thirty miles an hour. Just a pleasant breeze in the Hi Lo country.

As their breathing subsided, they stared across the vast land to the southeast and north. They could see into Colorado, Kansas, and the Oklahoma Panhandle. Although their psyches were on deer, there were millions of other specimens of life herein, mostly invisible to their cursory wide sweeping glance.

There were thousands of steers, calves, and lambs fat and ready to be rounded up and shipped to meatpacking plants around the nation. There were scores of horses in corrals and home pastures ready to be saddled to gather that production of beef made fat from the rich gramma and buffalo grass. And there were unseen humans to make all this work as a business, a way of life.

There were uncountable coyotes, bobcats, skunks, raccoons, badgers, foxes, eagles, owls, hawks, and rattlesnakes who had hunted that night and, if unsuccessful, were still doing so. There were rabbits, quail, doves, field mice, prairie dogs, ground and tree squirrels, sparrows, injured or sick calves and lambs, as well as barnyard chickens and turkeys that had been pursued, killed, and feasted on that night—or were still being hunted for another hour of this early light. There were vultures, ravens, magpies, and double-duty coyotes and innumerable insects and worms moving about to clean up the remains of the nocturnal kills. But to their own naked eyes it was infinite golden-grassed prairies and hills and the dark mesas with tops flat as aircraft carriers.

The two friends moved on up the mountain. They split apart to begin their hunt in deadly seriousness. If unsuccessful, they would meet at the bottom mouth of the strangely formed rimrocked canyon.

Luz almost got a shot in at a three-by-three buck, but he disappeared into some high oak brush, moved on into a gully and out of sight. Both men jumped several bounding does—three with fawns.

The timber on the mountain was sparse except in canyons and swales, where their roots were slightly protected from the eternal winds and they got more water from summer rains and snow melt-off of early spring.

All was quiet. Neither hunter had heard a shot. Each one was pleased by the silence of the other's gun. Hope and anticipation. Pride, at times as fateful as jealousy, insinuated itself unacknowledged into their beings. The bet was on and every step brought each one closer to a win.

Knowell, having a longer greyhound stride, reached the canyon first. He climbed on up to the rimrock and waited in an opening. For a time even his expert eyes could not see Luz. At last he spotted the movement down below perhaps a half mile. Luz still carried his gun at the ready. He moved methodically, surveying in every direction for movement as he neared an opening.

Knowell waved his arm back and forth from above.

Luz waved back. He silently pointed forward to the mouth of the rough, rocky canyon. Knowell nodded and moved out along the curving rimrock at the proper distance ahead of Luz.

Now both men moved at the same gait they had successfully ventured for so many seasons. Each heard his own heart pounding, pounding, pounding the blood that pushed it to their ears and to their brains, enhancing any sound, any movement. Hunter's blood. Even more. Time reversed and then caught up and reversed again. The earth stopped for an unmeasured spell to give the sun and the moon a brief respite. Then the machine-gun beating of their hearts put everything back in motion.

The huge buck jumped right out from under the overhang where Knowell had carefully walked. It bounded wildly through the brush around and over boulders at an angle towards the bottom of the canyon. There was no instant, sure shot.

Knowell, with all his ancestors' millions of years of hunting genes taking instant control, saw the opening in the bottom of the canyon where the noble creature intrepidly plunged. Everything, every tissue, nerve and every brain cell of Knowell Denny acted with exactness. He was moving his gun sights just ahead of the blurred animal.

The buck bounced into the opening. As he was at the apex of his leap across the clearing, Knowell centered the sights at just the right angle and just the right small area behind the shoulder blades. His hunter's aura left his body, followed the bullet, shattered the red heart into bits, and sprang back into place before the buck hit the other slope. It fell dead with only a slight movement of its hind leg in one last feeble instinctive move to escape.

Knowell was in a fog of the kill now as he, too, plunged recklessly for the bottom. He wanted to be there before Luz was. This action was alien to his surface nature. Even though he and Luz were true meat hunters, the size of the buck's trophy head was beyond anything he had seen before. Maybe in the world record category. Maybe.

As Knowell dodged around the last brush-wrapped tree into the opening, he was stunned. Luz had his hunting knife out to gut the deer.

He looked up smiling, saying, "Give me my hundred-dollar bill, amigo. There ain't ever going to be a bigger one killed on Sierra Grande than this one — at least not by a human." Still smiling, his attention went back to the job at hand.

The shock to Knowell's system could not have been greater if he had just witnessed the resurrection of Christ and a spaceship landing to pick up the great crusader at the same instant.

"What? What in hell do you mean, 'me pay you'? You pay me the hundred dollars, old friend."

For a moment Luz did not seem to understand. Then the smile slowly vanished. "I can't believe you, Knowell. You gone crazy on me? How come you're trying to claim my deer?"

Knowell stammered out, "Your deer? You gotta be kidding. I shot that big sucker."

Luz saw now that Knowell was serious. Unbelievable. *You know a guy most of your life, you think, and suddenly he is not that person at all,* he thought, then said aloud, "Listen, you crazy bastard, enough is enough. Just sit down and shut up while I dress out my deer. He's always been my deer. Always. I met him before. My God, don't you understand that? Oh, I guess I didn't tell you about that. Anyway, he is mine, Knowell."

Knowell sat down with his rifle held across his legs and stared grievously at Luz. His mouth and even his throat were dried up now. He rasped out with strain, "To hell with the money. If you touch my animal, I'm gonna blow your ass off."

"You're gonna what? What did you say to me? Did you threaten to kill me, Knowell?

"You heard it right, Luz boy."

Luz's naturally brown skin changed to a dark red now and almost as swiftly as a lizard's tongue he grabbed his rifle, whirling towards Knowell. The ends of the two rifle barrels were not over three inches apart when they both fired at exactly the same moment. Being the experienced hunters and fine shots they were, each blew the other's heart apart. They fell with the tops of their heads together, at the rear of the dead buck, where he had expelled several gut pellets that still steamed a tiny bit in the high-altitude cold.

Two days later, Herman Eubank, a lone hunter from Texas, stumbled upon the three kills. He nearly had a heart attack getting back down to his car parked on Highway 87. He drove to a nearby rest stop and called the sheriff's office at the county seat in Clayton.

The sheriff, a deputy, and the coroner drove to Hi Lo and gathered up a party to identify and remove the bodies. All three creatures were frozen stiff from the night's cold that reached near zero. After all the examinations and notes had been made, the deputy asked if he could finish dressing out the deer.

"It's been in the world's biggest icebox. The buck is as fresh as the minute it was shot."

The sheriff, like almost everyone else in the Hi Lo Country, loved venison. He instructed the retrieval party to go on down and wait for them at the highway, adding, "I'll just help Ol' Roy dress out this deer. No use wasting good meat." Then, giving his full attention to the deer, he continued, "I'll flip you for that head, Roy. Damnedest rack I ever saw. An absolute record-breaking head, no question about it. But"—he paused—"it'll never make the record book. Who'd get the kill credit?"

"You're right. Who would get the credit?"

The deputy shrugged his shoulders and continued the job that Luz had started. When he had just about gotten everything cleaned out, he discovered that the deer had been shot twice—one bullet had come in from between the shoulder blades on top, striking the heart. The other had come in from the side just behind the shoulder, also striking the heart. There wasn't enough left of that organ to fill a shot glass. The two best friends had fired perfect rounds at exactly the same instant so that neither had heard the other.

The deputy pushed his Stetson back, staining it with smears of deer blood without realizing it. He stared at the palm of his other large hand that held fragments of metal. Puzzlement.

He raised his head, saying, "Look here, Sheriff."

The sheriff squatted and stared at the upturned hand.

The deputy continued, "I'm holding more than one bullet here. The fragments were all in the heart area."

The sheriff asked, "What are you trying to say, Roy?"

"Aw, it can't be, no, sir, it just can't be. It looks like one of those bullets struck the other one right in the center of the heart. Course, that's impossible. Ain't it, Sheriff?"

The sheriff spoke softly, "I reckon the odds would be . . . oh, 'bout forty billion to one."

"Yeah," finalized the deputy.

It took the sheriff two weeks of sleepless nights to figure out what had happened. He enjoyed the free vension every day while he pondered the peculiar point of it all.

River Watch

LORI VAN PELT

The ghost story may be the oldest form of entertainment, chilling millennium readers and caveman listeners alike. Supernatural westerns, however, are rare. This is an oversight, as what region on earth is more densely populated by the ghosts of its past than the American West? Turn on all the lights and settle in with this haunting tale of tragedy and salvation by Wyoming rancher and writer Lori Van Pelt.

THE WIDOW WALKED INTO THE
river in winter, knowing not that such a deed had been performed
before. She stood for a moment on the shore of the deceptively
placid North Platte on a still December evening, emotions roiling
inside her as the icy water flowed past, at once beckoning and re-
pelling. She knew not that a century before she took these fated
footsteps, another broke the trail. She shook her head, letting fall a
curtain of auburn hair, releasing it from its fancy braid, the likes of
which I might have tried with my own locks had I taken a notion.

She stands, contemplating her fate, unaware of my presence. She
considered all that had been and all that might yet come to be, as I
myself had once done. I wanted to scream at her. I wanted to warn
her of the numbing frigid river, to push her back as sudden gusts
of wind might force her to retreat. But such behavior is not my
place.

Instead, I turn to my own memories, see myself in her image
on the snow-quilted bank. As she moves forward, I turn back.

Emmett Stoner, my dear beloved Emmett, stands alone near the
saloon door. He pushes open the intricately carved wooden half-
doors. They creak, swinging back and forth like a broken metro-
nome. The bartender has not yet seen fit to oil their hinges.

"I'll kill the man who did this," Emmett says. His voice, just a
notch above a whisper, vibrates with terse anger. "She deserved
better."

The happy hum of the saloon-goers faded into cold silence. Emmett brushed a stray lock of thick black hair from his forehead. I
had once thought it an endearing gesture, but that day after Christmas 1895 in the saloon, it looked ominous.

"Ah, Emmett," the bartender said, smiling, imparting a jovial tone to his words. "Come, sit and have a drink with us. I'll pour your favorite whiskey."

But Emmett shook his head. "I'll not drink again with such ruffians."

"Come, come, now. Your mind is a-grieving, friend. 'Twas indeed a tragedy." Already the bartender was filling a glass with amber liquid. "Was of no fault but the girl's own."

Emmett's eyes narrowed. "You're wrong, Duff. Someone drove her to it. And when I find out who, that man's dead."

Duff moved the drink forward. "Here you are. Sip it up, now. You can't go on living in the past, Emmett."

Emmett took the drink, downed it in a lengthy swallow. He licked his lips. "I must, Duff," he said. "There is no future now."

TEARS STING MY ALREADY FROZEN CHEEKS. EMMETT WAS MY BEST friend. He told no one my secret, but held it in his heart like a living thing, which needed nurturing and tender care. To watch him destroy himself on my account is almost too much for me to bear. A chill breeze beats waves into the darkness of the Platte's blue waters. The widow steps forward, stops. She teeters on the edge.

Indecision is a mighty coward. Her life has, to this moment, overflowed with the fulfillment of the wishes of others—children, grandchildren, and husband, who until his recent sudden heart seizure lay invalid for three years in their marriage bed. Her life has been much different from my own. Mine had not yet begun to blossom except for the dangerous love I felt for Amos Abernathy. In that, I was decisive. How very clear to me was the fact that we would share our lives together, that I would bear his children, and tell stories to our grandchildren in my old age like this widow walker has done. But my indecision on other matters sped me to my destiny.

I expected to burn in hell for that single night of shared desire. Instead, this icy river burned me, cauterized my very soul and catapulted me here. I live in a state in between the certain magnificence of heaven and the sure horridness of hell, but damned just the same. I chose. My decision overstepped the invisible boundary line and violated universal law.

On that sweet September night so long ago, I chose life. I chose to be with Amos Abernathy, to walk beneath the canopy of the cottonwoods and dared to speak of love. Amos was tall, slender, with sun-blond hair and sky-blue eyes and a thick mustache hiding his upper lip. He had come to Saratoga (he said) daring to risk all his money on a dream. A freighter, Amos dreamed of making his fortune by staking gold claims in the mountains.

"It will work, Lucy, I know it will," he told me, squeezing my hand as we traversed the bumpy knolls along the river.

"I've not heard of gold mines in these parts before," I replied.

Amos turned and rewarded my remark with a brilliant smile. "Exactly! That is the very reason that my idea will work. I'll be the first to find gold here. Let all those gold-diggers continue to starve in South Pass. Since '68 they've looked, and they've been fools. I'm staking my claim here and now in the mountains near Saratoga."

"I can see that this idea excites you," I said, thrilled by his exuberance. "But perhaps a little restraint will save you money in the long run?"

Amos shook his head. "Ah, Lucy. A minister's daughter to the core. Have you no sense of adventure?"

We stopped to lean against a sturdy cottonwood as the sun set, blazing an even deeper golden hue into the autumn-changed leaves. Amos reached down for a blade of green grass. Chewing it, he looked askance at me. "Perhaps your father would be interested. He could be my first investor." Amos paused for a moment as I thought about this. "Those who jump in at the beginning reap greater benefits at the end," he said.

I watched the sun set, reveling in the array of colors—several shades of mauve and peach. "No, Amos. My father would not agree. To him, this investment idea would sound greedy."

"I suppose, then, I am lucky that he allowed me to visit with his beautiful daughter."

I did not answer. My father did not know my whereabouts that evening. After supper dishes were washed and put away, I snuck out of the house, leaving him to watch over my younger brother and sister.

I had met Amos just a few days before. I hurried along Bridge Street, anxious to attend the meeting of the literary club. We met weekly in the ladies' parlor of Frederick Wolf's elegant hotel. Mrs. Wolf, hostess extraordinaire, baked delicious pastries for us to enjoy as we discussed new books and sipped hot tea in her sumptuous second-story room.

In my haste, I dropped my copy of *The Adventures of Sherlock Holmes.* As I bent to retrieve it, a suntanned hand reached down and picked it up for me.

He took off his hat, holding it to his chest as he read the cover. "Sounds fascinating," he remarked, handing the fortunately undamaged book to me.

"Yes, thank you, sir," I replied.

"Miss, I find it always a pleasure to help a young lady in need. My name is Amos Abernathy. If I may ever be of further assistance, I would hope you would allow me to do so."

His formality struck me as quite sincere, so I said, "Thank you, Mr. Abernathy. My name is Lucy Willoughby, and I am pleased to make your acquaintance."

Then I picked up my skirts, hurrying forward so as to not be late to the book discussion. But I turned back for just a moment. And in that moment, Amos had turned back as well, looking at me intently with his blue eyes. Heat sparked in my body. I felt my cheeks grow hot. "Good-bye, sir," I said.

Amos again tipped his hat. We met again at the piano recital given by my young students that Saturday. Inside the church, where my father had allowed this exhibition of musical excellence to take place, Amos was quite the gentleman. But my father whispered,

"Lucy, I do not like that young man. I believe he is quite smitten with you. You must watch your step."

I nodded, but secretly found Amos wondrously attractive. When he found a private moment with me, after the students and their parents had gone and my father had retreated into the sacristy to prepare for church the next morning, he asked me to come for an evening walk.

"The North Platte is beautiful at sunset, Lucy," he said. "I'll wait for you to join me this evening, then." With a smile and a flourish, he stepped from the church into the brightness of the afternoon. I stacked the remaining sheets of music I had been sorting, my heart filled with excitement.

"Lucy?"

His voice startled me from my memories. I looked up into his face, and swiftly he caught my chin with his forefinger and thumb and stole a kiss. My body melted against the rough bark of the cottonwood as the river swallowed the final flames of the sun.

I WATCH THE WIDOW. SHE TAKES A DEEP BREATH OF WINTRY AIR. She steps back—one step, then two. She watches the river. She begins to pace—two steps left, three steps right. Back and forth, back and forth, her movements mimic the subtle swiftness of the undercurrent tugging at my ankles.

She turns toward me, seeing only her own life. I see she has painted her face, wearing what must be her favorite shade of lipstick and rouge. I reach up and feel Grandmother's pin holding my own hair securely in place. I selected it for wear on special occasions with my burgundy brocade dress. I wanted to look pretty, as the widow surely does, though she wears men's trousers and a coat that appears to have also belonged to a man.

I run my fingers through the icy water. The sudden sting reminds me of another jacket, similar in color, that Amos wore the September evening we stood beneath the gnarled cottonwood. He removed his dark jacket in one smooth stroke, placing it on the ground.

"Please sit down, dear," he said, patting the fabric as he himself sat on the grass.

"Thank you," I said, still trembling with delight from the touch of his soft lips against my own. Again he reached for me and again I complied.

We consummated our love right here beside this very river in the cool evening air as the stars began blooming in a lavender sky. *Consummated*. A good word—for the flames of desire consumed us with greed. I had thought—wrongly—that such a tender man would love not just my flesh but my mind, too.

The water carries a broken twig past me. I look up and see the widow wading into the water. As it caresses her ankles, she stops, wincing. I watch, remembering the feel of Amos' hands caressing my body, delighting my skin with touch in places no man had seen before.

Full moonlight shone that night, and I feared discovery. But Amos reassured me that no one would see, as we were shadowed by the tall figure of the tree. The whisper of leaves above reinforced his words. As he held me, I gazed up into their delicate growth, imagining black lace like mourners wore.

"Sweet, sweet Lucy," my lover murmured between kisses. He placed a warm hand against my cheek. I shivered beneath him, partly from the thrill of the deed and partly from the chilling air. He hugged me to him, warming my flesh and sending my spirit soaring.

"Tomorrow, under this very cottonwood, my love," he whispered in my ear, "we'll meet again. But for now I must depart."

Quickly then, he dressed himself and helped me on with my dress. And I sat beneath the cottonwood for a few moments watching him walk away toward his dreams of striking the mother lode. I followed, my heart filled with dreams of a rather different nature.

The widow braces herself. She takes three steps more into the deepness of the water. I feel gooseflesh rise on my arms. The price that love exacted of me was too high to bear. The widow feels the same. I see it in her weary eyes and in the resolute set of her delicate chin.

The crescent moon barely lights this dark, oily river. Starlight is obscured by scudding clouds. The widow waited until the darkness would hide her. She chose a spot near the island where her husband fly-fished for years.

Her place is not so far from the cottonwood looming over me. I feel her temptation. She yearns for the cold water to envelop her and carry her to oblivion where one feels no pain and does not need to think.

Amos did not return the next evening near sunset, nor the next. I worried that some terrible accident had befallen him, but I dared not show my curiosity. As September melded into October, the price of my desire grew in my belly. Amos' child took over my body. By Thanksgiving, I found myself letting out my shirtwaists and adding hidden strips of cloth to the waistbands of my skirts. My father could never know of my incredible sin.

And it was then that Emmett Stoner earned my undying affection. He began to court me, sweetly, that fall. Unlike Amos, Emmett was dark-haired and clean-shaven with dark brown eyes. His kindnesses overwhelmed me. A simple squeeze of his hand after I played particularly well for church. A single sprig of sage plucked from the plants growing on his ranch.

"I will become known as one of the cattle barons, Lucy," Emmett confessed one evening as we sat sipping tea on my father's medallion-back sofa. "I know that I can make my cattle ranch profitable and comfortable."

I sipped tea from the rose-covered porcelain my mother had received from her mother as a wedding gift just months before my birth and her death. The china trembled slightly in my hand, making a musical sound against its companion saucer. "Many such ranchers have had similar dreams, Emmett. What makes you think you will succeed where others have failed?"

"A genuine love of the land, a fondness for the animals them-selves, and a healthy portion of dogged determination," he replied. We laughed.

I set my teacup and saucer on the table. Silence descended upon us.

I looked at Emmett and found him looking at me. Shy, he blushed furiously and looked away.

"Emmett, what's the matter?" Emmett had been my friend since we moved to Saratoga five years ago. We had both been just coming into our teens at that time. My father had encouraged Emmett, who had a strong tenor voice, to sing in church. As a result, Emmett and I had spent countless hours together rehearsing hymns and some-times playing secular tunes like *"Buffalo Gals"* and *"Oh, Susanna,"* when we thought no one was listening. "Have I embarrassed you?"

Emmett shook his head. A lock of black hair fell across his fore-head, making him look like the young boy he had been when we first met. He swept the hair back into place. "Lucy, you could never embarrass me."

"I'm glad," I said, and turned the talk to Sunday's hymns and the upcoming Christmas celebration.

"My home is almost complete at the ranch," Emmett blurted.

"Oh, how wonderful, Emmett," I replied, puzzled at his sudden change of subject. "I would love to see it one day."

"I would hope you would see it every day," he said.

I looked at him for a long moment. He cleared his throat. "What I am trying to say, Lucy, is that I would like for you to live there."

I did not know what to say, for his words unnerved me. He was not asking for my hand in marriage. I placed my hand on my stom-ach. Holding my secret close to me, I waited. Was it possible he knew of my indiscretion with Amos?

The silence lingered.

Emmett's face reddened again. "As my wife, Lucy."

I let the words fall into the quietness. I stood up and walked to the window.

"Oh, Emmett," I whispered, for I knew my next words would hurt him. In speaking, I felt my own heart ache. "I cannot."

He had come to stand beside me. He placed a gentle hand on my shoulder and turned me to face him. "I care for you deeply, Lucy. I would take good care of you, provide a good home for you and our children."

I nodded. "I know."

"We could marry on New Year's Day. Begin the new year with love and laughter and happiness."

I felt tears sting my eyes. Emmett wiped away the single stinging tear that rolled down my cheek.

"Is this happiness that makes you cry, Lucy?"

I shook my head no. He waited. When I could speak, I took his hand and led him back to the sofa. We sat, and I told him everything that had happened to me in the past few months. Emmett held my hand through the whole tale. Only when I had finished did he rise. He raked his hands through his thick dark hair. Frowning, he paced the room and stopped at the window.

"Whose child do you carry?"

"I'll not tell."

"You must, Lucy."

"No. It is my cross to bear, and mine alone."

He whirled, unable to contain his anger. "What kind of a man would leave a woman with child and not marry her and make a decent woman of her?"

I bit my lip. I looked at my hands, folded discreetly in my lap. I did not answer.

Emmett came and knelt beside me. He reached for my hand. "I am sorry, Lucy. I did not mean to imply that you are not a decent woman. I want to kill the coward who has done this to you."

"Then that would make you as cowardly as he."

Emmett considered my words. After a few moments, he nodded.

"Lucy," he said. "I would be most honored to be father to your child." He took my chin in his fingers and raised my eyes to his.

When I started to protest, he put a finger to my lips. "Think on it some first, before you answer."

Then he left me to ponder his kindness. But all I could think about was the stricken look that creased his face like lightning cracking the sky when I told him I carried the child of another man.

ON CHRISTMAS EVE, I PLAYED MY BEST. EMMETT'S STRONG TENOR voice filled our small church with hope and love and joy. He shared our evening meal with us, complimenting my skill as a cook and helping me wash dishes afterwards. Before he left, he took both my hands in his, whispered, "I look forward to your decision," and kissed my cheek. "Merry Christmas."

"What a kind and decent gentleman," my father said, having noticed Emmett's affectionate gesture. "I hope that you and Emmett are getting along well."

"Yes, Father. Emmett is a dear friend."

Father smiled. "I'll be in my room. I need to work on tomorrow's sermon some. Sleep well." He handed me the newspaper. "Gertrude's doing well as an editor," he remarked.

He referred to Reverend Huntington's daughter, who had for some years published the *Platte Valley Lyre*. Although Father was careful not to let his voice reveal it, he allowed an unspoken competition to seep into my mind. He couldn't have known that at that moment I felt inadequate when compared to Gertrude. She was a smart woman. During book discussions she always brought up points I would have never considered on my own. And she had always been kind to compliment me on my music and had printed news of my students' achievements and recitals. He handed me the newspaper. "Don't stay up too late, Lucy. Tomorrow is a busy day."

He didn't know I had already read it. He didn't know I had already seen the front-page wedding announcement. Amos Abernathy planned to marry Holly Whitmore on January 1, 1896. The couple planned to make their home in nearby Grand Encampment.

"I want to sit up and admire the tree for a while more," I lied. I felt sick inside.

"Very well, Lucy. Do as you please."

When he was gone, I took a candle from the branches of the Christmas tree. As quietly as I could, I stole into the night. The candle lit my path to the river and across the bridge to the tiny island and the cottonwood. My hopes that Amos would join me here had long since faded. The news report confirmed my worst fears, for Amos' marriage hurt me worse than his death could have.

I stepped into the cold water. I wore my burgundy dress, the finest I had. I did not want my father to fuss over my attire if they found me. I waded into the river, quickly, so I would not lose my nerve. The cloth billowed around me. My petticoats dampened first. The cold water set me to trembling violently. Every muscle, every bone, every sinew in my body cried for release. The urge to run was great, but I resisted. Years of being taught obedience to my parents and the heavenly Father did their work. Discipline conquered desire this time.

Teeth chattering, I tossed my candle into the water. The flame hissed as the water extinguished it.

I prayed. "Lord, I just want to rest in the arms of this mighty river. I have already disobeyed your commandments and I am mightily sorry. I know You will understand."

When the widow walked farther in, she was praying, too. "Lord," she said, "grant me peace within the waters of this river. My life has been unsatisfactory in your sight, I know. Please forgive me."

I shook my head. Why she sought solace in the river was beyond my understanding. She'd done plenty of good, righteous and godly things during her forty years of life. She had raised a family, cared for her invalid husband, baked meals for those who were sick or dying. She had not attended church every Sunday as I had done, but her beliefs shimmered through her deeds.

Emmett cried when he heard the news on Christmas Day. He

was the only one who ever knew I'd carried a child into the river with me as well. He found the note I'd left him in his hymnal. I'd placed it by the hymn *"Shall We Gather at the River,"* knowing he would seek solace in those tried-and-true words. My note said only, "Emmett, I'll not shame you, too."

A willow branch hidden beneath the water snagged the widow's trousers. Shivering, she struggled against it but could not pull away. She did not scream, but her frustrated "Oh!" carried to the banks.

Riley Stoner, the newspaper reporter, walked alongside the banks that night, as he was wont to do almost every evening. Gertrude's *Platte Valley Lyre* had long since faded into the *Saratoga Sun*. Wedding announcements no longer made the front page, but drownings and suicides did. Clouds parted, revealing the tiny moon. Its light shone on a bit of ice purling the water into a whirlpool near my skirt. Riley stopped.

Cupping his hands to his mouth, he yelled, "Who's out there?"

He was tall, and slender from riding horses during his spare time. At forty-three, he had not yet married, but several of the women in Saratoga had set their caps for him. He always wore a cowboy hat, perhaps a reminder of his days as a bronc rider. The light moved again. His face shadowed beneath his hat. Moonlight guided his eyes to the disappearing form of the widow.

"Oh, my God!" Frantic, he searched the bank for a stick. "Hang on! Hang on! I'm coming." Riley scampered toward the houses near the riverbank. He yelled and raised a ruckus until newfangled electrical lights shone out from their windows.

Riley raced to the river. Dazed, the widow floated among the waves, her foot dangling near the submerged willow. "I'm caught, I'm caught," she said.

"I'll help. Hang on, there. I'm coming." Riley crept down the bank as far as he dared. He anchored himself as best he could on the slippery slope. If he slid in, chances were good they would both die. Holding one end of the sturdiest cottonwood branch he could find, he reached toward her. "Grab the branch. Grab it."

As the cottonwood branch floated toward her, the widow reached for life again. The fabric of her trousers tore. She floated free of the willow's snare. Riley pulled her toward him. When the moonlight illuminated her face, he said, "Oh, Dr. Willoughby. You slipped into the river."

She came toward him, grateful for his strong arms around her as he pulled her onto the bank. A crowd had gathered. Whispers from the back echoed along the shore. "The veterinarian fell into the river. Riley saved her."

"You're from the paper," she said. He grabbed a blanket that a house owner tossed his way, put it around her shoulders.

"Yes," he said. "I'm Riley Stoner. You're lucky I came along when I did." Her suicide attempt was unimaginable to Riley, a broken rodeo rider with unquenchable spirit. A woman dedicated to the health of animals would surely be dedicated to preserving her own health, he thought. The word *suicide* never crossed his mind.

But when he told his fellow reporter the story of that December evening in 1995, a frown crossed his face. "She only told me that she slipped," he said.

The reporter nodded. "Lucky for her. This river had a suicide once a hundred years ago, practically in the same place."

"Really?"

"Yes. A woman named Lucy Willoughby drowned there on Christmas Eve in 1895."

"Lucy Willoughby? Are they related?"

"Lucy Willoughby is Dr. Anna Willoughby's great-great-aunt. Anna never took her husband's name, you know."

"Yes, I knew that." Riley sat down on the desk. "Lucy Willoughby?" he repeated. "They say my great-great-grandfather courted her before he married."

"Can I use that in my article?"

Riley nodded. "I'm going for a walk. Be back shortly."

He left the newspaper office and walked to the bridge. He stood in the center of the bridge's arch, gazing at the island named now

for veterans. In the gray December light, with two weeks to Christmas, Riley Stoner watched me from the river bridge. He could not
see my form as I saw his. But our spirits recognized each other.

I was punished for loving someone—the highest gift the earth
provides. And I, in return, punished someone who loved me, a debt
I could never repay. I held the tangled willow branch in my hands,
the piece of torn trouser fabric still clinging to it. Riley walked back
toward the newspaper office, hands in his pockets, deep in thought.

I walked the river, grateful for the merciful softness of waters
that no longer sting me but cradle me. I turn south, watching the
river.

Hewey and the Wagon Cook

ELMER KELTON

If you were to ask aficionados of Texas history to cast ballots in a popularity contest, the result might be a dead heat between Davy Crockett and Elmer Kelton. Kelton, author of *The Good Old Boys* and dozens of other novels of Texas old and new, has won more Spur Awards than anyone else in the history of the Western Writers of America. This tale of humor and trail-weary wisdom tells us why.

Chuckwagon cooks were expected to be contrary. It was part of their image, their defense mechanism against upstart young cowpunchers who might challenge their authority to rule their Dutch-oven kingdoms fifty or so feet in all directions from the chuckbox. Woe unto the thoughtless cowboy who rode his horse within that perimeter and kicked up dust in the "kitchen."

The custom was so deeply ingrained that not even the owner of a ranch would easily violate this divine right of kings.

Even so, there were bounds, and Hewey Calloway was convinced that Doughbelly Jackson had stepped over the line. He considered Doughbelly a despot. Worse than that, Doughbelly was not even a very good cook. He never washed his hands until *after* he finished kneading dough for the biscuits, and he often failed to pick the rocks out of his beans before he cooked them. Some of the hands said they could live with that because the rocks were occasionally softer than Doughbelly's beans anyway, and certainly softer than his biscuits.

What stuck worst in Hewey's craw, though, was Doughbelly's unnatural fondness for canned tomatoes. They went into just about everything he cooked except the coffee.

"If it wasn't for them tomatoes, he couldn't cook a lick," Hewey complained to fellow puncher Grady Welch. "If Ol' C. C. Tarpley had to eat after Doughbelly for three or four days runnin', he'd fire him."

C. C. Tarpley's West Texas ranch holdings were spread for a considerable distance on both sides of the Pecos River, from the sandhills to the greasewood hardlands. They were so large that he had to keep two wagons and two roundup crews on the range at one time. Grady pointed out, "He knows. That's why he spends most all his time with the other wagon. Reason he hired Doughbelly is that he can get him for ten dollars a month cheaper than any other cook workin' out of Midland. Old C. C. is frugal."

Frugal did not seem a strong enough word. Hewey said, "Tight, is what I'd call it."

Doughbelly was by all odds the worst belly-robber it had been Hewey's misfortune to know, and Hewey had been punching cattle on one outfit or another since he was thirteen or fourteen. He had had his thirtieth birthday last February, though it was four or five days afterward that he first thought about it. It didn't matter; Doughbelly wouldn't have baked him a cake anyway. The lazy reprobate couldn't even make a decent cobbler pie if he had a washtub full of dried apples. Not that Old C. C. was likely to buy any such apples in the first place. C. C. was, as Hewey said, tight.

Grady was limping, the result of being thrown twice from a jug-headed young bronc. He said, "You ought to feel a little sympathy for Doughbelly. He ain't got a ridin' job like us."

"He gets paid more than we do."

Grady rubbed a skinned hand across a dark bruise and lacerations on the left side of his face, a present from two cows that had knocked him down and trampled him. "But he don't have near as much fun as us."

"I just think he ought to earn his extra pay, that's all."

Grady warned, "Was I you, I'd be careful what I said where Doughbelly could hear me. Ringy as he is, he might throw his apron at you and tell you to do the cookin' yourself."

It wasn't that Hewey couldn't cook. He had done his share of line-camp batching, one place and another. He could throw together some pretty nice fixings, even if he said so himself. He just didn't fancy wrestling pots and pans. It was not a job a man could do a-horseback. Hewey had hired on to cowboy.

He appreciated payday like any cowpuncher, though money was

not his first consideration. He had once quit a forty-dollar-a-month job to take one that paid just thirty. The difference was that the lower-paying outfit had a cook who could make red beans taste like ambrosia. A paycheck might not last more than a few hours in town, or anyway a long night, but good chuck was to be enjoyed day after day.

Hewey was tempted to draw his time and put a lot of miles between him and Doughbelly Jackson, but he was bound to the Two C's by an old cowboy ethic, an unwritten rule. It was that you don't quit an outfit in the middle of the works and leave it short-handed. That would increase the burden of labor on friends like Grady Welch. He and Grady had known each other since they were shirttail buttons, working their way up from horse jingler to top hand. They had made a trip up the trail to Kansas together once, and they had shared the same cell in jail after a trail-end celebration that got a little too loud for the locals.

Grady was a good old boy, and it wouldn't be fair to ride off and leave him to pick up the slack. Hewey had made up his mind to stick until the works were done or he died of tomato poisoning, whichever came first.

It was the canned tomatoes that caused Doughbelly's first real blowup. Hewey found them mixed in the beans once too often and casually remarked that someday he was going to buy himself a couple of tomatoes and start riding, and he would keep riding until he reached a place where somebody asked him what to call that fruit he was carrying on his saddle.

"That's where I'll spend the rest of my days, where nobody knows what a tomato is," he said.

For some reason Hewey couldn't quite understand, Doughbelly seemed to take umbrage at that remark. He ranted at length about ignorant cowboys who didn't know fine cuisine when they tasted it. He proceeded to burn both the biscuits and the beans for the next three days. Another thing Hewey didn't quite understand was that the rest of the cowboys seemed to blame him instead of Doughbelly.

Even Grady Welch, good compadre that he was, stayed a little cool toward Hewey until Doughbelly got back into a fair-to-middling humor.

After three days of culinary torture, those tomatoes didn't taste so bad to the rest of the hands. For Hewey, though, they had not improved a bit.

Like most outfits, the Two C's had two wagons for each camp. The chuckwagon was the most important, for it had the chuckbox from which the cook operated, and it carried most of the foodstuffs like the flour and coffee, lard and sugar, and whatever canned goods the ranch owner would consent to pay for. The second, known as the hoodlum wagon, carried cowboy bedrolls, the branding irons and other necessities. It also had a dried cowhide, known as a cooney, slung beneath its bed for collection of good dry firewood wherever it might be found along the way between camps.

Like most of the cowhands, cow boss Matthew Mullins was a little down on Hewey for getting the cook upset and causing three days' meals to be spoiled. So when it came time to move camp to the Red Mill pasture, he singled Hewey out for the least desirable job the outfit offered: helping Doughbelly load up, then driving the hoodlum wagon. Hewey bristled a little, though on reflection he decided it had been worth it all to dig Doughbelly in his well-padded ribs about those cussed tomatoes.

The rest of the hands left camp, driving the remuda in front of them. Doughbelly retired to his blankets, spread in the thin shade of a large and aged mesquite tree, to take himself a little siesta before he and Hewey hitched the teams. A little peeved at being left with all the dirty work, Hewey loaded the utensils and pitched the cowboys' bedrolls up into the hoodlum wagon. He could hear Doughbelly still snoring. He decided to steal a few minutes' shut-eye himself beneath one of the wagons.

The cowhide cooney sagged low beneath the hoodlum wagon, so Hewey crawled under the chuckwagon. His lingering resentment would not let him sleep. He lay staring up at the bottom of the wagon bed. Dry weather had shrunk the boards enough that there was a little space between them. He could see the rims of several cans.

Gradually it dawned on him that those cans held the tomatoes he had come to hate so much. And with that realization came a notion so deliciously wicked that he began laughing to himself. He took a jackknife from his pocket and opened the largest blade, testing the point of it on his thumb.

Hewey did not have much in the way of worldly possessions, but he took care of what he had. He had always been particular about keeping his knife sharp as a razor. A man never knew when he might find something that needed cutting. He poked the blade between the boards, made contact with the bottom of a can, then drove the knife upward.

The can resisted, and Hewey was afraid if he pushed any harder he might break the blade. He climbed out from beneath the wagon and quietly opened the chuckbox. From a drawer he extracted Doughbelly's heavy butcher knife and carried it back underneath. He slipped it between the boards, then pushed hard.

The sound of rending metal was loud, and he feared it might be enough to awaken Doughbelly. He paused to listen. He still heard the cook's snoring. He began moving around beneath the wagon, avoiding the streaming tomato juice as he punched can after can. When one stream turned out to be molasses, he decided he had finished the tomatoes, at least all he could reach. He wiped the blade on dry grass, then on his trousers, and put the knife back into the chuckbox.

Whistling a happy church tune he had learned at a brush-arbor camp meeting, he went about harnessing the two teams.

Doughbelly rolled his bedding, grousing all the while about some people being too joyful for their own good. Concerned that the cook might notice the leaking tomatoes and the molasses, Hewey hitched the team to the wagon for him while Doughbelly went off behind the bushes and took care of other business. He had both wagons ready to go when the cook came back.

He had to fight himself to keep from grinning like a cat stealing cream. Doughbelly stared suspiciously at him before climbing up onto the seat of the chuckwagon. "Don't you lag behind and make me have to wait for you to open the gates."

Opening gates for the wagon cook was almost as lowly a job as chopping wood and helping him wash the cookware, but today Hewey did not mind. "I'll stick close behind you."

For a while, following in the chuckwagon's tracks, Hewey could see thin lines of glistening wetness where the tomato juice and molasses strung along in the grass. The lines stopped when the cans had emptied.

Hewey rejoiced, and sang all the church songs he could remember.

As he walked past the chuckwagon to open a wire gate for Doughbelly, the cook commented, "I never knowed you was a religious sort."

"Sing a glad song and the angels sing with you."

Hewey knew there would sooner or later be hell to pay, but he had never been inclined to worry much about future consequences if what he did felt right at the time.

He helped Doughbelly set up camp, unhitching the teams, pitching the bedrolls to the ground, digging a fire pit and chopping up dry mesquite. Doughbelly mostly stood around with ham-sized hands on his hips and giving unnecessary directions. The cowboys came straggling in after putting the remuda in a large fenced trap for the night. They were to brand calves here tomorrow, then move camp again in the afternoon.

Hewey had never been able to keep a secret from Grady Welch. They had spent so much time working together that Grady seemed able to read his mind. He gave Hewey a quizzical look and said, "You been up to somethin'."

Hewey put on the most innocent air he could muster. "I'm ashamed of you. Never saw anybody with such a suspicious mind."

"If you've done somethin' to cause us three more days of burned biscuits, the boys'll run you plumb out of camp."

The camp was thirty miles from Upton City, and even that was not much of a town.

"All I done was dull ol' Cookie's butcher knife a little."

Doughbelly started fixing supper. Hewey tried to watch him from the corner of his eye without being obvious. He held his breath when the cook reached over the sideboards and lifted out a can. Doughbelly's mouth dropped open. He gave the can a shake and exclaimed, "That thievin' grocery store has swindled the company."

He flung the can aside and fetched another, with the same result. This time he felt wetness on his hand and turned the can over. His eyes widened as he saw the hole punched in the bottom. "How in the Billy Hell . . ."

He whipped his gaze to Hewey. He seemed to sense instantly that Hewey Calloway was the agent of his distress. He drew back his arm and hurled the can at Hewey's head. Hewey ducked, then turned and began to pull away as Doughbelly picked up a chunk of firewood and ran at him.

"Damn you, Hewey, I don't know how you done it, but I know you done it."

The other cowboys moved quickly out of the way as Hewey broke into a run through bear grass and sand. The soft-bellied cook heaved along in his wake, waving the heavy stick of firewood and shouting words that would cause every church in Midland to bar him for life.

Cow boss Matthew Mullins rode up in time to see the cook stumble in a patch of shinnery and flop on his stomach. Like Doughbelly, he instantly blamed Hewey for whatever had gone wrong. "Hewey Calloway, what shenanigan have you run this time?"

Any show of innocence would be lost on Mullins. Hewey did not even try. "I just saved us from havin' to eat all them canned tomatoes."

"You probably kept us from eatin' *anything*. It'll be a week before he cooks chuck fit to put in our mouths."

"He ain't cooked anything yet that was fit to eat."

Mullins motioned for Hewey to remain where he was, a fit distance from the chuckwagon, while the boss went over to try to soothe the cook's wounded dignity. Watching from afar, Hewey could not hear the words, but he could see the violent motions Doughbelly was making with his hands, and he imagined he could even see the red that flushed the cook's face.

By the slump in Mullins's shoulders, Hewey discerned that the pleadings had come to naught. Doughbelly stalked over to the chuckwagon and dragged his bedroll through the sand, far away from those belonging to the rest of the crew. His angry voice would have carried a quarter mile.

"By God," he declared, "I quit!"

Mullins trailed after him, pleading. If he had been a dog, his tail would have been between his legs. "But you can't quit in the middle of the works. There's supper to be fixed and hands to be fed."

Doughbelly dropped his bedroll fifty feet from the wagon and plopped his broad butt down upon it. "They can feed theirselves or do without. I quit!"

Hewey had roped many a runaway cow and dragged her back into the roundup, bawling and fighting her head. He knew the signs of a sull when he saw them, and he saw them now in Doughbelly.

Mullins stared at the cook for a minute, but it was obvious he had run out of argument. He turned and approached Hewey with a firm stride that said it was a good thing he did not have a rope in his hand. His voice crackled. "Hewey, you've raised hell and shoved a chunk under it."

Hewey felt a little like laughing, but he knew better than to show it. "I didn't do nothin', and anyway the old scudder had it comin'."

"You know he'll sit out there and sulk like a baby. He won't cook a lick of supper."

"I've heard a lot worse news than that."

"You ain't heard the worst yet. Since he won't cook, you're goin' to."

"I ain't paid to cook."

"You'll cook or you'll start out walkin'. It's thirty miles to Upton City and farther than that to Midland. Which'll it be?"

Thirty miles, carrying saddle and bedroll . . . For a cowboy, used to saddling a horse rather than walk a hundred yards, that was worse than being sentenced to sixty days in jail. He looked at Doughbelly. "Maybe if I went and apologized to him . . ." He did not finish, because he had rather walk than apologize for doing what every man in the outfit would like to have done.

Mullins said, "You're either cookin' or walkin'."

Hewey swallowed. "Damn, but this is a hard outfit to work for." But he turned toward the chuckwagon. "I've never cooked for anybody except myself, hardly."

"Nothin' to it. You just fix what you'd fix for yourself and multiply it by twelve. And it had better be fit to eat."

"At least there won't be no tomatoes in it."

Hewey had always taken pride in two distinctions: He had never picked cotton, and he had never herded sheep. He had not considered the possibility that he might someday cook at a wagon or he might have added that as a third item on the list. Now he would never be able to.

He grumbled to himself as he sliced the beef and made biscuit dough and set the coffeepot over the fire. He glared at the distant form of Doughbelly Jackson squatted on his bedroll, his back turned toward the wagon. He figured hunger would probably put the old scoundrel in a better frame of mind when supper was ready, and he would come back into camp as if nothing had happened. But he had not reckoned on how obstinate a wagon cook could be when he got a sure-enough case of the rings.

At last Hewey hollered, "Chuck," and the cowboys filed by the chuckbox for their utensils, then visited the pots and Dutch ovens. He fully expected to hear some complaints when they bit into his biscuits, but nobody had any adverse comments. They were probably all afraid the cooking chore might fall on them if they said anything.

Grady Welch tore a high-rise biscuit in two and took a healthy bite. His eyes registered momentary surprise. "Kind of salty," he said, then quickly added, "and that's just the way I like them."

Hewey looked toward Doughbelly. He still sat where he had been for more than an hour, his back turned. Matthew Mullins edged up to Hewey. "Seein' as you're the one caused all this, maybe you ought to take him somethin' to eat."

"The only thing wrong with him is his head. Ain't nothin' wrong with his legs."

"At least take him a cup of coffee."

Hewey thought a little about that thirty-mile walk and poured steaming black coffee into a tin cup. Each leg felt as if it weighed a hundred pounds as he made his reluctant way out to the bedroll where Doughbelly had chosen to make his stand, sitting down. He extended the cup toward the cook. "Here. Boss said you'd ought to take some nourishment."

To his surprise, Doughbelly accepted the cup. He stared up at Hewey, his eyes smoldering like barbecue coals, then tossed the coffee out into the grass. He pitched the cup at Hewey. "Go to hell!"

"I feel like I'm already halfway there." Hewey's foot itched. He was sorely tempted to place it where it might do the most good, but he managed to put down his baser instincts. He picked up the cup. "Then sit here and pout. You're missin' a damned good supper."

Hewey knew it wasn't all that good, but he guessed Doughbelly would sober up if he thought somebody else might have taken his place and be doing a better job.

That turned out to be another bad guess. Doughbelly never came to supper. At dark he rolled out his bedding and turned in. Hewey sat in lantern light and picked rocks out of the beans he would slow-cook through the night.

Mullins came up and lifted Doughbelly's alarm clock from the chuckbox. "You'd better put this by your bed tonight. If he don't get up at four o'clock in the mornin', it'll be your place to crawl out and fix breakfast."

Hewey felt that he could probably throw the clock fifty feet and strike Doughbelly squarely on the head. He took pleasure in the fantasy but said only, "If I have to."

As Mullins walked away, Grady sidled up. "He's bound to get hungry and come in."

Hewey glumly shook his head. "He could live off of his own lard for two weeks."

Hewey lay half awake a long time, then drifted off into a dream in which he fought his way out from a huge vat of clinging biscuit dough, only to fall into an even bigger can of tomatoes. The ringing of the alarm saved him from drowning in the juice. He arose and pulled on his trousers and boots, then punched up the banked coals and coaxed the fire back into full life. He kept watching for Dough-belly to come into camp, but the cook remained far beyond the firelight.

After a time Hewey shook the kid horse jingler out of a deep sleep and sent him off to bring in the remuda so the cowboys could catch out their mounts after breakfast. He entertained a wild notion of intercepting the horses and turning them in such a way that they would run over the cook's bed, but he had to dismiss the idea. The laws against murder made no special dispensation for wagon cooks.

The cowboys saddled up, a couple of broncs pitching, working off the friskiness brought on by the fresh morning air. Grady Welch had to grab the saddle horn to stay aboard. Pride gave way to prac-ticality; he was still aching from the last time when he *didn't* claw leather. Hewey had to stand beside the chuckbox and watch the cowboys ride out from camp without him. He felt low enough to walk beneath the wagon without bending over.

Doughbelly rolled his blankets, then sat there just as he had done yesterday, shoulders hunched and back turned. Hewey went out to a pile of well-dried wood a Two C's swamper had cut last winter for this campsite. He began chopping it into short lengths for the cookfire.

He heard the rattle of a lid and turned in time to see Doughbelly at the Dutch ovens, filling a plate. Hewey hurled a chunk of wood at him. Doughbelly retreated to his bedroll and sat there eating. Angrily Hewey dumped the leftover breakfast onto the ground and raked it into the sand with a pot hook to be sure Doughbelly could not come back for a second helping. He hid a couple of biscuits for the kid horse jingler, who would come in hungry about midmorning.

Hewey was resigned to cooking the noon meal, for Doughbelly showed no sign that he was ready to come to terms. He peeled spuds and ground fresh coffee and sliced steaks from half a beef that had been wrapped in a tarp and hung up in the nearby windmill tower to keep it from the flies and larger varmints.

From afar he glumly watched horsemen bring the cattle into the pens, cut the calves off from their mothers, and start branding them. He belonged out there with the rest of the hands, not here confined to a few feet on either side of the chuckbox. He had been in jails where he felt freer.

Doughbelly still sat where he had been since suppertime, ignoring everything that went on around him.

The hands came in for dinner, then went back to complete the branding. Finished, they brought the irons and put them in the hoodlum wagon. Mullins told Hewey, "The boys'll drive the horses to the next camp so the jingler'll be free to drive the hoodlum wagon for you."

By that Hewey knew he was still stuck with the cooking job. He jerked his head toward Doughbelly. "What about him?"

Mullins shrugged. "He's *your* problem." He mounted a dun horse and rode off.

The kid helped Hewey finish loading the two wagons and hitch the teams. Hewey checked to be sure he had secured the chuckbox lid so it would not drop if a wheel hit a bad bump.

At last Doughbelly stood up. He stretched himself, taking his time, then picked up his bedroll and carried it to the hoodlum wagon. He pitched it up on top of the other hands' bedding.

An old spiritual tune ran though Hewey's mind, and he began to sing. "Just a closer walk with Thee . . ."

He climbed up on the hoodlum wagon, past the surprised kid, and threw Doughbelly's bedroll back onto the ground.

Doughbelly sputtered. "Hey, what're you doin'?"

Hewey pointed in the direction of Upton City. "It ain't but thirty miles. If you step lively you might make it by tomorrow night."

He returned to the chuckwagon and took his place on the seat, then flipped the reins. The team surged against the harness. He sang, "As I walk, let me walk close to Thee."

Doughbelly trotted alongside, his pudgy face red, his eyes wide in alarm. "You can't just leave me here."

"You ain't workin' for this outfit. You quit yesterday."

"Hewey . . ." Doughbelly's voice trailed off. He trotted back to where his bedroll lay. He lifted it up onto his shoulder and came running. Hewey was surprised to see that a man with that big a belly on him could run so fast. He had never seen the cook move like that before.

Hewey put the team into a long trot, one that Doughbelly could not match. The kid followed Hewey's cue and set the hoodlum wagon to moving too fast for the cook to catch.

Hewey had to give the man credit; he tried. Doughbelly pushed himself hard, but he could not help falling back. At last he stumbled, and the bed came undone, tarp and blankets rolling out upon the grass. Doughbelly sank to the ground, a picture of hopelessness.

Hewey let the team go a little farther, then hauled up on the lines. He signaled the kid to circle around him and go on. Then he sat and waited. Doughbelly gathered his blankets in a haphazard manner, picking up the rope that had held them but not taking time to tie it. He came on, puffing like a T&P locomotive. By the time he finally reached the wagon he was so winded he could hardly speak. Sweat cut muddy trails through the dust on his ruddy face.

"Please, Hewey, ain't you goin' to let me throw my beddin' up there?"

Hewey gave him his most solemn expression. "If you ain't cookin', you ain't ridin'."

"I'm cookin'."

"What about them damned tomatoes?"

"Never really liked them much myself."

Hewey moved over to the left side of the wagon seat and held out the reins. "Long's you're workin' for this outfit again, you'd just as well do the drivin'. I'm goin' to sit back and take my rest."

Supper that night was the best meal Hewey had eaten since Christmas.

A Woman 49er

JOANN LEVY

What is true courage, if not going on in the face of no hope whatsoever? JoAnn Levy invites us to look out through the burned-out eyes in the broken faces of all those pioneer women whose images still haunt us in photographs. She is the author of three books, including *They Saw the Elephant: Women in the California Gold Rush*; *Daughter of Joy: A Novel of Gold Rush San Francisco*; and *For California's Gold: A Novel*.

MARGARET STOOPED TO THE
hearth, wrapped her apron hem around the wire handle, and hefted
the iron kettle from its warming hook above the fire. As she stood,
the kettle in both hands, she felt the pain of the effort like a club in
her back. She submitted to it for a moment, and the smell of the
cabbage, too. Cabbage every night. They were all heartily sick of it.
The odor got into her skin. Sometimes she smelled it in the dark
when she'd lie awake, exhausted but sleepless, mystified by fortune's
revolution.

She saw clearly the wrong turn, knew the moment, called it back
in imagination ten thousand times, but fate remained immutable.
She and Jack had watched the ships come and go in Boston Harbor
all their lives. "Me a shipbuilder and never been to sea," he'd said
that portentous day, eyes on the horizon as if seeing California, the
golden rumors calling them like sea sirens. So much gold, the whal-
ers and sailors reported, passing hearsay like a church collection
plate, that the people there kept it in barrels and fetched it out with
flour scoops. From the talk, Margaret imagined herself gathering an
apronful of nuggets, collecting them up like hens' eggs. Not too late
for adventure, Jack had said. And she'd agreed. Why let riches pass
them by? Yes, let's do it. High hopes. Dashed to bits in this two-
room frontier cabin, her days as bound to ceaseless labor as sails to
a mast. The course of her life, and her children's, irretrievably altered.

She carried the heavy kettle to the table, the leather heels of her
best Albert slippers, worn out now, slapping across the tight pun-
cheon floor. Oh, this never-ending smell of cabbage, and oh, how
her back hurt. Some days the pain stabbed right through like an
arrow. The kettle weighed as much as Cassie, who cried to be lifted

up two dozen times a day. And how could a mother say no to her least and last, three years old and frightened of her shadow? Margaret knew she'd done that to the child, made her skittish with her own misgivings, fed the child fear in her mother's milk. As dried up now as herself. Seemed like she was always hauling or lifting something—water from the creek, a child into bed or bath and out again, a joint of beef to cut up, cabbages from the garden. She felt so tired her bones hurt.

The men's talk ceased as she thumped the kettle onto the plank table. Beneath the candle lantern suspended from the rafter, six expectant faces turned to her, three men to a bench. If her custom continued to increase, she'd get Susan to build another table and benches. A clever girl, and good with her hands like her father. Margaret brushed a wisp of hair from her eyes, wiped her hands on her apron, and picked up the ladle.

"Smells delicious, ma'am." The man sitting at the end of the bench on her right. A scarred face and a sullen, slit-eyed look, but his voice was all kindness. He took the filled plate from her hand with a respectful nod. Ma'am. When had she become a ma'am? When had she stopped being pretty and young and become old and tired? She couldn't remember. What had this one said his name was? She tried to remember their names, so they'd feel welcome and come again. She needed the trade. Proffitt, that was it. Ezekial Proffitt. Intuition told her he left trouble in his trail the way a horse left hoofprints. Next to him, Emil Bidwell, her one regular boarder, a strange bird. Perspired a bit too much for the climate. At the end, Ben Foster, and across from Ben, his partner, Dan Sutherland. Decent, hardworking miners, didn't drink or gamble their gold. Talked of sweethearts at home in Connecticut. Yale boys. They ate at her table when they struck a little extra pay dirt, a luxury for them, a godsend for her at two dollars a meal. Next to Dan, Jacob Rosen, the peddler who traveled through every few months, his worn frock coat as familiar to her now as the sound of his bell horse. He'd traded her candles for his meal, good candles, she could smell the tallow in them. A hard bargainer but honest. He'd sleep in his wagon and be off by daybreak.

She remembered all their names but this last one on her left, a handsome young man. He smiled as she handed him the warm, full plate. A sweet face. The others all had beards and mustaches. Most men in the mines backslid from civilization's habits, went wild, like boys out of school for summer. This one was new to the life here, still held to women's influence. No disappointment in his brown eyes yet, nothing but optimism. He must have come around the Horn or across the Isthmus, not by wagon. No hint he'd seen so much as the tail of the California elephant. Jim, that was his name, brother to Ezekial, as alike as Cain and Abel. He'd given her a jar of pickles for the table, put it into her callused work-worn hands like a bouquet of violets. They missed their womenfolks, all of them. If respect were gold, she'd be rich.

Margaret dug down inside herself for a smile to return to him, hauled it up like water from a well. Everything felt like effort, even the proper face for the six men sitting to her table correct as boys in Sunday School, looking at her like she was the preacher, or more likely, their own mother. Even Emil Bidwell, who had to be near her own age, nodding and smiling from behind his spectacles, his thinning black hair slicked and still damp with water from the horse trough. She felt old enough to be his mother. Truth be told, she felt more ninety-eight than thirty-eight.

Margaret dipped the ladle into the kettle and filled a third plate. Steam rose into her face with the smell of cabbage, dampening her brow. She felt wisps of hair escaping from the bun, more gray than chestnut now, pinned at the nape of her neck. She'd left off wearing a day cap. Civilization slipped from everyone in the mines. She'd even taken the ruffles off her petticoats to ease the washing of them. Practicality took the front seat in the wagon now, vanity the back. She'd avoided the mirror hanging from a wire in the bedroom after her mother's face surprised her in it. Until then, she'd still thought of herself as handsome. Until Jack's accident. Would she one day cease being amazed by the mirror's reflection? Or would she stare each time and think, Granny, when did you move in here?

"Boiled cabbage, barley, and beef," she said, handing the plate to Ezekial Proffitt. "Pass that down, Mr. Proffitt, if you would." She took another tin plate from the stack Susan had set out. Susan had cleaned up after feeding the children, set out all the little fixings for the boarders, the butter and bread, tin cups for the coffee, lined up the knives and forks in neat rows. God's blessing, her firstborn. Margaret heard her in the other room now, getting the little ones to bed after their baths, and George singing them a lullaby as hushed as the pines whispering above her roof. Different as night and day, all of them, her burden and her blessing.

Six living children, more than a woman might rightly expect to survive. Poor things, all crammed up together in one room. A two-room cabin, what passed for luxury in these parts. Not a candle on the Boston house they'd let go, relinquished for a chance at adventure, a ticket to California's golden lottery. "What do you think, Maggie, my girl, should we do it?" Jack's voice in her head like an echo. Both of them catching the fever, afire for adventure. Be careful what you wish for, you might get it. Hadn't her mother said that? She knew she said it to Susan. Mothers and daughters, they passed wisdom along, the daughters not catching the truth of it till they repeated it to their own.

Margaret filled and passed the last plate. The six faces smiled at her, like they were waiting for her to pick up her spoon and start. She'd say that for California, it put politeness for a respectable woman into men like good lye soap put clean into a wash. "You go ahead and help yourselves to more if you want it. There's plenty. And peach pie for dessert, too." Her boardinghouse voice, hauled up like her boardinghouse smile, what she imagined an innkeeper should sound like. Generous, obliging, happy to please. She remembered wanting to bake pies for people when she was a girl, always enjoyed cooking. Until now. Be careful what you wish for.

In the bedroom, Susan turned when Margaret slipped in to kiss the little ones good night. "Cassie's already asleep," she whispered. "Wore herself out, all that company giving her piggyback rides. I put her down in your bed."

Margaret sat down heavily on the edge of the bed. Sometimes even the weight of her skirts and petticoats seemed too much to bear. It felt good to get off her feet for a minute. She massaged the small of her back with one hand, resisting the temptation to curl up next to Cassie in the bed Jack had built from pine logs. No carved mahogany or turned bedposts now. "Sturdy, solid pioneer beds," Jack had said when he'd finished building them, putting the best face on it. He'd made a neat lattice of ropes to hold the mattress she'd fashioned from two sheets stitched together and filled with dried grass. One bed for them, one for Susan. An adventure. Margaret sighed. No sense crying over spilled milk. "That's good. She sleeps best with me." Margaret pulled the blanket around the tiny shoulders, and kissed her youngest daughter's forehead. The child smelled of soap.

A candle, set in a jar, glowed from the shelf nailed up by the door. It cast a dim yellow light over the two beds against one log wall and the five gunny bunks slung on the opposite. "The children will think they're fun," Jack had said, nailing gunny sacks to logs he'd set at right angles and fastened to the wall. A lark, an adventure then still, despite the sad truth that they'd thrown away Boston's comforts for California's rude surprise. Three bunks sagged from the weight of their young occupants. " 'Night, Ma," George said, up on one elbow in the bunk suspended above sleeping six-year-old Daniel. He ducked into his blanket as Margaret stood to come to him. He didn't like being kissed anymore, the man of the family now, too old for a mother's fussing.

In the other second-level gunny bunk eight-year-old Ellen murmured in her sleep. Margaret pulled a wisp of sand-colored hair from her mouth, and turned to Susan, hanging up the children's clothes on nails. "Eliza's sleeping with you?" Five-year-old Eliza objected to Cassie, 'the baby,' getting anything she didn't. She'd insist on sleeping in a bed, too.

Susan hooked Ellen's dress over a nail, a miniature of her own in blue-striped calico. "I don't mind, she's easier than Cassie." In the mirror next to the nail, Susan smoothed her hair from its center part and tidied the bun of rich chestnut fastened at the back of her neck. Margaret remembered her own hair had looked like that. How fleeting youth and beauty. She sighed. What had she done to her daughter, dragging her into this godforsaken country? The girl was clever. When she graduated from the female seminary at Mount Holyoke, Margaret had felt as proud as Susan herself. And all of it come to this. Be careful what you wish for.

Susan turned. "I can clean up, Ma. Why don't you go on to bed?"

Margaret brushed soot from her apron, a remnant of a brown windowpane-check skirt she'd cut up to make dresses for Ellen and Eliza. Washday tomorrow. No girl to come and do it here. No money to pay if there was. She rubbed her back with both hands. "More than enough for two to do." There always was.

At the table, the men were talking about Joaquin Murieta. If the subject wasn't getting gold, it was losing it—to bandits, traders, gamblers. Hard enough to come by, harder to hold on to. Margaret cleared the empty plates, stacking them together with soft clinking sounds. Susan collected the knives. "Keep your fork," Susan told Jim Proffitt, shaking her head. "For the pie." Margaret felt sorry for the young man, the way he looked at Susan. They all looked at her daughter that way until Susan let them know she found their attentions unwelcome. No man ever took Susan's fancy. "I'm waiting for the right one, Ma, same as you did for Papa."

Emil Bidwell wiped a hand across his mouth. "I saw him in Angels Camp. Almost, anyhow." He paused for effect.

Dan Sutherland planted his elbows on the table, coffee cup cradled in his hands. "Angels Camp? I heard he was at Moke Hill same time someone reported him at Sonora. Must be half a dozen Joaquins, the way the stories go."

Margaret reached past him for the butter dish. Ben picked it up and handed it to her. "Real good, ma'am."

They all chimed in then, like a handbell chorus, praising the food. Margaret nodded. "Pleased you enjoyed it. Pie for you in a minute." She wanted to hurry them, there was still so much to do. She longed to crawl into bed next to Cassie, hug the poor little thing to her like a doll, and sleep for a week.

Emil Bidwell picked up his fork and tapped the handle on the table like a timid bailiff calling court to order. Anyone else would have pounded a cup, Margaret thought, feeling sorry for his shyness. This was a rough country for the fainthearted.

"No, it was the real Joaquin Murieta in Angels, all right." Bidwell kept his eyes on the fork, turned it first one way and then the other, like he was looking for something. "He and his gang plagued the Chinamen down there like locusts come to Egypt. Rode in at night on their horses, thundering through the camp, scaring them into running. Not a one of those China boys carries a gun. Sitting ducks for bandits. Joaquin and his gang took them regular as going to the bank." He set the fork down, looked around the table. "Celestials are a clever lot, though. They moved all their tents together up on a hill, dug a twelve-foot ditch the whole way 'round, and filled it with brambles. Now they come and go by a plank they use for a bridge. Haul it in at night."

Ben Foster yawned. "Maybe it was Joaquin, maybe not. Seems nobody ever sees anything but a fast, black horse, a Mexican jacket, and a Californio hat."

Jacob Rosen said, "Could be anyone, and Joaquin getting the blame."

"Or the credit," Ben said. "Mexicans think he's a hero."

Margaret leaned one hand on the oak log that served for a mantelpiece and bent toward the dying fire with the long stick that served for a poker. Everything served for something else. Makeshift and make-do. That's what her life had come to. She poked the embers until orange sparks spit and popped and a small flame snaked to life around the last log. A gray finger of smoke twisted up the slate-rock chimney. The fireplace drew well. She'd say that for Jack Lockeford, he at least left them a tight house. Set right to it, when he saw how things were. "One thing at a time, Maggie, my girl. We'll just get us a shipshape house, start up a garden, and then I'll see about digging gold. Not so easy as we thought, maybe, but our chances are good as anybody's."

"I'll get more wood, Ma." Susan clattered the tin dinner plates into the bucket of water on the hearth.

Margaret put a hand on Susan's arm and shook her head no. "Get the coffee." She paused, willing away the pain in her back. "I'll serve up the pie." The men's talk was too lively, they'd sit all night to table if she kept a fire going, and there was cleaning up still to do and breakfast preparations to start. The Proffitt brothers looked like they meant to stay, good for her purse but extra bread to bake for morning.

While Susan filled the coffee cups, the aroma strong and hot, Margaret removed the pie from the iron Dutch oven she'd become proficient at baking in and set it on the table. It smelled warm and sweet and spicy with cinnamon. The men fell silent, watching her and Susan. Margaret cut into the flaky crust and dished up six pieces, spooning the juices over. Ezekial Proffitt forked a big bite into his mouth. "Reminds me of my ma's peach pie, ma'am. A real treat."

"I'm sure your mother's was better. All I've got here is those dried peaches that come from Chile, pressed into a round like a cheese."

Jacob Rosen licked his fork. "Good as fresh, missus, way you stew them up with butter and spices." He cocked his head in the direction of his wagon out front. "I got nutmeg this trip, you want to look?"

Emil Bidwell, digging into his dessert like a glory hole, looked up at the peddler. "You got any writing paper printed with California scenes? The miners like those illustrated lettersheets."

Margaret and Susan tidied the sideboard and swept the hearth. The men's forks clicked against their tin plates. Like the telegraph machine Jack took her to see in Boston, Margaret thought. Civilization. Memories. The men's talk turned to letter-writing. The peddler had a new lettersheet, he said, illustrated with the California elephant. Margaret knew all about the elephant, the mythic beast that smashed hope. The elephant was real. It had got her Jack.

Bidwell pushed aside his empty plate, brushed pie crumbs from the table to the floor. Margaret saw Susan look and shake her head. More sweeping to do. Bidwell pulled out one of his leather packets, spread it on the table, and withdrew a lettersheet to show the Proffitt brothers. "Five dollars to write a letter out. I've a nice hand, you see. Then another dollar to take it to the post office. Saves the boys a trip to town, and I pick up any mail that's come in. That's another dollar for the delivery."

And then Ben Foster and Dan Sutherland were saying good night, tromping more dirt from their boot heels into her floor, the door banging shut behind them. And the peddler was bowing and thanking her for her trade, and reminding her of the nutmeg, and Emil Bidwell following him out. In an hour, she'd hear the writer snoring in his tent tucked up against the chimney outside. And maybe the Proffitt brothers, too, them saying they'd maybe stay to breakfast. And Margaret was thinking that Susan was right, a room added behind the chimney would be worth the cost. Bidwell paid her a dollar a day for the privilege of his tent, but a regular sleeping room for travelers, there was money in that. She could charge maybe five dollars a night for those passing through, a little less to local miners with regular trade. This constant battle for a dollar here and a dollar there consumed her waking hours, every little thing being so dear, and her with six mouths to feed besides her own.

Susan swept, the broom a steady swish, swish. Margaret started the bread for morning, leaned into her kneading, the dough pliant in her floury hands. The stretching and pulling and pushing relieved her aching back.

"He seemed nice, Ma, didn't you think?" Susan splashed water from a bucket over the washed dishes, rinsing them in a pail.

Margaret brushed flour from her hands. She knew who Susan meant, recalling the smiles exchanged like welcome visiting cards.

"Nice enough." She set the dough to rise by the hearth, remembering youth, when life was all bright and unknown. Like California. A lottery. And winning still possible.

In the bedroom, Margaret undressed to her chemise in the dark, hearing Susan do the same, surrounded by the gentle sleeping sounds of the children. Outside, the wind whispered in the pines. Loneliest sound in the world, she thought, slipping silently into bed next to Cassie. Exhausted, she gathered the warm, sleeping child against her. She buried her face in Cassie's silky hair, inhaled the fresh good soap smell, and listened for Susan's regular breathing. Until her children slept, Margaret found strength each night to hold back the haunting image. But it would come then, insistent as birth, stealing the last of her strength.

It came now, tiptoeing into her mind like a thief. She saw her Jack again, smiling, as last she'd seen him smiling, brushing his hands in satisfaction over the final accomplishment, the snug cabin built, the pine furniture installed, the neat garden sowed. All first, foremost, he'd insisted, and only then the prospecting he'd dreamed of for months, like a child dreams of Christmas. "Well, then, I believe I'll just go down to the creek, Maggie, my girl, have a look around, get the lay of the land." He'd kissed her cheek, winked at her like Saint Nicholas himself. "Back by suppertime," he'd said, and whistling, disappeared into the pines.

She'd searched that night as far as she'd dared, she and the children calling, casting their feeble candlelight against the black forms of the soughing trees. Maybe he'd been kidnapped, or gotten lost, or injured and couldn't walk. Something, anything, but what her heart told her.

They'd found him the next morning. He lay where he'd fallen, the print of his boot still visible on the mossy stone where he'd slipped. The image returned each night as vivid and horrifying and fresh as though new from morning. Jack, just lying there, face down in the water, the creek babbling and washing around him, Jack Lockeford nothing more to it than a trapped log.

And Jack fell down, and broke his crown. The nursery-rhyme

words skittered like mice around the edges of the memory. Margaret couldn't remember when they'd forced themselves into the ritual that had become as much a part of her nights as darkness. Jack fell down, and broke his crown. The jingle chased the image from her mind. Then came the tears. She whisked them away with her hand.

It smelled of cabbage.

The Living Land

JANET E. GRAEBNER

The spiritual life of the American Indian was an intensely physical one as well. Janet E. Graebner, a native Minnesotan now living in Colorado, has published articles in regional and national business magazines, has worked as a consultant and editor, and is the author of two nonfiction books. In her spare time she studies Sanskrit and Lakota.

Aκíya walked quickly and quietly, his eyes fastened on the mountain in front of him. Like a woman certain of his intention, it beckoned him to climb the tree-darkened slope.

He obeyed the summons, shortening his stride to plant his bare feet better and grip the taunting hillside. His naked hard body blended with the surroundings: muscle and stone, brown flesh and earth, tenacity and endurance.

Toes curled into the dirt as his feet picked their way around red-ant hills, across broken shale, and over sage clumps that released silver-green pungency in the wet chill of the morning.

No sound issued in the false dawn. No stir of small animals or the visit of birds. Not even a sigh of exertion yet escaped his lips, for Akíya was in excellent physical condition, twenty-seven winters old, and an Oglala warrior of the Teton Lakhóta.

Looking over his shoulder to the south, he saw the land below spread wider and longer. Forward, the sky pressed down as the slope began to tilt up. The incline grew steeper. What had looked easily approachable from the valley now showed its true self as rugged terrain. Broken rocks, loosed from the eroding ledges above and exposing sharp white-gray edges, strewed his path, biting his feet. Others had lain for . . . how long? . . . their edges smoothed by wind and water and grit, their surfaces covered by a shield of gray-green lichen.

A rock-thrust tall as a lodge loomed before him, and as he skirted around it to his right, he saw the morning's first light fringing the horizon. The soft rosy colors gradually fanned into cartwheeling golds and oranges as Wi, Father Sun, began his daily ascent.

Akíya carried only a buffalo robe and a red clay pipe, its bowl sealed. It was safely tucked into an unadorned elkskin case and slung over his shoulder by a braided horsehair strap. His discarded breechclout and moccasins were snugged in the crotch of a tree below, earthly goods that had been abandoned in a sign of humility. To seek a vision one must come before Wakantanka, the great mystery, poor in the things of this world, bare of all but a sincere desire to receive Wakantanka's messengers.

He shifted the heavy robe for better balance and did not see the juniper root waiting to snag his foot. He stumbled, disturbing a rock, whose clatter as it fell broke the morning's silence. A magpie skreeked. A lizard scurried in front of him, scattering grains of sand as it slid under a rock. A startled rabbit broke from the brush to his left. Akíya smiled, pleased, for the rabbit was a good sign. In Lakhóta tradition, the soft, quiet little animal represented humility. Indeed, for this very reason rabbit fur bound the stem of the pipe he carried. The gentle animal lacked aggression and was not self-asserting, qualities which all vision seekers must possess when they journey to the sacred center.

Sweat beaded his body as the treed slope gave way to the wall of rock called *mato tipi paha*. Bear Lodge Butte, his people's sacred vision site. Lakhóta legend said its scored face was made by the claws of a boy-turned-bear who had chased his seven sisters. They raced to a stump, and in answer to their prayers, the stump grew, carrying the sisters out of reach as the boy-bear clawed its sides. Stranded, the sisters died and ascended into the sky to become the stars of *cansasa ipusye,* the Big Dipper.

Akíya looked around, half expecting to see the great bear. Then he dug his fingers into cracks and sought purchase with his toes. His goal in sight, he began to climb. By the time he reached a ledge under the lip of the butte, thin trickles of blood marked his passage.

A moment of uncertainty gripped him as he eyed the jagged edge rimmed by finger-long spikes of ancient rock.

Then, gathering courage, he pushed the pipe case around to his back and slipped the sling over his head to secure it across his chest.

He hefted the buffalo robe several times and grunted with the effort of throwing it over the edge. Stretching to grab the rim, he pulled himself up. His chest scraped against the sawtoothed sentinels. Bits of rock crumbled and fell away. He tightened his upper body, pulled strongly with both arms, and hoisted himself onto the top of the butte just as Father Sun crowned the horizon to bind with Mother Earth.

Akíya staggered to his feet, blinded by the sun-flashed designs spinning before his eyes. He faced east and raised his arms in greeting. "Father, I am ready."

When the sun had risen high enough for his vision to clear, he walked to the center of the butte. A flat rock about the length of a hunting bow had been placed there long ago to receive the vision quester's sacred pipe. He unslung the case and removed the pipe. Hanging from the middle of the stem was a small doeskin pouch that held his personal stone, round and smooth, wrapped in sage, the keeper of his protective spirit. Carefully he laid the pipe down with its stem pointing east. Beside it he spread his buffalo robe.

Three strides from the center, he found an arm's-length aspen branch discarded by a previous vision seeker. Dragging it beside him, he scratched a circle, its eye-measured distance from the center roughly corresponding to his body length.

Laying aside the branch, he returned to the rock and picked up the pipe, the keeper of truth. Holding it in both hands, he raised it horizontally to the west, where the thunder beings lived, and his voice rang out in prayer: *"Wakantanka unshimala ye oyate wani wachin cha!* Grandfather, Great Spirit, hear me, that my people may live! One is sending a voice, Power Above. I seek a vision to know the path to walk for my people."

Akíya repeated his prayer while facing the north, the direction of the white cleansing wind. Turning to the east, he offered his prayer to the power of light and wisdom. To the south, whence springs the summer power to grow, his voice again chanted: *"Ta-kuwakan,* Something Sacred, hear me, that my people may live!"

Then dipping the pipe stem toward the earth, he repeated the prayer for the fifth time. Lifting it skyward, once again his voice floated out over the land. Finally, raising the stem slightly higher, he acknowledged *Wahupa,* the word naming that which cannot be named. Wahupa, the center from which all life emerges, and through which all creation lives, and to which eventually all return. Wahupa.

He placed the pipe on the rock and began to walk slowly around the butte. The level surface was nearly as large as his people's village circle. A spare life clung here. Clumps of sage and some prickly leaf held fast in the dry soil, and humps of dirt were alive with ants. Pebbles and small rocks littered the butte, offspring of the elemental earth to which the grandfathers directly relate, and within each pebble lay the memory that it was once a mountain. Certainly at the beginning, he thought, Wahupa had commanded stone, something firm and lasting on which life shall sit and walk.

The Lakhóta had been coming here since before memory, so said the elders. But for the first time, Akíya regarded Bear Lodge Butte as more than just a mysterious reminder of the past settled on the plain. Under his feet trembled the power that gives birth to the land's shape; the initial thrust of hot, raw energy from deep within the earth that cracks its skin and permanently ruptures the original stone culture, separating stone families. The power that forever displaces boulders and relocates rocks, which gradually succumb to wind and water, then become worn and smooth and broken.

The sun rose higher as he walked. Grew hotter. Shimmering heat waves stimulated the land for which the *Teton,* they-roam-the-plains, were named, distorting it into unknown hills and gullies.

He circled one last time before lying down with his feet pointing east. He looked over his toes and his eyes fastened on the edge of the butte, then lifted to the late morning sun. Silently he petitioned the invisibles to intercede, that Wakantanka's messengers might be kind to him this first day.

The sun climbed higher. His underarms slicked with salty sweat. Ants found their way between his toes. Transparent-winged insects crawled along his sticky legs. His body's moisture drained away. The buffalo hair soaked up his sweat and his back began to itch.

He closed his eyes and willed his body to stillness. In his mind's eye flowed the thickwoods river below, where only this morning he had performed his bathing ritual. It seemed longer ago. He tried to recapture the water's coolness laving his body and trickling down the back of his throat. He ran his tongue around his lips, not yet dry and cracked. But he knew that before long they would split and bleed, the only moisture he would know during his stay on Bear Lodge Butte.

He sang softly. He sighed. He grew drowsy and slept. Dream-parts flickered.

MORNING RAIN, HIS SITS-BESIDE-HIM WIFE, FASTENED HIM WITH *her eyes, silently pleading that he not go on this quest. The journey's path was unsafe, traveled by white soldiers, and others who scratched Mother Earth for the yellow rocks that were of no use . . . Spare Hawk, his brother-friend, jumped from his horse during the fight at the river of the greasy grass, jerked a red sash across his shoulder, and pushed the dangling stake into the muddied blood, there to hold him in one place—the ultimate act of bravery—until a bullet found his heart. . . . The yellow-hair called Custer held a weapon to his own head. . . . A bloodied end of the red sash drifted on the death-scented air. . . . Ribbons of red flowed . . . so much blood . . . so much killing. . . .*

A SCREECH SPLIT THE AIR AND AKÍYA BOLTED UPRIGHT AS AN eagle swooped down, its curved talons extended. "I am not fat and juicy, friend," he shouted. "You will have to seek elsewhere to eat." The eagle shrieked again and wheeled away.

Hunger tightened his own stomach muscles, but neither food nor water would be taken until he left the butte.

As he lay there, his mind picked over the dream images, which came more often since their victory at the Greasy Grass, called the battle of the Little Big Horn by whites. To what end all this sadness, destruction, and bloodshed? Was there not enough land for all to live in harmony? And what do the white man's words "own land" mean? How could one possess Mother Earth?

His left hip, numb from lying still so long, began to ache. It had plagued him since the Greasy Grass, when he stretched from galloping horseback and tried to pull up the stake holding Spare Hawk, an intervention that only he, Akíya, could execute as a warrior and *hunka,* brother-friend. But he had failed, and the ache in his hip deepened, a lifetime reminder of his loss. Frustration gripped him and he pounded his fist against the benumbed joint. Then, chagrined at behavior unfit for a vision seeker, he stood and slowly kneaded his hip back to life.

Father Sun had completed his day's journey and was now dropping behind the rim of Mother Earth.

Akíya circled the butte, his eyes searching the land in the twilight. But the great plains offered little for eyes to lean on. Only the two shadowed hills to the southwest took shape, those called mother and child by his people, the smaller hill following just behind the larger one.

The darkness shouldered its way closer, and the evening's coolness felt good against his skin sucked dry by the sun. Discomfort pushed against his bladder. He stepped to the side and relieved himself, careful not to wet an anthill. Then he returned to the center and rolled into the buffalo robe.

Night's family emerged. Scurrying feet announced small animals tracing their passage. A nighthawk winged past his head. Insects landed on his face, drawn by its damp warmth.

The moon rose and the campfires of the departed ones began to fill the empty darkness. His eyes searched the spangled sky, seeking his mother and sister, killed three summers ago at Lone Woman Creek, and his father, who had earlier traveled the spirit trail. How to describe the pain of their absence? Words spoken by his father when Akíya received his first eagle feather flooded his hearing: *As long as a warrior has love for all things alive and all things dead, he will live twice but die only once.*

A part of him—the trained warrior—sought retaliation against the invaders of the land bestowed by the ancient ones. His heart quickened as his thoughts turned again to the fight at the Greasy Grass, recalling the women's tremolos of encouragement and the warriors' shouted *Hoka heys!* as they descended the hill, riding fast, then faster, like the wind, their eagle-wing-bone whistles fluting victory.

Beneath his horse's pounding hooves that day he had felt a surge of power from *inyan,* grandfather stone, and a loan of power from *thate* as the wind whipped him in the face. His horse fairly flew downhill. The day was his, theirs. Victory would not be denied.

Lying now on sacred ground, he again desired the same exhilarating power to bring a vision that would direct that part of him opposed to the vengeful warrior, that inner voice that he heard more frequently but did not understand. It contradicted the very core of his Lakhóta being. It was a prodding voice that spoke of bridging the differences with the white man. A voice that did not shout but whispered: *Bend like the willow.*

He shifted his position to ease his aching hip. Lying on his back, his eyes sought and held the star-that-does-not-walk, the star that leads a lost one home. His breathing slowed, and his heart beat in rhythm to the throbbing he felt underneath, movement of the earth-essential. It pulled him closer, like a child clutched to its mother's breast.

Quietly he lay, waiting. And the beat, from deep within the butte, pulsed steadily, each throb a command from its core to his: *Follow me, follow me.*

Akíya's eyes filled with the guiding star's light. Its brilliance covered him just before Earth's energy tapped at the base of his spine and spread through his legs and arms, tingling out to his fingertips. *Follow me . . . follow . . .*

• • •

A SOUND MORE FELT THAN HEARD RUMBLED ON EITHER SIDE OF him. He sensed the presence of the stone grandfathers, dark, substantial, ever-enduring. It was from them that he understood the call.

He felt himself lifted up by the force of their primal power and carried toward a cool light that spread wider and wider to allow him entry. As he passed through to the other side, he saw a tumble of people running from soldiers' bullets. Silent puffs of smoke spurted from discharged rifles. No sound came from running feet. No cry was heard from the mouths stretched in pain as bodies fell to the snow-covered ground.

He recognized the winding *canke opi wakpala*, the creek at Wounded Knee. Women and children huddled against its gritty banks. Soldiers pointed guns at them.

But there has been no fighting there.

Big Foot, leader of the Miniconjous, sprawled grotesquely, one still eye staring directly at Akíya.

But I just saw Big Foot three moons ago.

. . . Follow me . . . follow . . .

Again, the stone grandfathers' unvoiced force carried him deeper into Mother Earth. Like falling stars, images of destruction and despair flashed by him: A lone buffalo stood beside a dried wallow. . . . A staggering line of Hunkpapas headed away from the sacred hills toward the white grandmother's land in the north. . . . Across the plains metal boxes breathed fire and smoke. . . . Everywhere, like *heyapi*, head lice, people crawled across the land, digging, burning, slashing. . . .

One does not harm the land upon which the people walk.

. . . Follow me . . . , follow . . .

Through a curtain of snow, in the moon of the popping trees, he saw men and women on horseback, whites and Indians riding together, bundled in white man's clothes against the numbing cold. They had traveled a great distance and their fatigue was his, because he saw himself, dressed only in a breechclout and moccasins, riding alongside them.

The horses' breath hung in the air, and their muzzles were caked with frost. The lead horse was blindfolded to keep him calm.

The ghosts of Wounded Knee Creek still follow this trail.

The stone grandfathers' rumbling voice filled Akíya's spirit:

They ride to revere the dead and to leave the time of mourning behind, to begin anew, and to tell the world they lived, and will continue to live. You must begin the healing now, for it will take a long time.

Then the grandfathers began to sing:

There is someone lying on earth in a sacred manner.
In a sacred manner we have made him walk.

Their voices faded, and with the last sound Akíya found himself at a small watering hole surrounded by willow trees, each dipping gracefully curved branches to the earth. Beside the parent tree stood a sand-colored pronghorn. Its dark brown eyes gazed deeply into Akíya, absorbing his presence, until he understood the pronghorn's thought:

A wise leader knows when to bend like the willows
when it will be good for his people.
Where there is vision, the People live.

Then the pronghorn nudged him with her nose, and as he moved backward past the flanking stones, the light through which he had entered began to shrink in the distance until it was only a pinpoint. . . .

Akíya twitched as a gentle surge of energy traveled down his spine to ground itself in Mother Earth. He felt Father Sun washing his face and for a moment lay basking in the new day's life and the warmth of his vision, until excitement coursed through his body, compelling him to stand.

He raised his arms in greeting to Father Sun, then picked up the pipe carved from the sacred red stone found in the east. Red, the elders said, because the stone is partly made up of the blood of the ancients, ancestors of the Lakhóta who died in a great sweep of water. The other part awaits the smoke of understanding and peace, which comes about only through the efforts of a true leader. The pipe's power is sacred, they said. Use it carefully and wisely, and the People shall live. The small doeskin pouch hanging from the middle of the stem nodded agreement in the morning wind's breath.

The rabbit fur wrapped around the stem was soft in his palm. He looked closely at the delicately carved head of a pronghorn which formed the bowl. The tribe's holy man had given him the pipe, with the words that to see a pronghorn in a vision is rare. *Whoever meets a pronghorn as his spirit guide is a different kind of warrior. He is essentially a man of peace, a man of healing, a man who seeks the good of his people through harmonious relationships.*

Remembering this, Akíya sucked in his breath and shivered with the responsibility that was now his. An echo sounded within: *Follow me, follow . . . bend like the willows.*

The stone grandfathers had spoken. One was obligated to live the direction of one's vision. He blew out his held breath, relief and anxiety paired in the sound: relief for receiving a vision, anxiety for accomplishing its purpose.

And yet, he was filled with eagerness, too. He cupped the pronghorn bowl in his hands and accepted the reconciliation of his opposing faces, the warrior and the man of peace. He raised the sacred pipe in thanksgiving. "Wakantanka, you leaned down to hear me. The grandfather stones have led me. I will be as unwavering as they, as solid, a rock for my people to build on that they may live. I touch the earth as my witness."

A MOMENT LATER HE GATHERED UP HIS BUFFALO ROBE AND PIPE. He took a last look around, letting the special atmosphere seep into his every pore.

Just as he lowered himself to the ledge below, an eagle flew out of the west. It circled his head, talons curled closed, then sheared off with a piercing shriek.

Akíya watched him go, confirmed in the meaning of his vision. "You alone circle the highest skies, friend, closest to Wakantanka."

He shifted the buffalo robe for better balance and eased off the ledge. On the downward slope, his feet hugged the earth as pebbles rolled underfoot, racing him downhill.

The Last Days of Dominic Prince

RICHARD S. WHEELER

Richard S. Wheeler of Montana has been ranked "among the two or three top living writers of western historicals" (Kirkus Reviews). This tragedy of a latter-day cattle baron and his final conflict with the forces of political correctness contains all the elements that have attracted and maintained his huge and loyal following.

THIS IS ABOUT A RANCHER NAMED
Dominic Prince whose family had run scrub cattle in a remote desert
waste of southern Arizona ever since God kicked Adam and Eve out
of Eden. It's about a man who believed in the eternal verities: that
people would always eat beef, that ranching was good, that cattle-
men embodied an old and honored tradition in America.

And this is also about people with other ideas: that ranchers rape
the good earth, destroy the environment, fatten at the federal
trough, put saturated fats on our tables, and kill any beast that com-
petes for forage with their livestock. And it is about the way the
world changed in the sixties and seventies, and how a lot of people
began to celebrate nature and the environment, and how they got
caught up in the push to preserve what was left of the natural world.

But before I get too deep into all that, I have to tell you how I
got to know Prince. I'm an easterner, an advertising account executive with a big Lexington Avenue agency. So you would not expect
me to know anyone like Prince or to live in a remote corner of
Arizona as far from civilization as I could get.

But I had come to that place for healing, having wrecked my
marriage and career and damaged my reputation so spectacularly
that erstwhile friends just shook their heads. I won't go into all
that. This is about Prince, not me. I'll say only that I fled New
York after the divorce, quit my position—or was I pushed out?—
and ventured into the Arizona wilderness to put my life in order. I
had read Joseph Wood Krutch's *The Voice of the Desert,* and believed
that healing might come from the desert. That was where prophets
listened to God.

That's how I met Dominic. I drifted down to Sasabe, a sun-baked burg on the Mexican border, sixty miles of dirt road south-west of Tucson, looking for a place to acquire some wisdom for half a year or so. I ended up renting an adobe tin-roofed house squatting next to a windmill and mesquite corrals seventeen miles from the Sasabe road. It was grim, simple, stark, and ugly.

There, surrounded by rocky wastes, cholla, ocotillo, yucca, and stately saguaro cactus, I tried to mend myself and shake the city from my bones. Eventually I probed deep into the cholla-choked canyons of his ranch, alone under the relentless sun, my mind dwelling long on virtue and vice, sin and love, ambition and despair.

When I first drove out to Dominic's ranch, along gritty clay roads guarded by rattlers and gila monsters, I wondered what would happen when I asked to rent his empty adobe. I supposed he would just laugh at an urban man who was going to play cowboy a few months.

But Dominic was a larger man than that. He heard me out, agreed on a rental price of one hundred a month, and I moved in, along with a load of junk furniture from Tucson. When I bought an old dude-string horse and tack from a neighboring guest ranch, he extended the same courtesy, and if he was amused by a greenhorn fooling around with a gentle nag, he never let on.

Dominic's image is etched in my mind even now, three decades later. He never slouched, but stood bandy-legged and straight up, with innate dignity. His face had been stained the color of a chestnut by the ruthless sun, his eyes bleached of color and webbed by squint-ing. I discovered later that his family was Majorcan, but had been in the United States virtually from its birth.

"I have a man living in that little 'dobe out at the corrals," he said. "His name is José, and he don't speak English. He's Mexican and works by the month. He goes home the end of each month for a couple of days. He'll be no trouble."

That surprised me. Dominic didn't say so, but I suspected the whole deal was illegal, and that proved to be correct. I wondered how that could be, why the Border Patrol didn't clamp down. They had to know about José; their ubiquitous green four-wheel vehicles prowled that country night and day. But Dominic had his vaquero, and no one stopped him.

Later, after I had sunk some roots into the Altar Valley, I fashioned an explanation. That remote valley was a major conduit for marijuana and harder stuff coming up from Mexico. The feds needed the cooperation of local ranchers, who acted as their eyes and ears, to keep a lid on that traffic. I began to realize there might be an unspoken quid pro quo: If the ranchers helped the feds, the feds would not look very closely at the ranch help.

José received his pay in precious dollars at the end of each month, and then he would vanish from the little 'dobe behind my house, riding through the night back to Mexico, which he entered through an ordinary wire ranch gate far from the port at Sasabe. Dominic told me later that if José was being conscientious, he would fork over about ten bucks to his *esposa* for food for herself and the *niños* before heading for the nearest cantina and setting up the *cervezas* until he had blown the whole wad.

But sometimes he forgot to give something to his wife, and then the family would starve for a month, subsisting on simple fare, rice and pinto beans drawn from great burlap sacks, until the next payday. If José failed to return for work after a few days, Dominic would drive across the line in his old rattletrap and tell José it was time to report at the ranch.

And then I would wake up and discover José's ratty pony in the corral, and sometimes mesquite smoke drifting from the stovepipe of his 'dobe shack. All these comings and goings would occur at night, hidden from the cyclops eye of the Border Patrol units and aircraft.

Dominic visited almost daily, and I got to enjoy the sound of his clanking Ford pickup truck grinding up the slope to the old adobe. His truck had a rattle for every occasion, and sometimes rattled just for the fun of it. I can't imagine what taciturn old Dominic saw in me for a friend, and once I suspected he was keeping an eye on me for the feds, but that soon passed. We talked ranching, and sometimes Dominic invited me for a truck ride down wild and precarious two-rut trails that dropped into canyons, crawled up ocotillo-choked slopes, and burst into little green Edens where a few cottonwoods or palo verde had poked roots into moisture.

He usually carried with him a .25-caliber automatic, and I wondered why. It wasn't the weapon of choice for killing a rattlesnake or destroying a wounded cow. It lay loose on the bench seat of his pickup. When I began to patrol his ranch with him, the thing made me nervous because it inevitably bounced around until its barrel was aimed at my buttocks. I wasn't exactly relaxed when a loaded pistol in a careening truck was threatening to turn me into a soprano. On those occasions I delicately fingered the little firearm around until I was out of the line of fire. Dominic caught me at it once, smiled, and stuffed it into the crack between the seat and its back. We never saw a soul, neither a drug runner nor a harmless "wet," as the locals called an illegal immigrant. But that little shooter was Dominic's ace if he needed one.

Dominic was suffering hard times, but I gathered that most ranchers always suffer hard times. On a Sonora Desert ranch, there are good bad times, and bad bad times, and once in a generation, some bad good times. But never good good times.

"I'm tired of subsidizin' the beef-eatin' public," he said at least once every time we met. He knew plenty about ranching, at least the old-style variety. He ran no blooded cows, got much of his young stock from Mexico, and pastured it until it was ready for fattening at a feedlot. These ribby little Mexican *corrientes,* as common cattle were called, were admirably adapted to make a living in a harsh desert, and prospered where fancier cattle sickened or starved.

Occasionally he imported the *corrientes* through the Sasabe port, and those crossings were always festive occasions largely orchestrated by federal officials. The bawling, skinny, bug-eyed, multicolored, longhorned cattle were avalanched from Mexican semis by vaqueros with cattle prods, inspected by Agriculture Department veterinarians while still south of the border, and then forced to swim through vile-smelling sheep dip that massacred every varmint in the hides of the bony beasts. The stuff usually massacred a few cows, too, whose heads were poked deep into the brew to exterminate bugs in their ears. It didn't take much of that stuff in a cow's lung to kill it, and Dominic always figured on losing a few head.

There were usually endless and mysterious delays, and more federal officials than cowboys and truck drivers, but somehow the job always got done and semis drove the *corrientes* up to Dominic's spread, and the cowboys got down to the *cerveza* in the cantinas.

Thus it had always been, and always would be, as far as Dominic was concerned. But the world was changing. Dominic was almost unaware of it, living as he did in one of the most remote corners of the United States. Sometimes change burrowed into his hide like a screwworm fly. Every time he spotted a long-haired flower child wandering through Sasabe like some tropical orchid, he growled.

"Hippie," was his universal epithet. In his mind that was a fine and handsome substitute for all the derisions anyone had ever visited upon anyone else up until the year of our Lord 1972.

"Those damned hippies have never worked a day in their life," he'd say, skimming meaning out of it.

"Those damned hippies just want to shut down the world."

"Those damned hippies prefer rattlesnakes to beef."

"Those damned hippies . . ."

That was Dominic's litany.

I passed muster because I wore my hair short, never wore sandals, once held a high-paying job, believed in marriage, didn't despise soldiers, didn't burn flags and brassieres, had no use for Che Guevara, and didn't sound as though I wanted to harvest sugarcane in Cuba alongside the campesinos.

I don't really know what Dominic believed, or whether he had thought much about life. I once probed gently, wanting to know if he loved the Sonora Desert the way I did. I was ravished by its harsh beauty, its prickly flora, its brooding silence, its voluptuous blooms, its murderous reptiles, and its sheer grandeur. Not far to the north, the blue bread-loaf mass of Baboquivari loomed mysteriously, a sullen stairway to God, ready to inspire mystics. I don't think Dominic ever gave it a thought.

The more I probed Dominic's vast rancho, the more I awakened to the ways the silent thorny desert hid its treasures. In many a hidden arroyo the remains of a settlement endured: a tumbledown mesquite corral, a caved-in adobe or two, and usually a few yellow-clay graves, some protected by black wrought iron, others by weathered picket fences that had endured the sun a hundred years, but almost all without markers. The graves were all Mexican. They are a race very good at dying. And in every case, the fierce Sonora Desert had defeated the hopes and dreams of those who spun out their painful lives in those remote canyons. Each of those *estancias* filled me with great tenderness.

I loved the desert because of its beauty and mystery. I suspected that Dominic didn't love it at all, except as a home, and as the devil he knew rather than the devil he didn't know. When I told him how beautiful that vast, blistered, rocky land seemed to me, and how like a prayer, he turned silent.

It was a hard land populated by hungry people. José used a hunk of threadbare carpet as a saddle blanket, systematically grinding fistulas into the withers of Dominic's good ranch horses. Surely that was because he was so poor, I thought. I was horrified at the ruin of good horses, so I bought José a thick blue saddle pad, gave it to him as a *regalo,* gift, and thought I had preserved a good animal or two.

But the next day he again saddled up a ranch horse with the threadbare carpet. My saddle pad hung on the wall of his adobe. There it remained until his monthly excursion south of the line, and then it disappeared into Mexico, never to be seen by my eyes again. It probably bought him a dozen *cervezas*. There was more than poverty at work in all that.

Life on that border endured, unchanged, preoccupied with the only thing that counted in a harsh desert: survival.

That's how it went until one autumnal dusk, when Dominic and

José were riding back to the ranch headquarters after a hard day vaccinating cattle. Something caught Dominic's eye. There, scarcely more than ten yards distant, crouched a mountain lion, frozen in place and watching the riders approach.

Dominic told me later, "I didn't even think about it. I just saw that big cat, built a loop, and let go. It settled right over that lion's neck, and I dallied up and backed my horse. I had a lion on my line."

He told it casually, as if this were an everyday occurrence, rather than the first time on earth that a cowman had lassoed a mountain lion. But it was not a casual event.

The lion sprang away until the rope flipped him, and then turned on his tormentor. In two graceful bounds, it leapt straight at the panicked horse and sailed just over the mane, its claws flailing murderously. It landed on the other side, turned, and crouched to leap again, fighting the rope, even as Dominic fought his berserk gelding. But José had not been idle. Expertly he built his own loop and sailed it under the cat's haunches and yanked it tight. Swiftly the two horses backed until the ropes were taut. Dominic and José had the seething mountain lion headed and heeled, stretched between the two ropes by crazed horses, but no less dangerous for that.

Dominic slipped off his skittery saddle horse, found a stout piece of mesquite, and gingerly approached the raging lion. He brained the cat repeatedly until it died.

Shaking and distrustful, they surveyed their prize: an adult male puma, stretching around six feet in length not including its tail, a tawny gray color, perfect and unmarked.

It took some doing to load the lion onto the back of the saddler, which snorted and shied, but Dominic quieted the nag and led it back to the ranch house.

I didn't know about it for a day or two, but when I stopped by his house to pay the rent, he led me to his chest-type freezer and opened it. There, stretched across a bed of white-packaged beef, lay a lion so magnificent I could not have imagined a more perfect specimen.

"My God, Dominic!"

"He's big for a lion."

"Tell me about him!"

He grinned and shrugged. I had a tough time getting him to tell his story. He didn't want it known, and would just as soon have hidden it from the world evermore.

"What are you going to do?" I asked.

"I don't know. No taxidermist'll touch it without a tag."

So there the lion lay, in frozen magnificence. But the story didn't freeze, and soon it was whispered about the Altar Valley that Dominic Prince and his vaquero José had roped a mountain lion and lived to tell about it.

Stockmen quietly assured their listeners that never in the history of the world had such a thing ever happened. Prince had been catapulted into that mysterious realm of legend and myth. He had become the world's ultimate cowman, the John Wayne of all ranching people, a man of such courage and skill that he had triumphed over the most dangerous beast of the desert.

As for Dominic, he grew even more taciturn, deflecting questions or admiring comments with a slight grin. But I knew he was enjoying every moment of it.

"Better keep it quiet," he said. "Next thing I know, they'll want to fine me for it. And take away my lion."

As the days slid by, I brooded about that cat in his freezer and wondered what its fate would be. I didn't learn until weeks later, when he invited me into his spacious ranch home and showed me the exquisitely tanned lion pelt on the waxed plank floor in front of the fireplace, its jaws open, its saber teeth menacing, its yellow glass eyes peering up at me, its velvety pelt shading from dove gray along the spine to warm earth tones on the flanks, its claws no less menacing on the planks than in life.

"It's a flat six feet, butt to nose," he said proudly.

"How'd you do that?" I asked.

"Smuggled it down to Hermosillo."

"Ah! I didn't know they had taxidermists down there."

He looked pained. The things a New Yorker didn't know would fill several books. "Better than ours," he said.

"How'd you get him back?"

"Smuggled him in a heap of burlap bags. And don't you say nothing."

That made sense. No one at the port ever pawed through the rat's nest in the bed of his rattletrap truck.

He had even recovered the thick mesquite limb that had battered the cat to death, and now it stood beside his fireplace. I knew at once that all this loomed bright and shining in his mind; this was a feat unheard of, the very reason he had been set upon this earth. He had tenderly gathered the pelt and club and placed them at his hearth, the place of honor. Someday someone would spin a ballad about Dominic Prince and his mountain lion.

About José's role in all this, Dominic remained silent. He did not want the story to reach the ears of U.S. Immigration people, though I don't doubt they heard all about it within hours of the event.

José was more loquacious, and the story swiftly burgeoned through Sonora. Whenever Dominic slipped across the line to buy cattle or stop for some *cerveza,* he received a hero's welcome. Who could imagine such a thing? José was a hero. Dominic was a hero. What sort of hombre was this gringo?

That should have been the end of the story, but it was only the beginning. A tale like that won't die, so it crept outward like ripples on a pond, and the *Tucson Citizen* got wind of it.

A reporter called Dominic: Was it true?

Dominic, a man with a sophisticated knowledge of the border but little knowledge of the press, reluctantly owned to it, and the paper published the amazing story of the only man ever to rope a mountain lion and live. I saw these things unfold, bit by bit, and surmised that there would be more chapters.

I knew I could not tarry much longer in the desert, even though

I had come to love it. I had to earn a living, and in advertising employment is much like musical chairs. If I didn't get back into it soon, I probably never would.

Things returned to normal. Dominic stopped by for coffee, and the rattle of his old Ford was my cue to put on a fresh pot. He never spoke of the lion. I told him what the desert had done for me and what I hoped to take from the desert to New York. I especially wanted to take with me my newfound sense of sovereignty. In the desert, each man is a king.

In that lonely place I had read history, hiked, ridden my horse, and listened to the voices of the land, and the prophets, and my heart. I had begun to make my own decisions, set my own goals, establish my own values, and armor myself, as the cactus did, against the world. I knew I would be a stronger man when I went back east, better able to love and give and work.

But this is not about me; it's about Dominic.

One day he sat down with me, toyed with his java, squinted, and announced that some woman from Johnny Carson's staff had phoned him: Was it true? Would he be willing to talk about it on national TV? Would he be agreeable to a preliminary interview?

I saw the flesh around Dominic's eyes crinkle with amusement.

"I guess I will," he said. "It ain't a secret."

And off he went to New York.

They treated him graciously on the Carson show. I drove in to town to watch it at the cantina. There he was, a bandy-legged rancher in a new, stiff pearl-gray western suit, his face and hands the color of old saddles, responding reluctantly but firmly to each of Carson's questions. There, before a nationwide audience, Dominic told about roping, heading, and heeling the lion, and putting the great feline in his freezer. They liked that in New York. They don't see ranchers very often in the Big Apple, much less lion-ropers.

I pretty well guessed what was coming, but I kept quiet. Dominic returned, spent a day or two enjoying his life as a local celebrity, settled back to work—and then the mail came.

Not a few letters, but heavy canvas sacks full of mail, delivered

222

by the unhappy rural delivery man. Dominic stared, amazed, at the mounting pile of them, and summoned me to find out what to do with them. He couldn't imagine responding to all those people, and I assured him he didn't have to.

I had a hunch, born of years in advertising and public relations, that Dominic wasn't going to enjoy most of these, and I warned him:

"You know, Dom, the world's changing."

"Hippies," he growled.

"Yes, and animal-rights people and environmentalists."

He just growled, deep in his throat.

I wondered where his wife had vanished to. I scarcely had met her, even though I had dropped by his ranch house many times. She apparently had divided the world into men's and women's business, and made herself scarce when she thought she didn't belong.

"Well, how do you want to do it?" I asked.

"Just read a few. I'm no good with handwriting."

"Sure," I said, pulling a fistful of envelopes from one of the gray canvas sacks.

I slit one open and what I saw, in a woman's hand, didn't encourage me to read.

"Well, ah. . . ."

Dominic settled into a dining chair and wrapped himself in silence.

"Ah, she says, 'I saw you on Johnny Carson, and all I can say is you're the meanest man I ever met. What had that lion done to you? Nothing. But you just had to kill it to prove what a he-man you are. Now the world has one less beautiful lion. . . .' "

I eyed Dominic, who sat resolutely, revealing nothing.

I tried the next one:

"Don't you realize, sir, that lions are an endangered species, and that if they are killed off by thoughtless people like you, for no reason at all, the world will not only be an emptier and uglier place, but the life cycle will be disturbed? . . ."

Dominic sat like a Sphinx.

I pulled a scented blue sheet from an envelope: "There you go, raping the environment, just the way all ranchers do. You just can't stand to let any natural creature live, can you? You just have to show how big and tough you are, and before we know it, there won't be anything left on earth except your filthy cattle. . . ."

I looked at Dominic. Tough he might well be, but at five feet seven or so, he was scarcely big. His face remained expressionless.

I tore open another: "Well, now you have your reputation and you can strut around and be a big-time rancher. But the lion you killed for no valid reason was helping to keep nature in balance. Predators are vital to the whole cycle of life. Why did you do it? A real man, loving and sensitive, would not have even dreamed of such a vicious act. . . ."

Dominic looked stoic.

I read a bunch more that evening, twenty or thirty in all, scarcely a dent in that pile of letters. At least in that bunch, not a letter praised him, and the tone ranged from hostile to vicious.

"That's enough," he said, although the evening was young.

"Do you want me to read these and sort 'em, pro and con?"

He stared into the darkness. "I've heard enough," he said.

"You mind if I look at a few hundred?"

He shrugged. I took that for acceptance, and loaded a sack into my truck.

I spent a couple of days working through them. Most people expressed outrage, contempt, and an innate hostility toward ranchers, whom they stereotyped as dumb, greedy, ruthless, and parasitical. Most contained finger-wagging lessons in ecology, garnered from the media. A few did admire Dominic. To a handful he was awesome. Some messages were mixed, extolling his bravery and daring, yet scolding him for his destruction of a beautiful and proud animal.

I drove over to his place a few evenings later and reported my findings: in that batch, 387 hostile, 37 mixed, 4 favorable. Most attacked him on ecological grounds. A smaller number assailed him for cruelty. A large number described ranching and ranchers as rapists of the land, and they used terms so spiteful they shocked me. The whole world, it seemed, had landed on Dominic.

"It doesn't matter," he said.

There was something about the way he said it that awakened my concern. In the space of a few days, Dominic had aged. He slumped now instead of standing erect. Instead of listening quietly and joining in conversation, his mind seemed to drift to horizons unknown to me.

It did matter.

I spent my last weeks in the desert trying to buck him up, but he simply shrank deeper and deeper into himself, and began to let his ranch slide. Before, when José would linger south of the line too long, Dominic would go roust him out. Now he just drove his dirt roads and looked at his skinny little *corrientes* and did nothing.

I tried to fathom what was eating Dominic. I thought he would shrug off all the hostile mail. He had been tough and independent all his life; what difference did a bunch of angry letters make? He could go on living exactly as before . . . but that wasn't the way his life was spinning out now. It was as if four thousand angry letters had broken his spirit, even though he had read only the smallest fraction of them. The things people believed about ranchers hurt him.

"They don't know where their food comes from," he muttered one day. "Let 'em try starving."

That's how it went my last weeks in the desert, and when I finally packed up for New York, I could see he was still slipping day by day. A man can carry only so much hate on his shoulders.

Then I said good-bye. I drove over to his place to leave the key and tell him and his wife I was on my way, and to thank them for the desert interlude that had renewed me.

"Dominic, I've enjoyed every minute of it. You've taught me about life. You're good company. . . ."

I fumbled through the parting and finally drove away, haunted by the dullness in Dominic's eyes, and the slouch of his body, and above all, by the walls of silence surrounding him.

I did not like New York as much as I once did, even though I landed a new position at a fatter wage than before. Dominic gradually slipped from mind, and over the next year my sojourn in Arizona became an abstraction. New York was real; the Sonora Desert and its people, and Dominic Prince, had faded.

And then I received news of his death: a printed announcement on a card mailed by his family. And I knew that four thousand angry letters had become too much for any man to carry on his shoulders.

I grieved, and wished I knew how to keep the world from changing so fast.

The Two Trail Ride Tricksters

RILEY FROH

Riley Froh is a descendant of Texas settlers, cowboys, a Texas Ranger, and Margaret Taylor, who successfully defended her children from attacking Indians in the famous Fight at Little River. He is the author of several scholarly articles and two nonfiction books, *Wildcatter Extraordinary* and *Edgar B. Davis and Sequences in Business Capitalism*. In addition, he is a gifted humorist; but don't take this editor's word for it. Read his story.

"THIS HERE STORY IN THE *SAN-Antonio Light* gives me a great idea," Abner Butler said to me, setting off immediate alarms in my defense system. My concern was with any brainstorm Abner prefaced with *great*. The boy had a touch of larceny that any member of the Texas legislature could have envied.

"I'd just as soon not hear it," I said as he began to explain.

"Says right here that several organizations is goin' to sponsor a old-time trail ride from way down the country clear to San Antonio to culminate at the opening of the stock show and rodeo at the Joe Freeman Colosseum—with dignitaries from all over the state taking part."

"Oh, is that all?" I said with relief. "That don't concern us 'cause we can't go. That's a ride set up just for the rich folks."

"But it does concern us," Abner countered, "because we're going to stage a old-time holdup and give them dudes a taste of the real historic West. We'll make a killin'."

"There's goin' to be a killin' someday," I muttered, "but we're the ones goin' to get killed, and you're goin' to be the cause of it! Count me out."

"Better think about it," Abner said. His expression implied he knew something I didn't.

"You paid Mr. Carbe, didn't you?" I was never sure that Abner would part with money we owed somebody.

"There weren't no money to pay him with," Abner said, his tone a bit touchy.

"No money! Why not? That horse we bet on finished first. That gave us more than enough to pay off Carbe."

"Right," Abner said. "But our horse in the second race finished last."

"You didn't let our winnings ride?" I cried, knowing he did.

" 'Fraid so." Abner watched a smoke ring rise in the air.

I knew what he was thinking, and I didn't like it. But we had to come up with some emergency funds. Winston Carbe had caught us red-handed loading cotton seed out of the back of his gin at midnight. Abner believed it was cheaper and easier to get feed that way for our agricultural projects required by our FFA course at the high school. Carbe's night watchman pulled his pickup in front of our mules and blocked us off in the exit by the scales, and there we were, guilty as sin.

Abner's offer to put it back was refused. However, we accepted Carbe's demand that we go ahead and "buy" it at double the price, with a promise not to tell our folks and the law to boot. So we weighed out and left. Our winnings at the illegal quarter-horse track in the next county would have gotten us off the hook.

"Don't worry," Abner said cheerfully. "Carbe done give us a extra month to come up with the money—only now it's triple the price." He paused a moment to let that soak in. "Now, about that trail-ride robbery," he added craftily, with the expert timing of a born con man. He knew he had me.

A Texas trail ride was worth seeing. People are always trying unsuccessfully to recapture whatever the West really was, and reenactments of Indian fights, revolutions, bank robberies, buffalo hunts, stage holdups, and cattle drives are so common in the Lone Star State that you could probably attend one every weekend of the year. The trail ride attempted to enact some or all of the above, since it approximated a pioneer wagon train with anything thrown in to give it the authenticity it never quite achieved. Abner and I apparently were going to try to provide this one a taste of realism.

I will never forget the thrill in the air on that end-of-school afternoon we set out on our trail-ride project. On a typical Indian summer day which heralds a Texas fall, you can barely break a sweat with some exertion by about four P.M. Twelve hours later, the temperature is set at a steady, crisp sixty degrees, and it stays that comfortable even on into midmorning. You can't beat the weather for taking off on horseback, even to do something boring or legal. We were out on our adventure by five o'clock and it was grand. In fact, I was enjoying the natural beauty of a late evening ride so much that I hadn't even gotten scared yet.

The trail ride had come through town about noon so they could parade down Main Street before stopping at the fairgrounds for a siesta. The procession had to stay on the roads, so it was easy for Abner and me to head them off at the pass by cutting across the back tracks we knew so well. We were sitting our horses in concealment, waiting for them at the Geronimo Creek crossing.

"They'll camp on the other side and ford the creek in the mornin'," Abner observed.

" 'Pears that way," I agreed. "But whatever we're goin' to do, we got to do it tonight."

"Trust me," Abner said, "I got a plan."

Trusting my best friend was always risky; his scheme might be one he would make up as we went along. But I was already caught up in watching the splendor of the view from our elevated observation post. It truly was something to see.

The trail boss rode resplendent in his duded-up, movie-colored outfit, the Texas flag flying from the staff he had stuck down in his stirrup with his shiny boots and gaudy spurs. His great belly pooched over his belt buckle, giving him the appearance of a Texas lawman. Beside him rode his socialite wife, on a half-blind paint horse, her expensive leather vest matching her even more costly fine-tooled chaps, designed for show rather than riding in thick brush. She had her snooty head in the air, smelling whatever it was bad that made the corners of her mouth turn down.

Behind this pair of Dallas snobs, the riders, wagons, buggies, buckboards, and surries stretched back as varied and unusual as a New Orleans jazz funeral procession until it bent out of sight in a curve of the road in the distance, with everyone trying to outdo the others in garb and tack. Not even the Comanche warriors returning from the Victoria and Linnville raid of 1840, wearing all their stolen loot and plunder, had dressed in so extreme a fashion.

The sad thing is that only some of those four-wheel, horse-and-mule-drawn vehicles, dating back to the turn of the century or even earlier, were originals. Some were still in regular use in that Texas Centennial Year, including a 1906 Studebaker chuckwagon from the famous Ace-High Ranch. Now, why didn't more people think to preserve those relics instead of letting them rot out behind the barn over time?

"That bunch of greenhorns needs to be robbed," Abner said with contempt, but I knew it was sour grapes. Abner would have loved to have been a part of that show, if we'd only had the money. I know, because I was dying to join them, too. Every now and then we made out some young girls about our age among the riders, some of them almost as lovely as Abner's gorgeous sister Rachel.

"Well, ain't we about to do just that? Rob them blind, I believe we said," I said. "I know, I know, you're still formulatin' a plan."

"What's the matter, don't you trust me?" Abner grinned, knowing he didn't need an answer to that one.

We eased our horses upstream and watered them. Then we moved back down the creek to a spot right across the brook in the thick elms and staked them out. In his saddlebags, Abner had some canned goods he had pilfered from a delivery truck in a back alley in town, but soon the savory aroma of Bar-B-Q dripping over a mesquite fire wafted our way, and our cold fare didn't look so appetizing anymore.

"Let's get across the creek and scout 'em out," Abner said, but I knew he really just wanted something better to eat.

It was good and dark, so I followed him to a fallen pecan tree, which made a great log crossing, and soon we were crouched right outside the circle of firelight.

Not far away was a perfect set of large rocks for improvised picnicking, and beyond that was the line of saddle-sore folks queuing up for their grub. Soon, a middle-aged couple bowlegged it over to our spot, left their heaping tin plates on the flat stone surface, and then stumbled back toward the chuckwagon for their iced tea and pie.

"Now," Abner whispered, and we broke for the food worse than any two thieving coyotes we ever shot, retreated with the stolen meal like a couple of foxes leaving a hen house, and hustled to our place of concealment with as clean a conscience as any predator around. That hot feast was better than any stolen watermelon we ever cut.

Our dinner finished and somebody else's tin dishware mopped clean with the last of the sourdough bread, we settled back to smoke and pick our teeth with elm sticks we had sharpened. It was the pure contentment of outdoor life. Our surroundings became velvety with night. The frogs along the creek and the crickets in the weeds tuned up. Somewhere in the distance a train whistle mourned, and soon the coyotes echoed with their lingering wail from another direction. Today, millionaires pay big money to dude ranches to try to capture this sort of pleasant experience that was ours for nothing back in the 1930s. It always amazes me that modern historians have mainly recorded only the downside of the Great Depression. Certainly there were many Steinbeck-type Joads who poor-boyed it to California, but there were also numerous people below the poverty line that lived the good life that Abner and I did. And there were lots of folks who attended the University of Texas in the fall and spring, pledged expensive fraternities and sororities both semesters, and then toured Europe in the summer because their parents had the wherewithal to ride in that silly trail ride just across Geronimo Creek from us. This social class, which was numerous, has received very little attention from the professional scribes, and since history is what's remembered and what's written, when the rememberers are gone, only the transcribed record remains to make the past accurate or inaccurate, depending on the ability and honesty of the writer. More than likely, some award-winning study, written by a young person, well housed, well fed, and well clothed, will establish in print that the Depression was what Roosevelt said it was rather than a variety of experiences.

I will tell you this. That bunch of idlers right across the creek from us were living high, for the fiddles were tuning up for their nightly dance. I was ready to call the whole thing off, crash the party, and promenade with some of those rich pretty girls before somebody tossed us out as interlopers. About that time we heard two revelers stomping over in our direction to relieve themselves in the brush by the creek. Their voices reached us in slur as they laughed over the vulgar joke of two Texans doing the same thing off a bridge, one complaining that the water was too cold, the other that it was very deep.

"You two just hold it right there," Abner commanded, startling me with his harsh stage voice. "Don't move. I got the drop on you both."

"Well, well, looky here," said one of the drunks.

"Somebody done been lookin' at too many outlaw picture shows."

"I mean it!" Abner shouted. "Just throw your pocket books over here across the creek and you won't get hurt."

"Oh, we ain't gonna' get hurt," said the second inebriated fellow. "You are." He flung his empty Pearl bottle our way, where it thudded off a tree trunk without breaking.

"Yeah, try this on for size," said the first speaker, laughing as he sent his empty shattering into the rocks at our feet.

"Come on, let's leave Jesse James here in the dark. It's time to go rub bellies with the gals to that music again." And with that the two partygoers rambled off, arms over each other's weaving shoulders.

"I oughta plug them two in the hind end," Abner muttered.

"We oughta get ours in them saddles and get out of here," I said.

"Not without no money to show," Abner stated typically.

"Look, Abner, we done had a good ride and a great supper. Let's just go down there and dance a few sets and see where that leads. All them good-lookin' girls down there got money, or least-ways their daddies do. Maybe we can latch on to one of them and—"

"Money always marries money, so you can forget that. Besides,

Daddy don't allow no dancin' anyways. But speakin' of money, if we don't get some tonight, that skinflint Winston Carbe's gonna turn us over to the law, which will confiscate our horses, saddles, boots, and spurs, not to mention our liberty. So we got to leave here well heeled else we'll be coolin' ours in the county blockhouse. Now follow me."

I did, moved by the practicality of his logic if not its eloquence. We rambled down to our log crossing, scurried across to the other side, and sneaked back up to the circle of wagons. Within the enclosure, the dancers were cutting a Cotton-Eye Joe, moving counterclockwise in synchrony to the natural strains of stringed instruments. Draped around the outside of the bare dance ground, the other members of the trail ride sat or stood or slumped and kept time with the music by clapping the familiar beat.

"This just ain't workin' out," Abner said. "See, them kind of people is goin' to keep their valuables on them at all times. Really there ain't nothin' in them wagons 'cept baggage we could pick up anywhere. You know, changes of clothes and such. We sure don't need nobody's dirty drawers."

"Then let's just cut out of here," I said, somewhat relieved.

"Not so fast," Abner said, with a jerk of his head to the rear of our position. "There's a rig back yonder by its lonesome that's got my curiosity aroused."

I glanced around and, sure enough, there loomed a huge Conestoga that should have been reposing in the Smithsonian, sitting off under the shadow of a giant oak, the surrounding area illuminated brightly by the harvest moon. Something about the old relic did appear inviting, although I could not figure what. However, my partner possessed a sixth sense for locating plunder, even though this trait was consistent with a personality that at all times revealed a greater enterprise than discretion, standing always ready to embrace an opportunity of dubious legality.

We crept up to the covered wagon, where Abner indicated by sign that I was to stand watch while he entered the darkened interior. I saw him hump into the cavelike rear entrance made by the semicircle of canvas stretched over the frame hoops. There was a moment of silence. Then what can only be described as the blend of a scream and a yell, made by a very healthy female more angry than frightened, rent the entire surroundings. Next, a large, nearly naked form fell breech-birth out of the back of the wheeled conveyance, somersaulting heavily onto the earth before making an athletic backward roll to stand colossus-posed, powerful and awe-inspiring.

I knew immediately who it was. Only Mabel Marmaduke, local tramp of magnificent proportions, could be both that big and that sexy at the same time. A single woman and barmaid at the Two-Time Tavern, she had a trio of tow-headed kids who bore marked resemblance to three different prominent community figures. She had been referred to, though not named, in several of Abner's father's most lurid sermons denouncing wickedness and the temptations of the flesh. It was said that she had seen more naked men in her thirty-plus years than the community shower at the Austin YMCA.

I will tell you this. Since I beheld that substantial, dimpled Venus, clad only in a pair of Sears and Roebuck panties and a Montgomery Ward brassiere, and made marble by the ghostly moonlight throwing its oak-leaf-clustered shadows on her white skin, I have never seen anything more erotic. And since that night I have watched stripteases in Juarez, cheered burlesque in downtown Dallas, and viewed peep shows in New Orleans. But now the Amazon ceased yelling and started shouting.

You have to bear in mind that this bottle-blond giant also acted as part-time bouncer in the bar. (Of course, she bounced around horizonally after hours, too, but that was on another plane and for a different price.) She had the wind and the lungs to draw a crowd. Suddenly I realized that the music had stopped. With great effort I tore my gaze from my free one-girl girlie show to look behind me. Half of the trail riders had spilled out from the main wagons to stand in awe of this midautumn night's nightmare. I guess I would have just stood there and been captured had Abner not taken charge as usual as he alighted from the wagon.

"Not so fast, buster," Mabel said huskily, grabbing Abner's left arm just before his right-cross shove (not even Abner would hit a woman) sent his antagonist sprawling into my unwilling embrace. We went down heavily, the curvy creature's 160-plus pounds crushing both my wind and my libido.

"Rape," I screamed with what little air I had left, although it would take a combination of Freud and Jung to figure that one out, and then it still might only have something to do with a crushed cigar. Somehow I extricated myself from under that cursing, writhing female, for I saw Abner running for the team of large draft horses tethered out beyond the Conestoga.

"Don't just stand there. Get 'em!" screamed Mabel. Then in no uncertain terms she labeled both the trail riders and us with many unholy oaths, several extreme expletives, and some choice words never heard before but suitable to the occasion. Out of the corner of my eye, I saw a pudgy male form bounce out of the other end of the wagon and streak off into the darkness, holding up his pants with one hand and clutching a wad of assorted clothing in the other. But I was running in top form, and by the time I caught up, Abner had untied the Percheron and fastened a hackamore out of the lead rope. He helped me fix the Clydesdale the same way. I could hear the stampede of formerly dancing feet stomping toward us, with Mabel shrilly urging them on.

You have no idea how enormous those beer-wagon horses are until you stand right next to them. Swinging up on one's back is like vaulting upon the neck of a circus elephant, but we were hightly motivated, so we grabbed a handful of mane and clambered our way aboard—none too soon, I might add.

Trotting off on those giant equines was like running from someone in slow motion in a bad dream; in fact, we just barely gained enough speed to keep ahead of the mob thrashing after us, for the progress of our steeds was manifestly inconsistent with the intensity of our urgings. But our beasts had more wind than the men behind us, who gradually fell back as we beat it up the creek. We could hear them huffing and puffing to a stop in the rear.

"Get the horses and form a mounted posse, men," shouted one imaginative fellow who had obviously watched as many westerns as we had.

"They're already bringing some up. Now we'll get 'em," shouted an excited dandy, and, indeed, we could hear the kind of horses that we needed to be riding crashing through the brush and moving our way.

"Time to bail off," Abner said as he deftly threw his right leg up over the Percheron's head and twisted off the left side to hit stumbling toward the creek.

I did the same off the Clydsdale, although with a little less agility. Our two heavy work horses plodded only a short ways before pausing to graze. Abner had already plunged into the water and was wading hip deep for the other bank. I imitated his cold and unpleasant action, and the only good thing about the temperature was that the dark root I grabbed to pull myself out could not be a snake masquerading as a tree sprout.

We squish-squashed back downstream, staying well away from the watercourse but making way too much noise. At least the muddy liquid running out of the tops of our boots wasn't blood—not yet, anyway. Voices from the *posse comitatus* were not saying what I wanted to hear.

"Fan out, men. Beat them bushes. They can't get far on foot," mouthed the impromptu leader.

"Maybe they crossed over," suggested someone with imagination.

"I'll check the bank for sign," said an energetic trail rider.

"Yeah, you just do that," muttered Abner under his breath.

We had just reached our horses and were tightening the cinches on the saddles when even more alarming intelligence reached us from the campground. I recognized the voices at once as the two throwers of beer bottles.

"Yeah, right over there across the creek. Tried to hold us up, he did," bragged the one.

"But we fought 'em off with rocks," lied the other.

"Was there two of 'em?" bellowed Mabel, conjuring up erotic pictures in my mind. But surely she was dressed by then. Yet, *quien sabe*?

"Two! Mighta been twenty, for all we know!" fabricated the first liar.

But now the sounds of at least a score of horses could be heard splashing across the creek upstream. Soon they were breaking through the underbrush toward our place of concealment. We needed no prompting, for we were dearly departing the premises, picking our way quietly and easily up the slope, making for the county road. Who would have thought we would disturb a bunch of roosting crows, giving our position away? Now we could hear the crunching of hooves, cutting across right at us. Surging over the creek, reinforcements slogged up the way from the campground.

We hit the road at a gallop, but stragglers from the first party were cutting diagonally toward us through the woods. All of us, pursued and pursuers, funneled into the narrow lane of the fenced-off road as we distanced ourselves from the public bridge across Geronimo Creek. There was no way our sizeable lead was going to hold; the rich ride better horses just as sure as they have bigger bank accounts.

But right around Indian Bow Bend was a crossroads. Abner indicated by sign language that we were to cut left. I didn't feel comfortable with that move, but over the years he had gotten me out of as many scrapes as he had gotten me into, so I played the odds and reined my pony after him.

The vigilantes didn't see us turn since we had made the bend first. Abner was already signaling to stop and crowd our horses behind the twin oaks, old landmarks from stagecoach days. It didn't seem good judgment, but Abner was a gambler. I took the chance and skidded up to one side of the road while he whirled around on the other. We pushed our horses up under the massive limbs and as close up against the trunks as we could force them. The treetops touched across the dirt road, giving us the added help of shadow under the full moon. I held my breath and tried to keep my heart and lungs out of my throat as the horsemen thundered by. Thank goodness Abner flashed the stop sign to me, for I almost spurred off before the stragglers rumbled past also. Then he stopped me again before I could light out.

"Gimme your rope," he ordered. He was already tying his to his oak.

"I don't like this," I said.

"You ain't gonna like gettin' caught, either." He spliced the lines together with a Boy-Scout award-winning knot.

"Someone's goin' to get hurt," I said.

"It's goin' to hurt them a lot more than it hurts us." He laughed in that tone that really bothered me. "Here, ride up here. I got to measure this. Okay. Just the right height. See, them horses stretch their necks out at full speed. This ought to discourage them boys just fine."

I could already hear hoofbeats coming back down the road. Soon a sizable group was milling at the crossroads. There is no way anybody would appreciate the profane things Abner yelled at them about their ancestry, their hat sizes being geared small to fit their brains, their general low moral character, and their alleged incestuous relationships with next-of-kin. They bore down on us with a passion. I could feel the heat of their intensity as I urged my mount away.

Abner was at my side but looking back eagerly just as I was straining forward. However, I couldn't resist twisting around when I heard the sickening sounds. Thuds, oaths, grunts, snaps, crackles, pops, creaks, whinnies, snorts, and more curses rent the air as the worst pile-up since the great Central Texas train wreck occurred in full view. Thankfully, my fears of manslaughter did not materialize. Broken bones stacked up, but no necks snapped. The trail ride was turned into an ambulance procession. That was one movie stunt we tried that actually worked in real life, and for sheer physical damage to our fellow man, it was the worst thing we ever did.

When we hit the railroad crossing, Abner sped down the Southern Pacific right-of-way, which proved highly ingenious since this trail took us to a paved road, which we followed long enough to hide our tracks for good. By then we were back in familiar country. At just the right place, we left the asphalt, crunched across some rocky shale, jimmied the lock on a gate, and cut across some big ranches until our traveling evidence was obscured for good. Safe in the security of the back country, I felt like talking again. But my relief at escape soon gave way to gloom as our financial condition imposed itself on my thoughts.

"We're in for it now," I said dejectedly. "How we gonna pay that debt at the cotton mill now?"

"Oh, we ain't," Abner said lightheartedly. "Fact is, that bill's done been canceled and even reversed. I imagine we'll be able to pick up a little free cotton seed in the future in broad daylight from time to time as the need arises."

"I don't follow your reasoning," I muttered, still rather downcast.

Well, maybe that's because you didn't see what I seen tonight," Abner said tantalizingly. "You did figure there was someone else in that wagon, didn't you?"

"I caught a glimpse of someone streakin' for the brush as we was runnin' off, but I couldn't make out who it was."

"Oh, I can tell you who the unfortunate specimen was," Abner grinned. "And his wife—the one that actually holds the purse strings 'cause it's her family that really has all the money—is off at the Baptist Women's Retreat at Lytton Springs this very weekend. It would not do for her to get ahold of this particular piece of intelligence."

"Well, who was it?"

"A fellow by the name of Winston Carbe." Abner smirked, his face showing his best ironic, half-quizzical expression under the bright Comanche moon.

Laureano's Wall

MIKE BLAKELY

Who is to say that an electric light in the modern American desert is any less a threat to a way of life than the conquest of the Comanche? Not Mike Blakely, who offers an unlikely hero in the form of a simple Mexican craftsman. Blakely, whose *Comanche Dawn* was a finalist for the 1999 Spur Award for Best Novel of the West, is a well-known composer and performer of western music. He is also a former president of the Western Writers of America.

LAUREANO MADE THE MOST MAR-
velous walls of stone. He chose blocks and slabs that would lay one
upon the other with a permanence that rivaled bedrock. He scoffed
at mortar. Laureano built dry-stone walls with edges that seemed
perfectly square; rock fences that rolled with the contours of the
land; steps upon the hillside that begged ascension.

I met Laureano in Marfa, a small town situated in the open
mountainous country of far West Texas. I had taken a wrong turn
on my way to the Paisano Hotel to rendezvous with two friends.
Driving down some side street I had stumbled onto, I saw a man
leaning against a high chain-link fence surrounding a machine-shop
yard—the type of fence meant to keep people out, with strands of
barbed wire angling outward at the top. The security fence sprouted
from the top of a rock-and-mortar wall only about three feet high—
the kind of wall where the mortar oozed out from between the rocks
like hardened lava. The man I saw there sat on top of this rock wall
as he leaned against the steel mesh that rose above it.

He was Mexican, about thirty-five, I guessed, dressed in worn
khakis and a tattered straw cowboy hat resplendent with a feathered
hat band fifteen years out of fashion. I figured him for a local work-
ingman awaiting his ride home, so I slowed my pickup and pulled
to the curb. As I came to a stop, he pushed himself away from the
fence with a graceful economy of motion and took a step or two
toward my truck.

The tinted electric window lowered and I saw a look of curious
hope enter the man's eyes.

"Excuse me," I said. "I'm looking for the Paisano Hotel."

The man's eyebrows raised, and he smiled slightly, but seemed apprehensive of me. *"Sí,"* he replied after a pause. Then he placed his fist over his heart and said, *"Soy paisano."*

Now, my Spanish is not good, but I can pick up a word here and there. Some of my friends, fellow gringos, mistakenly believe that I am fluent in the language because I can order Mexican food with a fairly convincing accent. The truth is that my Spanish is woefully inadequate, but I like to speak what I know, and it thrills me no end to understand a complete sentence from a true Spanish speaker.

I understood every word spoken by the man looking cautiously into my truck window. More to the point, I understood the man by virtue of what he had said. First of all, he didn't know English. The only word he had picked up from my inquiry was the Spanish word *paisano*.

Literally translated, *paisano* means "countryman." More loosely, it describes someone who has been the same places you have been. A Mexican-American friend of mine who grew up in the *barrio* in Houston once told me that the word meant about the same thing as "home boy."

Along the border in Texas, the word also means "roadrunner." The bird. The *majados*—the wet ones—the ones from south of the border—the ones who cross the river illegally to work—the *mojados* consider the roadrunner one of their own. He must dodge in and out of the brush to hide from his enemies. He wears dull feathers. He works in the elements. He runs. He keeps his head down, and he runs.

I knew the man standing outside my idling truck was a *mojado*. An illegal alien. A wetback, to use the politically incorrect, yet time-tested Texas phrase. He was a *paisano*, and had owned up to it proudly, placing that weathered fist over his heart.

I took only a moment to process all these observances, yet I paused long enough to make the man nervous. He glanced both ways up the street. He was looking for an escape route in case I turned out to be a *migra*—an immigration officer. Yet, he needed work. Needed it badly. He was hungry. I could see this in his desperate eyes.

"*Necesita un trabajero?*" he asked for reassurance, speaking more slowly than before, as if he had sensed my difficulties with his language.

Again, to my relief, I understood every word. *Do you need a laborer?*

I had not come looking for cheap, illegal labor. But there was that hope in the man's eyes. He *needed* work. Yes, there was that. But mostly there was the fact that I understood him when he spoke. Maybe I could find some work for this man around the old house on my ranch. Maybe I could get him to talk to me. I have always wanted to speak Spanish. I don't really know why. It feels good when it rolls off the tongue. It expresses things English cannot. It makes the most common thought sound fluid and bright as quicksilver.

Once, while trying to speak Spanish to a Mexican woman working as a cook on a ranch where I was hunting, I was asked if I had seen any wild turkeys on my morning foray. I had failed to understand the cook's word for turkey—*guajolote*—and asked her what it meant. "*Ay!*" she had said, dismissing me in disgust with a wave of her flour-covered hand. "*No habla!*"

You do not speak! That had hurt. I wanted to speak. I could speak to this man, this *trabajero.*

But he was a *mojado,* I reminded myself. I knew it took place every day—the use of illegal labor. That wasn't so risky. A person could get fined or something. But I had gathered from rancher friends over the years that to *transport* an illegal could get a person in somewhat deeper trouble. For all I knew, the immigration service was staking the place out right now. The man there could be a plant. A decoy. That was entrapment, wasn't it?

"*Como se llama?*" I asked, stalling for time.

"Laureano."

In my obstreperous Spanish, I next asked Laureano what type of work he did.

All types, he answered.

Any specialty?

He built things.

What things did he like most to build?

Fences, he said. And walls. Walls and fences of stone. Walkways, too. Steps and paths. And patios. Of stone.

I pointed to the stone wall upon which Laureano had so recently rested. *"Como este?"* *Like this?*

He did not even look back. He only smiled, and shook his head. *"No, señor. Mas fina."* No, sir. Better.

"Me llamo Roberto," I said, sticking my hand out through the window to shake with Laureano. I had been Robbie all my life, but to Laureano, I would be "Roberto." Over the next minute or two, I explained that I owned a ranch in the Davis Mountains with an old ranch house that needed work. I was not going there now, I claimed, so I could not give him a ride. But if he could get there in the next couple of days on his own, I would give him work. *"Mucho trabajo,"* I said. *"Hasta Navidad."* Until Christmas.

"Bueno," he said.

I happened to have a photocopy of the map I had drawn up for my friends Grit and Damon, who were even now waiting for me at the Paisano Hotel. I was rightfully proud of the map, having designed it on my computer with all the roads marked and landmarks labeled, on a scale of one inch to ten miles, oriented to magnetic north. I handed the copy of the map to Laureano. He looked at it for about ten seconds in silence, then folded it and put it in his shirt pocket. I gave Laureano a five-dollar advance on his wages, making his eyes mist.

"Gracias, Señor Roberto," he said.

I told him I would see him in a few days, left him standing there, and went on to a convenience store, where I obtained directions, in English, to the Paisano Hotel.

I FOUND GRIT AND DAMON WAITING FOR ME AT THE PAISANO. Grit had flown his twin-engine Cessna from Houston, where over the last couple of years he had made a million dollars or more as a broker of natural gas, which he claimed gave him the right to fart wherever he pleased. Damon had driven a Subaru station wagon from El Paso and had picked Grit up at the Marfa municipal airport. Damon taught English and literature at the University of Texas, El Paso campus. I had driven my brand-new Ford diesel four-by-four pickup from Austin, where I had recently taken a new job as executive director of a national association, with a salary that enabled me to buy myself things like new pickup trucks for the first time since my divorce of three years earlier.

The last year had been a good one for me. Not only had I landed the new job, but I had inherited some six thousand acres in the Davis Mountains from an uncle I barely knew. This uncle had no children of his own, only a few nieces, and just one nephew. Me. I had never seen the ranch when I inherited it, nor had I even known of its existence. But I owned it now.

On my initial journey to inspect my new holdings, I had found a little old ranch house perched on high ground beside an ancient windmill. There were mule deer on this ranch, and I like to hunt. So do my friends Grit and Damon.

The three of us had played high school football together. I played both sides of the line at tight end and linebacker. Damon took the snaps. Grit ran the ball. Damon and I had made all-district. Grit had gone all-state, but he blew his knee out in the last game of the state playoffs. Since Grit *was* our offense, we lost that game in the final minute. He never played again, in spite of reconstructive surgery.

We had played basketball and baseball and had run track together, too, but it was football we always ended up talking about.

"Hey, boy," Grit said the moment he saw me at the Paisano Hotel. "We were just tellin' Darla about that time you blocked that punt against Cuero in the playoffs. Remember?" He got up and threw an arm around my shoulder.

There was a good-looking young waitress there waiting on them, her name, Darla, embroidered on her blouse. They were trying to impress her, I guess, with old football stories. I grinned at her and shook Damon's hand while Grit bear-hugged me. "You bet I remember. Coach Martin had drilled it into our heads for four years: 'Don't ever try to pick up a blocked punt and run with it. Just fall on it. *Fall on it.*' He must have told us a thousand times."

"So Robbie blocks it and falls on it," Damon added. "There wasn't anybody within fifteen yards of him. He could have walked in for a touchdown. When he gets back to the sideline, you remember what Coach Martin says?"

We were chanting in unison now: " 'Damn it, Chandler! Why the hell didn't you pick it up and *run?*' "

We laughed like drunken Shriners, and the waitress giggled politely with us.

"I don't know football," she said, shrugging. "I guess that's funny. I'll bring y'all some iced tea."

"Lone Star for me," Grit said.

We ate a big greasy dinner and decided to head out to the ranch in my new pickup. Neither Grit nor Damon had seen the place, and they were both as happy as if *they* had inherited it.

"Robbie, this truck suits you," Grit said on the way out of town. 'Bout time you got you some decent wheels. Hell, big rancher now. New pickup." About that time he let down the electric window on the passenger side, so I let mine down, too.

Damon was riding in the middle between the two of us. "Damn, Grit," he said. "Somethin' crawl up your ass and die?"

"I'm glad we're ridin' with you," Grit said, ignoring Damon. "I didn't much savvy that map you sent."

We drove forty-five minutes out of Marfa and turned onto a two-rut dirt lane that would lead us twelve miles off the highway to my ranch house. We drove up onto the summit of a high hill and approached the old frame-and-adobe house, standing clear and stark against the haze of the distant landscape. The windmill pivoted near the back corner of the house. The bunkhouse stood farther off to the left. An old privy stood well away from the ranch house to the right.

We stopped, got out, and slammed our doors. With the diesel motor off, the quietude was staggering, but welcome. The windmill pumped and wheeled. A hawk cried somewhere. We walked around to the back of the house to see the view, rocks and dry stalks of grass crunching under our heels. I had been here once before, of course, but the panorama still made my breath catch in my chest. The slope dropped off sharply below us beyond the backyard. Nothing but mountains and hills and grass and rocks and cactus lay under the cloudless blue sky. Not a road, nor a house, nor a barbed-wire fence marred the view.

"Oh, my God," Damon muttered. "You *own* this?"

"That draw's got deer in it," Grit said, pointing to a distant gash in the mountainside. "Mark my words, boys. If I was a big ol' buck, that's where I'd lay up."

We unpacked a few things, then sat out behind the house in cheap lawn chairs, admiring the scenery and drinking beer. We threw the aluminum empties in a pile. We liked the sound of a can crunching, then landing on the others in the pile at the end of a toss that we made to look like a quarterback's Hail Mary. We liked the sound of the windmill pumping, slow and steady, squeaking and clanking, then moaning somewhere far down the throat of the old well.

Dusk fell, followed by a moonless, star-speckled darkness.

"This is *God's* country," Grit said, his tone of voice revealing the expression we could not see on his face. "You can't see a light up here. No headlights, no porch lights. Nothin'."

"Hey, Robbie," Damon said, "can I bring my telescope out here? Look at the stars?"

"Bring anything you like," I said.

"Bring us a handful of them señoritas from Juarez," Grit suggested.

Finally, we lit the propane lantern and went inside to lay our bedrolls out on the floor. There was no electricity at the ranch house. Never had been. No plumbing, either, save for a single cold-water pipe leading into the kitchen basin. The scorpion- and black-widow-infested outhouse fulfilled the call to nature. The privy didn't even have a door, but didn't need one, as it faced away from the house. A person could sit in that outhouse and see some of the most marvelous scenery in Texas. Here we needed neither electricity nor plumbing. My ranch was basic, and that was what we liked about it. As we got horizontal in our bedrolls, we agreed to spend every weekend at the ranch until Christmas.

"Judy won't like it, but that's tough," Damon said. He had been married about two years to one of his former students, a pretty gal from New Mexico.

"That's right," Grit said. "You let 'em get you whupped, and it's all over. I ought to know."

I knew Grit. He was about to start grousing about one of his three divorces, so I muttered, "I'm goin' to sleep." I was still smarting over my own divorce, and just wanted to avoid the whole subject before my friends started asking how was Brenda, did I ever hear from her anymore, and how come I didn't have a new girlfriend yet.

Damon read my mind. "See y'all in the morning," he said.

"I'll try to be here," Grit replied, and we all chuckled ourselves to sleep.

THE NEXT MORNING I AWOKE TO THE STRAIN OF SOME NEW PRESENCE filtering in through the old screen door. It would fade, then get louder, then fade again. It consisted of scraping, grinding, thumping sounds. I fancied all kinds of creatures that might cause such a clamor, then finally concluded that it had to be human. My head felt foggy from all the beer the night before, and I didn't want to get up, but curiosity finally roused me, and anyway, my bladder felt like a football.

Shuffling to the screen door, I saw Laureano carrying, in both arms, a slab of stone up the slope. He lowered it to the ground as if it were a child, and lay it beside several others spread out near our pile of beer cans from the night before. I wondered who had dropped him off. I hadn't heard a motor. Perhaps someone had left him at the highway and he had walked the twelve miles up the dirt road.

I heard Damon stumble up behind me.

"Who the hell is that?"

"Laureano."

"Who the hell is that?" he repeated.

I hadn't told Grit and Damon about Laureano for fear they would rib me if he never showed up. To tell the truth, I didn't think Laureano *would* show up. I had given him five dollars for nothing. Why would he come work a day for me, when he could earn another five working for someone else? I had a lot to learn about Laureano.

"He's my *trabajero*."

Damon grunted and pushed his way past me, out through the door.

"*Trabajero*?" Grit said from his bedroll. "That means wetback, don't it?"

"Sort of."

"I'm damn proud of you, Robbie boy. New ranch, new truck. Your own wetback."

Without consulting me, Laureano had decided to build a low rock wall around our backyard. It would connect to the house and enclose our drinking and stargazing place. I told him he could build the wall if it didn't take too long, but then I wanted him to fix up the house for me, and the nearby bunkhouse for himself.

After breakfast, Damon and Grit and I toured the ranch in my pickup, which took a few hours. We came back hungry. Laureano already had the foundation of the rock wall established. How he made it appear so perfectly straight without stretching a line, I will never know. He had placed two parallel courses of stone on the ground, representing the outer surfaces of the wall. The open part between the two courses would be filled in later with less desirable stones and rubble. He already had one end of the wall against the house built up to a height of two feet. He had left an opening for a gate leading out toward the privy, and another leading the other way, toward the bunkhouse.

"Don't take ol' Loriando long to look at a horseshoe, does it?" Grit commented. It was one of those things he often said that didn't quite make sense to me. I think it was the punch line to an old joke or something. I also noted that he had mispronounced the name.

I corrected him: "Laureano."

"That's what I said."

After lunch, Grit and Damon took a siesta, and I went outside to practice my Spanish with Laureano. I gave him a sandwich and a Dr Pepper, and made him quit working. We sat in the shade against the north wall of the ranch house. He looked at his unfinished wall the whole time he ate. In a sorely misworded Spanish sentence, I asked him how he had come to learn the craft of dry-stone walling.

His father, and his father's father, had worked on a huge ranch in Mexico. On this ranch, bulls were raised for the fighting ring. All the fences on the ranch were made of native stone. The building and rebuilding of rock fences never ceased across mile upon mile of range. For two-thirds of his life, Laureano had lifted rocks into place. From rubble, he had given rise to order and beauty.

Finally, Laureano nodded at his wall and said, "*Necesito trabajar en eso rincón.*" He needed to work on that corner.

"*Bueno,*" I said, and lifted myself to my feet.

Laureano went back to work, moving to the steady rhythm of the windmill's machinations. I went to the bunkhouse to see what it would take for Laureano to set up his temporary residence there. Entering, I saw that he had already cleaned up a great deal, presumably while I slept off my drunk this morning. A folded sheaf of paper on the table caught my eye. It was my map that I had given to Laureano yesterday, now stained along the creases with his sweat. He had made his own marks upon the map with a pencil. On a straight line from Marfa to my ranch, almost halving the distance we had traveled by road, Laureano had sketched in landmarks. A spring. A windmill. A set of working pens. A dirt road he had crossed. He wrote no words, but his symbols were clear. He must have walked halfway into last night getting here. I vowed that I would never again refuse Laureano a ride, regardless of the legal consequences.

By the end of that weekend, Laureano had halfway finished the wall around the backyard. He worked even while Damon and Grit and I sat inside the rising enclosure. Occasionally, he would strike a rock with a grubbing hoe he had found in the bunkhouse to break the rock so it would fit where he wanted it. Mostly, though, he just chose the right rock for the place he needed to fill in, making it fit like a piece of a jigsaw puzzle.

"How long you think that wall will last without any mortar in it?" Grit said, watching Laureano work.

"It'll outlast you and me," I said confidently, though I had no experience with dry-stone walling.

"I bet it will," Damon said. "I'd like to put ol' Laureano to work around my place. I can see a big rock patio, and one of those fake waterfalls, you know, where you just pump the same water around and around."

"I can see another beer," Grit replied, "but I just can't reach it."

We had another round, then loaded the truck for the drive back to Marfa.

THE NEXT WEEKEND, WE RETURNED TO THE RANCH TO FIND A perfect wall around the backyard. It was high enough to set our little gathering place aside from the rest of the world, but low enough not to obstruct the beautiful panoramic view. In five days' time, Laureano had cleaned and organized the entire house. He had fixed the roof on the bunkhouse, replaced some rotten boards around the eaves of the ranch house, and tuned up the windmill so that it didn't have to pump all day to keep the concrete water tank full. When we arrived, the windmill was still and silent, and only the wind made noise. Laureano was hard at work on a stone pathway that wound gracefully toward the old outhouse.

"I'll be damned," Grit said. "A paved path to the crapper. That Lariando beats all I ever seen."

"*Laureano.*"

"That's what I said."

Damon positioned an artillerylike telescope on a tripod inside Laureano's wall. That night, after supper, he and Grit went outside to train the telescope in on some constellation Damon wanted to locate. I stayed inside long enough to put some edibles away in the pantry. I was just shutting down the propane lantern when I heard Grit's voice rise in anger.

"What in the hell! Robbie, get out here!"

I rushed outside in the dark and found Damon and Grit just inside Laureano's wall, staring out to the east. I didn't take long finding their source of aggravation. There, miles away, just over a low saddleback pass in the first range of hills to the east, rose the unmistakable glow of an electric light.

"Now, why did they have to put it there?" Damon groaned. "It's like they *wanted* us to have to look at it."

"Son of a bitch," I said, a vague feeling of nausea sinking into my stomach. It had been perfect. Stars. Moon. Dark space between. The Milky Way. Ursas major and minor. Scorpio. The belt of Orion. And now . . . General Electric. Someone at some ranch miles away had put up an infernal light on a damnable pole in the one place where we could see it over the low saddleback pass in the hills. Compared to the stars twinkling seductively above us, the sickly yellowish glow of that man-made light looked absolutely hellish.

"Laureano!" I yelled toward the bunkhouse.

Damon was training his telescope in on the wretched light.

When Laureano came from his quarters, I stammered a question in my broken Spanish: "*La luz. Quantos días?*"

He looked at the light. "*Hasta miércoles.*"

"Laureano says it's been there since Wednesday."

"That's a damn fluorescent yard light," Damon said. "On a friggin' pole, no less."

"Let me see," Grit said, pushing Damon aside.

"*Quien es?*" I asked Laureano.

He shrugged. "*El proximo rancho.*"

"He says it's on the next ranch over."

"I don't care if it's the governor's mansion," Grit said, his bulk bending over the telescope. "There ain't no call for it. No damn call for it whatsoever." He then began to cuss so magnificently that I wished briefly for a tape recorder.

I glanced at Laureano, and saw that he was confused and uneasy. "*Gracias,*" I said. "*Es todo.*"

He nodded, looked cautiously toward my two friends at the telescope, and turned back to the bunkhouse.

We continued to grouse about the light, then finally decided to ignore it. We found some constellation Damon had wanted to locate with the telescope—a magnificent smattering of glittering gems that prompted Grit to remark, "You mean that's it?" We forgot about the light on the next ranch for a while, but after we had all looked through the telescope, we found ourselves staring eastward at that one blemish on the nocturnal landscape.

"Hey," I said, suddenly inspired. "Let's go down the hill a ways until that damn light disappears over the ridge."

We grabbed our beer cooler and lugged it down the rough mountain slope. The neighboring light vanished a mere ten paces down the slope. We sat among the rocks and cactus and drank a beer or two, but it wasn't the same. The light had disappeared behind the crest of the ridge, but the hillside was uncomfortable. We wanted our cheap lawn chairs. We missed the comforting seclusion of Laureano's wall. It wasn't right. Someone else's electric light had chased us out of our own comfort zone. It just wasn't right.

I felt terrible—like it was my fault or something. My ranch had gone bad. My mind scrambled for a way to cheer up the boys.

"Hey," I said. "Y'all remember the halfback pass?"

"I remember it against Bay City," Damon chimed in, catching on immediately. Neither one of us wanted to hang around with Grit when he was mad, and this story usually cheered him up.

We had this one play, the halfback pass. It was sort of a trick play, and it always worked. Well, almost always. See, Grit was the best running back in the state at the time, but he could also throw the ball. Damon never claimed great athletic ability, but he was fast, and he made good decisions under pressure. He was one of the best option quarterbacks I ever saw. On this play—the halfback pass—Damon would pitch the ball back to Grit, then run downfield as a receiver. The defense almost never covered him, because he was the quarterback, and they were always after Grit, our all-state running back.

I was strictly a blocking tight end. I couldn't catch a ball to save my life, and everybody knew it. So, on this play, I'd run a pattern downfield, but I was just a decoy, to lure the defenders away from Damon as he came out of the backfield. Coach Martin loved this play because it demoralized the opposition. Except for that night against Bay City.

"I looked back and saw Grit scrambling," Damon recalled, "trying to dodge those two big Bay City linebackers. About then, I noticed that the defender covering Robbie had fallen down."

"Yep," I said, "I was wide open." Here we were, telling the story to each other as if none of us had been there.

"So Grit throws the ball to the open man, under pressure from those linebackers."

"Prettiest spiral you ever saw," I said. "Hit me right between the eight and the nine."

Damon poked Grit in the ribs. "That ball bounced off of Robbie and landed on the five-yard line. Remember? He could have walked in for a touchdown."

"Story of my football career," I said.

"You remember what you said to Robbie when he got back to the huddle, Grit?"

Grit was trying to play along, but his voice showed he was still mad about that light. "Yeah," he growled. "I said, 'Sorry, Robbie, I thought you were Damon. My fault."

I forced a laugh. "*He* apologized to *me*!" I blurted. "I missed the prettiest pass in the history of football, and Grit acted like it was his fault for throwing it to me!"

Damon threw himself back on the mountain in a shameless exhibition of moronic enthusiasm.

Suddenly Grit threw down his beer can and stormed up the hill. "Damon, shine that scope of yours back on that light," he ordered.

We scrambled up the slope behind Grit, and I watched as Damon apprehensively swiveled the telescope. Grit went inside the ranch house, then burst back out with his hunting rifle in his hand.

"Grit, what in the hell . . ."

"You just watch." He slammed a live cartridge into the chamber of the semiautomatic rifle, dropped to one knee, and took a rest on Laureano's wall.

"You can't be serious. That light is miles away."

"And this is a three-hundred Winchester Magnum," he blurted. "Damon, you let me know if I'm comin' close."

Grit hunkered behind the rifle scope, and a second later the big gun split the silence of the night with a thunderous roar. I saw Laureano appear at his bunkhouse door.

"Well?" Grit said, almost shouting. His ears must have been ringing even louder than mine.

Damon said, "Hell, I can't tell anything, Grit. It's dark out there."

I waved my hand reassuringly at Laureano. He must have thought we had gone loco.

Grit loosed another round, and another. Damon couldn't tell how close he was coming, of course, or even if his bullets cleared the range of hills to the east. Grit emptied the magazine anyway. Finally, he spouted another choice combination of profanities and stalked back into the house to put his rifle away.

THE REST OF THE HUNTING SEASON WENT LIKE THAT, OUR NIGHTS haunted by that ghostly glow of civilization to the east. We had our fun by day, however, and enjoyed the wild grandeur of my ranch. Grit killed a monster mule deer buck in the draw he had pointed out to us that first day. Damon and I failed to bag one, but it wasn't as important to us as it was to Grit. Laureano made quick work of skinning and butchering the deer for "*Señor* Grit" as he always called him, the name coming out like "Greet" in Laureano's tongue.

"That Lorenzio is handy as a handle on a bucket," Grit said, watching the *trabajero* hack quickly through the ribs of the deer carcass with a machete. Grit never spoke to Laureano, but spoke highly of him.

"It's Laureano," I said. "Oh, never mind."

One day I took Laureano to Marfa in my pickup truck, immigration laws be damned. We talked in Spanish the whole way to town. I learned about his wife, a textile worker, and their five children, including one baby girl he had not even seen yet. I imagined that when he went back to his home in Aguascalientes for Christmas, he'd probably get his wife pregnant again, then come north to look for more work. In a way I sort of envied Laureano. His life seemed like some great heroic adventure.

At the post office, Laureano bought a money order with his entire four weeks' pay and sent it to his wife. He walked away from the post office with empty pockets, a sad smile on his face.

I bought Laureano a new suit of work clothes at the western wear store, and he refused to even take off the new duds after making sure they fit in the dressing room. I then bought him a chicken-fried steak at the Paisano Hotel, and told Darla, the waitress there, that he was a wealthy Mexican rancher visiting the United States, which made the wrinkles around his eyes branch like wheel spokes when I explained it to him.

We stopped at the grocery store for more food and beer, then Laureano taught me more words on the way to the ranch. I was beginning to feel like Laureano's friend instead of just his employer. I noticed how worn his old straw hat was getting, and I came up with an idea.

In Spanish, I asked him what size hat he wore. He showed me

the tag inside, just above the sweat band. Six and seven-eighths. I told him I was going to bring him a new Stetson from Austin. A rich Mexican rancher should wear a fine straw hat. He smiled and sat in silence for a couple of miles.

"*Voy hacer algo para usted,*" he finally said. "*Un regalo.*"

He was going to make something for me in return for the hat. A gift. He would not say what it was he was going to make.

The days passed pleasantly with the crisp chill of autumn in the dry mountain air. Laureano began building a stone corral, though I never told him to and didn't plan on owning any horses. I asked him if the corral was the *regalo* he had promised to make for me, and he said no, he would make that in his spare time, otherwise it would not be much of a gift if I was paying him to make it.

Grit hunted, and managed to kill enough deer to use the tags on all of our hunting licenses and keep us all supplied with venison for the next year. Damon and I enjoyed each others' intellectual conversation while Grit was out hunting. And we watched Laureano work. We were all happy by day.

But the nights . . . the nights were sullied by *the light*. That damnable electric light. We would try to ignore it, but it would pulsate unnaturally over the saddleback pass to the east, tempting our gaze like some naked and lurid slut. We hated that light. We abhorred it. We never cussed it playfully. We profaned that alien bulb with deep-seated vindication and territorial ire.

Hunting season ended and we planned one last trip to the ranch before Christmas. Damon and I were to meet Grit in the afternoon at the Marfa municipal airport. We waited in my truck at the airport, with Laureano's new Stetson on the seat between us, while Damon graded term papers. We sat there for about fifteen minutes before Grit arrived. When he landed, he taxied to the fuel pumps.

"Hey, git in," he yelled. "Let's go fly the ranch."

The day was like a precious jewel, glimmering and full of facets, so Damon and I consented to a flight with Grit. I had never flown with Grit before, and never will again. He liked to roar over the mountain passes in such a way that we had to look up at peaks on either side. I remember marveling that Grit had not killed himself yet. I prayed that the odds would not catch up to him before he got me and Damon safely back to the airport.

"You need an airstrip on the ranch, Robbie. Tell you what. Hire the dozer, and I'll pay for it. Think of all the rock it'll push up for Loriendo to build stuff with."

I nodded, feeling slightly nauseated from all the unnecessarily abrupt maneuvers Grit kept performing.

"Hey, look at that mountain peak," Damon said, pointing ahead and trying to sound casual.

"I see it," Grit said with a groan in his voice that showed his disgust with our aerobatic cowardice.

We were over the ranch house in a matter of minutes. It looked strange from the air—tiny and isolated. Laureano's wall around the backyard was a postage stamp, the stone path to the outhouse a spider's web.

"Right here on the hill," Grit said, still thinking of the airstrip. He came in low and slow over the ranch house, demonstrating how he would land on the hill after the rocks were cleared and the ground smoothed by the bulldozer. He let the airplane get so low that I thought for a second he really was going to land. Then he poured on the fuel and made the twin engines pull us back into a steep banking ascent.

"Hey!" he yelled over the howl of the props and pistons. "You know what we're gonna do now?"

I shook my head, too afraid to speak.

"We're gonna buzz that son-of-a-bitchin' light!"

Scared as I was, I had to grin. We hurtled in a sweeping curve to the east, leapt the high point in the row of hills, and plummeted down toward the home of that gaseous nocturnal glow. As we dove like some fighter pilot in a John Wayne movie, engines whining to an ever higher pitch, I spotted two pickup trucks with campers on a plateau beyond the hills. The pole on top of which the light perched looked like a mere toothpick, but I saw it. It was someone's hunting camp. No electric lines led to the place. They had to have had a generator down there somewhere to keep that light burning. I couldn't believe it. We were being tortured by some bunch of deer hunters who had put a damn light on a pole just high enough to make it visible to us over the ridge and ruin our starry view. Grit flew so low to the ground that I thought he would knock the dang light off with his propeller.

As we screamed past the light pole and banked hard to the right, I saw four or five guys pour out of the two campers. Grit laughed and circled for another assault.

"Better let it go," I said. "They might get your tail number and turn you in or something."

"They usually don't think of that till the third pass," he said, as if he did this sort of thing all the time.

This time Grit buzzed the owners of the wretched light so low that he left them in a dusty cloud of prop wash. He was hooting like a Comanche as he barreled away to the north. Now he swung around the row of hills that separated the light from my ranch, and circled to take one last look at his proposed airstrip.

"Hey," Damon said, tapping Grit on the shoulder. "Who's that?"

"Where?"

"There. On the canyon rim, east of the ranch house."

Grit banked, giving me a glimpse of a man on the dirt road.

"That's got to be Lauriendo," Grit said.

"What's he doing that far from the house?" Damon asked. "Must be two miles."

"Maybe it's some other wetback," Grit said. "Let's go see."

The next thing I knew, we were dive-bombing poor Laureano. I saw him disappear into the shadows of a mesquite tree. Laureano knew how to hide.

"Damn, where'd he go?" Grit said.

"Let him alone," I yelled over the roar of the aircraft. "He probably thinks you're the damn border patrol."

"He knows I'm a pilot," Grit argued.

"No, he doesn't."

"You didn't tell him?"

"The subject never came up."

"What the hell do you two talk about all the time?"

"Mostly he just teaches me Spanish. I'm serious, Grit, leave him alone."

"All right," Grit said. "Hell, I didn't mean to scare him."

On the flight back to the airport, and during the drive out to the ranch, we would occasionally break out in chuckles and giggles over the way we had buzzed that light we hated so much. As we lurched down the twelve miles of dirt road, the sun set like a blazing slow-motion jump shot falling perfectly past the rim of the world. We didn't mention Laureano, but I was anxious to get to the ranch house and apologize for the way we had driven him into hiding. And I wanted to give him his new Stetson hat. Also, I had been wondering about Laureano's gift to me. He was going to make something for me, he had said.

Dusk had turned to twilight by the time we pulled up to the ranch house. I saw that Laureano had finished building the stone walls for the corral. I had expected this, so I looked around to see what else he might have started. Walking around the house, however, I couldn't find anything freshly constructed. This was curious, for Laureano worked quickly, and had been almost finished with the corral the weekend before.

His quarters were dark, and I hoped he was asleep in there, but something told me otherwise. I got my flashlight from the truck and went to knock on the door of the bunkhouse. No answer came. I walked in. "Laureano," I said, just in case. But I knew he was gone. I flashed the beam around the room and found the bed neatly made. All his personal effects were gone. He had three weeks' pay coming. I didn't even have his address in Mexico. I felt foolish and ashamed for having let Grit buzz him in the Cessna. I lay his cowboy hat on the table, hoping he might come back during the week to see whether or not I had left his pay, which I placed inside his hat. I didn't feel very good about it at all. I wasn't sure if I would ever see him again. It was a mean thing we had done.

Suddenly I heard Grit's and Damon's voices rise from the ranch house. They were hooting like coyotes, like sports fans celebrating a touchdown. I stepped out of the bunkhouse and trotted around back of the ranch house. I found them high-fiving inside Laureano's wall.

"What's going on?" I said.

"It's gone!" Grit sang.

"What?"

"Look," Damon said, pointing eastward.

I looked, and sure enough it was gone. The evil luminescence that had vexed us every weekend for months no longer glowed over the ridge of the saddleback pass in the first row of hills.

"Must have burned out," I said.

"Nope," Grit answered. "It's gone for good, compadre."

"What do you mean?"

"Look," Damon said, offering his telescope. He had already trained it on the place where the light had once burned.

Only the faintest vestige of twilight remained, but it was enough to illuminate the saddleback pass through the lens of the telescope. At first it made no sense. The saddleback pass seemed to have risen in altitude just enough to stamp out the glow of that cursed electric light to the east. How was that possible? Had they lowered the pole? Then I looked closer, and understood. I saw the seams and textures of the rocks placed by the hands of a master builder.

This was my gift. Laureano made the most marvelous walls of stone.

Going Home Money

JUDY MAGNUSON LILLY

Judy Magnuson Lilly is an associate member of the Western Writers of America whose short stories have appeared in *Louis L'Amour Western Magazine* and in *The Enchanted Rocking Horse,* a book of Christmas stories. Her compassionate tale of Annie Light, a homesteader broken by the land, should assure her active status very soon.

THE WIND WAS CLEVERLY STILL, Annie Light noticed, when the men swung into their saddles a little past dawn. Evander, his tanned face half hidden by a full beard, didn't even raise his voice when he said, "We'll be back in three to four days. Mind you keep the sow's food soft. I'll be planting wheat when I get back."

But by the time her husband and their neighbor Sam Brown had shrunk to dark moving objects against the northern sky, the wind had come out of hiding—up from the cracks in the bed of Dry Creek and out of the leafless trees along the Smoky. It whipped and flattened the winter-dried grasses that surrounded their homestead claim and cruelly danced over their baby's grave under the cottonwood tree.

All the while she saw to the chores, spreading gravel for the hens and feeding corn mush to the sow that was due to farrow in a week or two, she steeled her mind against the tiresome scream she had come to know over the past two years. Her silent husband praised the wind for bringing in the rain and then for drying out the hay. The wind was no enemy to him. It didn't wear at his mind and muscles as it did hers.

After tossing fresh hay for the cow and mule they called Old Luce, Annie gathered three warm eggs and hurried to the cabin. All about the dooryard, bits of ash and straw swirled and dipped like moths. It was a troubling sight, but she pushed the worry from her mind. With the wind this strong, a fire could be several miles away and still contributing fluff to the air. Besides, the Smoky Hill River, a mile south of their claim, would protect her against such a menace.

As Annie stepped through the heavy cabin door, she heard nine

275

chimes of the birdcage clock that sat on the wagon box, now used as a nightstand. "It'll see you through," Evander's wrinkled Granny Light had told her on the eve of their leaving for Kansas. "Evander's mighty like his grandpa. Lets go of his words hard like he's afraid he'll go stone dry."

Granny had been right about quiet Evander, with little enough to say over the garrulous wind so that he was no company at all. She never thought she'd hunger so for the sweet sound of a human voice to break up the lonesomeness of the prairie world that stretched and billowed around her. The old woman had been right, too, about the company of the little brass clock with its pierced work on the front and its hinged doors on the sides. While her young husband poured himself into his claim, the clock had tied Annie's soul to their families back in Indiana.

Annie put the eggs in a basket and took up her sewing. The morning passed slowly, each second marked by the tick of the clock. She huddled in a slat-back rocker, intent on a piece of denim she was making into a seed bag for Evander. Don't worry that the breeze from the open window seems to be blowing too warm for this early in April, she told herself. Or that it carried the unmistakable scent of singed hair and hide. Or that their livestock turn noses into the wind, watching something south of the river. Something she couldn't see.

Her small body tense under a gray, waistless dress, Annie back-stitched where the strap joined the opening of the bag, and then she looped the thread and drew the needle through the loop to make the stitch secure. "There now," she said aloud just to use her voice. "This'll hold a good weight of seed wheat when Evander sets to planting again."

She rose from the rocker and hooked the bag over its back. Over the noise of the rattling window shutters, she thought she heard her name called. Or was the wind playing its tricks? "Missus Light," it seemed to say.

She pulled open the door and saw two figures walking up the

lane, one leading a dun and the other a blood bay. She recognized them even at a distance: two bachelors who stopped now and then for food and talk. Annie knew them only as Lehman and Page. No Christian names. Just the two always together like bread and butter. They'd been partners at a hunting ranch on Thompson Creek till the Indian scares ran them out. The men often bought eggs from her and had a world of stories to tell.

"Don't want to alarm you, ma'am," called the shorter of the two. His name was Page, said to be a teacher of Greek before coming to Kansas eight years ago.

"Company's no cause for alarm," she said. "You're welcome to take a meal. Come in out of the wind."

The men tied their horses to the cottonwood, while Annie heated beans and pork on the cook stove and divided up the last of the cornbread. They sat down to eat on two homemade chairs and a wooden grocery box Annie kept under the table. Of the two, the man called Lehman, his long hair tangled into a beard, was more the hand for talking. Once he had told of the night he'd been caught in a stupendous thunder-and-lightning storm. Fearsome winds had swelled out of the darkness, sheared off trees, and hurled them through the air. "I watched dumbfounded," he had told Annie and Evander, his eyes wide under bushy eyebrows. "Lightning reached across the sky like spread-out bony fingers. But more strange was the balls of fire that played around my horse's ears and rolled off along the ground. I never seen nothing like it before or since."

It was Lehman who had brought the news that iron tracks were laid to Phillips Mill and beyond so that now a person could ride the railroad straight to St. Louis and even on to Warrick County, Indiana. As they ate, Annie told about Evander and Sam Brown being called to town to help jury a trial of the old Swede who lived inside a river tree. He liked to work a hired hand day and night but never liked to pay him, they said. Then she asked the men if they knew what might be spooking the livestock and making them stare off to the south.

Lehman spooned beans onto his plate and broke up the corn-bread. "I suspect the redskins are burning again. They do that this time of year."

"Not burning on purpose?" Annie put down her fork.

"That's what they do," Page agreed. "The Osage and sometimes the Kaw."

"They like to set fire to a stretch of dry prairie," Lehman con-tinued. "Let the grasses burn however they will. Then they sit back and wait for two, three days. Pretty soon deer, antelope, even bison and elk come scenting out the new green that's showing up from the scorched ground."

Lehman had finished his meal in good time and now tipped his chair back and lit a pipe. "Them redskins wrap rawhide around a ball of dead grass. Light it and trail that flaming ball behind a run-ning pony. The prairie burns from river to river."

Annie remembered how during the first spring while she and Evander still lived in the dugout, they'd seen smoke boiling beyond the river. A fire had never come close to them, but she knew the wind could choose to let it slide into the river, turning it to wisps of steam, or it could seize a flaming branch and roll it over treetops to the opposite bank.

"Doesn't the fire ever get out of hand?" she asked.

"Until lately, there's been nothing in the fire's way except more grass," Page said. "Not many claims yet where they burn. I reckon you're safe enough here."

Annie pushed away a half-eaten plate. The men were seasoned plainsmen, and their word should be comforting to her. But Lehman and Page were like Evander, fooled by the power of the wind. She said nothing as she listened to the cabin door groan on its iron hinges, and the branches of the cottonwood creak against a stiff gale.

Before the men left, Page drew a pouch from under his vest and laid several coins on the table. "We'll be back in a week or so. Could we speak for a few eggs, ma'am? Lehman's got a mighty craving for some, boiled, scrambled, or poached."

When the men had gone, the day felt lonesome again. The image of sweaty copper bodies trailing fireballs seared her mind, and Annie sought to fix her thoughts on something else. Once the dirty dishes were cleared and piled in the washtub, she remembered Page's coins on the table. The sight of them cheered her instantly. Annie crossed the hard-packed dirt floor to the wagon box. The little clock ticked away, as relentless as the wind. From behind the clock's brass side door, she drew a thin leather pouch, took it to the table, and shook out the contents. She smiled wide like a child as greenbacks and coins spread over the tabletop. How many times had she counted this money, making neat stacks, pressing it smooth with her hands? The coarse paper felt like strips of velvet. She had saved it little by little from egg money and money left by hunters and travelers for their meals. She hadn't meant to keep it hidden from Evander at first, but he was always busy, working through the daylight hours. The secret seemed to pour strength into her. Then to make the peeled log walls seem less crude and the days not as long, she devised a plan, constructed it as carefully as she had cut and stitched Evander's seed bag: With the money stored in Granny Light's old clock, she would board the train in Phillips Mill and ride it all the way to Indiana, where she could feast eyes on sweet, familiar faces she hadn't seen for two years.

Alone in the cabin, Annie thought of her white-haired grandfather's gentle hug and the sound of swaying willows outside her bedroom window. Instead of the thud and scrape of wooden shutters, she could listen to her sisters' laughter and her papa's fiddle music. The snarling, biting wind wouldn't find her there.

She was going home to Indiana.

THE DREAM CAME TO HER IN THE LATTER MOMENTS OF SLEEP AS an end to a fitful night when she thrashed and hollowed herself in the straw tick, the clammy muslin sheets binding her legs and arms. Perhaps she had allowed herself to dwell too long the night before on her family and home. Perhaps the unnatural warmth of the night would not let her relax. Or perhaps the glow of red on the horizon last night at bedtime troubled the corners of her mind.

Whatever it was, she dreamed she had walked up her folks' narrow lane past a field of corn shocks, past her brothers, who labored with sweaty backs along the haying rows, past her father, pitching fodder from the wagon into the feed trough of Old Jig and Jayne. As she paused before each dear face, it turned away, and when she tried to speak, the words became a foul stench in her mouth. She reached out to her father, but a brown mist crawled into her nostrils until she feared she couldn't breath. In desperation she lunged towards him and found herself crumpled on the earth floor of her cabin home.

Only a dream, she told herself. She lay still to sort out what was real. Forms lurked in the dimness of the room: the table, the cook stove, and the rocker. She could hear the steady beat of the birdcage clock. But her father's face was still clear in her mind and made her heart pound.

Then she noticed something. The choking, serpentine mist seemed to linger about in the shadows. Even awake she couldn't breath easily. The clock chimed five times. Dawn should be slipping through the unshuttered windows, but she could barely discern the window frames. She drew up her knees and hugged them. The darkness made her feel swallowed up and forgotten. Nagging her, pushing her to some kind of action, was the persistent thought: Where was the dawn?

Even before she went to the door and flung it open, she knew what she would find. The fire, still miles away last night, had found her, like the wind.

Annie allowed herself only a moment to stare from the threshold at a bar of crimson light lying on the tops of the river trees. The distance was too great to tell if the fire had jumped to the near bank. But already the wind was screaming. Already it had set about its work.

A gray haze scarred the rising sun, and the farmyard sat in shad-

ows. Annie knew its layout. Thirty long strides to the stable and
corral. She pulled off the rawhide strip securing the gate and jumped
back as the nervous mule and cow charged past. The sound of the
cowbell grew faint in the haze. The foolish chickens had to be
shooed from their roost in the eves of the stable. Flapping and
squawking they faded into the gray. Next she freed the sow, and
with the heel of her hand whacked its coarse back to start the animal
on its way.

How strangely empty the farmyard seemed now, void of the
living beings that had been Annie's only companions at times. A
new presence, too thick to be a mist, now weaved through Evander's
rail fencing and hovered over the fields. Suddenly Annie felt the stiff
wind grow warmer. A flash of light drew her eye, a light that seemed
to leap and swell in size. Instead of dancing on the treetops, it stood
between her and the river trees. The fire had crossed the river. She
knew it would come her way.

Inside, Annie fought to control her thoughts. She began to fill
Evander's seed bag with the framed likenesses of her family. Next
she eased the clock into the bag and hooked the straps around her
neck and shoulders. Her muscles tightened. Her mind felt both fear
and anger. All she owned was in this cabin: the rocking chair; the
old bed that had belonged to her mother's people; the linens, quilts,
and piece goods inside the wagon box that she had carefully protected from the dust and bugs and mice. She wouldn't let the fire
have it all.

With the bag slung over her back, she hooked an arm around
the back of the rocker and dragged it awkwardly outside. The air
was even warmer now and suffocating. Annie left the rocker and
seed bag in the fifty-foot-wide strip of plowed ground that circled
the cabin and outbuilding, and stumbled back for more. Grasping
the leather strap on the end of the wagon box, she pulled it across
the floor. Twice she stepped on her nightdress and fell backwards,
scraping her shins with the edge of the box. She reached the fireguard again, dropped her load, and returned to the cabin for whatever she could carry away. At last, she sank to the ground, exhausted

and breathless. Annie felt as if she'd been plunged into a bucket of pitch.

The wind was picking up and a dull sound rushed out of the piling smoke that rolled toward the farmyard. Suddenly the bank of smoke lifted, leaving in its place a wall of fire that danced at the southern edge of their claim. The wind howled. Burning embers, as thick as nesting bees, swirled in the wind until they caught in the outbuildings, the fences, the cottonwood tree, and finally the cabin.

Annie could barely breathe. The flame and smoke would overcome her if she stayed where she was, but she was too tired to move. When a loud clap brought her to her feet, she tried to muster some hidden strength. Pulling the straps of the bulging seed bag over her shoulder again, she began to run, bare feet maneuvering the clods of earth, her stride increasing as the roar grew louder behind her. A corner of the clock jabbed at her side. Hot air stung her back.

Annie Light's feet left the fireguard and flew over prairie earth that Evander had readied for wheat. On to the dry meadow grass she ran, her feet reading the direction she needed to go: wagon ruts running north to the settlement where Evander was and south towards the old Santa Fe freight road. Dry Creek lay not many yards ahead. But with the wind's help, the fire was gaining on her. Annie stumbled and fell to her knees at the edge of Dry Creek. She could run no more. Her nose and throat were full of ashes. Her eyes stung.

But as she waited to have her flesh melted from her bones, a sudden gust of cooler air rolled over her. She felt the intense heat behind her lessen. She turned her head and gasped. The cabin was alive with flame, and the cottonwood tree burned like a giant torch. But the fire hung in place; it was not advancing. The wind held it from her. The wind was turning the fire. It would grow weaker and burn itself out as it traveled Evander's finely worked ground to the east.

Annie couldn't watch any longer. She staggered through the creek bed, the seed bag still clutched to her side. Sam Brown's cabin stood whole before her. Inside, she sank onto the buffalo robe that covered a corner of the floor, the wild scent of it rising up around her, folding over her consciousness. With effort, she allowed her mind to think only of the feel and smell of the robe, until her exhausted body gave way to sleep.

HOW LONG SHE SLEPT, SHE COULDN'T HAVE SAID. EVANDER'S callused hands on her face brought her from a dreamless state. When she opened her eyes, she thought a stranger knelt beside her, his forehead heavily creased, his mouth pressed straight and grim. Finally she realized her husband, now clean-shaven, shook her and called her name. She buried her face in his rough shirt. Even on him, she could smell the smoke.

"Have you been over home?" she asked finally, pulling away, aching for him if he had not.

But Evander nodded. "I rode near as I could, looking for, well, checking the damage. The ground's still smoldering."

Did you find Luce? The cow?

"Sam's bringin' them. We came upon the stock near Lindgren's Ford. Seeing 'em made me feel some better. If you could free the livestock, you could surely get yourself from harm, I thought, but, God, Annie, I was so afraid."

He pulled her closer. "You're safe. That's all I care about. A burned-over prairie grows back thick and even, they say." Evander's voice was solid, but Annie heard an unfamiliar pitch. "I reckon we'll find out. If we stay."

She had almost forgotten. "I saved the clock, Evander. There's money in it. Money I've been saving. I suspect it won't go far, but it's something anyway."

His eyes held a look she could not decipher. She had seen it only once before: after the baby came and he had washed the sweat from her face. But it pleased her beyond anything he had ever given her.

Annie could feel a soft breeze from the open door. The seed bag had toppled on its side, and from it, the ticking of the clock filled their neighbor's cabin room. When the clock chimed, Annie thought of Evander's granny and her own family tending to the day's chores.

Perhaps if she planned carefully and bought only the barest necessities, a small portion from every egg sale could be saved and tucked behind the hinged door of her clock. Then one day she would climb aboard the train in Phillips Mill and visit their people in Indiana.

Thirteen Coils

LOREN D. ESTLEMAN

Western Writers of America President Loren D. Estleman is the author of more than forty novels, seventeen set in the historical West. He is a four-time winner of the Spur Award. Presented herewith: twenty-four hours in the life of a particular specialist.

IT OCCURRED TO ANDERS NILSEN
that if it weren't for having to wait at the train station he would be
quite contented to remain both a deputy sheriff and a Methodist.

His particular sect frowned upon all the standard vices, including
the use of tobacco, and although from the smell of it he doubted
he would ever appreciate the taste of smoke upon his tongue, he
thought the thousand little gestures involved with lighting a pipe or
a cigar or a cigarette, keeping it burning, and disposing of the ash
might make him look less the fool while awaiting the whistle's first
reedy blast.

Reading a book or a newspaper didn't answer. There was seldom
a space to sit on the benches, and anyway the words and letters had
a way of coming out backwards whenever he tried to concentrate.
His attempts to strike up a conversation with a fellow vigilant were
usually unsatisfactory; even law-abiding individuals felt uncomfortable in the presence of a man wearing a star and responded in mono-
syllables. And so to avoid pacing the platform and attracting
unwanted attention he was forced to lean against a post and find
something to do with his hands.

The fact that of late he had begun to form certain opinions about
criminal punishment only made the wait on this occasion less pleasant than usual.

He did, however, take pride in his powers of observation. When
the big new oil burner thudded up the tracks at last and the first
passengers allowed themselves to be helped down by a red-faced
conductor with magnificent white imperials, Nilsen amused himself
by guessing their occupations based on their dress and comport-
ment. The woman in the coarse woolen wrap and plain hat tied

under her chin with a scarf had to be a schoolteacher, for what other unescorted female would take such pains to prevent her ankles from showing on the steps? The shiny black bowler and loud plaid Inverness of the fellow behind marked him as a drummer even if he hadn't been lugging a sample case as heavy and bulky as a Wells Fargo box. Here was a butcher in his trademark straw boater and great belly. The disgruntled-looking older couple sold hardware, and barely enough to cover the rent on the shop. The farmer was as obvious in his suit, too short in the cuffs and ten years out of style, as if he'd left on his brogans and overalls; he scanned the platform with weather-faded eyes for a porter or someone to reassure him that the new plow—harrow? manure spreader?—he'd bought in Bismarck would indeed be delivered.

"Excuse me. I think you are waiting for me."

Nilsen shifted his attention from the farmer to the man who had addressed him. Clearly he was a banker, thick-set with spectacles and a well-trimmed gray beard in a charcoal suit with the faintest of stripes, quietly tailored and beginning to show genteel wear. His hat, fawn-colored with a narrow rolled brim and silk band, was set squarely on his head and he carried a black leather Gladstone bag, scuffed at the corners but hand-rubbed to a soft shine.

"I'm afraid you're mistaken." Nilsen spread his coat a little to show the star. "I'm meeting a man named Stone."

"Oscar Stone. Yes. Pleased to make your acquaintance."

He gave his hand to the man's dry, firm grasp in confusion. "Mr. Stone. Of course. Pleased. I thought—"

"—I would be tall and thin like a scarecrow, dressed all in black. That is the general expectation. I am sorry to disappoint you. You must have me as I am, you see." The tight smile in the gray beard acknowledged the existence of humor without partaking in it.

The deputy realized he was still shaking the old man's hand. Embarrassed, he let go abruptly—and became even more embarrassed that Stone might think he had acted out of revulsion. His gaze fell to the black bag. "Is that all your luggage? I'll carry it. You must be exhausted. I suppose you travel with your own, er—" He felt his face grow hot. He kept hurling himself against the shore of the man's damn implacability.

"Shirts and underthings, yes. I am not at all tired. The train did all the work. I have a trunk. You will want a porter to help with that."

The trunk was old-fashioned, long and deep and black, with painted metal corners, four leather straps buckled tight, and a brass padlock as big as a horseshoe. The contents shifted with a clank when Nilsen and the black porter lifted it onto the hand truck. It was heavy enough to contain a body. The deputy had not expected it to contain anything metal. It made him curious; but there was something about Stone that discouraged questions, although he was certain that any he asked would be answered without hesitation. The newcomer handed the porter a banknote and asked him to see that the trunk and his bag were delivered to the Czarina Catherine Hotel.

"Sheriff Connaught reserved a room for you at the Railroad Arms," Nilsen said.

"Please thank him for me, with my apologies. I am getting on in years and have come to depend upon my comforts. The Catherine and I are very old friends."

"You've been here before?"

"In '79, yes. The Mike Rudabaugh business. You don't know it? Before your time, I suppose. A successful effort. The sheriff's name was McAndrews. Unpleasant man."

"The governor threw Charlie McAndrews out of office ten years back. He beat a prisoner to death. The man turned out to be innocent. I'm in favor of jail over execution myself. You can always undo a wrong if the man you wronged is still alive."

"Yes. Well, that is the responsibility of the courts, isn't it? If it's a question of a man's life perhaps they will be more careful." He dusted his palms. "Is the Sugar Bowl still in operation? I'm famished. I never visit dining cars. The menu is limited and the swaying upsets my digestion."

"It's still the best place to eat in town. I'll take you. The sheriff lent me his trap."

Among the checked tablecloths, homely still-lifes, and chuckling crockery in the restaurant, Stone became animated. He looked around, eyes bright behind his spectacles, like an eastern tourist hoping to spot a frontier legend tying into a chicken-fried steak. "It has not changed. How reassuring. So much else has, you see. I stopped in Denver and did not recognize it."

He'd surprised Nilsen by ordering a bowl of tomato soup and a loaf of bread, warm from the oven and moist as a sponge, with buttered beans. The Sugar Bowl was known for its steaks and roast turkey. Stone ate fastidiously but with obvious enjoyment. The deputy contented himself with coffee and a slice of bread. Stone's appetite had for some reason deprived him of his own.

When the check came, Nilsen took it. Stone made no protest. He drank his water, wiped the corners of his mouth, and flung his napkin onto the table. "Let us go talk to your Sheriff Connaught."

MILT CONNAUGHT HAD THE REPUTATION OF AN EMOTIONLESS man, which was what had elected him. Tall and chiseled, the son of a Scots farmer who had broken his health and his legacy on the prairie, he was admired for his resolution and calm impartiality. He was no vicious McAndrews, but neither was he a mollycoddler. In twelve years in law enforcement, four as chief deputy, he had not once been questioned about the propriety of his arrests or his treatment of the prisoners in his charge.

Few were aware of how much his stoicism cost him in human suffering. He endured ulcers and insomnia, went through an envelope of headache powders a day, and was separated from his wife, who had gone to visit relatives in Joplin a month ago and had not written since. He carried a miniature tintype of her in his watch case.

When Nilsen entered the office with Oscar Stone, Connaught rose from behind his desk and shook the visitor's hand. He thought there was something foreign about the comfortable-looking fellow in banker's clothes; German, perhaps, although there was no trace of an accent in his precise speech.

"We don't usually bring someone in from outside," the sheriff said. "In the past it was the head turnkey's job, but there's talk of moving the capital here. That means promotions all around, and no one wants to get stuck in a position with no future. I hope you don't mind my being blunt."

"A dead-end job, yes." Stone's smile held no warmth. "I got it in the first place because no one else would volunteer. Nothing has changed."

"You'll want to meet the man, I suppose. He's a bad one. He took a farmer apart with a Stevens ten-gauge four miles outside town and raped his widow and slit her throat. He came for a cash box that was supposed to be hidden in the house, but he never found it. It probably never existed. There always seems to be a cash box involved but I've never heard of anybody ever finding one."

"Even bandits live on hope. Has he been weighed?"

He found the paper on his desk. "One hundred sixty-three and a half. We used the scales at Berger's feed store."

Stone rubbed the side of his nose. "I don't doubt Mr. Berger's honesty, but shop scales are not always accurate. They must be tested frequently and adjusted. Would he mind if I inspected them? I brought my own plates."

"I'll put it to him as delicately as I can. He's the kind to take offense."

"I'm sure he'll understand once the importance is explained. I once saw a man's head snapped clean off his shoulders because the fellow in charge misjudged the drop."

Anders Nilsen went a little pale. Connaught told him to see about having Stone's plates unpacked and brought around to Berger's. Nilsen went out. The sheriff liked the young man and thought him reliable, but he had too many convictions. If he stayed long enough to outlive his idealism he'd be a good deputy.

"If I put it to Berger that way, he'll go along. It would mean you suspect his scales are cheating him more than his customers."

"You are a diplomat, Sheriff. Unlike your predecessor."

"You mean McAndrews. There's a new century coming, no room for the likes of him. You may be retiring yourself soon. I heard they're installing an electric chair in Huntsville."

The gentle bearded face assumed an expression of extreme distaste. "I witnessed an execution by electricity last year in San Francisco. Barbaric. Flames shot out of the poor devil's head. It will be a dark day for civilization when such a thing replaces a short drop and a clean break."

"That's progress. The county bought me one of these new gas-powered self-loading rifles. It's sure as hell fast, but I don't know that it's a better weapon than my old Winchester."

"Thank you for reminding me. I assume there is a local ordinance against carrying firearms."

"Within the city limits. Marshal Henry will be enforcing it tomorrow."

"Splendid. Please ask him to close the saloons as well. If he chooses not to, I request that the prisoner be given a bottle of whiskey tonight. I will pay for it."

"What in thunder for?"

"It's a matter of respect. If the man must die before drunks, he should not be sober."

"That makes sense."

"Naturally I would prefer that everyone present abstain. Execution is serious business. In any case, hanging a man who is drunk or out of his mind presents complications. I cannot be held responsible for the outcome if he resists while I am trying to adjust the knot."

Something about Stone's unblinking calm brought a graphic image to Connaught's mind. Attending hangings was by far the least favorite part of his job, but he felt himself fortunate that he had never witnessed a badly botched one.

"The saloons will be closed. Do you want to see the prisoner now?"

"Please."

Morse Potter's surname wasn't Potter. At the age of six months he'd been rescued from the water barrel of a pilgrim wagon after his parents were killed by raiders. No one knew what the family was called, and so he was named for the field where the remains were buried.

When he was fourteen he'd used a hay knife to eviscerate the widowed farmer who reared him, stolen a mule and the wedding ring that belonged to the farmer's late wife, and left that country; he'd been on the run ever since. Running cost money. He had been unable to make that clear to either the clodbuster outside town or his slack-jawed woman, and that was why he was sitting in this cell instead of washing his feet in the Pacific.

"Stand up."

He didn't move or even raise his eyes. He sat on his cot with one boot off, trying to get a thumbnail under the head of a spike imbedded in the heel. He intended to use the spike as a weapon when they came to take him outside, or on himself if that didn't work. One good thrust under the corner of his jaw would spoil the show for everyone.

"Stand up or I'll have you hauled up by your ears." The sheriff sounded more tired than angry.

Potter stood, still holding the boot. Through the flat metal grid that circumscribed his world he saw that there was a third man present, a doctor or a watchmaker from his clothes and spectacles.

"Ask him to put on his boot."

"What's the matter, parson, you don't like the stink?"

The watchmaker spoke before the sheriff could open his mouth. "I need an approximate measurement of your height, to make sure I use the proper length of rope. I don't want you to strangle."

He gathered in his grin. "You're the hangman."

"I am. If you would?"

He stooped and tugged on the boot.

"Stand straight, please." The eyes were steady behind the sparkling lenses. "Five-feet-ten, I should judge, including the two-inch heels. I think one sixty-three and a half was somewhat parsimonious. One sixty-seven would be closer. We shall know once the scales are tested. Are you fully prepared, Mr. Potter?"

"Prepared for what, eternity? You a Christian neck-breaker?"

"Eternity lies outside my jurisdiction. What I mean to ask is, are you resigned to the fact that your life is ended?"

"What in hell business is it of yours?"

"Carrying out a sentence is an altogether different proposition when the man is stoic. In Cheyenne last year I was forced to stand by while the condemned was dragged up the steps, struggling and pleading. It was a most unpleasant business and could have been prevented with a simple injection of morphine."

"I ain't no coward."

"I am pleased to hear that." He turned toward the sheriff. "Do you observe the custom of a last meal?"

Connaught nodded, watching Potter. "He ordered steak and eggs and a pot of coffee. He'll be eating it in the morning."

"A healthy appetite is an excellent sign. Thank you for your time, Mr. Potter."

"I'll see you in hell."

"That is your privilege, of course." The two men left the cell area. Potter spat a white gob that flattened against the thick door connecting to the office.

STONE APPROVED OF THE GALLOWS AND SCAFFOLD, A PERMANENT structure built behind the courthouse of seasoned redwood, mortised and tenoned and treated with pitch against weather. The trap swung smoothly on a pivot, released when a lever was manipulated with a foot. It fell open with a thump and the hundredweight sandbag tied at the end of the rope shot through the opening and stopped with a thud and not too much bounce.

He was less satisfied with the rope, a stiff scratchy one of new yellow hemp.

"The phrase 'to hang with a new rope' is based on a misapprehension," he told Connaught. "It needs to be stretched and lubricated until it is as supple as full-grain leather. A noose that has been properly oiled will slide swiftly through the knot and provide the snap that is required."

"I'll put Nilsen right on it."

"That won't be necessary. I brought my own."

The sheriff stroked his jaw. It was blue-shadowed and his calloused fingertips made a scratching sound like a sanding block. "Do you enjoy your work, Mr. Stone?"

"Do you enjoy yours, Sheriff Connaught?"

"Some parts. Not this one."

Stone leaned a hand against the scaffold railing and used his handkerchief to polish the toe of his shoe where the lever had scuffed it. "When a man falls four feet and swings to a rest as peacefully as that sandbag, there is no greater satisfaction."

"You mean because he's paid for his crime."

"His crime? No. I am not a follower of the Old Testament. Whatever his deed, no man deserves to choke to death slowly or have his head torn from his shoulders like a chicken. I am a simple craftsman, like the fellow who built this scaffold. The sweetest sound to me is the clean sharp crack of a neck breaking at the second cervical vertebra."

They went from there to Berger's feed store, where under the glowering eye of the bald-headed proprietor Deputy Nilsen had removed the iron balance plates from the canvas sack in which Stone had placed them before packing his trunk. Each was embossed with its poundage, clearly enough to be read easily by the meatpackers in the Chicago plant from which they'd been acquired. Stone tested the scales personally, adding and removing plates to and from the treadle as indicated and grunting when the scales proved to have been weighing three and a half pounds light, as suspected. He told the storekeeper how to make the simple adjustment, returned the plates to the sack, and went out with the sheriff while Berger was figuring out on a piece of paper how many free pounds of feed he had let walk out the door since the last time the scales were tested.

"He's forgetting how many free pounds he bought the same way," Connaught said.

"It is the German temperament. I am Bavarian on my father's side and have seen it before."

He rode in the sheriff's trap to the Czarina Catherine, where he assured Connaught everything would be in readiness by noon of the following day.

"What time should I send Nilsen around to get you?"

"Thank you, I shall walk. I prefer to stretch my muscles before work."

The lobby of the hotel was as handsome as he remembered, paneled in red oak with pink marble on the desk where he registered, but he was not yet reassured. Out there, where things changed so rapidly and no tradition was older than ten years, the reputation of an establishment depended less upon the establishment itself than upon the character of whoever owned it at present. He was a veteran of western stopping-places and knew that a clerk in a stiff white collar did not necessarily mean a clean chamber pot in the room.

He accepted his key, shaking his head at the clerk's offer to summon a bellman to carry his canvas sack of weights. He'd noted the curious expression on the young man's long, pockmarked face, concluded from it that the reason for his visit was known to the staff, and chose not to expose himself to more gawking and possibly morbid questioning on the part of additional personnel. In most situations he was content to let others go on thinking from his appearance that he belonged to one of the more common professions. He only discussed his work at his own choosing.

His room to his relief was clean and comfortable, although not large, and located an inconvenient distance from the second-floor landing; all the prime space was already reserved for those who had come in to see the execution. He did not know how he felt about performing his work in public. The farther east he traveled, the more people he encountered who thought it barbaric that a man's death should be treated as a spectacle. He understood their distaste, but he also agreed with the late Judge Parker of Arkansas that a hanging carried out in private, as if it were some shameful act, was uncomfortably close to a lynching.

Oscar Stone hated lynchings. The possible injustice of the practice did not concern him so much as the shocking ignorance of those who would tie a bit of ragged rope around a man's neck and walk a horse out from under him, leaving him to twist and jerk and turn black in the face and stick out his tongue in a ghastly parody of death. He despised the untidiness, and he felt pity for the condemned. He himself did not judge a man by his crimes. In so far as he gave the matter any thought at all, it was his belief that murderers and rapists were born missing something vital and should be no more despised for this misfortune than a man with one leg or an infant with its heart on the wrong side. It was Stone's job, once the man was judged and sentenced, to remove him as an inconvenience both to society and to the man himself. Since it took only a little more effort and a certain amount of knowledge to do the thing quickly and without physical suffering, there was no excuse for doing it any other way.

The abominable electric chair he considered a throwback to the days of inquisition and torture. To send a jolt of galvanic current through a man and boil him in his own juices was no improvement over pouring molten lead into his eyes and ears. It was hideous to witness, created an indescribable stench, and would certainly result in transferring execution from the exhibition grounds to some black dungeon, bringing to pass the worst of Parker's fears. There was no more science in the thing than scalding a hog. Any fool could throw a switch.

He removed his hat and suitcoat and unpacked his satchel, laying out his shirts, collars, socks, and underclothes in the drawers of the rosewood bureau and arranging his shaving things on top. The lid of his trunk had been left open after the sack containing his balance plates had been removed, and now he took out the oilcloth bundle that filled the rest of the space, untied and spread it out on the bed, and inspected each of the four ropes coiled in a figure-eight inside. They were as flexible as silken sashes and nearly as smooth; their braided lengths, saturated with oil, slid like satin through his hands, which were even more thickly calloused than the sheriff's from years of bending and kneading various grades of hemp, thousands of miles of Indian (the best), American (the worst), and Chinese (inconsistent, but superior when not grown in times of drought or fire or bandit raids), but sensitive to the slightest break in the fibers. He found one in the first rope he selected and frowned at it, testing and separating the frayed ends with the ball of his thumb, then laid it aside. He had used it only four times. It was becoming increasingly difficult to find the hand-plaited variety he preferred. Machine-made ropes were not equal to the sudden and repeated strain he asked of them.

At length he decided upon one he had used eight times but had been reluctant to use again for fear he was expecting too much. The fibers were intact and when he worked in a fresh application of oil they accepted it without resistance. Years of search and trial had led him to sewing-machine oil as a lubricant; it was light and consistent and had a pleasing utilitarian scent. It dyed the hemp a golden saffron that he liked to think removed some of death's harsh sting. When that was done he wiped the excess from his hands and wound the rope into the traditional thirteen coils—one for each stripe in the flag, and for each of the original colonies. He slapped the tight hard tube against his palm to make sure it held. Then he returned the rest of the ropes to the trunk, rewrapped the one he'd prepared in the oilcloth, and put it in his satchel. In his vest and shirtsleeves he sat up in the comfortable leather armchair reading his travelworn copy of Marvel's *Reveries of a Bachelor* for thirty minutes before retiring.

The next morning was sunny and mild, and he did not mind the weight of the satchel as he walked the six blocks to the courthouse, where a crowd had already gathered behind it to pick the best spots. A deputy he had not met determined his identity and opened the gate in the low picket fence that surrounded the execution grounds to let him in. The old rope had been removed from the gallows by order of the sheriff and a stepladder provided. In his shirtsleeves Stone threaded the replacement through the staples and over the pulleys, allowing the noose to dangle five feet below the gallows arm and fixing the other end with a sailor's knot to a steel ring sunk in a concrete base buried in the earth beneath the scaffold. Anders Nilsen, sweating and fidgeting in a ready-made suit and celluloid collar and stiff new Stetson, helped him secure the noose to the hundredweight sandbag, then stood back as the hangman tripped the lever. The bag dropped without bouncing. Together they hauled it back up to the platform and the deputy carried the bag inside the courthouse while Stone readjusted the noose and reset the trap.

All this was hot work, requiring concentration. Folding his coat over one arm, he descended the steps and went into a private room in the courthouse to freshen up, washing his face and hands and neck with soap and water from a basin, putting on a fresh collar and cuffs from the satchel, and combing his hair and beard. He attended to these details with the same care he brought to his ropes and balance plates, a matter of respect for the gravity of the proceedings.

While he was adjusting his necktie, a commotion took place upstairs in the cell area. Someone shouted, something struck the floor above hard enough to dislodge a powder of plaster from the ceiling onto his coat where he had hung it over the back of a chair. Then silence. He shook the coat, brushed off the rest of the dust with his hands, and was putting his arms in the sleeves when Sheriff Connaught entered, red in the face but otherwise as implacable-looking as ever.

"Potter tried killing himself," he said.

Stone scowled at his reflection in the tin mirror above the basin. "How?"

"He got hold of a two-inch spike, I don't know where. He jabbed Nilsen with it while he was putting on the manacles to take him downstairs. It was just a prick, but when Nilsen grabbed for it Potter stuck himself in the neck. He's bleeding all over. Doc Pullen's up there. He was on hand to sign the certificate after the hanging."

"I won't hang a man who is half dead. It looks improper."

"That depends on whether the doc can stop the bleeding. We'll postpone if we have to."

"I'm expected in Fort Smith next week. If it can't be done by tomorrow I'll have to come back."

Connaught went out. Stone sat down on the chair and smoked a cigar. It was a vice he customarily denied himself until his work was done, but he'd left his book in the hotel room and he hated being idle. He pressed out the stub in the bowl of a scarred smoking stand just as the sheriff returned.

"We'll go on. It was a sticking-plaster fix. He missed the artery."

"Good."

THE EXECUTION TOOK PLACE TWENTY MINUTES BEHIND SCHED-ule. Stone was standing on the platform, listening to the leather-throated vendor hawking his pretzels among the crowd, when the back door opened and Sheriff Connaught came out carrying a shot-gun. A fat minister followed in a dusty coat reading from a Bible—*Yea, though I walk*—and behind him clanked the prisoner with man-acles on his wrists and ankles, braced by Anders Nilsen and another deputy. Potter appeared calmer than Nilsen, who had a bandage wound around his left wrist. Dr. Pullen, small and sallow, with glossy handlebars like a bartender's, brought up the rear carrying his black bag.

Potter had nothing to say. As Stone slipped the noose over his head, he saw his own reflection in the man's eyes, twin death masks in that familiar glaze of defiance and hate. He placed the coils be-neath the left ear, noting with satisfaction that the rope did not abrade the circle of white plaster pasted to the tender flesh under the jaw. He removed the black cotton hood from the side pocket of his coat and slid it over Potter's head. He no longer tried to imagine the blackness inside. It billowed in and out with the man's quickening breath—the first sign of fear he had shown, quite natural.

He adjusted the coils one last time—meaninglessly, an old habit—then stepped back off the trap, placed his foot beside the lever, and looked at the sheriff. Connaught hesitated. His throat worked once. Then he lowered his head a tenth of an inch. Stone kicked the lever. The hinge squeaked, the trap thumped. The black hood dropped out of his vision. The rope caught with a quivering twang, a gentle bass note heard only by Stone, drowned out for all others by a bang like a pistol report and under it the splintering crackle at the second cervical vertebra. The rope creaked, rotating a half turn to the left.

The crowd exhaled all at once. A woman whimpered. Another voice whispered a hoarse prayer.

Dr. Pullen waited below the scaffold while the body was lowered to the ground and the noose was removed. Through the square opening Stone watched as he bent over the prisoner, feeling for a pulse. The doctor straightened, looked down at his open pocket watch, and pronounced death at 12:21 *post meridian*. Stone shook Connaught's hand and walked down the steps while Nilsen and the other deputy lifted Morse Potter's body into the white pine coffin waiting on the ground, bound for a nearby buckboard and then Potter's Field. He would return later for his rope.

For luncheon he ordered a very large salad with bread and a glass of port. He never ate breakfast the day of a hanging and was ravenous. Although the restaurant was filled with people talking about the thing they'd witnessed, he had a table to himself. No one came to share it. When his salad came, the leaves white and crisp and beaded with moisture in a great polished wooden bowl, he inspected it carefully, then with a frown removed a shred of chicken with his fork and laid it on the edge of his bread plate. He hadn't eaten meat in twenty-three years.

The Purification of Jim Barnes

TROY D. SMITH

It takes more than a century of eastern-style civilization and a hellish war to destroy the essential Indianness in a man. Troy D. Smith offers a contemporary story of ancient beliefs, modern horrors, hope, and salvation.

JIM BARNES STEPPED OFF THE
Freedom Bird and walked into the World. Uncle Ray stood waiting
for him, eyes squinting into the Arizona sun and a cigarette dangling
from his lips.

"Glad you made it," Uncle Ray said, and Jim nodded.

Other words had begun to form in Ray's throat, but they could
not make the journey through his lips and into the air. He stared
uncertainly at Jim, and Jim could read the confusion in his uncle's
face. Uncle Ray did not recognize him, not entirely—he sensed that
the nephew he had helped raise was different, somehow. Jim had
what grunts called the "thousand-yard stare." His eyes focused into
the distance, into the future—not because it held out promise of
better things, but simply because it was not the present.

Through all those maddened months in the Vietnam jungles,
Jim's gaze had been fixed on the moment he was living now. Riding
that Freedom Bird across the ocean to a magical place called Home.
Now that it was really here his eyes had trouble focusing on it. All
his brothers-in-arms had their souls anchored to the same dream of
course, marking out the days until they were rotated out—not many
of them called an Indian reservation home, though. The Pimas and
Maricopas had been settled on one for generations. The place wasn't
much to look at, but there were no snipers or land mines there so
it seemed like a little piece of paradise.

The ride back to the reservation was a quiet one. Maybe Uncle
Ray was thinking about his own brother, who had never had a
homecoming. Jim Barnes Senior was instead rotated to Kingdom
Come, eighteen years ago in Korea—the younger Jim sometimes

imagined he could see the shadow of his father's ghost flitting through the Asian jungles.

He also remembered seeing another ghost when he was a child. It was a ghost that walked and drew breath and sought to cloud its eyes with whiskey. His name had been Ira—he was not a Maricopa like Jim, but a member of the Pima tribe which was so closely associated with Jim's people that they were almost as one. Ira was a big war hero. He had been a Mean Marine, and the whole world had seen the photo of him helping raise the flag on Iwo Jima.

Ira had not adjusted to life back in the States. He had fallen apart, and looking back Jim realized that Ira had the Stare too.

"How's Grandpa?" Jim said after a while.

"Same as always," Uncle Ray said. "Still goes around cussing at the young folks in general for not sticking with tradition."

Jim nodded. If Grandpa had his way, they would all be wearing breechcloths and bone breastplates.

Nothing more was said for the rest of the trip, and very little was thought—both men's minds were fuzzy and unfocused, their eyes on the flowing road.

The rest of Jim's homecoming was an extension of the automobile ride. Fuzzy and unfocused conversations, stilted words with family and friends who smiled with their teeth but whose eyes showed quiet panic. Panic and grief—Jim saw the realization in them that the Jim Barnes they knew was dead, had died in some foreign jungle.

He didn't see Grandpa during all that time. Grandpa was off in the desert somewhere, the neighbors said. Probably chasing a vision or a dream, or maybe just getting drunk. The old man was going to die in that desert someday, and no one would know about it until they tripped over his bones.

Jim felt his flesh slipping away like a snakeskin. He wasn't aware of the exact moment he became a walking ghost—he simply woke up one morning and saw that he was one, just like old Ira.

Others, even Billy Russell, saw him not as a ghost but as a demon. Especially after that night at the bar. Billy had been Jim's best friend since childhood, and was more than happy to accompany the vet on a drinking binge. Billy did not need the excuse of a war to drown his spirit in spirits stronger than him. Jim had started drinking soon after he returned, to silence the voices—he continued drinking to awaken them.

Jim had been stumbling, half drunk, when he jostled the arm of a man at the pool table. The man missed his shot—he spun and cursed, waving his cue at Jim, his threat obvious.

Jim's hand had snaked out and jerked the stick away, and he broke it in half over his knee. Then, with frightening speed, his right hand clamped tightly around the man's throat. With the other end he pressed the sharp broken end of the pool cue against the man's jugular. Jim backed him up against the wall, and the stick pressed tighter and tighter—the man made an ugly strangling noise.

Billy was frightened not so much by his friend's actions as by his expression. There was no rage in Jim's face. He was calm—as if this were the sort of thing one did every day.

"Let him go, Jim, you're killing him!" Billy said. Jim did not respond.

Billy grabbed his friend's arm—Jim's neck turned, so he could face his friend, and Billy felt a chill. He knew then that Jim could easily kill him, too. Could, and perhaps would.

Instead Jim let the whimpering man drop to the floor.

"What on earth is wrong with you?" Billy demanded.

"Killing is easy," Jim said. "Easier than most folks think." Living is hard, one of the voices said. Jim ignored the voices, like he had learned to ignore the rain which soaks your head in the jungle.

Jim kept on drinking. He woke up in jail, God knows how long later—the other inmates stared at him, sleepy and resentful, and he knew he had kept them up with his screams. Good. Let them hear the bullets cutting through the trees. Let them smell the blood for a while.

He was woken by a deputy, who informed him that someone

had made bail. Jim collected his belongings and walked outside to find his grandfather waiting for him.

"Thanks," Jim said as they walked to the old man's ancient Ford.

"It's time you had a vision," the old man said, not breaking stride or turning to look at Jim.

"I have more visions than I can shake a stick at, Grandpa."

"Nightmares," Grandpa corrected him. "Nightmares come from within. Visions come from beyond." The old man nodded. "Time you had one."

Jim slid onto the torn leather seat. He didn't bother to speak— he knew it would do him no good.

They drove out of town—into the desert. Grandpa lit a cigarette and puffed at it. He did not offer Jim one. Jim wished the old man had not torn the radio out of his car; it had turned into a very boring trip. Grandpa was apparently selective about which of the white man's "modern" items to reject: cars and cigarettes were okay, radios were not.

"Where the hell are we going?" Jim said.

"You'll see."

Jim sighed. "How'd you know I was in jail?"

"I been keepin' my eye on you, son. I knew how it would be."

Jim bristled, wondering what his grandfather was implying. The old man noticed, and nodded.

"I know what you're thinking," Jim's grandfather said. "You're thinking 'He don't know shit about me.' Well, you're wrong. You think you're the only man this ever happened to? Men have been going to wars forever, and coming back from them, too. When I came home from the first World War, I stayed drunk for a month."

"Yeah, yeah," Jim mumbled. "But then you pulled yourself up by the bootstraps and got on with life, by the sheer power of your Indian will."

"Hell no." He shifted in his seat, to look at his grandson. "When does the war end, Jim?"

Jim was confused. "What do you mean?"

"When does the war end?"

"That's what I'd like to know. Seems like it'll never end, not for some people."

"It ends when you are purified."

Jim shrugged. He didn't like playing word games.

"Did you take any scalps, Jim?"

Jim laughed at the unexpected comment. "Yeah Grandpa—I took scalps and counted coup. I also did rain dances, and they paid me in wampum."

Jim really did try to scalp a dead VC once. He was high at the time. The other grunts had expected it of him, since he was an Indian—he made a botched and bloody job of it.

"I bet you took something off the enemy at some time," Grandpa said. "As a souvenir."

Jim fished in his pocket and took out a cigarette lighter.

"Found this on a dead gook," he said. "It caught my eye. He probably took it off one of our guys, some poor stupid poge who wandered into the bad brush by accident."

The old man held out his hand. "Let me see it."

Jim handed it over to his grandfather and watched him examine it. It wasn't much of a lighter, really. Jim did not know why he kept it. Perhaps he kept it as a reminder that it was he who lived, not its previous owner. Grandpa handed it back, handling it with a strange sort of respect.

"We're here," the old man said, and the Ford rolled to a stop outside a weatherbeaten shack. It was probably the only structure for miles around, unless you wanted to count the tiny brush hut that stood forty yards away from it.

Jim stepped out of the car. He chuckled and waved his arms expansively. "So—this is what you're calling home nowadays, huh?"

"Don't laugh. See that hut over there?"

Jim nodded.

"That's what *you're* going to be calling home for a while."

"I beg your pardon?"

"Trust me," Grandpa said with a smile. It was a warm smile. "I know what you need."

"I need—a hut?"

Grandpa started walking around the hut, and Jim followed—knowing he would regret it.

"Our people have always been warriors," Grandpa said.

"Oh yes," said Jim. "We struggled against the Great White Father." The old man ignored his sarcasm.

"Against the whites, yes, but also against other Indians. Whoever pissed us off, really. And in all that fighting, we learned something."

"What?"

"We learned that a man can't come home from battle and slide right into a life of peace, there has to be a transition. The blood must be washed away."

"I'm betting that's where the hut comes in."

"It is the site of the purification ceremony. You have shed blood, and served with honor—but that part of your life is over. It's time to journey to another life—the life of peace."

"This doesn't involve self-mutilation, does it? I could never get into self-mutilation."

"Shut up and get in the hut."

"How long does this jazz take?"

"Sixteen days."

Jim's jaw dropped. "Sixteen days? Are you crazy? I can't sit in your stupid hut for sixteen days!"

Grandpa paused. "Excuse me," he said. "Do you have a job to go to, or a prior engagement, or a life of some sort I don't know about?"

Jim reflected. "You have a point there."

"Then get in the damn hut."

They walked the remaining distance to the tiny structure. Jim bent over and peered at the darkness inside. It was a very spartan setup—he had endured far worse discomfort, of course, in muddy jungles. But he had no choice then. He hesitated at the low doorway, uncertain yet drawn somehow. The ramshackle hut had an odd feel to it, a peculiar energy and presence—holy, Jim realized, then recognized the silliness of such a thought.

Grandpa was staring at Jim as if he knew his thoughts. The old man nodded, a movement so slight Jim almost missed it.

"You must sit facing west," Grandpa said. "You must fast all day—at night I will bring you food and water."

"But not much, I'll bet." Jim's words, though intended to be sarcastic, had lost their earlier bite. He was entranced by the darkness of the hut, and his tone trailed off in distraction.

"You will meditate—reflect upon your deeds—and if you are fortunate, a vision will come to you before the ritual is finished.

"Wear this." He dug something out of his pocket. It was a small leather pouch, strung onto a rawhide thing. He placed it around Jim's neck.

"Give me the lighter," Grandpa said—when Jim gave it, the old man placed it in the pouch. "This is your trophy from the enemy. In the old days it would've been a scalp—we gotta improvise a little on that one."

The old man gestured to the doorway. "It begins now," he said.

"That's it?" Jim asked. "I just go in and sit down—you don't shake a gourd rattle or something?"

"Gourd rattle," Grandpa mumbled. "What do I look like, a lunatic?" He chuckled, then casually turned his back and walked away. The old man did not even pause to look back before he entered his own shack.

Jim sighed and crawled into the hut. The darkness wrapped itself around him. He sat silent, waiting. He had sat motionless for hours on end before, never flinching a muscle, in the jungle—but today he had no idea what he was waiting for. He did not even know why he had agreed to his grandfather's ridiculous ritual.

Maybe it was the same reason he had volunteered to go to war. The same reason so many of his tribesmen, and members of other Indian tribes, had volunteered. The number of young Indian men slogging their way through Vietnam was proportionately much higher than their white counterparts. It seemed that every company had Indian soldiers. Invariably the other grunts would call these men Chief, or Geronimo. Or Tonto. Or something equally stupid. And they expected each Indian soldier to be a natural wizard of wood-craft, able to track their way flawlessly through the jungle, able to fight more fiercely—because they were Indians.

It was not true, of course, but many of the Indian soldiers wanted it to be. That's why they were there, really—trying to re-connect with the warrior traditions of their ancestors. Trying to erase the memory of the drunken generations which came between their ancestors and them. Trying, through combat, to reclaim the freedom and the pride.

And so Jim Barnes sat, in a dark, cramped hut. He sat and let his mind go numb, in an exercise which seemed foolish to his ra-tional mind, as it would to most civilized men's—in a hope, dimly felt and never vocalized, that the gamble would pay off and the magic would work, and draw his spirit to a home it had never known.

The invincible Indian brave—what fools those white soldiers from Indiana and Pennsylvania were to believe in such a myth. And what fools the Indian soldiers themselves were, to let themselves be sucked into it.

Private Gruder found out the hard way. Gruder had been eigh-teen years old, fresh out of school, a red-faced Iowa farm boy who still let the fear show. He had thought, naively, that because his more experienced comrades showed no fear, they felt none. And he at-tached himself to Jim Barnes, idolizing him like a kid brother. It was clear what Gruder was thinking—stick with the Indian and you'll be all right.

Jim savored it at first. He played the part of the mean green killing machine with the red skin and the black heart. But then he recognized the weight that was being placed on his shoulders, and he began to worry.

"Quit followin' me so damn close," he told Gruder one day when they were on patrol.

Gruder laughed. "I ain't gonna jump your bones from behind, Jim—you're too damn ugly. There's plenty of apes around who are more appealing."

Jim shook his head. "I'm hurt," he said.

Gruder was laughing, but not in his eyes—his eyes were floating in a sea of shamed fear. He took another step forward, bumping into Jim. Jim made a playful half swing at him.

"Quit crowdin' me, poge, you're makin' me nervous. You don't want to make me nervous."

Gruder nodded. "Don't want to make you nervous."

"Quit goofin' off up there," Private Stevens whispered from a few feet behind them. "I don't like standin' still in this friggin' jungle."

Jim picked up the pace a bit, his eyes scanning the foliage looking for any hint of a booby trap.

"You can crawl out of my ass now, Gruder. The trail is clear for the next few feet anyways."

Gruder chuckled, his relief evident. "Your word is good enough for me, Chief." Jim could sense his friend's body relaxing behind him, some of the pressure hissing out like air being let out of a tire. Jim kept walking forward. Gruder dropped several paces behind, Stevens a good distance behind the farm boy, as usual.

"We make a good team, Chief," Gruder said. "Like the Lone Ranger and Tonto, huh?"

"Better than Red Ryder and Little Beaver, I guess," Jim said, as he took one more step into the jungle—and felt the tension of the taut wire against his foot. He had just enough time, before the explosion, for a thought to form in his mind: I was careless, and I am going to die.

But Jim Barnes did not die. The mine was not directly beneath his feet—it was about four yards behind him.

Jim had seen his grandfather castrate a pig once, years before—he remembered the squeal the animal let out, so high in pitch that it tortured a man's ears. Gruder made that same noise, and it lasted forever. It bounced off the trees, vibrating the bones of every man in the platoon. It drowned out the echoes of the blast.

Jim had whirled around. Blood spattered him as he rocked on his heels, then fell to the ground—hot blood—and something wet slapped onto his face. Jim absently brushed it off—it was part of an intestine.

Gruder lay about five feet from Jim. The top half was Gruder, anyway—the bottom part was a mass of smoking red pulp. Gruder's jaw worked, silently now, up and down—up and down. His eyes were nearly popped from their sockets as they stared at Jim. The eyes pleaded, and accused, and died.

But before they died, the Indian knew, they had seen the truth in Jim Barnes's face. Jim had screwed up, and his buddy had been blown to bloody hell—his legs and his manhood smeared across the tree trunks—and as Jim fought to keep from retching, he felt his face flush for just a second with a wild joy.

Someone else was dead. Not him. Someone else. Jim wanted to laugh, and to scream in terror, but all he could do was climb numbly to his feet.

The other guys kept a much greater distance behind him after that. Jim was alone in the jungle. Despite the brotherhood and the camaraderie, he suddenly realized, they were all alone in the jungle, and always had been. Each of them carried his own private universe around with him, in his boots, a universe that would end the second he died. So screw everything else.

JIM BARNES WAS TREMBLING. HE SENSED SOMEONE IN THE DOORway. It was his grandfather.

The old man set a tin tray inside the hut. Jim did not speak, or even look up. He felt his grandfather watching him for several minutes. Watching him—seeing him. Then the old man trudged off. Jim did not know when sleep came, or if sleep came. He did not remember eating the food or drinking the water, but the next morning it was gone and Grandfather took the tray away. Time had become an elusive thing—something that was there but you could not quite put your finger on it.

Jim Barnes dreamed.

. . .

IT WAS ON THE SIXTH DAY OF HIS VIGIL IN THE HUT THAT PRIVATE
Stevens came. Like with Grandpa, Jim did not see the man approach
him—he just suddenly sensed, in the darkness, that Stevens was
there. Jim smelled the smoke from the doobie, accepted it when
Stevens passed it to him—he inhaled deeply. Just as he sensed Stevens, he could sense the heat of the jungle pressing in on him.

"Know what I miss, man?" Stevens was saying.

"What?"

"I miss TV. I miss *Andy Griffith*. And *Leave It to Beaver* reruns."

"Beaver Cleaver is probably out here with us somewhere, getting
his ass shot off. I heard he was."

"And Gilligan, man," Stevens continued, his eyes glazed but
good. "If we get wasted in this damn jungle, we won't never find
out if Gilligan ever gets off that friggin' island."

They shared another joint. Jim was passing it back when he
heard the rifle shot, saw Stevens slump back against the tree, heard
the sigh of life as it escaped through the other man's softly fluttering
lips.

Jim dropped to the ground and clutched his M-16. As if his M-
16 could save him from Victor Charlie, when Victor Charlie was
invisible. The very darkness of the night was a sniper, pumping bullets into Jim Barnes's soul. Dawn broke, eventually, and Jim crawled
away.

Gilligan will never go home. Everyone knows that.

GRANDPA FLUTTERED IN AND OUT OF THE PERIPHERY OF JIM'S
vision like a bird—never alighting, never slowing down. He came
and went many times. The days blended together like newsprint in
the rain.

Like it had rained that day in the village. Jim and his fellow
grunts had stood in the bush, just out of sight of the gooks, their

ears ringing with the sound of water pelting their helmets. The villagers went on about their business as usual, pretending they were unaware of the soldiers who watched them from silent hiding. There was no doubt that the sniper had run to this village, and that this village was probably his home. And that he was in there, maybe taking aim that very second at Jim Barnes or some other grunt.

Jim did not reflect on the ironies that day. That would come later. Jim did not think at all that day, he *felt*. He felt the adrenaline surge in his veins, knowing a firefight could begin any moment. He felt the anxiety and frustration of months in the jungle come to a boiling point—felt grief and rage at the loss of Gruder and Stevens and a dozen other friends, the rage never vented because the enemy always disappeared into the steaming trees rather than stand and fight.

He would dwell on the ironies later, though, no doubt about that. He would wonder if the feelings he had then were the same as those experienced by the white cavalrymen who made war on his people a century earlier. Substitute the thatch huts for tipis, after all, and the story became the same.

Jim would think back and remember herding the gooks into the center of their village. *Gooks*—like *redskins*—a dehumanizing term. He would remember the thrill he felt as he watched their shacks burn—because they were the enemy, and he hated them—as well as the shame, when he saw the tear-streaked face of a young girl, no more than thirteen.

He remembered the scream which echoed inside his head, never let out into the hot air, when in the corner of his eye he saw a movement and realized that one of the gooks had a gun. The air sizzled and popped and burned as a dozen rifles opened up on the crowd—tearing the flesh, not just of the armed villager, but of them all. They tried to run, but there was no time. The soldiers were screaming and shooting, the villagers were screaming and dying. When no more of the gooks were moving Jim started shooting the damn livestock—he could not stop squeezing the trigger.

Then he saw the girl's face again. Looking up at him, dead. He would never know if it was his own bullets which had ripped her torso apart.

There was no sound now but the crackling of the flames. One of the soldiers spoke.

"Man, these are some seriously dead friggin' gooks. These are by God confirmed kills for General Westmoreland to brag about on the evening news." The man giggled nervously, but no one else was laughing.

Like every man there, Jim Barnes wished he could have those villagers back again, alive, laughing and crying and being human. And like every man there, another part of him wished he could keep on killing them.

Jim knelt beside the dead sniper. It was a skinny bastard, barely in his teens. Jim searched the boy's pockets, but found nothing except a cheap cigarette lighter.

He choked on the smoke of the burning village.

NOW HE WAS CHOKING ON WATER. GRANDPA HELD THE CUP TO his lips, pouring it down his throat, holding him as he coughed.

NOW HE WAS CHOKING ON BLOOD. HE WAS IN A RIVER OF BLOOD, and the river flowed through a jungle. Jim was drowning. His clothes and skin were stained red.

A crow sat perched on a tree on shore. It croaked at him, fluttering its wings.

"Leave me alone," Jim said, but the bird stared at him—into his soul. Jim raised himself out of the blood—felt it pouring off him, wondering whose it was—and clambered onto the riverbank. He sank to his knees, then fell on his face. The crow was still there, but the jungle had turned into a desert. Then the desert became an ocean, its water fresh and pure and clean. . . .

. . .

JIM BARNES REALIZED THAT HE WAS IN A BATHTUB IN HIS GRAND-father's house. He did not remember taking off his clothes—for that matter, he did not remember coming here from the war hut.

"What am I doing here?" he mumbled.

"The sixteen days is over," Grandpa said. "Now you are washing off the sweat and the stink. So that you can walk outside, into the daylight, smelling fresh and clean—for the final ritual."

JIM STOOD BENEATH THE BRIGHT SUN, SQUINTING. GRANDPA'S backyard—or what passed for one—was crowded with people from the reservation. Most were older folks, but there were quite a few younger ones, too. Jim's uncle Ray was there.

Grandpa stood before a large clay pot. He was holding the cig-arette lighter up in the air.

"This is a trophy of war," he announced to the crowd. "My grandson is a warrior. I am the Keeper of Scalps." He plunged his hand into the pot and withdrew a leathery, hairy object.

"This is the scalp I took off a German in France, in 1918," Grandpa said. "I killed another German the same day, but the son of a bitch was bald. Here too is the scalp my great-grandfather took from an Apache. In here are all the trophies our people have taken, for generations." He dropped the lighter into the pot, along with the scalp he had held. Grandpa sank to his knees, and many of the older men began to chant.

After several minutes, Grandpa held up a hand. "I must listen," he said, and the chanting stopped. The old man cocked his head, as if he were trying to discern something in the rustling of the wind.

"I hear laughter," he said at last, and turned his gaze to Jim. "This means our people will still know joy."

The old man stood up stiffly and walked over to his grandson—he placed his hands on Jim's shoulders.

"You are part of this community, Jim," Grandpa said. "Your soul is clean. Your past is dead, and your future is with us."

Slowly, one by one, the onlookers approached Jim Barnes and embraced him. He felt hot tears on his skin, and knew that only some of them were his own. His grandfather looked on, and smiled.

Jim felt freedom fluttering in his chest like the wings of the crow. He reached down for the rage, but at the moment it was only a memory. The thousand-yard stare was gone as well; he could see only the faces of his neighbors.

Jim Barnes had come home.

Mother George, Midwife

PATTI SHERLOCK

Epistolary fiction—stories told through journal entries and letters—can boast of a long tradition going back to Daniel Defoe's *A Journal of the Plague Year*. With meticulous attention to language and period detail, Patti Sherlock employs the form to its best advantage. If you don't know this story's historical inspiration, you will have a hard time anticipating the ending.

From Effie McDermott, twenty-eight-year-old wife of Hiram McDermott, farmer, Idaho Territory, 1889:

I would have died without her help.

I believe that. The labor went fine and I wasn't in bad pain until the baby's head started to come out. Then things went haywire and I wanted to give up and die from the misery. But that woman stayed close beside me, sponging my face and speaking words of encouragement even when I was screaming like a crazy woman.

It took two hours for the baby's head to get free, and she didn't leave my side. She'd wipe my face and whisper, "Effie, have courage. Everybody's real proud of you." That wasn't exactly true, because Hiram had left the house after the first couple screams and didn't come back until after midnight. Even Mama had to leave a couple times and walk down by the river to get herself calmed down. But Mother George knew how to say the right thing, and it inspired me to believe that everyone thought I was brave.

When she wasn't holding my hand, she was trying to turn Robert. Even though her hands are large, she's gentle as a deer, and she kept working to ease that baby out. I figure Robert and I neither one would have made it without her patience.

There's hardly a person around here who cares that she's Negro. Or part Negro. No one knows for sure about her background because she doesn't talk about it. I've probably pried more than anyone; I talk plainer to her than I do to my sister Lucy. Lucy's got a tendency to take everything I say to Mama, and then Mama gives me a lecture about how I should appreciate Hiram and my children, how we are getting a place put together that we can be proud of. So I've stopped talking to Mama and Lucy, but I talk to Mother George.

One time I asked her, "Don't you want more than this life here offers?" I was talking about pretty things and pretty houses. I went to Denver once on the train, and oh, my, the pretty big houses there and the pretty dresses on the women. Even the horses glisten.

After spring breakup, we have dances once a month until late fall. Hiram thinks we ought not to go; we're Methodist and don't dance. But most of our neighbors dance, because Mormons don't think dancing is sinful. Hiram says, "They don't think plural marriage is wrong, either." But I persuaded him into going.

No one dresses very fancy for the dances. Well, the unmarried girls make pretty dresses for themselves, but once you're married and have children, you don't have time to sew for yourself.

Mother George sews beautiful clothes and she looks so elegant in them. She buys watered silk and lace trim and pearl buttons and makes herself the most lovely dresses. I don't know how she finds the time, working her own place like she does. I said to her, "Don't you wish you had a better place to wear those pretty dresses than the schoolhouse?"

She looked at me, out of those big, warm eyes, and didn't say anything. I said, "Do you remember how it was when you were a girl, how you wanted to grow up and do exciting things and go wonderful places? And here we are in this forsaken place, working like slaves."

Her face didn't have any expression at all. I felt bad I'd been so careless. I suppose the word *slave* has a meaning to her that I can't comprehend. I forget that some people have terrible hard things in their background and Mother George is probably one of them. I've read how it was down there for the coloreds, the horrible things that happened, and how mistreated they were.

If she doesn't understand what I'm longing for, though, she never lets on. She listens better than anyone. I suppose that's why she went into the kind of work she does. Because she has a big heart.

One time I asked her if she knew a way to stop the babies from coming. I know that's a sin, but I've got four healthy ones and I wouldn't mind stopping there. Go up to the Ozone Cemetery and count how many women we've lost in this valley in the past ten years, and you can understand why I want to quit now. Mama George didn't look shocked, and I could tell by her expression that she did know a way.

I kept deviling her until she told me. It's been three years now and no babies. Hiram comments on it, but I'd never tell him what I'm doing because he'd feel tricked. I couldn't give Mother George away, either. Hiram would blame her more than me, because she's a darkie.

From Sister Lucretia Sutton, plural wife of Isaiah Sutton, blacksmith:

Black crows with black crows and white crows with white crows, that's what I've always said. I don't know why she wants to be here with us and not with her own kind. One other family of nigras is here, but they're fifteen miles away, and in winter I don't think she gets together with them at all.

I'm not ashamed of my views. The darkies are the ones who ought to be ashamed. Our Prophet has told us that the dark races were cursed, and I think we can see that Heavenly Father has not favored them.

At a dance once, Madame George asked me how I liked being a plural wife. Can you imagine her saying that? I gave her a cold look, and I hope she realized how rude she'd been. The truth is, I never intended to be a second wife, and it has its difficulties. But the Church was entrusted with the principle, as well as the restored gospel, and I follow it. I don't think an unmarried woman who isn't even white needs to look down her nose at me.

But don't think it's just the color of her skin that troubles me. She's odd in other ways. My mother knew something about coloreds and their rites and ceremonies, and she said they're in league with Satan. People are starting to depend on Madame George and her herbs, but I think we ought to trust our own doctors or even Sister Lindquist, who knows something about healing plants and also is a good Christian.

My daughter Libby gets annoyed at me and says when she and Tom have a baby she will have Madame George in, like her friend Eva did. I told her, and I meant it, "I don't want that woman touching my grandchild. Honor your mother, Libby," I told her, "and go stay in town at the maternity home when your time comes, and have a clean, white doctor."

From Wendall Ritchie, farmer and teamster:

She knows how I feel about her, even if I haven't put it in so many words. I stop and visit at her place a couple times a week, and at the dances I end up talking with her most of the night.

At the last one, I asked her to dance with me. She shook her head and looked flustered. I figure she's embarrassed about her size. I've noticed, though, a big woman can be lighter on her feet than a small one.

Oh, you think I should worry about what people would say? Well nobody says anything to Randall Anderson, who's got himself a Flathead wife. I think Georgia may be part Indian, too, because of the shape of her face, and she's not as dark as most Negroes I've seen. Well, no, I haven't seen many, hardly any at all. But the Bixby family, they're black as obsidian. Georgia's skin is the color of fresh-tanned leather and her hair don't kink much. She couldn't wrap it around her head in that big braid if it did.

I wonder if she even knows what she is. I asked her once, when we were walkin' up by the stream, what her first name was. She gave me the funniest look. I said, "I feel kinda odd callin' you Mother George or Madame George, and us the same age. You must have a first name, and that's what I'd like to use." She said, "I don't know." I said, "You don't know your first name?" She said, "My family got all split up. But you could call me Georgia, if you like." So that's what I do.

You thought my mother wouldn't like it? Mama doesn't mind. I've talked to her about it. Mama respects hard work, and she looks at what that woman has put together for herself and the way she's available to the women in this valley, and she figures Georgia's got to be a fine person no matter what color she is. I've only ever heard of one other woman around here provin' up on a place all by herself; most women have filed on behalf of their brothers and fathers.

Mama did say, "Wendall, I wonder if your children would feel welcome. Or if it'd be hard for them."

I said, "Would you welcome them?" She said, "I'd love them if they came out striped." I said, "Maybe others would feel that way, too."

Look at Hiram's wife. She thinks awful high of Georgia. She puts her babies in the wagon and rides up to visit with her once a week.

You may be right that marrying her would upset some people. But I don't think anyone would try to enforce that law that says it's illegal to cohabitate with someone who ain't white. If they did enforce it, we'd have a lot of squaw men settin' around in the territorial prison. Besides, with us getting statehood, a lot of things might change.

Yessir, if I was to guess, I'd say marriage is where it's headin'. I can't think of no one I admire more than her.

I do figger she likes me, too. I ain't had a lot of experience with women, but you remember Annie Talbot? A gentleman knows when not to say much, but her and I were pretty stuck on each other before her daddy married her off as second wife to old LaVar Pierce who's got the bank. So I know a little about how a woman looks at a man she cares for. Georgia looked at me just that way when I forced her into dancin' with me. Smellin' all pretty of lavender, she put her arm around my neck and held herself tight against me. There is for certain somethin' between us. Them brown eyes told me that.

From Bobby McDermott, nine years old, son of Effie and Hiram McDermott:

Papa teases me that I got a Negro mammy. Mother George helped me be born, and Mama says neither of us would have made it without her. Maybe that's why she likes me so good. She's nice to my sister and brothers, and to Abe Olsen and his sisters, too, but I spend the most time with her. Me and my brothers and sister go up to visit her when Mama goes, but these past few months, Mama has let me ride up there by myself. No matter what Mama George is doin,' she's pleased to see me come. I've hammered boards on her barn and helped her string barbed wire and poured wax on top of jelly. She says, "Bobby, I don't know how you got so talented." I asked her once if she didn't want to have children of her own, and she said, "But what if they weren't as helpful as you? Then I'd be disappointed."

For Christmas, she made me a flute out of willow and she's been teaching me to play it. She says I got a knack for it, and even Papa likes to hear me play.

He doesn't like me going up there so much. Says if I got time to squander, I ought to spend it with my own brothers and sister. But I get my chores done fast on the days I'm going visiting, and he likes that part.

From Effie McDermott, 1890:

Madame George is dead. When I heard the news, I felt like someone had shoved a hot poker in my side.

Last night, I got on my knees to Hiram and asked for forgiveness. I told him about using that plant to keep the babies from coming. He got in a fury and slapped me, but only twice. Said he had a mind to send me back to my mother, but I pleaded and said I never would do anything like it again, ever, and as God is my witness, I won't.

He didn't blame Mother George, said I was the one who should have known better. He said he was glad I wouldn't be running off there anymore, that I'd spent too much time at her place when I had work to do at home. Everybody is having a hissy fit about the rumor, but Hiram didn't take on about that much. He's just relieved I'll be home more.

There comes a time in a woman's life when she looks at her life and the errors she's made, and yearns to start over. The Bible is full of stories of how people saw their mistakes and corrected themselves and that's what you're going to see in me. I'm going to stop wanting things I can't have, I'm going to be grateful for the good husband I've been given, and I'm going to avoid people who encourage my weaknesses.

Mama and Lucy are planting a windbreak at Lucy's place and I'm going to help them. Hiram wants to see me spend more time with my mother and sister.

I don't know if I'll go to the dances anymore. One way a person can keep away the wickedness of this world is to not succumb to worldliness oneself.

From Sister Sutton:

I told Lydia, "What did I say about her being peculiar? Just thank Heavenly Father this came to light before you got in a family way." Isaiah said the undertaker told him it was heart failure, but I'm inclined to think the Lord had a hand in it. A person can't scorn God's laws without paying a price. And a person can't deceive the People of God without incurring God's wrath.

I don't think there will be a funeral. Some of us are packing up to move, because those who believe in plural marriage can't vote now that Idaho is a state. Isaiah wants to leave. Second time in his life he's moved because of persecution.

But that's not why there won't be much of a funeral. Tell me, who would go to it, in view of everything?

From Wendall Ritchie:

I don't know what to think. I don't. I'm stunned, and I think it'll take me a while to get over it.

Mama came down last night and said, "There's more peculiar things happen in this world than we can ever be prepared for." And she's right.

Mama said, "Don't let this take away from the pleasant memories."

I said, "Mama! How can you say that? They're not pleasant memories anymore." And she said, "We can't know what kind of heartache another person has. Mother George cleared a parcel of land and put up a neat little place with hardly any help at all. Never once in ten years did she turn down a woman who was birthing and needed help. That's what I'm going to remember, when everyone else is sniffin' around this scandal like a pack of wolves."

I can't feel like she does, though. I just don't know what I'll feel when I get down the road a ways.

But I'd appreciate it if you wouldn't bring up what I told you about her and me at the dance. Don't bring it up at all.

From Bobby McDermott:

I don't see how she coulda been a man. Benjamin's daddy is the undertaker and the undertaker gets to see people without no clothes. Benjamin says all those years she was just pretending to be a woman. But I don't believe it. I used to sit on her lap and when she hugged me, she had tits. Not as big as Aunt Lucy's, but big.

Boar hogs have tits, but they never do grow out like a sow's. I don't think she coulda been a man and had tits that had grown out.

There's been so much whispering, I don't know what they're gonna do about a funeral. I like funerals because of all the food, but that's not the reason I want to go to hers. I thought I might could slip the flute into the box with her so she could be buried with it. Wherever she's gone to, I'd like her to be able to play it and think of me. I'd never play that flute again, 'cause it would make me too sad and lonesome.

NOTE: In Bonneville County, Idaho, during the homesteading era, a midwife called Mother George or Madame George acted as a nurse, unofficial doctor, and good neighbor, while also running a ranch of her own. Women especially appreciated the care she gave them when they were having babies.

Mother George was known for her large hands. She was such a big woman, she wore men's shoes. When she was being readied for burial, her secret came to light.

Dove's Song

RANDY LEE EICKHOFF

Readers of *The Fourth Horseman*, Randy Lee Eickhoff's epic novel based on the life of Doc Holliday, know that he has the ability to inhabit the skin of another human being as if he were born inside it. We offer in evidence this story of immense individual courage.

NOW SHE WALKED IN THE BRIGHT
frozen winter morning with a buckskin band holding her long white
hair back away from her tan, seamed face. Her skin had its own
pattern of branching wrinkles while two knobs of color showed high
on her cheekbones, a dull red burning under the tan. She walked
slowly through the deep snow in the shadows of the birch trees,
moving a little from side to side with her burden. She wore an
unadorned dress made from an elkskin, spotted here and there from
old grease spills and smelling heavily of wood smoke.

Dove—she seldom remembered anymore the name she had been
born with so many winters before—moved on tired feet through
the birch and aspens. Here and there, a dead leaf showing traces of
autumn color still clung stubbornly to dried limbs. Her breath
showed in the air in front of her and she sang softly to herself in a
reedy old voice as she walked. Sometimes she sang the songs of
ancient warriors who had sung them around the council fires of her
youth. Sometimes she sang the songs she and her playmates had
made up when they were young and picking chokecherries along the
Bad River bottom where the tribe had held its summer camp in
happier days. Occasionally, strange notes would spill from her thin
lips with strange words. Not many, maybe only one or two—and
she would mouth them carefully to the child wrapped in a five-point
Hudson Bay blanket in her arms.

"Bu-fu Da-muh"

She did not remember having heard them before, and convinced
herself that the words were medicine words that would make the
fever go away and let him swallow. He no longer cried in her arms
although he still whimpered now and then when she stumbled on

343

a root over the path hidden beneath the snow and jarred the little body. She promised herself that she would rest whenever she came to the gnarled limbs of an oak, but all too often she forgot her resolution and when she finally did come upon an oak tree, she stared at it for a moment, trying to recall from half-forgotten memory why that tree should be so special. Finally, she would give up on memory and move away from the tree, her feet following by memory the bare trace of the familiar path to the fort.

Her eyes flickered around the woods as she walked, watching the birds dance impatiently upon the bare branches of the trees. Squirrels briefly chattered angrily, then fell silent until long after she had passed. Somewhere a woodpecker rattled against the bark of a cottonwood, making a grave and hesitant noise in the still air.

Now and then, the branches of the bushes quivered. Dove changed her singing words to a chant: "Stay away, Brother Fox; stay away, Brother Squirrel; Brother Wolf and Brother Coyote, let me pass. Stay away, Brother Rabbit; Stay away. . . . I have a long way, a long way."

And on she went, following the small stream away from the Washita River where The People had erected their lodges on land the soldiers had told them to use, her song rising again as she wove her way through the silent woods. A mourning dove sounded from a hollow, and she smiled a stumpy-toothed smile and sang back in answer to her sister.

The stream bent around a hill, hugging the rocks so tightly she was forced to abandon the path and wade through the snow as she climbed over the hill. She panted as she strained against the hill.

"My feet are tied to the rocks of this hill," she said to the child in the voice old people use to proclaim their age to others. "The hill wants me to stay and become a part of it."

When she got to the top of the hill, she paused to catch her breath and looked half fearfully behind her to see if she was being followed. A shadow moved within the deeper shadows of the trees. For a brief moment, her heart fluttered as she strained her tired eyes, trying to determine the shadow. But it stayed still in the line of trees and finally she shook her head and looked past the trees toward the lodges of The People, but she could not see them for the trees.

Her son had been very angry when she tried to tell him to take the child to the white shaman at the fort. . . . *You are a stupid old woman! The white man is our enemy! What would he do with an Indian baby? . . . But, the child . . . Enough! Go to the fire with the rest of the women! That is all!* . . . She had tried to tell him to look into the child's throat and see the white spots there that the white man's medicine would be able to take away. But he had angrily pushed her away, shouting at the shaman to work his magic and show his power to the rest of The People.

"Up on the hill and now back down the hill to the trees. Yes, that is the best way. Follow the water. Follow the water," she said to the child.

Her eyes opened their widest, and she started down slowly, her mind again set on her task. But before she got to the bottom of the hill, the spears of a yucca plant caught her dress.

She stood still for a moment, then tried to pull the dress free, balancing the child in the crook of her arm. He felt familiar there, and for a moment she was confused about where she was, looking for the chokecherry bushes, listening for the voice of Fawn, her best friend who always chose her first for their games and whose brother had been her husband. She frowned, trying to remember where the others were. She took a step and the yucca pulled at her dress.

"Why do you try to stop me?" she asked the yucca. "I thought you were a chokecherry bush, but you are only a soapweed. Why do you stop me?"

She tugged, and finally her dress slipped free. She stood trembling for a moment before daring to continue down the hill towards the stream.

The sun slipped off the water, dazzling her with its bright glitter. She bowed her head away from its brilliance, watching the patterns from the branches dance and writhe upon the snow. There is magic in the patterns, she thought. Magic from He-Who-Watches. If only I could walk in that magic.

But the elusive patterns slipped away from her feet, remaining tantalizingly out of reach, disappearing in the spears of silver grass that grew clumps between the aspens where the snow had not reached them. Spare bright drops of frozen moisture still sparkled from some, but she knew that would not last. She raised her head and looked at the sun.

"The sun is going high," she said to the child. But he didn't answer and heavy tears ran down the seams in her cheeks. "The sun is passing faster than I can walk."

At the foot of the hill, she paused for a minute to rest, laying the child on a bed of dead leaves gathered in the hollow of a cottonwood while she knelt to drink from the stream. The water flowed through a hollow log that an ancient one had laid there to make a spring. The spring had been there long before she had come to the tribe. Some of the older ones believed First Warrior had made the spring for The People for it had been a part of The People's hunting grounds long before time in the village's memory.

She broke the thin sheet of ice over the water and drank. The water was cool and fresh and had the slightly tannic taste of fall, and she drank deeply. After a minute, she felt better. She rose and turned back towards the child, but her foot slipped on the wet leaves and she fell. She looked in surprise at the ground so close to her eyes. She rolled over on her back and looked up at the sky showing through a hole in the cottonwood branches. A puff of white cloud moved by, looking like a shaggy buffalo.

She remembered when her father Crow killed the white buffalo the third year after he had found her on the prairie. The People had honored him greatly then, and he had given her her name that night at the council fire. She had repeated it after him, the word strange but light upon her tongue, nearly getting away before she caught it and brought it back: "I am Dove."

She frowned as another name stirred in dusty memory, but she could not recall it. The leaves were cold against her face and a light breeze fluttered across her. She felt herself becoming dreamy, floating above the earth, and when the little boy brought her a stick with

346

meat charred on the outside with juices rolling richly from it, she thanked him, reaching for it. But her hand gathered only empty air.

"Bu-fu Da-muh," she said again, taking heart in the medicine words. Her fingers moved, but still remained empty. She sighed. The medicine words did not work as often now. Maybe they were becoming worn out, too.

The child muttered from its leaf bed. She sighed and pushed herself painfully to her feet.

"Getting old. Forgetting," she said. She took a small piece of pemmican from the bag around her neck and placed it in her mouth, chewing it carefully with her worn teeth. She picked up the child and pulled a fold of blanket from its face. Her skin felt like dried parchment against his cheeks as she pursed his lips, then bent and let her saliva, heavy with the juice of the pemmican, drip into his mouth. He screwed his eyes tight as he painfully swallowed.

. . . *There is a white sickness in him. It is the white man who has brought this to our children. We must drive the white man from the land before the white sickness will go away.* . . . She had tried to tell the shaman that she had had a dream about a gray-bearded man with strong medicine, but the shaman did not believe her and had turned away from her, shaking pollen over the child and muttering ancient charms.

She turned and began following the stream again. It went deep, deep down between tall cottonwoods meeting high overhead. It was as dark as a cave. She came to a log barring her path, its sides rough with old bark, dark green moss growing heavily down the sides. The log was too high for her to climb. She had to kneel and creep and crawl under it, spreading her knees to help take the weight of herself and the child, stretching her fingers wide against the ground for balance. She sang to herself and the child so neither of them would be scared if she happened to get stuck under the log.

At last, she was safely on the other side, and she rose and leaned back against the log, breathing deeply, watching the puff of her breath rise away from her. A dead cottonwood stood at the end of the clearing opposite her. Its bone-white branches stretched emptily towards the blue sky. A raven sat on the lower branch, looking at her.

"Who are you watching?" she asked it. "Go away. We're not ready for you." The raven's beady eyes rolled in its head and then it flew slowly away, heavy wings flapping in the still air. She remembered then about snakes and looked fearfully around her but saw none, then remembered that snakes did not come out in the winter. She sighed and continued her way across the clearing, beginning her song again.

She crossed the dead leaves, listening to their dry shuffle and crackle beneath her feet. A small breeze rubbed the branches of the trees above her, making them rasp in the silence. The path she thought she was following seemed to disappear. She paused, trying to think if she should continue following the stream or cross up and out of the trees onto the prairie and the hills. Which would be shorter? she wondered.

Then there was something tall, dark, and thin in front of her. She became frightened and stared at it. She thought she heard the drumming of hooves and then the faint notes of a bugle and gunshots, but when she raised her head, cocking it like a dove to find the sound, it disappeared. She looked again at the thing in front of her.

"You there!" she called to it, but it did not answer.

"Spirit, go away!" she said. "You are blocking my way!"

Slowly, she walked to it. When she came closer, she saw it was only a young sapling hiding in the shadows of its older brothers, its nude branches fluttering like a ragged coat in the slight breeze.

"My eyes are too old, too old," she said. "I should be at home, sitting in the sun in front of our lodge."

She went on, weaving her way through the new strand of trees that whispered all around her. Ahead, she saw quail strutting around the edge of a thicket, the plumes dancing on their bobbing heads.

"Walk nice, walk nice," she said. They scooted back into the underbrush at the sound of her voice. Disappointed, she continued on, following the stream, making her own path now beside it.

The sun had risen high and as she labored, she grew hot now, and imagined dragonflies buzzing around her, trying to drink the salt of her sweat. She swung her head at them, shooing them away. Near the water's edge, willows grew, their long, thin branches like long thin filaments of lace. She heard the water gurgle as it bubbled over the gravel, the sound cool and clear. She felt thirsty again, but she did not know if she could kneel and rise again to her feet, so she licked her dry lips and told herself that she wasn't thirsty and continued on, singing.

She thought she heard a noise behind her and turned to look. A shadow moved in the shadows. She stumbled and fell to one knee. The child whimpered in her arms.

"Hush, now," she said. She looked over her shoulder again at the shadows. This time she could make out its lines: a black wolf. Or maybe it was a coyote. She couldn't be sure.

"Old woman, the shadows are coming for you and will take you if you do not move," she told herself.

Her hand closed around a rock. She picked it up and threw it at the shadow. It flinched and moved away. She found another rock and threw it again from memory because she could no longer see the shadow now. She waited, listening. She saw an old, cracked hickory nut on the ground beside her. She reached out and took it in her fingers, rolling it around, remembering the gathering along the Snake River when she and Fawn had startled the bear and had been forced to run into the raging water along the rapids to get away from it. She smiled at the memory and how Fawn had looked with her long black hair hanging over her face in wet strings, and Fawn laughing at her, huffing and blowing in the water, trying to get her breath.

The child moved in her arms, again reminding her. She placed the hickory nut in the small pouch with the pemmican and pushed herself to her feet, her muscles aching and shaking with the effort. A wave of dizziness washed over her. She refused to close her eyes for fear that she might fall again. A bird flew by and she thought it was a dove. Taking heart in this as a good omen, she slowly took a step, then another, each step a conscious lifting of one foot against straining muscles.

She started as a man dressed in blue with a heavy cloak around his shoulders stepped from the shadows in front of her. She stared at him in confusion, then recognized him as a soldier.

"What are you doing here?" he asked. He looked warily past her, staring down into the darkness from which the stream came, his hand on the pistol at his belt. He was young; she could see that. He frowned and asked her again what she was doing beside the stream. She did not know what he said, although some of the words sounded dimly familiar. She tried to hold the child out to him, but her arm had cramped, locking the child to her.

The soldier moved closer and stared suspiciously at the bundle as she unwrapped the folds from the child's face. He frowned and gingerly touched the child's forehead.

"He's burning up!" he exclaimed. He took the child from her. Her arms dropped with relief as the burden was taken from them. The young soldier jerked his head to his right, away from the stream. "Come on!" he said roughly, gesturing with a hand. "The fort's that way. The doctor will know what to do."

She did not understand what he was saying, but nodded and tried to keep up with him as he led her away from the stream and trees and up the hill. But his legs were too long and too young as they impatiently pushed their way along a path through the deep drifts.

The fort stood on the crest of the hill, and they were nearly to it before she could smell the wood smoke from the stoves. The soldier waited impatiently beside the gate for her. There were other soldiers there, too. They stared curiously at her as she limped after the young soldier, following him to a log building at the back of the stockade. Some children played around the steps in front of the building. They stopped and stared at her. She felt odd, out of place because of their stares, and stopped, looking at them as if she had never seen children like them before. They stepped aside, and she slowly followed the young soldier up the steps.

"Hey, Doc!" the soldier called as he entered the building. "See what I found! The kid's really sick."

A gray-bearded man wearing a long white coat took the child from the soldier and laid him on the table. Her heart leaped as she thought she recognized the man from her dream. Gently, he unwrapped the blanket. The child whimpered as the gray-bearded man probed gently with his fingers.

"That's a Hudson Bay five-point blanket," the young soldier said. "The trappers used to trade them with the Indians for pelts back in the old days. A five-pointer was worth a lot of pelts. No ordinary squaw would have one like that. What's wrong with the kid, Doc?"

"Diphtheria," Gray Beard said. He shook his head. "It doesn't look good. Still . . ."

He looked at the old woman. Sweat on her face made the wrinkles shine like a fine-meshed net. "Is this your grandchild?"

She stood stiff and silent in front of him, trying to comprehend his words, her face solemn and rigid. The young soldier made an impatient gesture. "She's an Indian, Doc. She don't understand."

"An Indian with gray eyes?" Gray Beard asked. "I don't think so." He pointed at the child on the table and then to her. "Yours?" he asked.

She recognized the word or thought she did. She opened her mouth to tell him the child's name and the name of its father, her son, but a strange word came from her lips, a medicine word, she thought.

"Yes," she said.

"We might be able to help him. You should have brought him in sooner. But there is a chance, even now. You're very lucky. A load of serum came in on the last supply train. But he'll have to stay here for a long time. Do you understand?"

He smiled at her and she felt the warmth of his smile and knew the medicine word had worked. He seemed to be waiting for her to say something, so again she repeated the word.

"Yes."

And then the dream returned again, the dream she had hoped was gone forever, and she remembered the bearded man fighting the enemy and yelling at her to hide, and she ran away, running over the prairie, then crawling into a small hole in a clay bank above the Washita. She covered her ears, trying hard to stop the screams coming from the bearded man and the tired woman who had bathed her and dressed her and sang to her, "Beau-ti-ful dream-er . . ." She waited long after the screams stopped before crawling from her hole and going back, but the horses and the furs were gone and the bearded man and white woman were naked, with bloody patches showing from where their hair once grew. She sat down beside them and cried until the stench drove her away back to the Washita. She drank the cold water and wondered what to do, and then she heard the coyotes and ran down the river away from their noise until she found her father, Crow, riding on the horse the bearded man once rode, and he smiled at her and lifted her up on the horse and took her to her new home.

She blinked and discovered the two soldiers looking curiously at her.

"Yes," she said again because she thought they wanted to hear her say it again.

Gray Beard nodded in satisfaction. "Good. You'd better take her over to Major Reno. Colonel Custer will be wanting a report when he returns from Black Kettle's village."

"Yes sir," the young soldier said, giving her a strange look. "Wisht I coulda gone along with Custer. Them red bastards been looking for a fight for a long time."

"Oh, yes," Gray Beard said. "That is why Black Kettle flies the American flag over his village and why he stays in his camp instead of going north with those hotspurs like Roman Nose who left his village. They're tired of fighting. That's why they stay there. They're already beaten."

The young soldier sniggered. "They sure will be after Custer gets done with them."

"Do what I told you." Gray Beard looked at her. "You don't know how lucky you are. Probably never will."

"Yes sir," the young soldier said, giving her a strange look. "How long do you think she was with them?"

"A long time," Gray Beard said. "Long enough for her to forget who and what she was." He turned back to the child. "Now do what I say: Take her to Major Reno."

The young soldier took her by the arm and gently tugged her toward the door. She started to follow him and then stopped, staring back at the child.

Gray Beard saw her concern and smiled reassuringly. He nodded.

"Go on," he said gently.

"Yes," she said. The word was beginning to sound familiar to her, and this frightened her for she did not understand why she was beginning to understand the word. She said the medicine words then. "Bu-fu Da-muh."

The gray-beard looked at her and smiled. "Yes, that is a lovely song."

She nodded, not understanding, but feeling that she did, and turned and followed the young soldier from the building, stumbling over the threshold, nearly falling down the small steps. The young soldier caught her arm, steadying her. She smiled at him, and he jerked his hand away as if he had touched something distasteful. A sadness swept over her. She felt very tired, and the sun's heat did not seem to draw the chill from her as they began to walk over the parade ground. Halfway across, a band began to play and soldiers rode in through the gate. The young soldier pulled her out of the way and paused to watch the cavalry trot in through the gate to the strains of "Garryowen." Some of the soldiers had run rawhide strips through black scalps and hung them over their saddles in front of them. A few had brightly colored blankets tied behind their saddles while others carried different trophies: bows and quivers of arrows, a few old rifles, knives and hatchets stuck in their belts, a coup stick she recognized as having belonged to her son.

"I'll be damned!" the soldier beside her breathed gently. "It must have been a massacre! And I missed it."

353

He spat in disgust and gave her a resentful look, then sighed and gently tugged at her arm. She turned to follow him to a low log building. The soldier helped her up the three steps, then motioned for her to wait as he knocked on a door and entered. Dimly, from the trees beside the stream at the bottom of the hill, she heard the mournful cry of a dove's song.

Sepia Sun

DEBORAH MORGAN

Deborah Morgan has published stories in *Louis L'Amour Western Magazine* and three anthologies, *Lethal Ladies II*, *How the West Was Read*, and *Tin Star*. Her stories have been reprinted in two collections, *The Fatal Frontier* and *The Best of the American West*, and she recently signed a contract to create a new mystery series set in the world of antiques. "Sepia Sun" is a slice-of-life story about a veteran female photographer determined to "freeze history once again for the ages."

SHE INCHED FORWARD IN LINE, stooping and carefully nudging her valises alongside her as she did so. She was anxious to register and get to the work at hand. The train upon which she had journeyed into Bismarck arrived behind schedule—recent snows and a heavy volume of travelers for the holiday season being the cause—and when she caught sight of the hotel's crowded lobby, she found herself for the second time that day mentally adjusting her own schedule to compensate for the light she would lose.

A wisp of a woman by all outward appearances, she was white-complexioned and wore her black hair cropped short (she'd done so ever since posing as a male during the Civil War a quarter century before). Her hair was beginning to thread with silver, as if the silver nitrate stains she'd suffered for years in her profession had finally penetrated her skin, coursed through her veins and, at last, had woven glittering strands into the black. Dressed all in black, from her trademark beret to her suit of the latest design from Paris, she garnered more than a few glimpses from passersby.

But she did not notice the attention paid her by strangers. Her large dark eyes were busy, working much like the lenses of her trade—letting in and filtering light by degrees, adjusting the aperture, altering the shadows cast upon everything surrounding her.

Thin winter light angled through the high windowpanes in pale shafts, causing the baubles and foil that decorated the great evergreen in the far corner of the hotel's lobby to glitter and wink. To the layman, the woman would appear mesmerized by the flickering light. In truth, her artistic vision was stimulating her mind, and the two forces were searching for a way to capture with her cameras the twinkling stars. This puzzled her only briefly and she was, once again, aware that time was ticking away at itself.

At last, she stepped up to the lobby desk.

The clerk was a tall man about half her age with sharp, angular features and wearing an impeccably tailored suit coat of gray wool. He didn't look up from his ledger.

"Pardon." She emphasized the second syllable, revealing a French accent that only showed itself when she was either excited or irritated.

"No vacancies, miss." Still he did not look up.

Her jaw clenched. She resented his assumption that she had merely wandered in off the streets looking for a room. "Rooms are being held for me. If you will check under—"

"Miss." He looked at her. "Madam, rather. There are no rooms at the inn, as it were." He smirked, obviously amused at his turn of phrase.

"For Lautrec." She placed a calling card on the cold white marble of the counter. "Mademoiselle Lautrec."

The man frowned. "I have a suite of rooms for Lautrec, but they are for a gentleman by the name of Mike Lautrec."

"*I* am Mike Lautrec. Michelle, actually, but I'm known professionally as Mike. If I *were* a gentleman, I'd be the only one present."

Tight-lipped, he slid the calling card into his palm and studied it. It read, in bold print:

Mme. Michelle "Mike" Lautrec
Daguerreotypist

"Dag-ear—"

She pronounced it for him. "I use other techniques now, but continue to use this title in homage to the great inventor, Louis Daguerre."

"My apologies, mademoiselle. I had no idea you were a woman. I mean, that the reservation was for a woman." Obviously flustered, he seized a large, tasseled brass key from its numbered cubbyhole on the back wall and walked the length of the counter. "My name is Colin Barnes and I will personally escort you to your suites." He started toward a double doorway just off the lobby.

Mme. Lautrec made no move to follow him. "Shouldn't you inquire whether I have baggage that needs tending?"

He stopped and turned. "Yes, of course. Do you?"

"Yes, of course."

Barnes motioned to an old man in a tiny cookie-tin hat and short jacket—both of red wool trimmed with gold cording. His dark trousers were too short. The uniform reminded Mike of an organ grinder's monkey she frequently saw in the Montmartre district of Paris as a child. She doubted the bellman could hoist her valises, let alone handle any of her trunks.

"Sir," she said, smiling. "With all due respect, you are going to need help. I'm quickly losing the light for my work and I have several trunks." She pointed toward the main entrance of the hotel.

Just inside the stained-glass doors was a large collection of steamer trunks of various sizes and two pine crates as large as coffins. Standing sentinel was a small man with white hair and beard, and skin dark as tobacco. In his hands was the plantation-style hat Mike had given him as an early Christmas gift to replace his sombrero, which had been stolen by highwaymen. He wore a black suit of tasteful design and his boots were polished to a shine.

The old bellman mumbled something about there not being that many strong backs in all of Bismarck, then excused himself to set about disproving his statement.

Mike led Barnes toward the old Mexican. "My assistant, Candelario Ruiz. Candy, Mr. Barnes will be showing us to our rooms."

When the elderly bellman arrived with an assemblage of chefs, janitors, other bellmen, and a parade of hand trucks, the entourage made its way to the Governor's Suite.

Barnes threw open the doors of the suite's main entrance with a grand gesture, revealing a massive room opulently decorated in aubergines, pinks, and golds. He pointed out the large water closet, obviously expecting the lady to be impressed with its convenience and design. Yet, all these lavish appointments were lost on her.

Mike glanced quickly about, scrutinizing her surroundings. She had included a list of needs in her telegraph to the hotel the day before and was both surprised and grateful to find that they had been seen to. A long table had been placed in the water closet where she would create the darkroom and there were three long tables arranged end to end in the main room.

Candelario supervised the placing of the trunks, then dismissed the helpers and began the tedious process of unpacking.

Barnes pointed out an entrance to an adjoining room. "Your subject will be waiting through these doors. You can expect everything to be ready for you by four o'clock."

"Thank you," Mike said distractedly. "Now, if you will excuse us."

Ignoring her, he peered into one of the crates. "This will be quite an experience for you, I imagine. I assume, anyway, that you've never photographed an Indian chief."

She paused finally, removed her hat and jacket, and hung them on the hall tree. She turned to the young clerk and eyed him evenly. "I've photographed presidents and kings, Mr. Barnes. I've photographed African witch doctors and Russian czars. And I've photographed Indian chiefs. Many before you were born."

"Perhaps that's why I've never heard of you."

"I doubt it. It's probably for the same reason you assume I've never photographed Indians. Because I'm a woman."

She turned away and walked to the large windows on the west wall. Snow had begun to fall. Dusk would come early. Rapidly, she began untying the drapery cords that were thick as ropes and pulled the purple velvet panels over the glass.

Candelario turned to Mr. Barnes. "You must leave now. Señora Mike begins her work."

After a moment Barnes nodded and left the room, quietly pulling the doors shut.

Mike seized both of her valises and retreated to the water closet. There, she changed into work smock and apron, opened the trunks that Candy had placed under the table, and began assembling her darkroom.

While she worked, she thought about the first time she'd met today's subject—the only chief she'd ever met that she *hadn't* photographed.

It was 1875 and she was making obscene profits traveling throughout the Black Hills with her darkroom wagon. She'd been constantly warned about being on the roads alone, but that had never bothered her. She had guns and she knew how to use them. A gun, however, was as useful as those parasols the size of bread plates when one contracted the influenza.

Her profession had saved her. A small band of Sioux discovered her, fevered and delirious, and took her and the wagon back to their camp. They were fascinated with the odd vehicle and its paraphernalia. One enterprising brave decided that the tribe's great medicine man would make the woman well and she in turn would show them what magic was contained within the wooden boxes and foul-smelling liquids she carted around.

She recovered and, with the interpretive aid of a French trader who was wintering with the tribe, photographed any and every tribe member who would grant permission.

The medicine man was not one of them. Instead, he'd asked for a stereoscope and a stack of studio cards—the "two-picture" cards, as he called them—to be viewed through the apparatus. She'd rarely met anyone who wasn't fascinated with the three-dimensional stereoscopic prints. At the time, it had not seemed enough payment for the care she had received. Now she was grateful for an opportunity to repay her debt in full.

Once she had the darkroom arranged, Mike joined Candelario where he was assembling the tripods.

Everything had been unpacked and she inspected the array of cameras, checking the smoothness of the shutter movements and examining the lenses for any flaws. Candy's pride in the equipment showed and this pleased her greatly. The oaken panels of each camera had been rubbed and buffed to gleaming and the brass trappings of the boxes were polished to a brilliant shine.

She moved on to the glass plates and checked the edges of each with the beveler.

Carefully, she carried the stacks of glass plates to the darkroom and closed the door behind her.

The water closet was as close to ideal as she could get without being in her own studio. Working in the field for much of her career had taught her resourcefulness, and she would never have an aversion to putting those skills into practice. But she'd put in her time wrestling equipment onto battlefields and into caves. She'd stayed awake nights aboard steamships and trains, guarding her costly cameras and the accessories they required. Today, however, time was everything and she appreciated the conveniences at hand.

She unstacked several trays for the chemical and water baths and placed them on the table. Beside these, she placed funnels and a container of silver salts.

Then, one at a time, she carefully lifted the apothecary jars from between the padded compartments of her valises and placed them beside the trays. She could live without a man, or clothes, or good wine. She could not go on without her elixirs.

Her chemicals. The sticky, noxious collodion and the potassium iodide were first, followed by silver nitrate to sensitize the glass plates that would become the negatives. Then the pyrogallic acid and hyposulphite for developing and fixing the images.

She placed a stack of dark slides on the table; these would hold the plates after they were sensitized. The glass plates must be prepared one at a time and rushed to the camera for the shot. Then she would race back to the darkroom, work frantically developing the negative and fixing it in hypo before the water bath.

At least here, she and Candy wouldn't have to haul water. The wet-plate process had to be completed in minutes, and couldn't be done without a good supply of water.

She remembered Gettysburg. She'd just photographed a dead

soldier and the shot had all the elements of a gripping image—the light, the composition, the face of the soldier. But she needed more water. She had become so obsessed with developing the negative that she'd fought a man, whose arm had just been blown off, over a pail of water. Now she shuddered, though she didn't know whether it was from the memory of what she'd done or the fear that she might repeat it. Sometimes, the mad driving force behind her art frightened her.

Art. She had trained in Europe, learning from such brilliant masterminds as Daguerre and Niepce. That training was being compromised with new inventions and improvements—as they were so loosely called—that were putting little camera boxes and rolled film into the hands of anyone who would spend a few dollars. Thus the thinking of the general population had been altered and she fought to bring more recognition to her art.

There was a rap on the door and she jumped.

"Señora Mike?"

She opened the door.

"Oh, señora, by the looks of you, you have been on another mind journey, *sí*? Do not do that to yourself today."

"You're right, Candy." She wet a cloth in the basin and mopped her face as she walked back into the main room.

Candelario Ruiz had been with her for almost twenty-five years. He knew her better than anyone. It was both a blessing and a curse.

"How are things coming along out here?"

"The cameras are all in place, señora."

The mantel clock chimed four, Mike Lautrec took a deep breath, then turned to her assistant. "Shall we freeze history once again for the ages?"

"*Sí*." Candelario spoke solemnly, stationing himself at the worktables.

She opened the double doors leading to the adjoining room and stepped through.

• • •

WHEN SHE SAW THE GREAT MAN, SHE SMILED TENDERLY. "AH, maker of strong medicine. Things are very different from last time we met, no? Do you remember? You saved my life." She bowed slightly.

She'd been nervous about this assignment. Her emotions had run high with the news, and her schedule had not wanted to allow the trip. But she was compelled for many reasons to juggle everything in order to be there for him. His way of life was disappearing, and the honor of having been chosen to record this event was not to be taken lightly. She owed him, and she believed with every fiber of her self that he would have known had she declined.

When she saw him, though, her training, her years behind the shutter, her artistic instinct all took over and her trepidations vanished.

"I had hoped to see you again, *vis-à-vis*. But not like this." She walked to the platform, draped with white buffalo hides, where they had Sitting Bull lying. She stroked his hand, surprised that it felt warm to the touch. "You're like a sepia sun, my friend. Bronzed and warm and shining strong golden light on a nation as you slip past the horizon."

She stood for a long moment admiring him, his black braids woven through with beaded strips of fawn leather and his hands resting on an antelope-hide shirt quilled in amber, gold, and vermilion. Beside him was a red stone calumet and a pouch of what she knew would be the finest tobacco that could be found for his journey.

She studied with a trained artist's eye the light and shadows and how they played off the deep lines and crevices of the man's bronzed flesh.

Without traceable thought, she walked to the camera in the center. "I'll do good by you today, Chief."

Ducking under the black cloth of the camera, she adjusted the height of the tripod, inched it forward; adjusting, inching, modifying, until the shot was perfectly framed. "There."

With a glowing lucifer she ignited the magnesium in the flash pan as she squeezed the rubber bulb. The shutter clicked and the flash powder flared and popped and belched a cloud of smoke upward.

She watched the smoke lift and wondered if the chief's great Ghost Dancer spirit was hovering above the scene, waiting for the smoke, waiting for yet another ceremony to end before he could move on and join the Indian Messiah.